By Anne McCaffrey
Published by The Ballantine Publishing Group:

DECISION AT DOONA
DINOSAUR PLANET
DINOSAUR PLANET SURVIVORS
GET OFF THE UNICORN
THE LADY
PEGASUS IN FLIGHT
RESTOREE
THE SHIP WHO SANG
TO RIDE PEGASUS
NIMISHA'S SHIP
PEGASUS IN SPACE

**THE CRYSTAL SINGER
BOOKS**
CRYSTAL SINGER
KILLASHANDRA
CRYSTAL LINE

**THE DRAGONRIDERS OF
PERN® BOOKS**
DRAGONFLIGHT
DRAGONQUEST
THE WHITE DRAGON
MORETA: DRAGONLADY OF
    PERN
NERILKA'S STORY
DRAGONSDAWN
THE RENEGADES OF PERN
ALL THE WEYRS OF PERN
THE CHRONICLES OF PERN:
    FIRST FALL
THE DOLPHINS OF PERN
DRAGONSEYE
THE MASTERHARPER OF PERN
THE SKIES OF PERN

*By Anne McCaffrey and Elizabeth
Ann Scarborough*
POWERS THAT BE
POWER LINES
POWER PLAY

With Jody Lynn Nye:
THE DRAGONLOVER'S GUIDE
    TO PERN

Edited by Anne McCaffrey:
ALCHEMY AND ACADEME

THE
SKIES
OF PERN

Anne McCaffrey

A Del Rey® Book
BALLANTINE BOOKS • NEW YORK

A Del Rey® Book
Published by The Ballantine Publishing Group
Copyright © 2001 by Anne McCaffrey

www.delreydigital.com

ISBN 0-345-43469-2

Map drawn by Mapping Specialist Ltd., based on map by Niels Erickson.
Oceanography information by P. Barr Loomis; ocean current maps by Marilyn Alm.

Manufactured in the United States of America

First Hardcover Edition: April 2001
First Mass Market Edition: January 2002

10 9 8 7 6 5 4 3 2 1

This book is respectfully dedicated to
Steven M. Beard, Ph.D.
for putting my world in my hands.

Acknowledgments

THE LONGER I WRITE in the Pern series the more unusual the circumstances become and the more I need the help of special friends and even more special experts in various fields.

In this book, my cry for astronomical help went out again to Dr. Steven M. Beard and Elizabeth Kerner. Necessity required me to add a Cosmic Impact Consultant in the person of Scott Manley of Armagh Observatory, which I also visited to see telescopes and to learn how to arrange for a cosmic impact on exactly the site required, with digital embellishments and proper readouts. I also had the pleasure of dining at the Armagh home of Dr. Bill and Mrs. Nancy Napier and meeting some of their colleagues for a lovely April evening.

Marilyn and Harry Alm—and the exceptional oceanographical help of P. Burr Loomis—provided me with splendid maps and diagrams so that I would know where I was on Pern.

I owe a particular debt to Georgeanne Kennedy who rallied me to keep to the "real" story line when I had a tendency to go off on tangents because there are so many people on Pern. Thanks also to Lea Day, Elizabeth Kerner and Elizabeth Ann Scarborough who kindly read original draft material and gave me invaluable support. Last but scarcely least is my appreciation for my editors, Shelly Shapiro and Diane Pearson, who helped me refine this latest adventure on Pern. I am deeply grateful for their input.

I would also like to thank http://science.nasa.gov/headlines/

y2000 for their excellent updates on what is happening in and about this world.

Music played while writing: Jerry Goldsmith—*The Ghost & the Darkness* and other sf theme music

Percy Grainger—*Piano for Four Hands* (2 volumes)

Elgar—*Enigma Variations*

James Galway—various CDs

Mendelssohn's Italian Symphony

Inspector Morse CD

Janis Ian—various CDs

Manuel Barrueco plays Lennon & McCartney

Tania Opland and Mike Freeman—*Masterharper* and other CDs

THE SKIES
OF PERN

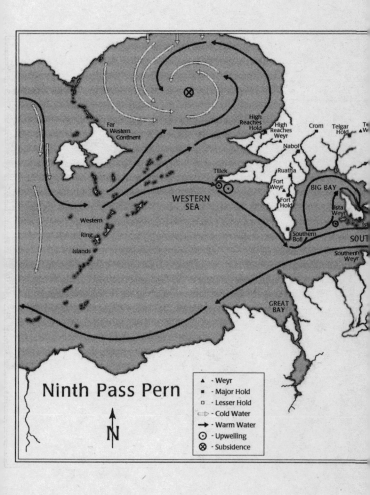

Ninth Pass Pern

N

- ▲ - Weyr
- ■ - Major Hold
- □ - Lesser Hold
- ⇨ - Cold Water
- ➔ - Warm Water
- ☉ - Upwelling
- ⊗ - Subsidence

Far Western Continent

High Reaches Hold
High Reaches Weyr
Crom
Telgar Hold
Nabol
Tillek
Ruatha
Fort Weyr
Fort Hold
BIG BAY
Ista Weyr
WESTERN SEA
Western Ring Islands
Southern Boll
SOUTH
Southern Weyr
GREAT BAY

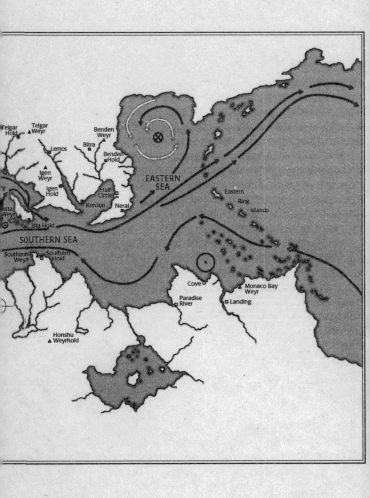

Introduction

Ours not to ponder what were fair in Life,
But, finding what may be,
Make it fair up to our means.

WHEN MANKIND FIRST discovered Pern, third planet of the sun Rukbat, in the Sagittarian Sector, they paid little attention to the eccentric orbit of another satellite in the system.

Settling the new planet, adjusting to its differences, the colonists spread out across the southern, most hospitable continent. Then disaster struck in the form of a rain of mycorrhizoid organisms, which voraciously devoured all but stone, metal, and water. The initial losses were staggering. But fortunately for the young colony, "Thread," as the settlers called the devastating showers, was not entirely invincible: both water and fire would destroy the menace on contact.

Using their old-world ingenuity and genetic engineering, the settlers altered an indigenous life-form that resembled the dragons of legend. Telepathically bonded with a human at birth, these enormous creatures became Pern's most effective weapon against Thread. Able to chew and digest a phosphine-bearing rock, the dragons could literally breathe fire and sear the airborne Thread before it could reach the ground. Able not only to fly but to teleport as well, the dragons could maneuver quickly to avoid injury during their battles with Thread. And their telepathic communication enabled them to work with their riders and with each other to form extremely efficient fighting units—wings.

Being a dragonrider required special talents and complete dedication. Thus the dragonriders became a separate group, set apart from those who held land against the depredations of Thread, or those whose craft skills produced other necessities of life in their Crafthalls.

Over the centuries, the settlers forgot their origins in their struggle to survive against Thread, which fell across the land whenever the Red Star's eccentric orbit coincided with Pern's. There were long Intervals, too, when no Thread ravaged the land, when the dragonriders in their Weyrs kept faith with their mighty friends until they would be needed once more to protect the people they were pledged to serve.

After one such long Interval, when Thread renewed its violence, the dragonriders were down to one single Weyr: Benden. Its courageous Weyrwoman, Lessa, rider of the only gold queen, Ramoth, discovering that dragons could move through time as well as space, took a desperate gamble and flew four hundred Turns into the past to bring the other five Weyrs forward in time to renew the defense of Pern.

Circumstances encouraged exploration of the southern continent and there Lord Jaxom, rider of white Ruth; his friend, F'lessan, rider of bronze Golanth; Journeywoman Jancis from the MasterSmithcrafthall; and Piemur, Harper at large, discovered the most important artifact in the settlers' original Landing: AIVAS—Artificial Intelligence Voice Address System.

With the myriad files of information that the colonists had brought with them, Aivas was able to restore lost pieces of information for all the Crafthalls. He was also able to teach them how to rid their world of the cyclical dangers of the erratic satellite, inaccurately called the Red Star.

F'lar and Lessa, Benden's courageous and far-seeing Weyrleaders, were the first to encourage Lord Holders and Craftmasters to end the domination of Thread and start a new era on Pern. Almost all Lord Holders and Craftmasters agreed, especially since Aivas could provide them with new methods and technologies for improving health and quality of life.

Those who considered Aivas an "abomination" attempted to stop the splendid project, but were defeated. Instructed and trained by Aivas, the young riders and technicians were able to transport, by means of the dragons, the antimatter engines of the three colony ships—still in orbit above Landing—and place them in a massive fault on the Red Star. The subsequent explosion was visible from much of the planet, and people rejoiced to think they would finally be rid of Thread.

Now, though, Thread continues to fall, because the swarm already brought in by the Red Star has not yet completely passed by Pern. Dragonriders and harpers have explained to those who would listen that this Pass is the last one Pern will have to endure.

They must now start planning for a Threadfree future, making use of the Aivas files, full of helpful but not overly sophisticated technology that will improve life for everyone on Pern. Even the dragonriders, for centuries the defenders of Pern, must fit themselves for new occupations. The questions are: Which technologies can be adopted without disrupting the culture of the planet? And how will the dragonriders integrate themselves and their splendid friends into the new Threadfree society?

Prologue

CROM MINES—5.27.30–PRESENT PASS
AIVAS ADJUSTED RECKONING–2552

THE JOURNEYMAN ON DUTY in the prisoners' quarters at
Mine 23 in the western foothills was the first one to see the
bright, almost bluish streak in the sky. It was coming from
a southwesterly direction. It also appeared to be coming
straight at him, so he shouted a warning as he scrambled
down the steps of the guard tower.

His yells attracted the attention of other miners, just
coming up from the shafts, tired and dirty from a long day of
digging iron ore. They, too, saw the light—coming straight
at the hold. They scattered, yelling, diving for the nearest shelter under ore carts, behind the raw mounds of the
day's tips, the gantry, back into the shaft. There was a rushing
noise of thunder rumbling from the sky—and not a cloud in
sight. Some insisted that they heard a high-pitched shriek.
Everyone agreed on the direction from which the object
came: southwest.

Suddenly the high stone wall that surrounded the prison
yard was breached, showering pieces of rock that rained
down on the other sections of the minehold and causing
miners to fall flat, covering their heads against the fragments.
A second explosive noise followed the first, punctuated by

screams of terror from those in the prison quarters. There was
the stink of very hot metal, a familiar enough smell in a place
where iron ore was smelted into ingots before being shipped
to Smithcrafthalls—only this stink had an unusual acidity
that no one could later accurately describe.

In fact, from the moment the journeyman shouted his
warning, only one man of the several hundred in the minehold kept his head. Shankolin, imprisoned in the Crom mines
for the past thirteen Turns, had waited for just such an opportunity: a chance to escape. He heard the wall shatter, of
course, and saw a moment's reflection of the blue-white light
in the small window of the heavy door that was the only
entrance to the building. He threw himself to the left, diving under a wooden bunk just as something large, hot, and
reeking pierced the wall where his head would have been. It
hissed as it plowed down the main aisle and buried itself in
the far corner, dropping through the wood planks, smashing a
corner pillar, buckling the wall, and causing part of the roof
to collapse. Someone was screaming in pain, pleading for
help. Everyone else was howling with fear.

Wriggling out from under the bunk, Shankolin took just
one look at the opening made by the meteorite—for that was
the only thing that could have caused the damage just done—
and, realizing that he could see straight across the yard to the
shattered wall, he reacted instantly. He dove out of his prison
and sprinted to the broken wall. On his way, he made certain
that there was no one on the guard walkway or in the end tur-
rets. They must all have abandoned their posts as the meteor
streaked toward the minehold.

He heaved himself up and over the broken wall and ran
down the hill as fast as he could to the nearest cover of
straggly bushes. Crouching behind them, he caught his breath
while he listened to the continued sounds of confusion from
the minehold. The injured man was still howling: the guards
would have to tend to him before they did a head count.
They'd probably want to have as close a look at the meteorite
as possible. The metal types were valuable. Or so he'd heard,
once his deafness had lifted. He didn't hear everything, but

he heard enough. He had never let on that he had recovered from the skull-ripping sound that that abominable Aivas had emitted when Shankolin had led men, picked by his father, Master Norist, to destroy the "abomination" and end its evil influence on the people of Pern.

Having caught his breath, Shankolin rolled down the slight incline until he felt it safe to rise to a crouch and make his way to the sparse forest. He kept turning his head this way and that, listening for any sound of men coming after him. Crouching, he ran as fast as he could down the dangerous inclines. He could hear the pebbles and stones rattling and bouncing ahead of him.

One thought dominated: this time he would make good his escape. This time he had to be free—to halt the progress that the Aivas Abomination was inexorably making, destroying the Pern that had survived so long, as his father had told him in a hushed and fearful voice. Master Norist had been horrified to learn that the Weyrleaders of Pern believed that this disembodied voice could actually instruct them on how to turn the Red Star from its orbit and prevent it from ever swinging close enough to Pern to drop the avaricious and hungry Thread. Thread could eat anything, herdbeasts, humans, vegetation—it could even consume huge trees in the time it took a man to blink. He knew. He'd seen it happen once when he'd been part of the ground crews assembled by the Glasscrafthall. Thread truly was a menace to bodies and growing things, but the Aivas Abomination had been a more insidious menace to the very minds and hearts of men and women, and from its disembodied words a perfidious treachery had been spread. His father had been amazed and disheartened by all the impossible things the Abomination had told the Lord Holders and Craftmasters: of the machines and methods that their ancestors had used; equipment and processes—even ways to improve glass—all of which would make living on Pern much easier.

At that time, when everyone was extolling the miracle of this Aivas thing, his father and a few other men of importance had seen the dangers inherent in many of these smooth and tempting promises. As if a mere voice could alter the way a Star moved. Shankolin was firmly of his father's mind. Stars did not change their courses. He agreed that the Weyrleaders were fools, inexplicably eager to destroy the very reason why the great dragons were basic to the preservation of the planet! He agreed because he was so close to the end of his journeyman's time. He was eager to prove himself acceptable to his father, to be the one of his sons to receive the secret skills of coloring glass in the glorious shades that only a Master of the Craft could produce: which sand would make molten glass blue, which powder caused the brilliant deep crimson.

So he had volunteered to be one of those to attack the Aivas Abomination and end its domination over the minds of otherwise intelligent men and women.

He was into the stream before he realized it. His right boot hit a slippery stone and he fell, striking his face on another rock. Dazed by the blow, he was slow to push to his hands and knees. The chill of the water on his wrists and legs helped to revive him. Then he saw the drops of blood landing on the stream and floating pinkly away. He explored the cut on his face, wincing as he realized the slash started at his forehead and continued down one side of his nose to a gouge in his cheek—as jagged a cut as the rock that had made it. Blood dripped off his chin. Holding his breath, he buried his face in the cold water. He repeated the process until the cold water had somewhat stemmed the flow of blood. Even so, he had to tear off the tail end of his shirt to tie a rude bandage to stop the blood running from his forehead. Once he cocked his head, listening for any sounds of pursuit. He couldn't even hear avians or the slithering of snakes. His running might have startled them away. With water still dripping from his soaked clothes, he got to his feet and sniffed at the slight breeze.

During his long Turns of deafness, his other senses had intensified. His sense of smell had once saved his life, even if he had lost the tip of one finger. He'd caught the rank odor of gas being released just before the mine wall had collapsed. Two miners had been buried alive in that fall.

Blood continued to drip from his cheek. He took another patch from his shirttail and held it to the gouge. He looked this way and that, wondering how to proceed.

There were men in the minehold who boasted about their success in tracking escaped prisoners. Bloodstains would make their job easier. He looked anxiously about him, but the stream had swept the blood away. It was fortunate that he'd fallen in the middle of the stream: there'd be no blood to be found.

Perhaps the meteorite had delayed pursuit. There'd been more injured and no prisoner count had been made. Maybe that meteorite was of more importance to the miners. He'd heard that the Smithcrafthall paid well for such pieces falling from the sky. Let them waste time sending a message to the nearest Crafthall. Let them give him enough time to reach the river.

If he kept to the water, he'd leave no bloodstains or scent to be tracked. Eventually this stream would reach the river and then the Southern Sea. He'd have to keep holding the bandage on his cheek until the blood clotted. He was still a bit woozy from his fall. He'd find a stick to help him keep his balance and to check the water's depths. He spotted one farther down the bank, sturdy and long enough to be useful. A few cautious steps forward in the stream and he reached for it. He gave it a pound or two to be sure it wasn't rotten. It would do.

He walked through a moonless night, slipping occasionally in muddy spots or dropping into unexpectedly deep pools, despite using the stick to avoid them. When his cheek stopped bleeding, he shoved that bandage in a pocket. The one on his forehead was adhered to the dried blood, so he left it in place.

By dawn, his feet were so cold and clumsy in the soaked heavy mining boots that he stumbled more frequently and his teeth began to chatter with the chill. When the stream broadened and he was more often up to his waist than his knees, he could go no farther. Seizing hold of shrubs that lined the stream, he clambered out of the water and hid himself in the thick vegetation, curling up to preserve what warmth remained in his body.

Nothing disturbed him until the ache of an empty belly finally roused him. It was far into the morning for the sun was well up. He had come much farther than he had thought possible. His rough work clothing had partially dried but the minehold emblem woven into shirt and pants would mark him as a fugitive. He needed food and new clothing in whichever order he could get them.

Carefully he emerged from the bushes and, to his utter astonishment, saw a small cothold directly across the stream that was now wide as a river. He watched the cothold a long time before he decided that there was no one working inside or nearby. He waded across the river, his bruised feet feeling every rock, and hid again in the bushes until he was sure he heard no human sounds.

The cothold was empty but someone lived here. A herder, perhaps, for there were hides pushed back on the rough sleeping platform made supple by long usage. Food first! He didn't even wash the tubers he found in a basket by the hearth. Then he saw cold gray grease in the iron skillet, set a-tilt on the hearth. He dipped the raw vegetables into it, relishing the salt in the grease as flavoring. The worst of his hunger momentarily assuaged, he searched for more to eat and a change of clothing. As a younger man he would never have filched so much as a berry or an apple from a neighbor's yard. His circumstances were as much altered now as the tenets of conduct his father had beaten into him. He had a duty to perform, a wrong to right, and a theory he must confirm or forget.

His stomach churned with the raw, greasy food he had eaten. He had to eat more slowly or lose everything. Vomit was a hard smell to hide. In a tightly covered container that would protect its contents from vermin, he found three quarters of a wheel of cheese. He thought how long such food would sustain him in his escape—but the fewer traces of his passing were noticeable, the better. While the cotholder might not notice the loss of a few tubers and grease in a pan, the disappearance of too much cheese would be a different matter. So he found a thin old knife blade in the back of a drawer and sliced off a section of cheese, enough to provide him a small meal but, he hoped, not enough to be instantly noticed. Almost as if his restraint were being rewarded, he found a dozen rolls of travel rations in another tin box and took two. He would surely find more food if he was not greedy now. He believed in that sort of justice.

He removed the bandage on his forehead, a painful task even when he had soaked his face in the cold stream water. One or two spots bled a little, but as no blood trailed down his face, he left the wound open to the clean mountain air.

He went back to the cothold to look for clothing but found none. He did take one of the older hides. He could not count on finding shelter, and though this was the fifth month, the nights could still be chilly.

Leaving the cothold, he investigated the tracks that led off in several directions. A flash of sunlight on something metallic caught his eyes and he whirled toward the river, afraid that he had been discovered. It took him much longer to locate the source of the reflection: the oarlocks of a small boat. Under the thick shrubbery along the bank, the boat was almost invisible, tethered to a branch with a rope so worn by constant rubbing against a half-submerged stone that the slightest pull would part the last strands.

He provided the pull and, stepping carefully into the boat, used his stick to push out into the current of the river. Perhaps he should have tried to find the oars, but he felt an urgency to be away from this cothold and as far down the river as possible. The little craft was just long enough so that if he cocked his knees, he could lie flat and be unseen from the shore.

That night, when he saw the glowbaskets of a sizeable small holding—not a large enough one to have a watchwher on guard—he propelled himself to the bank and tied up the boat by the tether he had mended with strips of his tattered shirt during his long day afloat.

Luck was with him. First he found a basket of avian eggs left on a hook outside a side door to the beasthold. He sucked the contents of three, and carefully deposited three more in his shirt, tucked into his waistband. Then his eye caught the shirts and pants drying on bushes by the flat river stones where women would have washed them. He found clothes to fit him well enough and corrected the positions of others to make it appear that what he had chosen might simply have fallen into the river and drifted away.

In the beasthold for a second look, though the animals moved restlessly in the presence of a stranger, he found bran and an old battered scoop. Tomorrow he would boil the bran and add the eggs for a good hot meal. Suddenly he heard voices and immediately returned to his boat, pushing it carefully out into the current and lying down, lest he be seen.

The night swallowed the voices and all he heard was the gurgle of the river in which the boat moved so silently. Above him were the stars. The old harper who had taught all the youngsters at the Glasscrafthall had told him the names of some of them. Indeed, the old man had mentioned meteorites and the Ghosts that appeared in bright arcs in Turnover skies. Shankolin had never believed that those bright sparks were the ghosts of dead dragons, but some of the younger children had.

The brightest stars never changed. He recognized the sparkle of Vega—or was it Canopus? He couldn't remember the names of the other stars in the spring sky. In trying to recall those names and when he had learned them, his mind inexorably returned to Aivas and all that . . . that *thing* . . . had done to him. He'd only recently heard, in a repetition of very old news, that his father had been exiled to an island in the Eastern Sea with the Lord Holders and other craftsmen who had tried to stop the Abomination.

Now that the source was silenced, they'd be able to talk men and women into returning to their senses. The Red Star brought Thread. The Dragonriders fought Thread in the skies, and people lived comfortably enough between Passes. That had been the order of life for centuries—an order that should be preserved. When he had heard that the Masterharper of Pern, a personage Shankolin had admired, had been abducted, he had been deeply disturbed. But his ears had been blocked for Turns before he gradually recovered some hearing and learned about that part of the incident. He had never clearly heard why the Masterharper had been found dead in the Abomination's chamber. But it, too, had been dead—"terminated," one of the miners said. Had Master Robinton come to his senses and turned off the Abomination? Or had the Abomination killed Master Robinton? He felt eager to discover the truth.

Once he got down Crom's river—perhaps Keogh Hold would be far enough—he could make plans and see just how badly the Abomination had interfered with Pern's traditions and way of life.

Gathers began in springtime, when the roads dried of winter snow and mud, and he could simply blend into the crowds, and perhaps find more answers. He was hearing more and more these days, even the shrill song of avians. Once he caught up on current news, he would be able to plan his next moves.

Surely not everyone on Pern would want tradition degraded or would believe the lies that the Abomination had spouted. He called to mind those whom he knew had been seriously disturbed by the so-called improvements promulgated by Aivas. By now, eleven Turns since the Abomination had terminated, some right-minded, thinking folk would realize that the Red Star had not changed course simply because three old engines had blown up in a crack on its surface! Especially when Thread continued to fall on the planet—as indeed it *should*, to be sure that all Pern was united against the menace of its return, century after century.

AT A GATHER—6.15.30

"I don't know why it had to mess up time," said the first man, morosely fingering a pattern in the spilled gravy in front of him.

"You're messing up the table," the second man said, pointing.

"He had no call to mess up our time," the first man insisted, rather more vehemently.

"Who?" Second was confused. "He? It?"

"Aivas, that's who or it."

"Whaddya mean?"

"Well, he did, didn't he? Back in '38—which should be only 2524." The holder scowled, his thick black brows coming together across the wide bridge of his thick nose. "Made us add some fourteen Turns allasudden."

"He was *regulating* time," Second corrected, surprised at his companion's vehemence. The holder had seemed a pleasant enough companion, knowledgeable about music and knowing all the words to even the latest songs the harpers were playing. With his third wineskin, his temper had deteriorated. And possibly his wits, if time or how folk numbered Turns was bothering him.

"Made me older'n' I was."

"Didn't make you smarter," Second said with a rude snort. " 'Sides, Masterharper himself said it was all right on account there were dis- ah, disk—" He paused and used a belch as an excuse while he recalled the exact phrasing. "—there'd been inaccurate timekeeping because of Thread falling only forty Turns once instead of fifty, like it usually did, and people forgetting to account for the disk—"

"Discrepancies," the third man put in, regarding them superciliously.

Second gave a snap of his fingers and beamed at Third for finding the word he couldn't recall.

"The problem is not what it did," First went on. "It's what it's continuing to do. To all of us." He made a flourish that included everyone at the Gather, all laughing and singing, oblivious to the dangers in this continuation.

"Continuing to do?" A woman who had been standing nearby slipped into a seat several places down the long Gather table, on the opposite side from First and Second.

"Pushing things on us whether we want 'improvements' or not," First said slowly, eyeing her in what illumination dimly reached their side table. He saw a thin woman, with an unattractive face, a pinched mouth, a recessive lower jaw, and huge eyes that glowed with an inner anger or resentment.

"Like the lights?" Second asked, gesturing toward the nearest one. "Very useful. Much more convenient than messing with glowbaskets."

"Glowbaskets are traditional," the woman said, and her petulant tone carried into the shadows beyond the table. "Glows were put here for us to cultivate and protect."

"Glows are natural, and have lighted our holds and halls for centuries," said a deep, censorious voice. Startled, the woman gasped and put her hand protectively to her throat.

Certainly First and Second, who had thought they were having a private discussion, were annoyed by the intrusion until the big man stepped out of the shadows. As he slowly walked to the table, the others watched his deliberate advance, noting the size of him. He sat down by Third, bringing the number seated there to five. He wore a strangely shaped leathern cap that hid most of his forehead but did not cover the scar on the side of his nose and cheek. He was also missing the top joint of the first finger on his left hand. Something about his scarred face and his purposeful manner compelled the others to silence.

"Pern has lost much lately and gained little." His unmaimed hand lifted to point to the light. "And all because a voice—" He paused contemptuously. "—said to do so."

"Got rid of the Red Star," Second said, shifting uneasily.

Fifth turned his head toward Second, regarding him so unblinkingly that his scorn was nearly palpable.

"Thread still falls," Fifth said in that deep, disturbing voice that seemed to use no inflection.

"Well, yes, but that was explained," Second said.

"Perhaps to your satisfaction, but not to mine."

Two men seated at a table opposite the group looked over with interest, and gestured at First to let them join in. First nodded his head at the two, and Sixth and Seventh hastily climbed into vacant spaces among the others.

"The voice is gone," First said, when the two newcomers

were settled and he was guaranteed the group's full attention once again. "Terminated itself."

"As it should have been terminated before it was allowed to pollute and corrupt the minds of so many," Fifth went on.

"And it has left so much behind," the woman said in a despairing tone, "so much that can be misused."

"You mean the equipment and new methods for manufacturing all kinds of things, like the electricity that brightens dark places?" Third could not resist teasing such somber and humorless people.

"There was no good reason for that . . . thing to turn itself off like that, just when it was beginning to be useful," First said resentfully.

"But it *left* plans!" And Fourth sounded as if that was suspicious.

"Too many plans," Fifth agreed, deepening his voice to a lugubrious and ominous level.

"What?" Third prompted him. Fourth's eyes rounded with fear and anxiety.

"Surgery!" In that expressive deep voice the three syllables were dramatically drawn out as if he spoke of something immoral.

"Surgery?" Sixth frowned. "What's that?"

"Ways of mucking inside a body," First replied, lowering his own voice to match Fifth's.

Sixth shuddered. "Mind you, sometimes we gotta cut a foal out of its dam or it strangles." When the others regarded him suspiciously, he added, "Only a very well-bred foal we can't afford to lose. And I saw the healer once remove a pendix. Woman would've died, he said. She didn't feel a thing."

" 'She didn't feel a thing,' " Fifth repeated, investing that statement with sinister import.

"The healer could have done anything else he liked," Fourth said in a shocked whisper.

Second dismissed that with a grunt. "Didn't do her any harm and she's still alive and a good worker."

"I mean," First went on, "there's a lot of stuff being tried in the Crafthalls, not just the Healers—and when they make mistakes, it can cost a man's life. I don't want them fooling around with me, inside or out."

"Your choice," Second said.

"But is it always 'your' choice?" Fourth wanted to know, leaning forward across the table and tapping her finger to stress her point.

Third also leaned forward. "And what choices are we being given—to decide what we want and need—out of all those files Aivas is supposed to have left us? How do we know we want all this technology and advanced gadgets? How do we know it'll do what *they say it will*? Lot of people saying we got to have that; ought to have this. They're making the decisions. Not us. I don't like it." He nodded his head to emphasize his distrust.

"For that matter, how do we know that all that hard work—and I had to work my arse off some days down at Landing—will work?" Seventh asked with some rancor. "I mean, they can *tell* us that it's going to work, but none of us will be alive to see if it does, will we?"

"Neither will they," Third said with black humor. "Then, too," he went on quickly before Fifth could start in again, "not all of the Masters and Lords and Holders are keen to just latch on to all this new junk. Why I heard Master Menolly herself . . ." Even Fifth regarded him with interest. "She said that we ought to wait and go carefully. We didn't need a lot of the things that that Aivas machine talked about."

"What we *do* have," Fifth said, raising his deeper, oddly inflectionless voice above Third's light tenor, "has worked well enough for hundreds of Turns."

Third held up a cautionary finger. "We gotta be careful what new junk gets made just because it's new and seems to make things easier."

"But you have electricity?" Sixth said enviously.

"It's done naturally—we use sun panels, and they've been around forever."

"Ancients made 'em," First said.

"Well, as I said," Third went on, "*some* things will be

useful, but we've got to be very careful or we'll fall into the same trap the Ancients did. Too much technology. It's even in the Charter."

"It is?" Second asked, surprised.

"It is," Third said. "And we can do something to keep us traditional and unsullied by stuff we aren't even sure we need."

"What?" First asked.

"I'm going to think about it," Fourth said. "I don't hold with someone hurting people, but devices—things we neither want nor need—can be broken or spilled or got rid of." She looked to Fifth to see his reaction.

Third guffawed. "Some folks tried that. Got their ears deafened . . ."

"The machine's dead," First reminded him.

Third snarled at being interrupted. "Got exiled for hurting the Masterharper—"

"I did hear that the Masterharper died in its chamber. Perhaps the Masterharper had realized how insidious that Abomination was. Could he have terminated it?" asked Fifth.

The woman gasped.

"That's a very interesting idea," Third said softly, leaning forward. "Is there *any* proof?"

"How could there be?" First responded in a horrified voice. "The Healers said Master Robinton's heart gave out. From being bounced around during his abduction."

"He was never the same after," agreed Second, who had grieved as sincerely as the rest of the planet for his death. "Heard tell there was a line printed on the screen. Stayed there for a long time and then disappeared."

" 'And a time for every purpose under heaven,' " murmured Sixth.

"Couldn't have been Master Robinton that put up that message. Had to have been Aivas," Seventh said, scowling at Sixth.

"Something to think about, though, isn't it?" Third said.

"Indeed it is," Fourth said, eyes blazing.

"There are other matters to think about: what that . . . Aivas machine"—though Fifth's odd voice had no inflection, his scorn for Aivas rippled down the table—"has insinuated into our way of life, corrupting the traditions by which we have survived so long." Fifth had no trouble dominating the conversation again. "I do not—" He paused. "—approve of harming a living thing." Again, he left a significant pause before he continued. "But permanently removing items that can have dangerous effects on innocent people is another thing. It would be wise to make certain that such new materials and objects should never see the light of day."

"Much less glowbaskets or electricity," Third said in a facetious tone that was not well received even by Second. Fifth and Fourth glowered so repressively that he recoiled.

"I go along with removing some of those gadgets and new junk," Second murmured, but he didn't sound entirely convinced. "It's more that some of us," he added, glancing from one face to another, "never seem to get our fair share."

"I agree wholeheartedly. Like dragonriders getting what *they* want first," Third said. "Get *our* share."

"There are more folk than you might think," Fifth said in his compelling voice, "who have genuine doubts about improvements from all this Aivas stuff. Machine oughtn't to know more than a human *being* does."

First gave another emphatic nod of his head and rose. "Be right back with some other right-thinking human *beings*."

By the end of the evening, there were over twenty "right-thinking" men and women, discussing in low voices the possibility that the Aivas machine—the "Abomination" seemed as appropriate a name as it had been for the original protestors—might not have the good of *real* people at heart, it being a machine and all.

No one exchanged names and hold or hall affiliations, but they all agreed to meet at the next Gather, if they could. They agreed to find out who else might wish to organize a protest about undesirable and possibly detrimental changes that were introduced as "progress."

*   *   *

It surprised First and Second, but not Third, Fourth, Sixth, and Seventh—and especially not Fifth—who continued to use those numbers as their Gather identities, that many people had grievances, small and large, real or fancied, that needed to be aired and perhaps addressed. Fifth never again spoke about the synchronicity of the death of the Masterharper and the Abomination, but that little rumor bound many to the cause who might not have given it much credence. Master Robinton had been very popular, and if—*if*—that Abomination had been responsible in any way for the Masterharper's death, then that was cause enough to ally against it. If devices or procedures they couldn't understand were sponsored or suggested by the Abomination, distrust or fear—along with that damaging rumor of *which* death had been first—supplied an impetus that could be successfully channeled into action.

There were those who found fulfillment within the group and in the planning, and with a certain perverse joy in subtly thwarting "progress" with minor deeds of damage. But for others, such "minor" deeds—which did not cause real alarm in Hold and Hall, or have deeper consequences in preventing the making and distribution of more and more abominable devices—were not enough.

Though it caused some distress to healers to find the latest shipments of new preparations from the Healer Hall missing from their shelves, it did not immediately occur to them that none of the older remedies were ever stolen.

If a Crafthall, manufacturing parts for new devices, found work damaged by "accidents" or acids spilled on packing crates, they put stronger locks on their hall doors and kept eyes open for strangers visiting in the area.

If the Printer Hall found discarded sheets missing from the bin in which the ruined paper had been placed for recycling, none of the apprentices thought to report the matter.

Then the Lilcamp traders, who were transporting some valuable components from one Smith Hall to another, found the carefully packed crates missing one morning and reported it to Master Fandarel at Telgar Smithcrafthall. Fandarel sent an indignant message to Masterharper Sebell, reminding him that this was by no means the first time delicate items had mysteriously disappeared on the way to Smith Halls. One of the healer journeymen had casually complained about having to resupply new medications to a rather large number of healers, working in isolated areas. Fandarel, Sebell, and Masterhealer Oldive began to notice such depredations.

It was Master Harper Mekelroy, better known to the Masterharper as Pinch, who sifted through such incidents and found a pattern to the thefts and pillaging.

PART 1

Turnover

TURNOVER AT LANDING—
1.1.31 PRESENT PASS AIVAS—
AIVAS ADJUSTED TURN 2553

SINCE IT WAS not at all unusual for dragonriders to be found poring over the volumes in the extensive Aivas archives, F'lessan, rider of bronze Golanth, was not surprised to see a girl wearing the shoulder knots of a green rider from Monaco Bay deeply engrossed in study. What did strike him as odd was that anyone at all was here in the main archive reading room during Turnover. Tonight the planet, north and south continents, would officially celebrate the beginning of the thirty-second Turn of the present and, hopefully, final Pass of Threadfall. Even through the thick walls of the building, he could hear drums and occasionally the sound of the brass instruments from Landing's Gather Square.

Why wasn't the girl, especially a green rider, out dancing? Why wasn't *he*? He grimaced. He was still trying to overcome the carelessly lustful reputation that he had earned early in this Pass. Not that he was any different from many bronze and brown riders. "Just more noticeable," Mirrim had told him in her candid fashion. Mirrim had astonished everyone, including herself, when she had Impressed green Path at a Benden Weyr Hatching. Being T'gellan's weyrmate had mellowed her natural assertiveness, but she never spared him her blunt opinions.

The girl was engrossed in her study of a foldout page depicting Rukbat's planetary system, spread across the tilted reading desk. Not everyone's reading choice certainly, F'lessan thought.

Many of the younger riders, who would see the end of this Pass in sixteen Turns, were studying to become proficient in another craft. In that way they would be able to support themselves once the traditional tithe to the Weyrs ceased. While Thread still fell, Hold and Hall would continue to support the dragonriders, in exchange for aerial protection against the voracious organism that could destroy anything but metal and stone. But when Thread ceased, so would that support. Those riders whose families owned holds or halls might simply be reabsorbed, but weyrbred dragonriders like F'lessan had to find another way. Fortunately for F'lessan, he had discovered Honshu, in the foothills of the great Southern mountain range, and since the Weyrs had wrung out of the council that loosely governed the planet the concession that dragonriders might claim holdings on the Southern continent, F'lessan had claimed Honshu as his. He had based most of his argument on the fact that he intended to restore and preserve the Ancient habitation and its splendors for everyone to enjoy. He had used every ounce of his considerable charm and every jot of guile with other Weyrleaders, Craftmasters, and Lord Holders in order to secure that title to himself. And once the formidable intelligence of the Artificial Intelligence Voice Address System—Aivas—and the combined might of all the Weyrs of Pern had diverted the orbit of the menacing Red Star, he had begun to spend all the time he could spare from his duties as a Benden Wingleader in refurbishing Honshu.

F'lessan had never been a studious youngster—his interests as well as his concentration span had been limited to escaping lessons whenever he could and having the greatest amount of fun. Impressing bronze Golanth had imposed discipline at last, because there was no way he would neglect his dragon. He had learned a determination and focus that had resulted in his becoming one of the most adept riders, held up as a fine example—at least of riding—by weyrlingmasters.

Honshu had become another passion. The Ancient holding, with the splendid murals in its main hall, had exerted a strange compulsion on him from the start: to preserve the ancient treasures found there and to discover as much as possible about its founders and residents. With the boyish impudence that was his most ingenuous characteristic, he had appointed himself Honshu's guardian and caretaker. He had worked harder than anyone else in clearing out the muck and mold and restoring the fabric of the place. Tonight he had a puzzle he wanted to solve. He had specifically chosen this time to come to the Aivas facility, hoping to be its sole visitor. He preferred not to share his research—his fascination with Honshu was at odds with his reputation.

You protect Honshu. I like being there very much, said his dragon, Golanth, from where he had settled himself in the hot noontime sun among the dragons who had brought their riders to Landing's Turnover festivities. *Good sunning places, clear water, and many fat herdbeasts.*

Still paused quietly on the threshold of the reading room, F'lessan grinned. *You found it. We'll keep it.*

Yes, Golanth agreed amiably.

F'lessan stuffed his riding gloves into the Turnover gift of a fine carisak, giving the wide cuffs a good push; the new wherhide leather was stiff, despite the good oiling he had given it yesterday evening. The carisak had been presented to him by Lessa and F'lar. He rarely thought of them as "mother" or "father": they were his Weyrleaders, and that was more relevant. His birthing day, his Impression Day—the day marking the advent of Golanth into his life—and Turnover were, however, always recognized by some gift from them. F'lessan didn't know if this was occasioned by their need to remind him of his parents, or themselves of their son. Fostering was the rule in a weyr, so no child was without several people, not necessarily the birth parents, who took special interest in him or her. As F'lessan grew up and saw how easygoing life was in a weyr, and the conformity required of children in the holds, he was as glad he'd been weyrbred.

He gave the gloves one more shove to store them completely, but still he hesitated to enter the room. He didn't want to disturb the single reader who was so engrossed in her study that she was unaware of him standing there.

No one has ever disliked your company, said his dragon.

I don't like to break into such concentration, F'lessan replied. *How do we know she isn't studying an alternative occupation for After?*

Dragons will always be needed on Pern, Golanth said stoutly.

Golanth was fond of making that observation. Almost as if Golanth, too, needed to reassure himself. Maybe it was just the mind-set of a bronze dragon—or more likely Mnementh's in particular, since F'lar's great bronze took a keen interest in the subtle tuition of any bronzes hatched on Benden's sands. However, succeeding F'lar as Weyrleader of Benden was most certainly not in F'lessan's future plans. F'lessan earnestly hoped that F'lar would lead the Weyr out of this Pass: a triumph in itself, over and above what F'lar had done at its beginning with the slender force he'd had available then. Being Wingleader suited F'lessan's blithe personality, especially now that he had claimed Honshu as his special domain. Now, if the Weyrleaders—or rather F'lar—would just come out and say that he and Lessa would retire there, no one would dare contest his claim.

Unlike the position of Lord Holders, the Weyrleadership was not hereditary. A good example was the recent stepping down of R'mart and Bedella of Telgar. To establish the new leadership, the challenge had been for the best bronze in the Weyr to fly the first junior queen ready to mate. J'fery, rider of bronze Willerth, was now Telgar's Weyrleader, and Palla, golden Talmanth's rider, was Weyrwoman. F'lessan knew them both well, and knew they would lead Telgar Weyr well under Threadfree skies.

If we don't make the arrogant mistakes that the Oldtimers did, F'lessan added to himself, *and expect to continue re-*

ceiving the perquisites due the Weyrs during a Pass, once there is no more Thread.

A movement brought him back to the present. The girl's boots scraped over the stone floor as she recrossed her ankles. She was hunched forward over the reading desk and now leaned her elbows on the table. Her profile was well lit by the softly disseminated light, and she had thinned her lips over whatever it was she was reading. She frowned, then sighed over the wide page. F'lessan saw the well-defined arch of a black eyebrow as her frown relaxed. She had a long and very delicately formed nose, he observed with mild approval. Her hair, a midbrown sparking with red as she moved, was clipped short on top to reduce sweating under her helmet. Left long at the nape of her neck, the wavy mass reached halfway down her back, where it was neatly cut off in a straight line.

She turned her head abruptly, suddenly aware of his scrutiny.

"Sorry. Thought I'd have the place to myself," F'lessan said genially, striding forward, his dress shoes making very little sound on the stone floor.

Her startlement suggested to him that she, too, had thought she could study in solitary quiet. She was in the act of pushing back her chair when he held out a hand to prevent her from rising. Most riders knew who he was: he made a habit of flying Thread with the two southern Weyrs and usually attended every Impression. The latter was sheer indulgence on his part, for at each Impression, he and Golanth reaffirmed their lifelong commitment to each other.

Now that he could see her full face, he recognized her.

"You're Tai, aren't you? Zaranth's rider?" he asked, hoping he remembered rightly.

You always do, Golanth murmured.

She'd Impressed, unexpectedly, nearly five Turns ago at Monaco Bay. She'd come south, though he couldn't remember from where. There had been so many people flooding through Landing since Aivas was discovered in 2538. While she couldn't be much older than her mid twenties, he wondered if she'd been part of the workforce during those astonishing five Turns of Aivas. After all, Aivas had demonstrated a distinct bias for green dragons and their riders.

F'lessan stepped forward, extending his hand to her. She looked embarrassed, dropping her eyes as soon as their hands had clasped politely. Her handshake was firm, if brisk almost to the point of rudeness, and he could feel some odd ridges, scars, on the back of her hand and on her forefinger. She wasn't pretty; she didn't act sensual, the way some green riders did, and she was only half a head shorter than he was. She wasn't *too* thin, but the lack of flesh on her bones gave her a slightly boyish appearance.

"I'm F'lessan, Golanth's rider, of Benden."

"Yes," she said, shooting him a sharp look. Her eyes were set at an unusual upward slant, but she looked away so quickly he couldn't see what color they were. Oddly enough, she flushed. "I know." She seemed to gather breath to continue, "Zaranth just told me that Golanth had apologized for disturbing her nap on the ledge." She flicked him another almost contrite glance, awkwardly clasping her left wrist with her right hand so that the knuckles turned white.

F'lessan grinned in his most ingratiating fashion. "By nature, Golanth is very considerate." He gave a little bow and gestured toward the volume open on the reading desk. "Don't let me disturb your studies. I'll be over there." He pointed to the far right.

He could just as easily work in the alcove as in the main room and not intrude on her solitude. In no time at all he had collected three of the records he thought most likely to contain the information he sought, and brought them to the smaller reading desk in the alcove. A narrow window gave him a view of the eastern hills and the barest sparkle of the sea. He seated himself, placed the piece of paper that he had brought with him on the table, and started riffling through the thinly coated plastic pages of the COM Tower records. He was looking for one name: Stev Kimmer, listed in the colony records as Stakeholder on Bitkim Island, now called Ista Hold. He needed to find any connection between Kimmer and Kenjo Fusaiyuki, who had been the original Honshu Stakeholder.

In his careful clearing of debris in the ancient dwelling place, he had found the initials SK carved or etched on several surfaces: on the metal worktop in the garage of the ancient sled and on several drawers. No other inhabitant had defaced or initialed anything. The only SK not listed as going north in the Second Crossing—when the Thread-beleaguered colonists had resettled at Fort—was Stev Kimmer. Previous research revealed that the man had disappeared with a sled after Ted Tubberman's illegal launch of an appeal for help from old Earth. Kimmer had not been seen again. The loss of a functional sled had been officially regretted; Kimmer's absence had not.

The interesting point in F'lessan's earlier search was that Ita Fusaiyuki had continued to hold at Honshu and resisted every invitation to move north with her children. Other colonists, like those at Ierne Island and some of the smaller holds in Dorado, had hung on in the south as long as they could. Eventually all, save perhaps those at Honshu, had immigrated. There had been no reference to Honshu or the Fusaiyukis in the early records at Fort Hold.

The initials, S and K, were distinctively carved. F'lessan needed to find any other samples of Stev Kimmer's handwriting to be sure of his identification. Not that it mattered, except to him. With atypical zeal, F'lessan yearned to complete the history of Honshu itself as accurately as possible: who had lived there, when they had left, where they had gone, and why.

Honshu was also an excellent example of colonial self-sufficiency. Clearly it had been occupied by quite a few people and designed for many more: a whole floor of bedrooms had never been furnished. Then, all at once and in some hurry, considering details like drawers left pulled out in a workshop that had otherwise been meticulously kept, everyone had left. Twelve of them at least. To judge by strands of moldering material, even garments had been left behind, folded on the shelves, in drawers, or hanging in closets. The fact that all the utensils were still stored and hung about the capacious kitchen argued that, wherever the inhabitants had gone, they hadn't needed to bring along household equipment. Storage canisters filled with desiccated remnants indicated that few, if any, staples had been taken. There were homely artifacts like rusted needles, pins, and scissors. There had been no human bones to suggest a sudden annihilation from attack or disease.

Although all the other entrances to the interior of Honshu had been shut, the heavy doors to the beasthold had been propped open, suggesting that the Ancients had released their livestock but had left the creatures access to a refuge.

He turned page after page of the daily comings and goings from Landing, neatly recorded by the Tower duty officers. He saw again the reference to Kimmer's defection with a much-needed operational sled.

S.K. involved in the Tubberman launching. Observed on a northwestern course. Suspect that's the last we'll see of him and the sled. ZO.

F'lessan had already tried to find any notes in Kimmer's handwriting from his time as Stakeholder at Bitkim. There had been none from either him or Avril Bitra about their mining operations, though the Minercrafthall still excavated the occasional fine gemstones from the clay at their original site.

He closed the final volume with a frustrated soft *whoosh*, and then glanced apologetically over his shoulder for disturbing the quiet. He noticed that the surface of Tai's worktable was covered with bound volumes. Idly he wondered if she was having any more luck with her research than he was. Craning his neck he could read the spine on the book facing in his direction: Volume 35—YOKO 13.20-28/. The last four digits, which would be the relevant Turn, had been overwritten in red marker to read 2520. The correction had been made in the precise numerals only Master Esselin could produce.

Stuffing the note with the replica of the initials back into his belt pocket, he rose with quiet agility, trying not to scrape the chair on the stone floor. Collecting the volumes he had been consulting, he returned them to the proper shelf. He stood for a moment, fists jammed into his belt, glaring at the rows of records that would not produce the answer to his puzzle. Was there a reason why he had to identify SK? Who would care? He did, for some obscure reason he didn't understand. He made sure the books were properly aligned on the shelf. Master Esselin was very particular about how his precious volumes were returned.

Hearing Tai get to her feet and push back her chair, F'lessan swiveled around to see her picking up the outsized book she had been studying. She hefted it up, pirouetting gracefully on tiptoe to return it to the special shelf in the case behind her.

"I hope you had better luck," he said with a rueful grin.

Startled, she lost her grip on the awkward, heavy tome. One edge was wedged against the lower shelf. She struggled to get it up again and into its assigned place, but her hand slipped. Knowing how difficult Master Esselin could be about damage to any artifact in his custody, F'lessan leaped across to catch the volume, just managing to keep one corner from impacting on the stone floor.

"Not a bad save, if I say so myself," he said, grinning up at her. Why was she regarding him as if he were dangerous? Or shifty? "I've got it. Allow me?" With what he sincerely hoped was a cheerful smile, he took the volume from her nerveless fingers and shoved it safely into place.

That was when he saw the raw scrapes on the back of her left hand.

"That looks nasty. Seen a healer?" he asked. He reached out to examine the injury, at the same time fumbling in his belt pouch for numbweed.

She tried to pull free of his grasp.

"Tai, did I hurt you?" he asked, instantly releasing her fingers. He quickly displayed the distinctive green glass jar used for numbweed.

"It's nothing."

"Don't try that on me," he said, mock stern. "I'll get Golanth to make Zaranth tell on you."

She blinked rapidly in surprise. "It's just a scrape."

"This is Southern, Tai, and you should know by now that even well-tended wounds can develop some peculiar infections." He cocked his head at her, wondering if he should try a coaxing smile. He had the jar open and passed it under her nose. "Smell? Just reliable old numbweed. Fresh made this spring. My own private supply." He used the tone that had been effective with his sons when they were tots. He held out his hand again, palm up, wriggling his fingers to overcome her reluctance. "Someone might grab that hand later when you're dancing and that'd really hurt." As if on cue, music from the square swelled into an audible finale.

She relented and, almost meekly, extended her hand. He lifted his palm up to steady her fingers as he turned the numbweed jar over the scrape, waiting for a glob of the semiliquid stuff to ooze down.

"It's easier to let it take its own time," he remarked idly, all too aware of her nervousness. The gouges weren't deep, he noticed, but went from knuckles to wrist. She should have taken care of it immediately. It was, he judged from long experience with injuries, several hours old. Why had she ignored it?

She gave a little gasp as the cool numbweed flowed. Expertly, F'lessan tilted her fingers and they both watched the salve slowly cover the scratches.

"At Turnover one is more apt to require fellis for overindulgence than numbweed." That wasn't a particularly clever remark, F'lessan said to himself and gave his head a little shake. "There! That'll prevent infection."

"I didn't realize it was quite so bad. I was in a hurry, you see." She gave the reading room a quick glance.

"Trying to work without interruption." He chuckled, hoping that wouldn't offend her as much as his smile seemed to. "That's why I'm here. No, wait a few moments longer to let the numbweed set," he added when she started to move.

He pulled out a chair, indicating that she should seat herself as he dragged another over for himself, switching it around so he could straddle it, resting his arms on the top. She propped her arm on the table, watching as the numbweed changed from clear to opaque on the scrape. Trying to appear more solicitous than overbearing, he let the silence lengthen, wondering what he could ask without giving additional offense. He didn't usually have problems striking up conversations. He was beginning to wonder if he should have just left her alone in the reading room. Just then the significance of all those *Yoko* records made sense.

"May I ask why you're interested in the Ghosts?"

She stared at him in such astonishment that her mouth, with its very well shaped lips, fell slightly open. He gestured.

"Why else would anyone be looking over Turns of the end of the thirteenth month? When the Ghost Showers occur?"

She looked everywhere but at him and then, suddenly, blurted out, "I often do some research for Master Wansor and he'd heard that the Ghosts—which we can't see down here—but you'd know about them since you're from Benden—" she stopped, swallowing as if she'd said something untoward.

"Yes, I know that they are not visible here in the southern hemisphere, and yes, they do appear extremely bright and numerous right now. I did notice. In fact, many people have noticed," he went on encouragingly, "but, having lived in Benden Weyr all my life, I remember that on other occasions, they have been as bright and as numerous. I have studied some astronomy, so would a Benden dragonrider not totally untutored in his local starscape be any help to you?"

"Personal observations are always admissible," she said rather primly. "Others have noted," and she gave him the ghost of a smile, pointing to several of the volumes, "their brightness and numbers occur in cycles of seven Turns."

"That's right, because I was three when I saw the pretty lights and asked about them, and this is the fifth time I've seen them so brightly in their hundreds. Here, I'll help you put those heavy books away. Spare irritating your hand."

She seemed about to hesitate, but he stacked five volumes

deftly on one arm and walked to the proper shelf. She hastily gathered up more.

"Did you have any luck with your research?" she asked when they had finished racking.

"Actually, no," he said. "But there may not be a source."

"With all this?" She indicated the full ranks of shelving around them.

"Aivas didn't know everything," he said, once again managing to startle her. "That's not heretical, you realize, because he couldn't have recorded anything after the Second Crossing."

"I know."

There was an odd note in that simple agreement that he didn't dare query.

"The answer to my puzzle probably doesn't even exist," he added.

"What puzzle?" She inclined her body slightly in his direction.

Ah, she's curious. That's good. "Initials." He reached into his belt and found the slip of paper. "S.K." He smoothed it out to show her. She frowned slightly, puzzled but not totally reserved. "I believe the initials are Stev Kimmer's," he said.

She blinked. "Who?"

"A real villain—"

"Oh! The man who absconded with a functional sled after the Tubberman launch?"

"You know your history."

She flushed, ducking her head. "I was very fortunate to be accepted to the Landing School."

"You were? I hope you were a better student than I was."

"But you were already a rider," she said, startled into looking directly at him. Her eyes were an unusual shade of green.

He grinned. "That didn't necessarily mean I was a good student. If you're still studying," and he gestured at the shelving, "then you learned good habits. Did you stay on here when you finished schooling?"

She glanced away from him, and he couldn't imagine what he had said to alarm her.

"Yes," she said at last. "I was fortunate. You see," she explained hesitantly, "my father brought us all here. From Keroon. He was a Smithcraft journeyman and helped—here."

"Oh?" F'lessan drawled the exclamation out encouragingly when she faltered.

"My brothers were his apprentices, and my mother took my sister and me to the school, in case we were lucky enough to be accepted. My sister didn't like school."

"Not everyone does," F'lessan said with a self-deprecating chuckle. Her quick glance gave him the impression that she had taken to learning as a fire-lizard to the air. "So . . . ?" he prompted.

"Then, during the last Turn when everyone at Admin was so busy, Master Samvel sent me here to work. My father was anxious to find a good place to hold and they went off."

And, F'lessan thought from the sorrow in the set of her shoulders and dejected attitude, she had never heard from them again.

"Did anyone look for them?"

"Oh, yes," she said quickly, glancing up. "T'gellan sent out a full wing." She looked away again.

"No trace at all?" he asked gently.

"None. Everyone was very kind. I was apprenticed to Master Wansor—I read for him. He liked my voice."

"I don't wonder at that," F'lessan said. He had already noticed how expressive her voice could be.

"That's how I came to be at the Monaco Bay Hatching and Impressed Zaranth."

"Reading to Master Wansor?"

"No," she said in an amused tone. "He liked to have someone telling him what was going on. So we were seated to one side of the Hatching Ground."

F'lessan chuckled. "Yes, I remember. Master Wansor had to push you at Zaranth. You didn't know what to do: respond to the hatchling or tell Master Wansor what was happening."

The smile that lit her face and her green eyes was evocative of the sense of incredulity and wonder that overwhelmed anyone lucky enough to Impress a dragon. His smile answered hers and both were silent for a long moment in fond reminiscences of their Impressions.

"You're still keeping up with your studies?" F'lessan asked, indicating the old tome she'd been studying.

"Why not?" she asked, with a wry grin. "It's as good an occupation for a dragonrider as any."

After a pause, she asked, "Have you tried the Charter?"

He blinked. "The Charter?"

She waved toward the special case where the original Charter of the Pern Colony was housed.

"Kimmer was an original colonist, wasn't he?" she said. "He'd've had to sign his name somewhere, even as a contractor, wouldn't he?"

F'lessan got to his feet so fast he had to catch the chair from falling. His movement startled her.

"Now, why didn't I think of that?" he exclaimed with exaggerated self-castigation. He strode to the airtight case that held what was considered the most valuable, and venerable, document on the planet.

Fort Hold had ceremoniously returned the Charter to Landing. Indeed, no one had known what had been stored in the thick container that had been gathering dust with other Hold treasures until Aivas had told them what to look for. Aivas was certainly the only intelligence that had known the combination of the digital lock. Inside its airtight case, the Charter had been revealed to be pristine. Upon close examination, Masterwoodsmith Benelek remarked that the plastic-coated pages could not have been damaged by anything short of being chopped into little pieces by very sharp blades. Now the Charter was enshrined behind some of Master Morilton's clear thick panes, mounted on a mechanism—also an Aivas design—that turned its pages to the one required.

"The capital letters would be similar, wouldn't they? Printed or written," F'lessan muttered. "Your research skills are better honed than mine." He shot her an appreciative grin. "Let's get to the end . . . Ah, contractor, contractor," he said under his breath as the pages shifted in sequence to the final ones containing signatures, many of them mere illegible scrawls. There were three sections: the first, of the Charterers; the second, longer, included the names of all the Contractors; while the third listed all minor children over five years of age who had come with their parents on this momentous venture.

"There," Tai said, her right index finger tapping the glass so that he could find the bold handwritten *Stev Kimmer, Eng*.

With careful fingers, F'lessan smoothed his note on the glass, just above the bold, and legible, name.

"Couldn't be anyone else," Tai said. She ran her finger down the listings. "No other S.K."

"You're right, you're right. He's here. It's him." With his characteristic exuberance, F'lessan grabbed her by the waist and spun her about, forgetting the reserve she had shown any of his overtures of friendliness. "Oops!" He dropped her, staring in mute apology.

She staggered a little off balance and instantly he steadied her.

"Thank you very much for finding it so quickly. I was looking so hard I couldn't see," he said, giving her a quick bow.

She had a very nice smile, he thought, as the corners of her wide mouth curved up, showing her teeth, white and even, accented by a tanned complexion that was as much heredity as exposure to southern sun.

"Why was it so important to you?"

"Do you really want to know?" he asked with the ingenuousness that could still surprise people.

Her smile deepened, causing two dimples to appear in her cheeks. He didn't know any girls with dimples.

"If a dragonrider finds it more important than"—she tilted her head toward the noise of very loud dance music—"Turnover eating and dancing, it must be important."

He chuckled. "*You're* a dragonrider and you're here."

"But you're F'lessan and a bronze rider."

"And you are Tai and a green rider," he countered.

The dimples disappeared and she looked away from him.

You are a bronze rider and you are F'lessan and she's shy,
Golanth said. *Zaranth says she wants to make something of
herself for After. She never wants to be beholden to anyone
else ever.*

Like all dragonriders, F'lessan said with considerable
irony.

Not even to other dragonriders, Golanth added, slightly offended by Tai's utter independence.

"We were getting along quite well when you found Stev
Kimmer's signature for me," F'lessan said gently.

Be very careful, his dragon said softly.

"I think the numbweed is dry enough now," he added. "I
know I'm hungry and thirsty and, while I would prefer to go
back to Honshu, I have to put in an appearance out there." He
nodded in the direction of the music.

"Is that where Stev Kimmer went? To Honshu? Why
would that be his destination?"

"Ah," and F'lessan held up a finger, "that's part of the
puzzle I've got. I did find his initials on surfaces in the Hold,
and yet the records Ita Fusaiyuki kept until a few months after
Kenjo's death make no mention of him."

"She died there?"

F'lessan shook his head as she absently followed his slow
drift out of the Archives room.

"I don't know that. Aivas has records of messages sent to
her, urging her to come first to Landing to cross north. So she
was still alive during the Second Crossing. Or someone at
Honshu was."

"I promised I'd lock up," Tai said, pausing in the entrance
hall to enable the alarm.

F'lessan nodded approval. All archival material, whether
here or at a Hall or Hold, was provided with safeguards
against natural—or unnatural—accidents.

Outside, both stopped on the wide top step. The quick tran-
sition from twilight to full tropical night had occurred as they
talked. Below them, spread out in festive splendor, were the
lights, sights, and sounds of Turnover. More enticing were

the luscious aromas of the fine feast awaiting the revelers. As one they inhaled the odors and then, again simultaneously, turned slightly to see the round blue lanterns of massed dragon eyes on the heights, the blue denoting the dragons' own enjoyment of the happy scene. The music came to a raucous finale and the sound of laughter and excited chatter drifted back to them.

"The harpers are setting down their instruments," F'lessan said, pointing to the platform. He rubbed his hands together. "That means it's time to eat and I'm very hungry."

He looked around at her: she was exactly the right height for him. But would she dance if he asked her?

"I am, too," she admitted and tilted her chin just slightly.

He made a bow and swept his hand gracefully, indicating they should proceed.

"You've got long legs. I'll race you to the roast pits." And he took off, hearing her laugh before he heard her boots scrabbling in the beach pebbles that lined the path.

Tai, who knew rather more about Benden Wingleader F'lessan than he was aware, surprised herself by responding to the challenge. Despite all the tales she had heard from Mirrim about the bronze rider—including dire warnings about his fecklessness—he had acted considerately and courteously toward her in the library. She'd been surprised that he appeared to know his way around the shelves. He had certainly prevented her from getting in trouble with Master Esselin, who had his own ideas about what dragonriders should study. Especially green female riders. After Tai's first distressing encounter with the pompous Archivist, Mirrim had comforted her with a tale of how nasty Esselin had once been to her, in the early days of the discoveries at Landing, before Aivas was discovered, and how MasterHarper Robinton himself had acted on Mirrim's behalf. The fussbudget was the main reason Tai tried to pick unusual hours at the library: times when she wouldn't have to deal with the persnickety old man.

Fortunately the path from that wing of the Archives was wide all the way down to the open area where the Turnover festivities were being held. Now that the sun was down, lighting had come up so they didn't have to watch where they put their feet. F'lessan was ahead of her, as he passed the Aivas section, but he slowed and looked to his right with a respectful bend of his head. Tai knew that he'd been very much involved with Aivas, almost from the day of discovery, so his reverence was understandable. She slowed, too, as much from surprise as to nod her own respects. Then he lengthened his stride and so did she, trying to catch up. She wasn't a Runner, but she was no drag foot either and really wanted to catch up. Riders kept fit—it was part of their dedication to their dragons—and running was good exercise.

She ran into the dragonrider when he abruptly stopped, rounding a curve and trying to keep from knocking over a couple who were so involved in each other that they were oblivious to their surroundings. His halt and turn were close to acrobatic as he kept her from tripping over him.

Contrary to what Mirrim had led Tai to expect in F'lessan's behavior, he held her no longer than was necessary for her to regain her balance. His eyes were merry with amusement as he jerked his head at the still unmindful pair, lost in their private world.

"Let us not be an obstacle in the path of true love," he murmured to her and gestured that they circle around the lovers. He was breathing only a little hard from the run, though no more than she was.

They made the detour and then, the race forgotten, loped easily side by side toward the roasting pits. Diners were just beginning to assemble.

There was always an evening breeze at Landing, and that dried the sweat on her brow as they stood in line. They arrived just before the crowd streaming from the square. By the time they were served roast beast and quarters of grilled avians, and took their choice from steaming bowls of tubers and vegetables, the line at the serving tables had tripled its length.

"Where shall we sit?" F'lessan asked her, looking around.

"Surely you're joining your friends?"

"Ha! No one in particular. I wanted free time at the Archives. Look, over to our right, there at the edge. A quiet table." He raised his voice. "Hey, Geger!" A wineman glanced their way. "Serve us, will you?" F'lessan pointed and, putting his free hand on her elbow, steered her in that direction.

The wineman converged on the table just as they arrived.

"White? Red?" F'lessan asked her before turning to the wineman. "D'you have any Benden there, Geger?"

"Well, seeing as it's you, F'lessan, yes, I can get one." The wineman put his fingers to his lips and his shrill whistle pierced the happy noise of the crowd. Across the square, where skins of wine were hung in display, another wineman looked toward them. Geger flagged his arms in a private code and the man waved in reply. "That'll be three marks, bronze rider."

"What?" F'lessan demanded.

"I'll pay my share," Tai said quickly, reaching for her belt pouch.

"That's robbery, Geger. I could have bought from the source for one and a half."

Tai was amused by the outrage in his voice.

"Then you shoulda done before you got here, F'lessan. And you know three marks isn't high for cold white Benden." The last three words were delivered in a slow cajoling drawl.

"But three?"

"I'll give—" Tai began, but F'lessan flapped his hand sharply at her.

"Geger and I are old friends," he said, his eyes sparkling. There was a firm edge to his voice. "Aren't we, old friend?"

"Even for old friends, three marks for a '30 vintage cold white Benden is a good price at Turnover." Geger was not to be moved by any consideration of friendship.

"Benden marks," F'lessan said, sticking his jaw out.

"Benden marks are, to be sure, the best. Almost as good as Harper Hall."

F'lessan passed over the three marks just as the other wineman arrived with the skin, a large one.

"Good Turnover," Geger said, tipping a salute to F'lessan and a wink at Tai.

"Well," F'lessan commented, feeling the skin, "it's properly cold." He unplugged the small end, gesturing for Tai to supply glasses from those on the table. He filled both deftly, restored the plug, and laid the skin under the table. "Safe skies!" he said in the traditional toast. Quickly she touched her glass to his.

"I think it *is* a '30," he added after a judicious sip. He grinned broadly. "You know, three marks isn't that bad for a vintage Benden white."

His remark caught her taking her first sip and she nearly choked on it. Three marks would have been out of her reach even at a Turnover celebration when everyone tended to spend freely. She hadn't brought much with her; once she'd completed the declinations that Erragon wanted, she hadn't expected to do more than get a quick meal here—and maybe listen to the harpers awhile—before returning with Zaranth to her weyr down by Monaco Bay. She didn't have a great many marks in any event, though like many other green riders she could be hired to deliver small packages and letters almost anywhere in Southern, when she wasn't involved in Weyr duties or researching for Master Wansor at Cove Hold.

"Thank you, bronze rider," she said.

"I'm F'lessan, Tai," he replied with gentle chiding and a smile lurking in his eyes.

She wasn't sure how to respond to that.

"Let's eat," he suggested, taking his belt knife from its sheath. "I think from the smell of it the Landing cooks have used their special sauce. What more can one ask for on a Turnover night?"

Tai wouldn't have asked for this much, she mused as she picked up a clean fork and started on the roast tubers, her favorite.

The wine was the best she'd ever tasted and so was the food.

"How's the hand?" F'lessan asked after they'd eaten in hungry silence for a few minutes.

"My hand?" Tai looked down at it. "Oh, truly nothing now. My thanks again. And I usually do keep numbweed handy. I just didn't . . . today." In truth she had a big jar among the supplies in her weyr, but she did not have one small enough to fit in her belt pouch.

"How'd you do it?"

"Oh, probably when I was scrubbing Zaranth this afternoon. She hunted today and needed a good wash." Hunting and bathing Zaranth had taken longer than Tai had planned. Knowing that the Archives were more likely to be unoccupied on Turnover days, she'd been anxious to get there—and not careful enough to avoid barnacle-covered rocks when rinsing the stiff brush she used on Zaranth's hide.

"That can happen," he said with rueful agreement. "Are you weyred along the coast or inland?"

Tai tried not to freeze at the question: bronze riders with an eye to mating with Zaranth the next time she was "ripe" always wanted to know where she could be found. Zaranth wasn't even close to her cycle. "Coast," she replied quickly. Almost too quickly. "Do you spend a lot of time at Honshu?"

"Coast, huh? See much of the Monaco dolphins?"

She made herself relax. She was being overly suspicious. "Yes, I do." She smiled. Thinking of her dolphin friends always made her smile. It seemed to have a similar effect on F'lessan, who grinned back at her. He had such a merry smile. Just as Mirrim said he had.

"Natua has a new calf. She showed him off to Zaranth and me," she said, quite willing to talk about dolphins.

"She did?" F'lessan was really interested. It showed in the way his eyes sparkled and his whole face lit up. "Golanth and I must take the time to admire him."

"She'll show him off to anyone, she's so proud."

"I'm better acquainted with the Cove Hold and Readis's pods, you see," he confided in her.

"I know," she replied.

"Quite likely," he said, shooting her a teasing glance. "Dolphins like nothing better than to gossip. They can spread news faster than Runners. We have too many animals on this planet who can talk back to us humans."

She gave him a startled look and then let herself chuckle. "I suppose we should be grateful that fire-lizards can't talk."

"A large mercy," he agreed. "It's bad enough they sing!"

"But they add such beautiful descants."

"I suppose so," he replied amiably.

She knew that Lessa, his mother, had a prejudice against fire-lizards. Mirrim had said it was because no one had known how to control the creatures when they were first brought to Benden. Did F'lessan share her bias? She didn't know what to say to change the subject. He spared her by speaking first.

"What has you so interested in Rukbat system charts?"

"Ah!" She was grateful for the change in topic. "Well, I'm close enough, being at Monaco Bay, and I was an apprentice . . ." She floundered a moment.

"So you said . . ."

"So I'm often asked to check out figures on the original charts, which are much too valuable to be anywhere else."

"Good Master Esselin." F'lessan's tone was facetious.

She flushed. "He doesn't really approve of me, even if Master Stinar entrusts me to take *Yoko* updates to Cove Hold, because I'm only a green rider."

"There's no such thing as '*only* a green rider,' Tai. A wing never has enough green riders," he replied so staunchly that she was startled enough to catch his eyes. "That's the Wingleader in me talking. Besides which, Master Esselin is a pompous old hairsplitter! Ignore him."

"I can't. And weren't you hoping to avoid him, too?"

"Whenever I can. He," he told her, dropping his tone to a whisper as he leaned across the table to her, "doesn't approve of *me* being in Honshu."

"But you found it," she said, surprised.

"Yes," he said, nodding with an air of mischievous satisfaction. "And I take great care of its treasures."

"So I've heard."

"So you *have* heard some good of me?"

She knew he was teasing her; she knew she was often too solemn. Even Mirrim said she shouldn't be quite so conscientious, but that was just how she was. She just didn't know how to respond to levity. As if he hadn't noticed her uncertainty, he reached for the skin.

"More wine," he said briskly.

She hadn't realized her glass was empty and obediently held it out.

"Does Erragon let you stand any night watches with him at Cove Hold?" he asked.

"Yes. I'm a good timekeeper." *Conscientious* was what Erragon called her, just like Mirrim.

"Time is a critical factor in astronomy," he replied.

She was surprised that he knew that.

"Did you study much astronomy?"

"Not as much as I should have, but I'll catch up." He wasn't teasing now. He was quite serious. "And to good advantage, since we must look beyond our traditional duties. I like people who think ahead."

"You certainly are, with Honshu."

His expression altered again, as if he, too, had considered his future—which put another dimension to the outwardly lighthearted dragonrider. He grinned, impulsively covering her hand with a reassuring pressure.

"Yes, I've plans for Honshu." Then, in another abrupt change, he added, "I'll just get us second servings before the roasts are all gone."

She wouldn't have had the nerve to go back for more to eat, but F'lessan took her plate before she could protest. Slightly awed, she watched as he chatted with the cook while the man carved generous slices from the roast.

All the tables around them were filled now with boisterous diners, enjoying the excellent Turnover meal. Though several called cheerfully to F'lessan as he made his way back, he returned the greetings without stopping to chat. He wasn't at all what she'd expected based on Mirrim's tales of some of his pranks at Benden Weyr. Well, that had been Turns ago, before he'd Impressed. He did have a serious side to his nature, along with that most amazing sparkle in his eyes. She should be wary of such a sparkle. Mirrim had said he had been very much a bronze rider! Maybe she should slip away while she had a chance. But that seemed very discourteous. She had barely touched the second glass he'd poured.

A bright chord of music cut through conversations and she saw that harpers were ranged on the platform, ready to entertain the diners. Moreover, there'd be new music for a Turnover. She'd intended to stay that long. She reached out for Zaranth's mind, but the green was obviously enjoying herself on the heights with the other dragons.

F'lessan deftly placed the dish before her. It was piled so high she wondered where she'd put all that food.

"I brought you some of the things I like, too. Fresh from the ovens." He topped off their wineglasses. "With music! Good!"

He had no trouble putting away his second helping of Turnover food. Nor did she, but then, her parents had raised her to "eat what's on your plate and be thankful." She took a hasty sip of the white Benden; she hadn't thought of her family recently. Her life with them had been so different from the one she now had—even before she had Impressed Zaranth. Zaranth—and Monaco Weyr—was her family now, and closer to her than she had ever been to her bloodkin.

Determinedly she concentrated on something else and the music caught her up. Sometime during the first round of songs, their plates were removed and a basket of southern fruit, northern nuts, and sweet cakes was deposited on the table. Klah was also being served and F'lessan, she noticed, drank more of that than the wine, which he continued to savor in sips.

It was expected that the diners would join in the chorus of the ballads. When F'lessan opened his mouth to join in, she was astonished. *He* complained about fire-lizards? *They* could harmonize, and were supplying descants from wherever they were perched. He couldn't even find the melodic line! He wasn't quite a monotone, but so near to one that she hoped the lusty voices around them drowned him out. Yet he was—well, not exactly singing, although he bellowed out the right words—carrying on as if he didn't care. He merely waved to those at the nearest table, who were grimacing at him and vigorously indicating that he should either shut his mouth or go elsewhere.

Should she try to drown him out? She had an alto range but at least she sang on pitch and with reasonable musicality. He was gesturing broadly—urgently—for her to sing. His merry eyes caught hers, and from the mischief in them, she suddenly realized that he knew very well how badly he sang and didn't care. That he was willing to show such a defect in a culture that apotheosized music, and certainly encouraged vocal talents, astonished her. Mirrim might criticize his fickleness and breezy attitudes to weyrmates, but why hadn't she mentioned his flawed voice?

Now, still lofting his hearty non-tone, he cupped his ear to indicate that he couldn't hear her singing. Out of pique, she took a deep breath and joined in—hopefully loud enough to cover his performance. Vigorously, he approved her efforts, amiably marking out the tempo with both hands. He *did* have a good sense of timing. At the rousing end of the final chorus, he closed his mouth but applauded enthusiastically.

"Why do you sing, when you know you can't?" she demanded in a low voice.

"Because I do know all the words," he replied, not at all abashed.

She had to laugh and waved her hands helplessly. This group of harpers had finished their stint and F'lessan stood up, surveying other tables, waving to someone who waved back, though he made no effort to leave her side. Then suddenly he was hailed.

"Thought we heard your bellow, F'lessan!"

Tai saw the unmistakable figures of T'gellan and Mirrim making their way toward them. That wouldn't do at all! While the bronze rider was urging them to join him, Tai got to her feet and, pausing only to take her wineglass with her—the white Benden was too good to be abandoned—she slipped into the shadows and away.

She heard him welcoming the bronze and green riders.

"T'gellan, Mirrim, you'll never guess who I met at the—"

His voice broke off as he realized that she had gone. She halted in the darkness, waiting for him to identify her. She'd never hear the last of it from Mirrim.

"Geger," he called after a beat. "D'you have more white Benden?"

Tai hurried away.

That was silly, Zaranth said.

You know how Mirrim can be.

Why would she object?

You know Mirrim, Tai replied.

You're silly. Then Zaranth asked wistfully. *Do we have to go now?*

No, love. I want to listen to the music. I can do that from any part of the Square.

You'll have to stand. Everyone who can be is at Landing's Turnover.

Don't tell Golanth where I am, Tai said, remembering the proximity of the two dragons on the heights.

Why not?

Just don't.

Oh! As you wish. Zaranth sounded confused.

It's all right.

Tai found herself a place to stand at the edge of the throng and listened to the splendid music. She made her glass of Benden white last through the concert. It really was the best wine she'd ever tasted.

It was when she was making her way back to the heights that she heard the crashing. Glass? Rather a lot of glass, by the sound of it. An accident? She ought to see what was happening. That was much too much noise for a simple mishap.

BENDEN WEYR—1.1.31

Lessa, Ramoth's rider and Benden's Weyrwoman, emerged into the winter night air, shivering as the crisp cold struck. At least the blizzard blanking out High Reaches and a good bit of Tillek Hold had not marred this last night of Benden's Turnover. She wrapped the long fur-lined coat about her and wished she'd put her gloves on, too, though the basket of hot pastries, which Manora had pressed on her as they left, kept her right hand warm. When F'lar finished closing the panel on the rousing chorus of the latest Harper ballad, she slipped her left hand between his elbow and the rough hide of his jacket. He slung the wineskin over his left shoulder and pressed her hand tighter to his side.

Out of habit they both glanced across the Bowl, which was eerily silent. Opposite them, on the ledges to the Weyr-woman's quarters, they could see their dragons in the moonlight. Blue-green, two pairs of dragon eyes winked open and followed the progress of their partners across the flat, frosted Bowl.

Belior, its brightness better than a glowbasket, lit the eastern arc of the huge double crater, throwing the entrances to the individual weyrs into darkness. The moon illuminated the watchdragon and his rider, striding up and down the Rim to keep warm.

"Don't dally, girl," F'lar murmured, shrugging into the warmth of his jacket and lengthening his stride.

"If I had a Harper mark for every time I've crossed the Bowl," Lessa said.

"Add those to mine and we'd be as rich as Toric."

Lessa gave a snort and, her breath misting before her, quickened her steps. Maybe they should have gone south, where Turnover could be conducted on sun-warmed beaches and the more temperate southern night. But Benden Weyr had been home to her for thirty-five Turns now, and F'lar's for all of his sixty-three. Although they had made their traditional appearances at Benden Hold on Turnover First Night and heard marvelous music at Ruatha on the second, they preferred to end the celebration here. She was glad enough to be able to enjoy some quiet time after the frenetic pace of this Turnover Past.

She wondered if, at the end of this Pass—"After," as people referred to it—he would want to leave Benden. Or maybe, if he could not bear to leave the splendor of the Weyr, at least spend the worst of the cold months in the south. Maybe not *in* Honshu, which F'lessan had repeatedly invited them to share, but nearby.

She understood, on one level, that the prospect of "After" did not obsess F'lar: "During" was his responsibility, and hers. Finishing this Pass honorably and still as Benden's Weyrleader—even knowing Thread would no longer threaten Pern—was his committed goal. Especially since they had both made such a point of urging their younger dragonriders to learn an alternative skill, Lessa kept trying to insinuate After in their private conversations to see what he'd really like to do then. Idling on a sandy beach in Southern would quickly bore a man who'd always been active. And, if he would not contemplate the options, maybe she'd have to make the decision for both of them for where they'd live After. Only where?

Suddenly both dragons reared, staring up into the night sky, the color of their eyes briefly reflecting the orange of alarm. Startled, Lessa glanced over her shoulder and grabbed F'lar tightly.

"Oooh!" she exclaimed. The night cold was nothing to the fear that surged through her, making her heart race at the brief trails of fire in the north. Then she was disgusted with her primitive reaction to what she now knew were meteorites burning up in the atmosphere. As a child she'd believed her nurse—that those flares across a night sky were the Ghost Dragons of the First Pass.

"Erragon said we'd have a lot of Ghosts this Turn." F'lar chuckled at the old explanation, his breath puffing white. "So long as they keep their distance." Another flare caught his eye, barely a finger length in the northern sky. His sigh drifted white in the frosty air.

"There really are a lot more of them this Turn, as Toronas complained last night at Benden. They certainly are bright. Why that one—" She pointed her finger, following the arc in its path before it blinked out. "—looked like it might land."

"They never have."

"Well, you heard Toronas. All that nonsense about it is all"—she altered her voice to mimic the Benden Lord Holder's slightly nasal speech pattern—"because we let Aivas change the orbit of the Red Star and this is the result of meddling with things we don't know enough about."

F'lar laughed, because her imitation of the Benden Lord Holder was so accurate. "One of the reasons Aivas delayed the blast was to put the Red Star far beyond affecting any other of the planets in this system. The mathematics was accurate to the tenth decimal point. Or so Wansor assured me at the time. Or ask F'lessan. He's into astronomy with that old telescope in Honshu."

"I might indeed ask F'lessan," she said. "It's something like this that would agitate the Abominators into doing more harm than they've already done."

"You think they're behind some of those peculiar incidents of vandalism Sebell reported?"

"Who else would be that vindictive and destroy only *new* medicines or materials, or waylay traders carrying components from one Smithcrafthall to another?"

"Let's talk about it in the weyr. It's far too cold to dawdle out here, woman."

He tugged her into a jog, throwing an arm about her shoulders to prevent her from slipping on the icy ground, and they quickly reached the stairs up to her quarters.

Are you two coming in? he asked the two dragons, who had not moved from their ledges.

We will watch the Ghosts until they leave, Mnementh said, a hint of amusement in his voice.

As you wish, F'lar said.

"Silly beasts," Lessa murmured, smiling as she pushed aside the entrance curtain. Sometimes she wished she had a hide as impervious to weather as a dragon's. Or was it just that this winter was unusually cold?

Between is colder, Ramoth remarked.

Once she was inside, Lessa swiftly made for the nearest heater unit, putting Manora's basket, still warm, on the table as she passed it and stripping off her long fur. She hung it on the hooks to the left of their sleeping room.

"I didn't think we'd have to worry about Abominators again," she said with a weary sigh.

"N'ton checked the island where we exiled those that were convicted of abducting Robinton." F'lar's expression was austere, his lips thinned. He kicked the heavy curtain rather more forcefully than was needed to be sure that the hem excluded the cold drafts. "In fact," he added, his face altering to a less forbidding look, "there were some youngsters, since several spouses went with their men."

"Oh!" Lessa paused. "And the earlier group, who were caught damaging other Crafthalls? The ones who were sentenced to the Crom mines?"

"Ah, now, there's a possibility." He shrugged out of his jacket and would have dropped it on the chair but Lessa pointed sternly at it and then at the hooks where she had hung her fur. He grinned, scooped it up, and hung it with exaggerated care.

"Go on," she urged him, knowing he was going to tease her before he answered.

He got two glasses from the cabinet and deftly poured wine from one of Morilton's elegantly carved glass bottles. He handed her a glass, then stepped backward until he was close enough to feel the heat from the radiating unit on his legs.

"That meteorite—the metallic one that everyone in the Smithcrafthall is going on about—smacked a good-sized hole in the prisoners' quarters and broke one man's leg. It wasn't until evening that a count was taken. One was missing. One of those—" F'lar's lips thinned with remembered anger. "—who were involved in that attack on Aivas. He was deafened. Big man. Should be easy to find. He's missing the tip of his first finger on his left hand."

He took a sip of his wine, savoring it. Lessa allowed him that enjoyment.

"But he hasn't been found yet, has he?" she asked at length.

With a wave of his wineglass, F'lar dismissed the problem. "Telgar, High Reaches, and Fort Weyrs have been alerted. Runners carried the news along their traces and warned the traders."

Lessa gave a cynical snort. "Some of the traders are not above harboring a holdless man."

"According to the Mine Master, this man kept himself to himself. Seemed to dislike new things."

"Made by Aivas, of course," she said in a caustic tone.

F'lar raised his eyebrows. "By Aivas, of course."

"Do you think this one man is responsible for all those thefts and vandalism? Too wide a spread."

"Quite right, but there are enough people with petty grievances against hold and hall who might delight in causing trouble here and there." He rocked back and forth on the balls of his feet, relishing the warmth. "I don't consider that as serious a problem as deciding what more refinements"—he pointed to the heating unit—"we can safely introduce."

"No one has objected to having better lighting and heat," Lessa said. "After all, solar panels came with the Ancients. So did hydro-engineering and generators. We just have to speed up the education process to produce the *necessary* improvements that will reduce drudgery After."

"I don't approve of life being made too easy," F'lar remarked.

"You were never a drudge," she said caustically, reminding him of her ten Turns spent as one.

"Don't forget that this Weyr was scarcely luxurious until Thread started falling again."

"How could I?" She grinned at him, her eyes alight with laughter. "But that doesn't mean an indiscriminate release of technology. The Crafthalls are the worst offenders there."

"You mean, you object to what Master Oldive is doing in surgical procedures and more effective medications?"

"Of course not," she said with a scowl. "But I don't think everyone agrees with some of the surgical stuff." She gave a little shudder.

"You would if your life depended on correcting an internal problem, like your guts protruding out of your belly because the stomach lining had ruptured," F'lar said with a humorless laugh.

"Sharra said it's called a hernia and is not life-threatening," she responded in a brusque tone. Then, in an abrupt change, she exhaled. "I take the point. We have to educate others to do so."

"Agreed, and we have to get our younger riders to educate themselves, too, for After."

"Well, some will have no trouble," she said. "They don't consider it beneath their dignity to deliver messages or transport urgently needed bulk items. Tagetarl sent us a copy of the dictionary that he copied from Aivas's files with definitions of technical terms. Far more current than anything the Harper Hall has. Sebell said he's got orders from every major hold, nearly all the minor ones, and most of the halls."

"Then maybe understanding and defining a technological vocabulary will become wider spread."

His facetious tone caused her to grin. "That wouldn't hurt. But it's the older riders, who show absolutely no interest in supporting themselves After, who worry me. Why is it so belittling for a dragon and his rider to extend their abilities in other quite respectable pursuits? They *know* that living in Southern is not a matter of flinging up some fronds to cover a hut on the white sands and picking ripe fruit off the nearest tree. They won't even consider helping the beastherders to keep the feline predators from causing witless stampedes into gorges and ravines even if dragons have always killed their own food. Dragons don't share their kills, even with their riders."

It was F'lar's turn to chuckle at her acerbic remarks. "If you're hungry enough, I suppose roast feline can be tasty."

"Sharra said it's tough and often tastes more of fish than flesh."

"We've sixteen more Turns of Threadfall, love," he said, refilling her wineglass.

"Now," and she gave him a sly look, "if Benden's Weyrleader should make a decision as to what he will do After?"

He chuckled indulgently as he held Manora's basket of delicacies out to her. The spicy odors wafted her way.

"What is Manora tempting us with?" she wondered, unfolding the napkin.

"They certainly smell palatable. You take your pick."

She did, delighting in the flaky pastry and the spicy filling. "I think," Lessa mumbled through her full mouth, "that she plans to go from one end to the other of the recipes she had us download from the Aivas files."

"It's a shame she never got down to speak to Aivas. He'd've liked her."

Lessa grimaced. "If you remember, we offered to take her many times and she refused. There was always too much to do." She licked the last of the pastry flakes from her fingers.

F'lar sat down and she noticed the bone-weariness evident in the slow way he settled his body in the comfortably padded chair across from her. Only with her did he have the luxury to relax. If she missed the painful stiffness that indicated his bones were aching, Mnementh would tell her and she'd make him take a dose of the medication Oldive had made to relieve the problem.

"Is there ever enough time?" she asked.

"There should be." He scowled, sweeping back the forelock that was silver now. "There should be all the time in the world After."

"Have you decided where we'll go After?"

He frowned, brushing the inquiry aside. She fretted at his reluctance. They certainly should have their choice of residence, barring beautiful Honshu in deference to F'lessan's proprietary interest in it. But what—and a dreadful thought arose from the deepest part of her mind. She did not refuse that flash of unnecessary alarm; she did hold it deep in her thoughts. What would happen if Ramoth should fail to rise to mate in the coming Turns, as Bedella's Solth had done recently? R'mart had gratefully retired to Southern with his

Weyrwoman. But somehow Lessa had always assumed that she and F'lar would remain Weyrleaders until the end of this Pass. There *would* come a time, even if it wasn't imminent, when Ramoth would not feel the challenge of fertility. Lessa gave her head an impatient shake, smiling as she remembered the most recent time Ramoth had risen gloriously to challenge the bronzes and Mnementh had vigorously conquered. Her grin broadened as her dragon caught that thought. But Mnementh lived in constant danger of injury.

He is strong and clever fighting Thread. He evades score and ash as nimbly as any green, Ramoth responded in stout support. *Mnementh is the only bronze I will ever accept and there isn't another as daring. Even if he sleeps more than he used to. Be easy.*

With the bond between the riders so acute, F'lar invariably knew when Ramoth had spoken to her rider. He cocked one eyebrow at his weyrmate.

"What's on her mind?" Then he chuckled. "Or yours?"

"When are you going to make up your mind where we'll go After?" she asked with a hint of exasperation, as if that was what occasioned Ramoth's remark.

F'lar gave her a long patient look. "We can go where we want. Be certain of one thing: we shall not be dependent on anyone." Briefly his jaw settled into an inflexible line.

"That will make a very nice change," she said at her driest.

"We could see if one of those eastern islands would suit."

"What?" She scowled fiercely at him, realizing that she had risen to his bait. He chuckled again. At least he was in a good mood.

"I know the weather here's terrible but I've spent all my life in this pile of rock." He shot her a look to see if she would disagree.

"Rock is cool in the summertime," she agreed diffidently, then added in a nostalgic tone of voice, "When I think of how much history we have made here . . ."

"Indeed. And how many changes have occurred since we became Weyrleaders."

"Too sharding many losses in the past Turn, too."

" 'There is a time for every purpose under the heaven,' " he quoted softly.

Tears welled quickly in Lessa's eyes at that reminder of Robinton—and Aivas. Two Turns and a few months were not enough to distance that double loss.

"I miss Robinton so much."

"Who doesn't?" F'lar replied softly, lifting one hand briefly in resignation before he continued. "I was thinking more of Laudey and Warbret. And good old R'gul." He let out a sigh of remembered frustration.

"We must be charitable," she reminded him in her more usual caustic fashion. The bronze rider had been a thorn in both their sides despite his outward acquiescence to F'lar's Weyrleadership. There was always the hint, when R'gul took orders from F'lar, that he, R'gul, would have done differently. "He did obey, you know, and his wing thought highly of him as a leader."

F'lar grunted, twirling the stem of his glass and apparently absorbed in admiring the ruby color.

"I'll miss Laudey," she went on after nibbling at a pastry, "although I do like Langrell as Igen Holder. Very nice person."

"Handsome, too."

She shot him a glance. "He needs a good wife."

"He'll have no trouble." F'lar poked at the contents of the basket before selecting a triangular pastry and popping it in his mouth. "Not bad."

She found another of the same shape. "No, it isn't." She licked her lips.

He sipped his wine, regarding her from the corner of his eye. "Do you favor Janissian for the Holdership at Southern Boll? That's another issue for the next Council to decide."

"Boll has an historical precedent for Lady Holders, you know."

He nodded, waiting for her to continue.

"Certainly Lady Marella has been directing the Hold unofficially for a long time, saving Sangel's face. She got Janissian educated at Landing, too."

"Groghe likes the girl. Old enough to take Hold. Well respected."

Lessa shrugged. "Jaxom says she's as organized as Sharra is. He'd be glad to step down from the position of youngest Lord Holder."

F'lar stretched out his right leg, grimacing as the tendon resisted full extension. He gave a sigh.

He's all right, Mnementh told Lessa privately, waking from his nap.

All that dancing he tried to tell me he didn't enjoy, Lessa replied.

"We need younger minds dealing with all the changes," she said aloud.

He turned his amber eyes on her, amused and slightly condescending. "Young heads can be as certain that they are right as the old ones. And no experience to draw on." He ate another pastry, licking his fingers as the juice within leaked. "Idarolan's been studying astronomy with that journeyman of Wansor's. He got Morilton to make him some special mirrors for a telescope to set up on that bridge of his down at Nerat's Ankle."

"For all that I like Curran as Masterfishman, I'll miss Idarolan's sly wit in the Council." She took another tidbit and then a sigh escaped her lips after she swallowed. "I shall miss them. I'll miss them all."

F'lar reached over the table to cover her thin, small, but remarkably capable hand, squeezing her fingers.

"We both shall, love." He picked up his glass. "To absent friends."

She raised hers, the glasses touched, and they finished off their wine.

Simultaneously they rose. F'lar slipped his arm about her slender shoulders, drawing her against his body as they walked in step to the sleeping room.

Lessa didn't think she'd gotten to sleep before they were both roused by angry dragon trumpeting.

SOUTHERN HOLD — 1.1.31

Toric was recovering from too much wine consumed the night before. The red had definitely been too young to be potable, even if it had come from his own vineyard and therefore was handy and cost him nothing. Except this morning's headache. Well, it took time to establish vines and, considering the cost of the starts from Benden, he had been eager to see some return on the investment. MasterVintner Welliner's estimate of how much wine he would be bottling from the hillsides under cultivation was inaccurate, too. If this year's press was not up to what he'd been led to believe he could expect, he'd have a long chat with Welliner. Toric slowly opened dry eyes in his aching skull.

"You're getting old, Father," Besic said. He handed Toric a steaming mug. "Mother's compliments."

Toric stifled a groan as he took the mug. Though he knew from experience that Ramala's morning-after cure was efficacious, the steam was slightly nauseating and he averted his head before attempting the first gulp.

Besic settled himself in the sling chair, stretching his legs out and crossing his ankles, thumbs hooked in his belt as he regarded his father with a bland expression.

"Hosbon's here. Sailed in from Largo last night. Got here at dawn."

Toric nearly dribbled the potion down his chin at the unwelcome news. Had Besic timed that remark until he had the cup to his lips? The two men tolerated each other warily, not because of Blood ties but out of begrudged respect. Toric grunted and drank as fast as the heat, and the taste, allowed.

"I told him that you were busy."

"I am," Toric said. The liquid made him belch and left a vile taste in his mouth. He stood, balancing himself on his bare feet, to prove that he was capable of overcoming the previous night's excesses as easily as ever.

He strode to where Ramala had laid out fresh clothes and

stepped into the new short trousers and matching loose shirt that would be comfortable during the heat of the day. He growled as he had to sort the rank cords against his right shoulder. Nuisancy things. As if everyone didn't recognize the Lord Holder of Southern. That caused him to snort, as any reminder did of how he had been gulled by the Weyrleaders. From the corner of his eye he saw the smirk on Besic's face, as if he read his sire's thought.

"Didn't you think to bring in—"

Besic interrupted him by pointing to the breakfast tray on the table.

Despite the fact that the pounding in his head was easing, Toric was still in a foul humor. "What's on Hosbon's mind? He's always at me for some concession or other."

"He's a good holder," Besic said, knowing not only that his approval counted for nothing in Toric's opinion but also that, by being scrupulously fair, he could sometimes irritate his sire.

Toric waved his hands dramatically. "Is the man never satisfied? First it was a drum tower, then a pier, and a sloop and a crew."

"He gets results."

"So—what does he want this time? A hold dragonrider?" Though there was always a dragonrider available to Lord Toric, the relocation of Southern Weyr still rankled. It was irksome, too, that the Weyrleader, K'van—the impertinent scut—so punctiliously performed his duties to the Hold that Toric never had grounds to fault him. He had managed to swallow that mortification, since he really did prefer not to have the constant traffic of dragons overflying the harbor, but perhaps he should not have taken issue with K'van over the matter of Weyr support to subdue the rebels and that sharding Denol on Ierne Island.

"Why, he wants to celebrate the end of Turnover with his Lord Holder," Besic said, getting to his feet. "Dutifully listen to whatever harper reads the Report. And, quite likely, to see what other craftsfolk he can lure to his hold."

"Hasn't he got enough?" Toric demanded, seething.

"Some can't get enough," Besic murmured, reaching the door as he delivered that parting shot.

"Get out! Get out!" And Toric lunged, aiming a kick at his son. Besic didn't so much as look back over his shoulder. So Toric kicked again at the heavy yellow wood door, which slammed satisfactorily, echoing down the stone hall. Besic knew his father too well!

Limping because he'd caught his bare toes on the wooden edge, Toric wheeled and attacked the food on his tray. The tonic had cleared his head and now his stomach grumbled, as much with hunger as with irritation.

Where would Hosbon put more craftsfolk? He'd already enticed some of the best-trained people from Landing once the Great Bang had been accomplished, supposedly ridding the planet of Threadfall forever. Toric was not at all convinced that Aivas had known what it was doing: imagine blowing a whole planet off its course with the stuff left in long-dead engines! Still, in sixteen Turns—or was it seventeen in this Pass?—the end of Thread meant he could proceed with his plans to develop the small portion of the southern continent that he had been able to wrest from the sharding Benden Weyrleaders. That inequity would always infuriate him.

He made an effort to calm himself. Ramala was certain his indigestion came from stress. He should take his meals calmly and eat slowly. He was, after all, Lord of an important Hold, no matter how much larger it should have been.

His Lady Ramala was already chatting with Hosbon, seated in the main hall. She rose when Toric entered. "Perhaps you would both like more klah. There's still time before Harper Sintary makes his report. Is your wife here?"

Hosbon gave an almost imperceptible wince. She was here, and if they'd arrived by dawn, she'd have had plenty of time to spread marks about, Toric thought, his humor revived by Hosbon's discomfort.

"Yes, join us for klah, Hosbon. Come outside. It's a fine day for our first one of this Turn!"

Toric clapped the man heartily on the shoulder.

"I'll just bring fresh klah," Ramala called after them.

Toric indicated the way to the smaller of the two tables that were situated on either side of the Hold's entrance. A small awning shaded it from the bright sunlight. He took his usual chair, arranged so that anyone sitting opposite him had the sun glaring into his face. "Now, what's on your mind, Hosbon?"

The man was no fool, but he settled himself, elbows on the table, and leaned forward. There was little danger of being overheard, slightly above and well back from the entrance to the Hold.

"I am wondering if you know what the subjects of today's Report will be?"

"Of course I know, *and* what's to be voted on," Toric replied with some heat. "I had to sit in on the sharding meeting, didn't I? Boring trivia, with the Council insisting that the 'original intent' of the Charter be followed."

Toric did not approve of the publicity regarding the Charter: a document so old that it should be regarded as an artifact, rather than guidance for this planet's needs—not twenty-five hundred Turns after it had been promulgated. And harpers were holding "discussion groups" to be sure children and drudges could recite it by rote. There were a few provisions that he would like to see quietly annulled and the clauses that named the perquisites of major landholders extended. He would live to see the last day of this Pass, and he certainly intended to exert his not-so-small influence when the Charter was reviewed—After—and suitably altered once dragonriders were no longer needed. Toric had endured many boring hours to be sure no one in the Council slipped in any more surprises on him. He was developing a few surprises of his own.

"Is that all?" Hosbon was plainly disappointed.

"Oh, there'll be the usual reports from Landing, premises and promises." Toric dismissed them with a wave of his hand. "The availability of printed texts for those wishing to improve themselves." He snorted. "I—" Then he stopped himself. "And you know that any 'improvement' will stay here, in Southern and in Largo." He inclined his head tactfully at Hosbon as he recalled Besic's reason for Hosbon's visit. "You have such a growing number of craftsfolk there. We wouldn't want to lose any of them. Did you find any new recruits this Turnover?"

"None that I would dare tempt from here, Lord Toric," Hosbon said with oily deference. "Not," he added quickly, "that we don't always need more."

Toric merely nodded. Generally he approved of Hosbon. The man came of a Bloodline that had produced many sensible holders who knew how to get the most out of their workers. Looked like a much younger version of his sire, Bargen, even to the pale eyes in a deeply tanned face and a body that had sweated off excess flesh. Anyway, Hosbon had older brothers, and now that he'd had a taste of holding in a decent climate, he'd not want to return to frigid High Reaches.

"So I will bring back news of this meeting and the Report for my holders." Hosbon's lips twitched slyly.

"As well you do," Toric replied, allowing his eyelids to close briefly in acknowledgment of the tacit understanding. Just then Ramala emerged from the Hold entrance carrying a tray of refreshments, so he added, "We will discuss it later."

They had time to finish the klah and most of the little spiced rolls before the big bass Harper Drum boomed to announce the imminence of the public meeting. The deep sound echoed off the cliffs, reverberating to the ships at anchor in the deep harbor, vibrating along the stones of the Hold and, it felt, into one's very foot bones.

As Toric rose and strode up the wide shallow stairs carved out of the rock path that led to the cleared space on the height, he glanced down to the other levels of the Hold complex. In small groups, holders were surging up from the wharves where numerous small craft bobbed beside buoys or were tied to the pilings. He moved through the crowd, toward the platform on the southern edge of the Gather area where a single Harper sat, holding the traditional scroll that contained the Report he would shortly read. Toric looked from right to left, occasionally awarding a brief smile to those who deserved his favor. Since he had taken over Southern thirty-one Turns ago, twenty-four self-sufficient holds had been established under his direction and tithed to him. He could see representatives of each holding—significantly fewer from the more distant ones—and identified the shoulder knots of many journeymen of various crafts. With an all-too-fleeting moment of satisfaction, he took the six steps to the platform, two at a time, defying anyone—especially Besic—to assume that he had been the worse for wear earlier that morning. The Harper, Sintary, had been suggested by Robinton himself as suitable for the position of Master Harper for Southern. Robinton had been one of the few northerners whom Toric had respected, so he had not appealed the appointment. But he had come to regret that decision, for Sintary was a subtle and stubborn man who took his position as Harper so seriously that he had agreed to no changes even when Toric had suggested several minor alterations to the traditional teaching. The old Harper was very popular, with a dry sense of humor and an ability to improvise lyrics about local incidents that made him a very difficult man to discredit. Toric had tried; he kept hoping that an opportunity might yet arise and he could indisputably be able to send Sintary away.

With a curt nod at his intransigent Harper, Toric turned to face the audience. Holding up his hands, he brought conversations and laughter to a halt. Even fire-lizards stopped their flitting about and disappeared into the forest curving about the space.

"Master Sintary needs no introduction," Toric said, lifting a voice that had once carried above storms. "I see you have a scroll to read us today, Master Harper."

Master Sintary rose, giving Toric a bland stare for such a terse introduction. Toric enjoyed giving subtle jabs, especially to harpers and dragonriders. And where were the dragonriders who should be here? Toric glared out across the tanned faces, looking for the Weyrleader. If K'van hadn't come . . . Then Toric located him on the left, where trees and the ferny shrubs of this highland formed a bordering park. He counted at least fifteen dragonriders and the three queen riders! Shards! He could make no complaint that they had been delinquent in performing this Weyr duty.

Sintary had taken two steps forward, an easy gesture of his hand waving Toric to the other chair on the platform. Deftly unrolling the traditional scroll with his right hand, he proceeded to read, winding it up with the skill of long practice.

Toric took the chair, crossing his arms on his chest. He was almost as annoyed now as he had been this morning when he'd awakened. The dragonriders were in attendance. They—and far too many other people—would eat of the feast a Lord Holder was required to produce. And how could Sintary make himself heard so effortlessly? He hadn't even raised his voice, just intensified it with some harper trick.

To occupy the time it would take Sintary to get through that thick scroll, Toric surveyed the polite faces below him. Spotting his brother, Mastersmith Hamian, Toric uncrossed his arms, because Hamian had assumed a similar stance. Hamian and his new Plastics Hall. Plastic indeed, when he should be working metals: especially that lode of—what was it called? box-something—that produced very lightweight and malleable ore. Toric hadn't encouraged his young brother to pursue his Mastery in the Smithcraft only to have him fritter his skills away on some Aivas nonsense. The summarily exiled MasterGlass-smith Norist had been right to call the artificial intelligence an Abomination.

The sun was now midheaven, and even in his loose clothing, Toric was beginning to feel the heat. Packed rather tightly together, the crowd was becoming restless, fanning themselves and shifting weight from foot to foot. Those who had no one to leave their children with were beginning to sidle to the edge of the crowd, taking the fretful whingeing brats away.

Was the Harper speeding up the tempo of his recital? Well, why not? The scroll would be displayed on the notice board when the reading was over. He caught the change of pace and heard Sintary's concluding remarks.

"Now, I can start taking your private petitions, which, I as-sure you, will be scrupulously dealt with."

Sharding Harper Hall, meddling with what was Hold busi-ness. His holders had no right to complain. They worked hard and they got what they deserved.

Toric quickly scanned the assembled to see if any petitions were being removed from belt pouches or dress pockets.

Sintary finished reading. Cheers, loud calls, whistles, and other raucous noise welled up, and that combined with the heat brought back Toric's headache. While the bloody Harper descended the steps, Toric went down the back way, into the cool shade. He needed to find Dorse. The man had said he would be back by now from his latest trip north.

His public duty completed, Sintary stepped off the plat-form, aware that Toric had scooted off as soon as he could. Just as well. The Harper could collect petitions without Toric's interference. He whipped open the sack he'd brought for the purpose and, securing the scroll of the Report under his belt, took the petitions shoved at him as soon as he reached the bottom of the steps.

"They'll be read, I assure you. Harper's word on it. Thank you. Yes, the Council will see this. Thank you. It will take time but this will be read." He repeated these phrases as he made his way through the crowd to post the Report. "Yes, yes, this will be read." It became a litany. "They'll be read's" to the left, a "harper's word on it" to the right, and "let me through, thank you" as he made his way forward until he reached the notice board. He handed the scroll to the appren-tice in harper blue and held it flat to be tacked up.

The days of laborious copying by cramp-fingered appren-tices were now well gone. Council reports were printed by Masterprinter Tagetarl's speedy presses on some of the new heavy paper, made in rolls and then plastic-coated so the no-tice could not be easily defaced. Copies had been sent to every major and minor hold to be read on this day of Turn-over. Even Toric would have to let it remain displayed, at least until the Turnover crowd had all departed to their holds.

Which, knowing Toric's ways, would be as soon as possible. However, judging by the number of small craft, it would be the work of two days, at least, to clear the harbor.

Not that Toric was a bad Holder. Quite rightly, he insisted that everyone earn his or her right to hold on his land. The man had had to put up with the vagaries of the Oldtimers as well as incursions by thousands of folk streaming south, hoping for easier living. For all the tribulations the immigrants left behind, they acquired as many new ones here—but many of their supposed grievances would be minor.

Sintary left most of the eager petitioners behind as they began to read through the Report or went to look for shade, food, and drink. He was given two more crumpled sheets on his way down to the Harper's hall and slipped into a small entrance when he spotted Dorse and one of the hard-faced men Toric used as guards hurrying up the stairs. They were busy watching their feet, but he particularly didn't like the obstinate and sly expression on Dorse's features. Sintary knew that Dorse often did "errands" for his Lord Holder.

When the two men had passed around the bend out of sight, Sintary continued on his way. That's when he heard the crash of glassware and the dull sound of an axe hitting wood. But Dorse and the other man were on their way up. So who was throwing things about?

With the petitions weighing him down, he decided to get them safely to his hold before he returned to investigate the noise.

HEALER HALL—1.1.31

Masterhealer Oldive eased back from the worktop, closed eyes bleary from peering so long into the microscope, and sighed deeply. So similar and yet the samples did not match anything from Aivas's pathology files sufficiently to call them the same virus. Ah, what splendid, and frightening, new dimensions for learning—and Healing.

Slowly, aware that his body was cramped from inactivity,

he extended one leg as far as he could from the rung of his stool. Letting it hang down, and gripping the seat of his perch, he stretched the other leg. Then he raised his arms as far as his deformity allowed before rotating his neck to ease those aching muscles.

"Oldive?"

"Oh, my word, Sharra!" He swiveled the stool so that he could face her in the corner where she, too, had been single-mindedly peering into her microscope. "I didn't realize you were still here."

This laboratory was such a pleasure to work in and today he and Sharra had it to themselves, since anyone with any sense was up at Fort Hold's Gather Square enjoying themselves. Through the wide expanse of special triple-plated glass, he could see the banners displayed from the windows of the Hold and yet not feel the cold that was gripping the northern continent. While he wished he could be in two places at once—and right now, one of them would by preference be the large sunlit Landing Healer facility—he was still luxuriating in the new headquarters at Fort. "Head quarters"—such a lovely concept and such splendid "quarters,"—with sufficient teaching rooms and airy dormitories, as well as more aspiring healers than ever before. More need of them, too, he admitted.

"We do get involved, don't we?" Sharra commented with a tired smile. "Have you been able to identify that virus?"

He shook his tired head.

"Could it be one of those mutations that are mentioned in Pathology Records?" she asked. "Considering what we've learned about such things, there's been plenty of time for them to alter from the specimens Aivas had."

"And that would account for the fact that the plague can decimate otherwise healthy holds," Oldive said sadly. He gave himself a little shake. No sense being morbid. "But such things have been with us a long time and are, fortunately, not upon us right now. While this *is* the last day of Turnover, and you should be with Jaxom and your children."

"They are all very well occupied with Ruatha's festivities," she said fondly. "Jaxom had to read the Report and accept petitions. I could do much more here than sit there and be bored, you know." She indicated the slides that she had been studying. She kneaded the nape of her neck, arching her back against having hunched so long over her instrument. "Will we ever have one of those electron microscopes that Aivas mentioned?"

Oldive permitted himself a chuckle as he carefully descended from the high stool. Had his spine developed normally, he would have been tall; his legs were long. They were the same length, but the malformation of his backbone had resulted in a pelvic slant. With a slight lift in one shoe, his limp was barely noticeable.

"There are so many calls on Master Morilton's skills," he said ruefully, and gestured to the cabinets filled with special glass products, the myriad paraphernalia that had been created by the Glass-Smith for healer use.

"A start, of course, on the quantity needed to equip all Healer Halls," Sharra said in an acid tone, "especially when the Council unanimously—for once—agreed that the Healer Hall has priority. We are concerned with the health and well-being of everybody, not just new gadgets that we've done without for twenty-five hundred Turns."

Though Oldive completely agreed with her, he raised a hand in gentle rebuke as he walked across the airy room to the small stove where the klah pot was kept warm. Someone had brought in a tray of food. He flipped back the napkins and saw the generous servings. When had these been brought? The meatrolls were still warm. He oughtn't to concentrate to the exclusion of everything else.

"Someone brought some food," he informed her.

"Oh, yes, I should have told you," she said contritely as she slipped off her stool and joined him. "I just wanted to finish that tray of slides." She poured klah for them both.

"Oh, we do very well, my dear Sharra," he said, talking around a mouthful of roll. "We have achieved all this—" He gestured around them. "—and Morilton is considering dedicating one Hall to nothing but Healer requirements." He glanced back at his workstation and his unidentifiable virus smear. Then held up his hand as an odd sound impinged on the silence of the laboratory.

Sharra listened hard. "Sounds like breaking glass. Breaking glass!" She repeated, setting down the mug and rushing to the door. As soon as she'd opened it, the noise was far more audible, and far too close.

"Meer, Talla," she cried, calling for her two fire-lizards.

"What's the matter? What's going on? What clumsy apprentice has been let loose?" Oldive cried.

Despite his physical disability, Oldive could move swiftly, but Sharra, after one startled look to her right, hauled him back from the threshold and closed the door, throwing the latch.

Ruth!

The white dragon might be asleep on Ruatha's fire-heights, but he'd respond to her mental call from any place. Meer and Talla arrived, midair, mouths open to shriek panic, but Sharra's stern command aborted that instinct.

"I don't know who, Oldive," she said, dropping her voice to a whisper, "but there are people crashing about in the still-room as if they thought no one would hear them."

Once again the intrepid Masterhealer attempted to leave the room and she caught him by the arm.

"There shouldn't be anyone else here but us," he said grimly. He had given leave to even the lowliest apprentice to enjoy this last day of Turn's End.

"But there are," she said, her eyes sparkling with anger as she opened the door to the noise of considerable destruction. A shadow fell across the long window of the laboratory and she grinned, pointing. "However, we shall deal with it."

Oldive gasped at the sight of a white body, wings outstretched, all but plastered against the glass, his eyes flashing the red and orange of alarm.

Ruth! Sharra said, relieved that he had responded so quickly. *Tell the Hold's fire-lizards to attack the intruders.* Fire-lizards held Ruth, the white dragon, in awed respect and would obey him without question. She gave him a very clear mental image of what she had seen in her brief glimpse down the hall. Meer and Talla cheeped once and disappeared. Scant seconds later, both she and Oldive heard loud cries, angry fire-lizard bugles, shouts of pain, and more banging and crashing.

Sharra opened the door wide enough to see down the hall. A mass of fire-lizards was trying to enter the stillroom. Then the mass split into several groups, which zipped off, screeching challenge, swooping down the stairwells at each end to the other levels of the hall.

There are several groups throwing things about in the Hall, Ruth told her. *That is wrong. Fort dragons come.*

She and Oldive watched as the fire-lizards drove four people out of the stillroom. They could hear human cries echoing from other points. Oldive groaned in dismay.

"They'll be damned sorry they ever thought of this," she told him angrily as she started purposefully down the hall. "Damned sorry."

"I never thought of—intrusions—when we built here," Oldive murmured, shaking his head in bitter denial of the event as he followed. He'd been so proud of this new Hall, with its marvelous equipment, its spacious and well-organized facilities. The previous quarters had been better protected in the angle between the Harper Hall and Fort Hold. But the Healer Hall was usually so busy that, on a normal day, no unauthorized persons would have been on this floor.

Sharra reached the stillroom first. The reek of spilled liquids and wet herbs was nothing to her appalled survey of empty shelves, cabinets with broken doors, glass shards everywhere. Even the marble worktops had been cracked. She slammed the door shut to spare Oldive the sight.

"Everything's ruined," she said tersely and pulled him toward the stairs, dreadfully certain now by the sounds of screams and shouts from the lower floors that there would be more damage elsewhere.

Fire-lizards drove the intruders out of the Hall where the humans were halted by the sight of a dozen dragons, their wings spread to form an impregnable wall, their eyes whirling red with anger. More dragons hovered overhead, their wings casting dark shadows on the scene below. Shouts and drumbeats echoed down Fort's rocky canyon, confirming that reinforcements were on their way. The cowering vandals were herded into a knot, clothes rent by fire-lizard beaks and talons, bloodied hands raised to protect their faces. While no dragon would hurt a human, the fire-lizards were under no such restraint and darted in to peck or claw when anyone in that huddle moved.

Call them off now, Ruth, Sharra said, pausing to catch her breath on the broad top step, *and thank them for coming so quickly. We need the wretches alive and able to tell us why they despoiled a Healer Hall.*

Though some of the wild fire-lizards looked as if they would disobey, a second rumbling bark from Ruth caused them to disappear, leaving the dragons to stand guard. When the dragons did not advance, one of the men uncoiled and stood up, glowering at Sharra and Oldive.

"Why are you here?" the Masterhealer asked at his sternest. He counted fifteen men and women in front of him, a sufficient number to trash more than his fine stillroom. His heart sank at the destruction they must have done. "Why have you destroyed the very materials and medicines—"

"The Abomination must be halted!" a man shouted, his body taut with his fanaticism. "Its taint removed forever from Pern."

"Abomination?" The word made Sharra shudder. That's what some people called Aivas. And those Abominators had kidnapped Master Robinton to force the Council to shut Aivas down because of the technology he represented. They'd tried to prevent the restoration of the technology that their ancestors had used and that many, many people wished to revive. Oldive caught her eye and his expression turned bleaker still.

The others began to chant, shaking their fists in the air, undeterred, as if they now realized that the dragons would not harm them.

"Vileness must be expunged!" the leader went on, louder, more daring. "Erase abominations."

Sharra began to shiver in the cold. Oldive's face looked pinched. Though she could see nothing beyond the high interlaced wings of the dragons, she could hear the pounding of hooves on the hard-packed road, the rumble of a cart, and shouts of many voices. Lioth, bronze dragon of N'ton, the Fort Weyrleader, cocked his head as if he had understood the taunts, his eyes beginning to whirl with orange spurts.

They're coming, Sharra, Ruth said and craned his head ominously toward the protestors. Their chanting noticeably faltered as the sound of hoofbeats and shouts penetrated to the dragon circle. Their leader rallied them to greater efforts.

"Tradition must be upheld!" He glared around him, his angular face and burning eyes inciting his followers. "Halt abominations."

"Turn back to tradition at Turnover!" screeched one of the three women, waving a bloody hand at Ruth, who frowned down at her.

"Our petitions have been ignored!"

"We protest the Abomination!"

"And all its works!"

"Abomination! Abomination!"

Stoically, Sharra and Oldive endured the chanting.

Smoothly, as humans neared, the dragons began to close their wings and give way, to allow the reinforcements a clear path to the despoilers. Lioth stepped closer to Ruth; Sharra knew that his rider, N'ton, would be in the vanguard. But it was two of Lord Groghe's sons who arrived first, riding bareback on a gray runnerbeast that wore no more than a headcollar. Haligon hauled it to a stop just short of the captives, doing a flying dismount to confront them. Such was the fury in his face and manner that the group backed away from him.

In one of those irrelevant observations that can occur even in moments of crisis, Sharra noted that gray hairs marred the brown of Haligon's fine Gather clothes. Horon, taking a belligerent stance next to his brother, was equally untidy.

A group of blue-clad Harpers, led by Masterharper Sebell,

arrived on foot, to increase the force. The cart, driven by N'ton and crammed with holders, some clutching clubs, nearly rammed into them. With an enlarged audience, the prisoners renewed the volume of their defiant messages.

"Destroy all the Abomination's devices."

"Purity for Pern!"

"Turn to Tradition."

"Avoid abominations!"

The holders began booing from the cart as they jumped down, clubs raised threateningly. Those in Healer green continued to where Sharra and Oldive stood on the top step.

"See what damage has been done, Keita," Oldive ordered in a low voice to the Healer journeywoman who rushed to him. A convulsive shiver ran through him. "Check the infirmary first."

Sharra was wracked with compassion for him. "A cloak for Master Oldive," she added urgently, suddenly realizing that she was feeling the cold seep through the adrenaline rush of the last few minutes.

"Harpers!" Sebell said, gesturing for his men to help. "Assist Keita."

Over these orders, the chant continued in rabid cadence—until Lord Groghe reached the scene. As well his mount had been saddled, Sharra thought, just as someone threw a fur-lined wrap over her shoulders, for Groghe was no longer agile enough to ride bareback like his sons.

"Abomination away!"

"Restore our tradition!"

"Shut up!" Groghe bellowed, the volume of his voice as intimidating as the powerful runnerbeast he pulled up just short of knocking the leader down. The man rocked back and it was then that Sharra noticed that he, and the rest of his vandals, had the effrontery to be wearing green: not the genuine Healer green but close enough to answer how they had been able to gain access to the Hall.

At his most fearsome, face suffused with fury, eyes protruding, Groghe stared down at the man. He looked larger than life, fine in his Gather clothes with a cape billowing out over his mount's rump.

The silence was palpable. Then it was broken by a plaintive moan.

"I'm bleeding," one of the women said in a mixture of outrage, shock, and horror as blood dripped from her face to her upheld hand.

"You can bleed to death for all I care," Sharra snapped, furious.

"Head wounds invariably bleed freely," Oldive said, descending the wide steps. Sharra hurriedly followed. Throwing back the corner of the cloak someone had put on his shoulders, Oldive reached into the belt pouch that he always carried and drew out a bandage to staunch the wound. Although the woman shrank away from him, her eyes wild, he was able to assess the long gash on her head. "It will require stitching."

The woman went white with shock, a look of absolute horror on her face before she folded in a faint.

"No!" cried the leader, dropping to his knees to shield her body. *"No!* No abomination! Spare her that!"

Groghe let out a contemptuous oath, his mount dancing nervously. All the onlookers echoed Groghe's reaction and cries of "shame" were loud and angry. Oldive, however, turned a look of mixed compassion and rebuke on the protester and sighed with genuine regret.

"Let her bleed, Healer!" someone advised.

Others around Oldive mockingly repeated "No, spare her, spare her."

"Healers have been stitching wounds as needed for the past two and a half centuries," Oldive told the leader with quiet dignity. "Still, she is unlikely to bleed to death."

"More's the pity," was the quick gibe from a spectator.

Oldive held up his hand and the crowd turned respectfully silent as he went on. "The laceration is long and shallow. If the scalp is not stitched, there will be an unsightly scar. The hair must be cut away to prevent infection. Numbweed would reduce her discomfort." He paused and then added in a wry tone, "Numbweed flourished on Pern long before our ancestors arrived."

With each of Oldive's sentences, the prisoners had moaned or writhed. The leader glared at the Healer.

"By giving my advice freely, I have fulfilled my duty as a healer," Oldive said stolidly. "It is up to you to accept or reject."

"Spare her! Spare her! Away, abomination," cried several of the prisoners, lifting their hands in entreaty.

Oldive gave a slight nod of assent. "Her healing is now in your hands." He turned from them, outwardly composed. Sebell stepped solicitously to his side, and he acknowledged the tacit support with a little nod.

Just then, Journeywoman Keita came storming out of the Hall, other healers behind her, all shaking their heads, visibly devastated by what they'd found.

"They've smashed every piece of Morilton's last shipment!" she cried, glaring at the culprits, hands clenched at her sides. "It'll take months to replace our supplies. The stillroom's a complete shambles! Every sack, canister, and bottle in the treatment rooms has been emptied, and what they didn't burn—" She paused in her telling to take a deep breath before she could continue. "—they urinated on!"

Before Groghe could intervene, a holder launched his club at the prisoner nearest him, whacking the man to his knees.

"No!" Groghe roared. *"No!"* The crowd wavered but its forward surge aborted. "I am Lord Holder. I mete out punishment. And they *shall be punished*!" His face was livid with fury that anyone would usurp his prerogative. He legged his big mount forward. "You!" He jabbed a finger at the leader, who skittered to one side on his knees as the runnerbeast's hooves came very close to stamping on his feet. "Name! Hold! Craft!"

"Notice that they're wearing dark green, Lord Groghe," Keita said in a taut voice. There was an angry murmur for the additional insult.

"No rank knots or hold colors," Sebell said, walking around the vandals, closely observing them.

"I'll ask you once more!" Groghe said. "Names? Holds? Crafts?"

He—and the crowd—waited with brief patience. The prisoners looked more obdurate than ever.

"Search them!" Groghe said with a wave of his hand. More than enough erupted from the crowd to obey. "I said 'search them,' not strip them," Groghe added when he observed the force used.

"Why not? Maybe the cold will loosen their tongues," suggested a burly holder wearing Fort colors and a journeyman's knot.

The vandals found their tongues only to protest vehemently against such handling.

"We have rights!" the leader cried, surrounded by willing searchers.

"You just lost 'em. Not answering the Lord Holder!" the holder bellowed, roughly turning out the leader's pockets, scattering a few quarter marks on the frozen ground.

Suddenly Keita pointed to one of the women, whose shirt and jacket were opened to expose a red and inflamed chest.

"I recognize her," the journeywoman said. "She came to the Hall for ointment to ease a rash."

"Come here!" Groghe gestured to the woman.

"You will not touch her with your abominated hands," the leader said, shaking himself loose of his searchers.

"You had no problem with my abominated hands when you wanted something to stop the itching," Keita said as she pulled the woman out of the group. "And from the look of it now I'd say you didn't even use the salve. Well, I hope you itch forever!" She released her and the woman sidled hastily back to her companions.

"Keita," Oldive asked, "can you remember exactly when she was here? If she gave a name or any details?"

Keita nodded and dashed up the stairs to the Hall.

"No doubt she had a good look round the Hall, as well," Sebell said.

Nothing more significant was discovered on the vandals'

persons. Groghe ended the search and the prisoners adjusted their rumpled clothing.

Sebell spoke up. "The clothes and boots they're wearing will tell us where they were made, and we've weavers and tanners enough at the Gather to make such identification."

Then Sharra gave a bark of laughter, pointing to travel stains and scurf on the worn boots. "They're not dressed for the Gather, are they? In fact, they've done some hard riding. Could they possibly have stabled their runners in the Hall's beasthold for a quick escape? And left interesting items in their saddlebags?"

She saw several of the vandals flinch and laughed again as Groghe roared for Haligon to check. The Hall's stabling was to the west of the main entrance. A half-dozen holders accompanied Haligon on the search.

"Stuffed in here, Father!" Haligon shouted back. "Still saddled. Eating their heads off."

"A gallop to the harbor and a ship to sail away in?" N'ton asked.

"It's been done before," Sebell said, his eyes narrowing with anger, his expression grimmer than ever.

"Would you be kind enough to check Fort Harbor, Weyrleader?" Groghe asked N'ton.

"My pleasure, Lord Holder." Pivoting, N'ton singled out four riders, standing by their dragons. As soon as the dragons were aloft, fire-lizards appeared, shrieking glad cries and following them in graceful fairs.

"Rather stupid, really," Groghe said, easing himself in his saddle and staring down at his prisoners. "Never considered the possibility of discovery, did you? Thought you'd do the dirty and get away without being seen?"

The leader looked arrogantly in another direction, but the rough body searches had considerably subdued the others; most of the bluster was drained out of them. Two looked dismayed as Haligon and the others led the mounts out for inspection. Willing hands emptied the saddlebags onto the ground, spilling out the usual camping gear.

"Fifteen of them, aren't there?" N'ton said, rubbing his

jaw. "One of my sweepriders saw such a group camping in the Trader clearing by Ruatha River a few days back."

"He didn't report it?" Groghe demanded, offended.

"To me, Lord Holder, as he reported all those heading toward all the Turnover celebrations," N'ton replied with a diffident shrug. "He mentioned them wearing Healer green."

Groghe harrumphed at that detail. Who'd know these were not legitimate folk, braving the discomfort of winter travel for the magnificence of Turnover feasting and dancing? Who'd have thought the Healer Hall would be attacked?

Sharra, standing close to Oldive, could feel the man beginning to shake. The cold was penetrating her boots, and he was only wearing soft leather shoes.

"You must go in, Master. This has been a terrible shock to you," Sharra murmured and began to withdraw him from the scene.

"No, I must stay. It is my Hall they have defiled." He hunched into the wrap, pulling it tighter against him.

Sebell stepped close, offering Oldive a small flask.

"It's some of that fortified wine of yours," the Masterharper murmured. Oldive gratefully took a hefty swig.

"Father!" Haligon's cry was triumphant as he held up a thin wallet. He hastened to put it in Groghe's hands.

As the crowd watched in anticipation, the Lord Holder made an exaggerated inspection of the wallet's contents.

Groghe held up a piece of paper by an edge. "What? You make use of abominations?" he cried, eyes glinting with malice as he turned to the leader. "No less than a map printed by Master Tagetarl's *abominable* press. Useful things, abominations!"

Sharra tried not to grin at Groghe's style; he'd always appeared so pragmatic. Mockery was unusual for him, but today the gatherers loved it. Dancing and singing was all very well, but this was the most unusual diversion! They must remember every detail to tell missing friends and kin in hold and hall.

"B?" Groghe read by dropping the single sheet to eye

level. "That's you?" He fixed the leader with an inquiring look.

"One of 'em comes from Crom, Lord Groghe," shouted a holder busy examining a runnerbeast. "Brand on this one's rump. Under the mud!" He shot a disdainful glare at the prisoners for such shoddy animal care.

"This one's Crom, too," a harper reported.

"They could have been stolen," N'ton remarked. "But even that's significant enough to start a search there for stolen runnerbeasts."

"B?"

"Father," Horon began, "if there's a B, could there also be an A and C, and Abominators raiding other healer halls today, when they're apt to be empty?"

The sound of distant drumming echoed down the canyon, startling everyone. As one, heads were turned toward the Harper Hall Drum Heights.

"I'm sorry you're right, son," Groghe said with a weary sigh as he, and the others familiar with the drum messages, identified the source—Boll—and the message: vandalism.

Sharra became rigid with renewed anger as the message provided crisp details. "Janissian sending. Healer hall destroyed. Two journeymen and one apprentice injured!"

"Don't hold with hurting healers!" Groghe cried and his mount danced as he tightened his legs in angry reaction and barely missed knocking into the intruders. The Lord Holder began to give crisp orders.

"Use the cart. Take 'em to the Hold. Horon, put them in one of those rooms on the lower level." His expression was malicious. "One without abominable lights. No contact with anyone for any reason. Give 'em only water. Bottled water!"

The onlookers cheered.

"Him!" And Groghe's finger jabbed at the leader. "Take B to the small room. N'ton, Sebell, we'll question him there. Will you attend, Master Oldive?"

"I must oversee . . ." The Healer waved vaguely at the Hall. Sharra moved to support him.

"Yes, yes, of course, you've better things to do with your

time, Master," Groghe agreed, circling his mount while he decided what else needed organizing.

"But she's unconscious," cried the woman with the rash, pointing to the wounded one who was still in a heap on the ground.

"Then she can't object to being handled by abominable hands," Groghe said dismissively, motioning to the nearest men to put her in the cart that had been backed up to receive its load of prisoners. There were certainly enough hands and clubs to ensure that the prisoners quickly obeyed.

"Take all that gear up to the Hold, lads," Groghe told the men still inspecting the saddled runners. "Bring me that bony-backed Crom nag. Haligon, throw B over the beast and tie his hands. I'm not about to stay here in the cold any longer. I've other duties today." He made his mount pivot on its hindquarters, for a final survey of the scene. He kneed it to the stairs as Master Oldive, with Sharra and Sebell beside him, started to ascend.

"Dreadful display of ignorance. Dreadful," Groghe said bending from the saddle to sympathize with the Healer. "You took no hurt, Master Oldive? I shall deal with that rabble to the full extent of my power as Lord Holder. They expected to wreak their worst and disappear to the pits they came from. Ha!" The runnerbeast sidled, sensitive to his rider's anger. "Abomination! I'll show them abomination! I will find and punish all who perpetrated these outrages."

Oldive shook his head sadly. "I doubt they will be the last."

Sebell shot him a wary glance, pursing his lips tight.

Groghe scowled fiercely. "I thought we'd got rid of the lot of 'em after . . . after . . . the problem at the Ruatha Gather. Didn't I see Ruth here?" he added, looking about.

"He's probably gone for Jaxom," Sharra replied.

Groghe cleared his throat and reined his runnerbeast back to where B was being trussed aboard the nag. Haligon, bareback on his gray, held the lead rope. Standing up in his stirrups, the Lord Holder addressed the crowd.

"Any of you who care to help the healers restore order to their Hall will be well rewarded," he shouted, circling again to be sure all heard his message. "Let's clear the way, then. Thanks for your help, every one of you."

He led the way back to Fort Hold, Haligon just behind him while those not tempted by his reward followed at the brisk pace he set.

The dragons and riders who had not gone on search sweep sprang off into the air and, with great wings working, made the short flight back to the square.

They were halfway up the canyon when the air exploded with new arrivals of dragons, from several directions. Surprised, Meer and Talla set their talons into the cloth on Sharra's shoulders.

"What else can have happened?" she cried in alarm. She recognized not only Ramoth and Mnementh, but also Golanth carrying F'lessan, and Heth with K'van.

"I fear Master Oldive may be right," Sebell murmured, "that the attacks here and at Boll were not isolated."

Ruth, the last to arrive, uttered a squawk of surprise and agilely winged in under the others who were still hovering. He dropped precipitously to the ground, a maneuver that sent a sharp current of air up to lift the skirts of Sharra's coat. Her compulsive shudder was stilled when Jaxom's arms encircled her.

"Did they attack Ruatha, too?" she cried, horrified by the thought of all her carefully prepared and preserved medications destroyed.

"No, no," Jaxom hastily reassured her, hugging her tight.

"But Boll was attacked."

"I heard the drums." He held her tighter.

Alerted by the arrival of more dragons, Groghe came galloping back, his cloak flying and his expression fiercer than ever. He dismounted very agilely for someone his age and joined the newcomers. In that brief interval, Sharra fretted that Ruth had inadvertently alarmed too much support. F'lessan might not be annoyed by a needless summons, but she doubted the Benden Weyrleaders would be so charitable. Not when they were close enough for her to see their stern expressions. They both looked tired.

"The Healer Hall, too, huh?" F'lar said in a far too accurate assessment of the scene as he strode over toward Sharra, Oldive, and Sebell.

"What d'you mean by that, F'lar?" Groghe demanded.

"The same sort of thing has happened at Benden Hold and Landing," F'lar said.

"And Southern," K'van said, nodding courteously to Lessa and Sharra.

"We had just got Toronas calmed down when F'lessan contacted us," Lessa said, her voice as weary as her face.

"This can no longer be considered random damage," F'lar said, "but a planned and coordinated attack!"

"Let's go inside," Oldive said, his voice low with fatigue.

"The dining hall is warm—and wasn't touched," Keita said encouragingly, appearing on the top step.

"We could all use something hot," Sharra said, urging Oldive to lead the way.

"These incursions were far too widespread not to have been planned," Lessa said when they had all been served klah fortified with the Healer Hall's restorative liqueur. "Making too much good use of the laxity everywhere at Turnover."

"Not well-enough executed or timed, though," F'lessan remarked sardonically. "One of T'gellan's green riders investigated the sound of breaking glass and forestalled a more comprehensive destruction." His usually amiable expression was harsh. "T'gellan is questioning the three that were caught."

"The Benden Healer was not as lucky," F'lar said, "though his journeywoman says he'll recover. Our wings will search until full dark."

"Sintary got just a glimpse of the vandals," K'van said, and added in an apologetic tone, "The jungle's too thick to hope we'll find them easily."

"We've got *this* lot," Groghe said with great satisfaction as his fist came down on the table in emphasis.

"That leader looked an obstinate sort," Sebell remarked. "The kind who might die for a principle."

"I doubt the others are of similar fortitude," Sharra said wryly. "Scalp Wound is a moaner."

"Itch's rash is going to spread all over her body," Keita said, passing around a tray of tiny, hot Gather rolls.

Sharra tsked-tsked in mock pity. "Let them get thirsty, too?"

"Thirsty, Itchy, Scalp Wound?" Lessa asked pointedly.

Sebell explained and Lessa's grin of understanding turned into a wide yawn.

"My apologies, but we didn't get much sleep last night," she said.

"There are guest quarters here, Lessa," Oldive offered quickly.

"We're not that decrepit," F'lar said stiffly.

"Maybe you're not, F'lar," Lessa said, rising slowly to her feet, "but I was looking forward to a good night's sleep eight hours ago. And I would be grateful for some of it. Anywhere."

"Of course, of course," Groghe said. "You're always welcome at Fort."

"And Ruatha," Jaxom and Sharra said in unison, knowing how much Lessa liked to visit at her birthplace.

The Benden Weyrwoman shook her head with a rueful smile.

"Ramoth and Mnementh are already ensconced in the sun on Fort's fire-heights," she said, rising. "I'm for a quiet room. Here." She pointed downward. "No Gather noise."

"Shards! I have to get back to the Gather. Explain this mess and collect petitions," Groghe said, getting his feet under him to stand. "Those Abominators can bloody wait. Do them good."

"If anything will do that wretched lot any good," Sharra added bleakly.

Keita hurried forward, to escort the Benden Weyrleaders to guest rooms.

"I must return to report to Lord Toric," K'van said ruefully, pushing back from the table. "I doubt he'll appreciate that he's only one of many targets."

"Toric does indeed prefer to be singular," F'lar said, lifting a hand to acknowledge K'van's uneasy truce with the Southern Holder.

"We'll keep him informed," Groghe promised with a curt nod of his head. He had his own quarrel with the testy man. "Landing, Benden, Boll, Southern? How, ah, many targets could there be?"

"I wonder did they count on blizzards at High Reaches?" Lessa asked drolly and followed Keita out of the dining hall.

F'lar paused briefly. "F'lessan, are you coming with us?"

"No, sir, though I'm tempted. I want to see if that green rider's all right. They messed her about before her dragon arrived."

As the meeting broke up, no one was tactless enough to voice the customary Turnover good wishes.

Before Groghe, Sebell, and N'ton reached the Gather Square, more drum messages came rolling in.

"Alert," Sebell said, translating the initial beat and setting himself to hear more bad news, "from the Smithcrafthall."

"Not Fandarel, too? He's been extraordinarily conscientious in locking his Halls and stores against incursions. Ah, yes, I see . . ." Groghe's face relaxed into a pleased expression as the drumrolls ended. "They tried! I wonder what he'll find out from them. Oh, shards, everyone's waiting!"

They could all hear the harpers playing a sprightly tune to a sparsely populated dance square. Around all four sides, knots of people were warming their hands at the braziers, murmuring among themselves, and anxiously watching the progress of their Lord Holder on his big mount.

"Father!" Horon's shout reached their ears as he came down the wide hold steps at an almost dangerous clip. He rushed over, waiting till he was close before he gasped out his message. "Father, we've found something you have to see!"

"Later, Horon, later."

"It's extremely important."

"Sharding Abominators! Thought we'd seen the last of their kind," Groghe said impatiently. "Sebell, go see what's so bloody important. I'd better deal with them." His gesture indicated the waiting Gatherers. "Damnable way to start Turnover." With that he kneed his mount to a trot all the way to the harpers' platform. The tune was brought to a conclusion with a flourish that Sebell wryly approved, and the crowd flowed forward to hear what the Lord Holder had to say.

Sebell caught the eye of the nearest person in harper blue, an apprentice girl who rushed up to him.

"Worla, I'll be at the Hold with Lord Horon. Bring me the text of all the messages coming in. I'll send any replies directly to the Drummaster." He summoned his gold fire-lizard, Kimi. Holding her to his shoulder, he and Horon jogged up the wide staircase to the freezing expanse of Fort's upper court. He heard the cheers as Lord Groghe stepped up on the harpers' platform.

"So what is so important, Horon?" Sebell asked once they were out of the wind.

Horon gulped. "The most—ghastly . . ." His face contorted with revulsion.

"Abominator cant?" Sebell was surprised.

Horon gave a shudder. He opened the door into the Lord Holder's five-sided office. A table had been set up on which the vandals' gear was spread. Grainger, the trusted steward of Fort Hold, was busy searching a saddle pack.

"That!" Horon pointed to a thin pamphlet with a dirty cover, its pages roughly fastened by crude stitches. His nostrils flared and it was plain he wanted nothing more to do with it. Grainger's expression was similarly revolted.

Sebell bent over to examine the pamphlet: obviously a very amateurish effort. Why, Tagetarl's youngest apprentice could have done a neater job. In bold block letters—similar to the single letter on the vandal's map—the title of the pamphlet read *Tortures of the Abomination*. Yes, the same hand had made the B.

"Just—just look inside, Sebell!" Horon flicked his fingers, his mouth contorted with revulsion.

Sebell lifted the cover and only stern self-control kept him from slapping it shut. He could see what had made Horon squeamish. The picture was, indeed, revolting to look at. It depicted shapes, indecently colored, of unusual appearance and what looked like knives holding flesh back from what could be a long incision. A caption had been blacked out. Underneath, again in the black block lettering: "A body laid bare, pulsing in torture. It could be yours."

"It's all like that. Revolting pictures," Horon said. "Where could they . . . get such things?"

Impassively, Sebell flipped several more pages and found one picture he actually recognized. The compound fracture of a human tibia, the flesh colored an unrealistic pink against which the ivory bone nauseatingly contrasted. He'd seen such an injury in a hill hold, Turns before. The printed caption read "Shattered by blows." Sebell made out page numbers, almost obscured by the dirty finger marks, and, right by the margin of the picture, "Fig. 10" and "Fig. 112." Checking, he found none of the pages were sequential and realized that the pamphlet was comprised of random photographs, undoubtedly removed from a perfectly proper medical text released from Aivas's comprehensive records.

"Kimi." Sebell turned his fire-lizard's head toward him, one finger stroking her neck affectionately. He scribbled a quick note on the pad he kept with him and tucked it in her message cylinder. "Take this to Keita at Healer Hall. You know her." He projected a vivid image of Oldive's discreet journeywoman. The little queen made a throaty noise and disappeared from sight.

"Revolting to us, perhaps," Sebell said, negligently pushing the pamphlet away from him, "but instructive to a Healer when not used as . . . disinformation."

Horon shuddered.

"Those photographs are quite likely of surgical procedures. Those are not well understood as yet," Sebell went on, looking directly at Horon. "Your own grandfather died of a burst pendix that the then Masterhealer could have removed. Such an operation was known—and successfully performed."

Horon's face was pale as he nodded his understanding.

"Healers have recovered much lost or imperfectly understood information," Sebell said. "Master Oldive has been training his most skillful men and women to perform surgery that will greatly lengthen life and improve health." He gestured disparagingly at the pamphlet. "That was deliberately produced to misinform people. To undermine one of the most basic rights of the Charter, the treatment of ills and wounds. You know," he said, pointing at Horon, "that when Master Oldive offered treatment, that stupid female rejected him. She's been well schooled in the delusion. No one is *forced* to accept healer help. Certainly no one's bones are broken in torture! Not by Healers!" He dismissed the pamphlet with contempt.

There was a scratch on the door, which swung open. The burly minor holder who'd assisted with the prisoners peered round the door.

"MasterHarper, Lord Horon?" He entered at Horon's wave. "I thought you'd like to know that they're talking."

"Talking?"

"The prisoners. Naming each other, at least. I thought you should know."

"Indeed we should," Sebell said. "That could be most useful."

The half-open door hit the man in the back as someone else tried to enter.

"Master Sebell?" A man in proper Healer green with a master's knot came in, breathless.

"Ah, Master Crivellan, just the person to explain what exactly we have here!" And Sebell slapped the dirty pamphlet in his hand. As Crivellan stared down at it with some apprehension, Kimi slipped into the room and resumed her perch on Sebell's shoulder. "Crivellan's particular skill is surgery. Do tell us what these pictures actually depict."

BACK AT LANDING — 1.2.31

As soon as the warm air of Landing's morning hit him, F'lessan realized how tired he was.

You need to go back to Honshu and sleep. There is no Fall for two more days, Golanth told him as he circled above the panorama of Landing.

"I just want to check on Tai. They kicked her around a lot. Persellan said she'd be badly bruised but the gash on her cheek wouldn't scar."

She's not here. Golanth stretched his head skyward and stroked his great wings for height.

"Surely she's in bed in her weyr?" F'lessan said.

Zaranth is sitting by the sea.

"Zaranth is by the sea?" F'lessan echoed in amazement.

Tai is in the sea, Golanth informed him. *Shall we go there?*

"By all means." Hearing that she was well enough to go swimming, F'lessan was annoyed with himself for having been so concerned. So concerned that he had left what would have been a fascinating session at Fort. He wondered if T'gellan had had better luck questioning Landing's captives.

Golanth went *between* and came out again, circling, skimming the brilliantly turquoise and blue sea. Dolphins immediately tail-danced to greet him, squeeing their welcome. He was as well known as Ruth was to the various pods along the southern continent. Golanth swung shoreward until F'lessan saw the swimmer: a black spot in the sea.

Swimming is good for aches, Golanth remarked.

"Quite likely," F'lessan replied with uncharacteristic sarcasm.

The swimmer was Tai. She seemed to be treading water as they overflew her.

"Come in!" F'lessan yelled through cupped hands. Then he pointed to the shore.

Craning his neck backward, he saw that dolphins accompanied her. Well, maybe she wasn't being so reckless, then.

Yes, she swims with Natua and her new calf.

Were you listening then, last night? He never knew when Golanth was. Last night seemed a very long time ago.

I like dolphins. Flo is with them. And here come others from the pod.

Close to land now, F'lessan could see Zaranth sitting upright on the shore, watching her rider. Golanth landed, dipping his head politely to the big green and managing deftly not to churn sand onto her. Draped on Zaranth's neck ridge were a towel, a shirt, and shorts. F'lessan slipped off Golanth's back and took a moment to shuck off his flying gear, wishing he could strip and swim.

You could, you know.

Golanth! F'lessan should have grown accustomed to his dragon's teasing.

Then he saw Tai limping out of the water and, grabbing the towel from Zaranth's back, he jogged down to the edge of the sea. Only because he knew that his flying boots would take a long time to dry did he resist the impulse to continue into the water. Her body, legs, and arms were covered by bruises. Persellan had done a neat repair of the gash on her right cheekbone.

"What's wrong, F'lessan?" she asked anxiously, splashing the rest of the way.

"What are you doing?" he demanded, looking but not looking—as was polite—at her long lean figure and her long, lovely legs.

"Admiring Natua's calf," she answered tartly, taking the towel from his hand and wrapping it about her. "There he is." She pointed to the dolphin heads, large and small, bobbing as they watched her safely landed. "Salt water's good for wounds, you know."

"And washed off all the numbweed." He reached for his belt pouch. He had seen her wince when the towel rubbed against one of the contusions.

"I brought some with me," she said, pointing to her clothes.

"And I suppose Zaranth can apply it?" He gestured to the bruises running down her back.

"Why are you angry with me?"

F'lessan let his breath go out in one exasperated sigh and glanced around him, looking for a good answer. Even the right one.

"I'm sorry. I was worried."

She gave him a little smile. "Thank you. Zaranth was doing all the worrying I needed." She shot a fond glance at her green dragon, who had been joined by Golanth, sitting beside her in much the same pose, an arm's length taller at the shoulder. "How bad was it at the Healer Hall?"

F'lessan blinked, time-disoriented. Landing was half a day ahead of Fort.

"Give me your numbweed and I'll apply it while I tell you."

He did tell her—in perhaps more detail than was possibly discreet, but she was a rider, already involved, and deserved to know.

On her part, Tai was grateful that he could spread on more salve. The salty water had stung the cheek cut and the scrapes, although it had been good for the bruises. The solicitude of the dolphins had been another balm. When dolphins went to the aid of humans in the sea, they didn't stop to consider the consequences: they acted. Everyone else had lectured her on how foolish she had been to burst in on the vandals. She didn't bother to justify her actions. Of course, she hadn't had any reason to suspect what she'd found: men swinging hammers and crowbars with such fervent expressions of enjoyment on their faces that at first she'd thought they'd gone mad. She had wrestled a bar from one man's grasp, her interference confusing him enough to loosen his grip. She poked him hard in the groin and then, once he'd dropped to his knees, she started swinging the bar indiscriminately around her. She'd been so furious that she really hadn't thought of the danger to herself. The very idea of someone destroying healer remedies—some of which might be needed before the night was over—had given her a strength, and an agility, she hadn't known she had. But what would have happened to her if that vandal had managed to complete the

swing of his hammer? She flinched, remembering how close
it had come.

"Didn't mean to be so heavy-handed," F'lessan said in
quick apology. "I'm nearly finished."

"Not your touch, F'lessan," she replied. "It's the thought
that there are still Abominators, causing willful damage for
some perverted reason. You'd think that a healer hall would
be the last place to be attacked! For any reason!"

He screwed on the cap of the numbweed jar with an angry
twist, and then stared out across the sea, turning his head
northeast, in the general direction of the islands where the
first Abominators had been exiled after the abduction of
Master Robinton.

"There's no chance, is there," she asked, following his gaze
and dreading the answer, "that they've been rescued and are
responsible for these new attacks?"

F'lessan shook his head, rolling up the sleeves of his
rumpled Gather shirt. The sun wasn't up very high yet, but
even here by the sea, the air was getting warm with the
new day.

"I suspect riders will investigate. Do you know if T'gellan
learned anything?"

Tai shook her head, her lips twitching in amusement.
"Green riders are the last to hear. Besides, Persellan sent me
to my weyr. I went, but I couldn't get comfortable."

"Hmmm. That's understandable, considering the number
of bruises I just tended. Have you fellis to take?" He had returned her numbweed jar and now fumbled in his pouch.

"Yes, I do," she replied and rose to her feet. "I help Persellan, you know. I've all I need." She grinned. "Except my
arms don't bend to reach the awkward spots. Thanks. I think I
will be able to rest now."

"Promise?"

She cocked her head at him in mild reprimand. "You're the
one who needs to rest, bronze rider. Thank you for your concern." She extended her hand toward Golanth. "Zaranth will
take me back."

And I will take you, F'lessan, Golanth said, rising to all four feet, *to Honshu.*

For a confused moment, F'lessan looked after Tai's towel-draped body striding across the white sands to her dragon and saw her begin to dress.

It will make sense when you've had some sleep, Golanth remarked as rider and dragon watched the green make a graceful spring into the air, neatly down-winging to gain altitude and quickly reaching a gliding height on a sea thermal. *Zaranth's a good size for a green. You're sweating. It'll be cooler, and much nicer, in Honshu right now.*

F'lessan rolled down his sleeves, shrugged into his riding gear, and jumped to his dragon's back.

"Then let's get there, please, Golly."

They were already airborne when a horrible thought crossed F'lessan's mind. What if yet another gang of Abominators had broken into Honshu during one of his absences and smashed some of the brittle artifacts?

You are silly-tired, Golanth said with exasperation. *It takes days to walk there. Not even a runner trace to guide a stranger.*

"Runners!" F'lessan exclaimed. "The Runners should be asked if they've seen any suspicious groups out on their tracks!"

Someone else will remember to do that. We're going to Honshu. With that, Golanth took them *between.*

FORT HOLD—LATE NIGHT—1.1.31

The Benden and Fort Weyrleaders, along with Lord Jaxom and Lady Sharra of Ruatha Hold, joined Lord Groghe, his sons, Masterharper Sebell, and Master Healer Crivellan at a late private meeting in the small dining room. Not as lavishly decorated for Turnover as the Main Hall and located on the inside rank of the Hold's main reception area, the warm, comfortably sized room was partly wood-paneled, and hung with a mixture of tastefully arranged portraits and landscapes of varying styles and periods.

Since the possibility that the Abominators exiled in 2539 had somehow escaped their remote island occurred to others during the afternoon, N'ton had gone with one of Sebell's most discreet men to make certain that those men and women were all present and accounted for. The island was one of many in the long eastern archipelago, its precise location known only to N'ton; even the most diligent search by other dissidents would have been unlikely to find the inhabited one.

"At the time I wasn't all that certain everyone involved in the shameful business of abducting Master Robinton was apprehended," Groghe said brusquely after N'ton delivered his report.

"Those involved in the original attacks on Aivas and the Crafthalls were sentenced to labor in the mines," Jaxom said, his expression as bleak as Groghe's. "Do we know if they are still in custody?"

"Most are registered as dead," Sebell replied. "Of the two remaining, one escaped when that meteorite tore through the minehold. A search was initiated, of course, but it's believed he must have died. The terrain there is difficult to traverse— little vegetation, not much of it edible. He was deaf and not considered very bright. I don't think we have to worry about that one." He dismissed the problem with a wave of his hand.

"Then let's deal with today's atrocities," Lessa said, restlessly trying to find a comfortable position, her slender body taut with indignation at the scope of the destruction. Impatient as ever, she wanted answers before she could go back to Benden with an easy mind. She and F'lar had gotten some rest at the Healer Hall and had an excellent dinner in Fort's smaller dining room. However, the ability to sense people's thoughts—and sometimes to cloud their perceptions with the strength of her mind—could be useful in extracting or confirming truths. Aivas had said she was as much a telepath as any of the dragons. F'lar called it "leaning on people," though she had never been able to cloud *his* mind. Still, though it was an enervating process and one she disliked being required to use, she had leaned on people to advantage on a number of occasions. Tonight would probably be another. "How many in total, Sebell?"

"Benden, Landing, Southern, here, Southern Boll—trouble avoided at Crom because the healer was stitching a wound and the patient's relatives beat off the 'drunken louts.' Then caught them when they tried to sneak back in," Sebell said with wry amusement. "Bitra's healer chased two off, and Nerat was locked up too tight, though an obvious attempt had been made to break in. Haven't heard anything from Keroon. That makes twenty-three apprehended while damaging Healer property, and nine who were detained for damaging three separate Glass Halls. Master Fandarel says there were prowlers at the SmithCraftHall but no harm done. Benelek was working late. In view of the number of attempts, he thinks there may have been one on the Computer Hall, too. They're frequent enough."

"I hadn't realized there were so many," Groghe said, twisting his glass until the wine came dangerously close to the rim.

"Then there's less possibility that these were all random, local disgruntlements," F'lar said.

"If there hadn't been so many, and such emphasis on healer halls," Lessa said, frowning slightly, "I might attempt to understand their reasons for such attacks. Especially at this time of a Turn when petitions are part of the celebrations, a clearing away of grievances to start a new Turn in good heart. Nor would they give their hold and hall affiliations. I know there are still many who survive—quite well—as holdless. But that doesn't give them the license to attack halls and deny such services to others. Did I understand correctly, Groghe, that the prisoners became thirsty enough to talk?"

"In a manner of speaking, yes." The success of that tactic briefly cheered Groghe. "Not having anything but bottled and abominated water worked well, though not quite as I'd thought. Zalla, the Scalp—" Groghe chuckled at the nickname she had acquired. "—was terrified that tunnel snakes would be drawn by the smell of blood and eat her alive. She got everyone else so worked up they dropped more information than we could have anticipated. Isolating their leader helped. No real discipline in the bunch." He harrumphed at such moral weakness before he went on.

"The 'B' on the map stands for 'Batim,' the leader's name. He comes from Crom, evidently served as a guard at Crom Hold, but he's been elsewhere, too, strictly for pay. Three are from Bitra, five from Igen, the others from Keroon, Ista, and Nerat. All have one thing in common." He gave an apologetic nod to Master Crivellan. "They have what they think are good reasons to mistrust healers. Viscula, the Itch, blames the Craft for not ridding her of her rash. Lechi is missing fingers due, he claims, to healer incompetence. Another blamed healers for not saving his family from fevers. They do not"— he held up his hand to forestall an obvious question—"know from whom Batim received his orders."

"How, or if, he received any at all is almost as important," Lessa said, her tone cross. "He can't have been acting independently. There were too many other such incidents to consider this a random event."

"Lady Lessa," Haligon put in, raising his hand. "The Runners have been asked to tell us what messages have been delivered to Crom, to whom and sent by whom. That will take time."

She gave a snort. "There're always fire-lizards to bring messages and no record of where they came from or to whom they belong."

"Even fire-lizards have scruples, my dear," F'lar said dryly. "Also, Turnover is a very good time to move freely."

"Was it just healer and glass halls that were attacked?" Jaxom asked.

"No, some of Morilton's were," Sebell said, tapping the pile of drum messages in front of him. "Those who specialize in making equipment for healer purposes. Anyone else who had break-ins would have drummed in by now. Only Landing and Toric's Hold were attacked in the south."

"Cove Hold?" Lessa asked urgently.

"Not with D'ram's Tiroth on watch, my dear," F'lar reminded her. "Has T'gellan made any progress questioning the ones he caught?"

"Again, all three men had grievances with healers."

"By destroying medicines and equipment, they achieve nothing but the enmity of the people who must now wait to be treated," Master Crivellan said, his tone distressed. "And delay our discovery of the cause and the cure for acute rashes. Or learn enough to repair crushed fingers. There is so much we *don't* know and then we're damned because we can't remedy all conditions." He gave his head a quick shake. "I apologize."

"No need to, Crivellan," Groghe said gruffly reassuring. "Anyone with an ounce of common sense knows how dedicated and loyal healers are. We cannot change minds and attitudes overnight or spread knowledge planetwide. It all takes time."

"And then something as vile as that," the Master added, pointing to the pamphlet in the middle of the table, "has no trouble getting spread around." He was still obviously shaken by the perverted use of the medical diagrams.

"All the more reason to be sure the truth—" Lessa paused to stress the word. "—is circulated. And countered when such perversions," she added, waving at the pamphlet, "are discovered."

"Such damage is easy to do," Sebell remarked, "and very hard to undo."

"Runners listen and are listened to," Haligon put in hesitantly. "They are welcome everywhere, too." All eyes were on him and he cleared his throat nervously. "People believe what they say."

"Harper Hall often hears of . . . rumors, inconsistencies, minor problems," Sebell said, "but I wouldn't care to involve Runners too much. They are as vulnerable on their routes as healers."

"But faster on their feet," Haligon said with a little smile. "And able to deal with danger."

"If they would be willing just to listen a little harder right now," F'lar suggested, raising an eyebrow.

Haligon nodded. "I'll ask."

"Anything that will prevent a repetition of today's attacks," Lessa said firmly.

"Any assistance would be welcome," Crivellan added urgently, leaning toward Haligon. "Master Oldive is going to be terribly upset by that vileness. He's had such plans for the extension of healer services. If such untruths are circulating, healers may be discredited, or endangered. So often they travel alone and great distances."

"Any healer who requires the assistance of the Weyr need only let us know," F'lar said, looking to N'ton, who nodded vigorously in agreement.

"The problem often is that we can't know how serious an injury or a condition is when we're called to attend," Crivellan said.

"How many healers have fire-lizards?" Sharra asked, acutely aware of how useful hers were.

"Not many here in the north," Crivellan replied regretfully.

"I thought healers had priority on Master Bassage's little hand units." Lessa turned to F'lar.

The Weyrleader's expression was rueful. "They do and Master Bassage is working as diligently as possible, but the materials come from various sources and have to be hand-made. Again, it all takes time."

"Oh, some have been delivered," Master Crivellan hastily admitted, "but not enough, and even then," he added with a little shrug, "the things don't work in deep valleys."

"The benefits of Aivas's technology are often ambivalent," F'lar remarked.

"They require work," Groghe announced bitingly, "determination, and application. Too few of this generation want to work."

"We know the problem, it's the solution that eludes us," Sebell said. He sounded and looked tired.

"Shall we deal with the problem of this Batim?" Groghe asked, regarding Lessa with a benevolent eye.

"For all the good it's likely to do," Jaxom remarked, hooking one arm over his chair back.

"He might just let some clue drop," F'lar said blandly.

Groghe gave a sharp nod to Haligon, who rose and left the room. "He's been cleaned up. He'll undoubtedly start claiming his 'rights.' His sort usually does."

"And the rest of his crew?" Lessa asked, frowning.

"And the—ah—Scalp's injury?" Sharra asked, not at all solicitous.

"Oh, you heard her reject Oldive's offer? Magnanimous of him when you think what she'd just done. However," Groghe continued with a malicious grin, "they've been fed, and washing took care of the dried blood and other dirts."

"You had them washed?" Lessa asked.

"They objected strenuously to being hosed down," Groghe said, "and Haligon said they complained that the food they were given was too salty."

Lessa grinned at Sharra, who also felt that some deprivation was very much in order, but Master Crivellan was dismayed by the news.

The door opened to admit Haligon, followed by the prisoner, propelled into the room by two guards. No longer in bogus Healer green, he was clad in a patched shirt and too-short trousers from which his hairy legs protruded. His feet were bare and his lank hair was still damp. His expression was both arrogant and sour, expecting the worst and prepared for it. When Batim realized who was present, he twitched his shoulders defiantly and strutted right up to the table. Involuntarily, his eyes darted to the bread, cheese, and fruit on the table and he licked thin, dry lips

"I want my clothes. I demand my rights," Batim said without preamble.

"Sorry about the clothes, Father," Haligon said, clicking his tongue apologetically. "I really couldn't present him in what he was wearing. Beyond cleansing."

"I have my rights," Batim repeated.

"Which do not,"—Groghe's fist came down hard on the table, bouncing plates and glasses—"include destroying the Healer Hall."

"Abominations! We destroyed abominations! I have rights."

"Not in my Hold you don't!"

"What is your Hold?" Lessa demanded, almost idly.

"If any would claim you," Groghe continued contemptuously. "We know you came down from Crom."

Batim twitched a lip derisively.

"Sometimes it's what's not said that speaks for itself," Sebell remarked across the table to Lessa, who shrugged indifferently.

Batim glared at the Harper, who took a sip of wine, ostentatiously savoring the taste in his mouth before swallowing.

"Holdless then, are you?" Groghe remarked. "Viscula left a Crom hill hold to follow you, didn't she? Minsom, Galter, and Lechi are Bitran. They're often so gullible, those Bitrans." He gave a pitying shake of his head. "Small wonder Zalla has such a great fear of tunnel snakes, coming from Igen Caverns. Bagalla, Vikling, and Palol—" He stopped naming the other prisoners as the sneer on Batim's face deepened. Leader he might have been, but he had no loyalty to those who followed him. That also was information—of a sort. "Ah, well, not that that matters. They chose to follow you."

F'lar pushed back his chair, impatiently cutting through the air with one hand. "This is such a waste of time, Groghe. Do let me take him for a short dragon ride. If *between* doesn't loosen his tongue, I'll just leave him there and that's the end of the matter."

That startled the prisoner. Master Crivellan stared in shocked astonishment at the Benden Weyrleader.

"Why bother Mnementh, F'lar?" Jaxom commented, flicking an indolent hand. "When we'll know by morning where those Runner messages originated?"

"Runners don't talk," Batim protested.

"They may not," Lessa agreed with a wickedly innocent smile, "but they keep records of acceptance and delivery, don't they? In case anyone wishes to trace the progress of . . . important messages." Clearly Batim hadn't considered that at all: She could see his impudence wane. "Traders would remember where they sold enough green cloth to outfit fifteen people." He hadn't considered that either. "I hate to keep thinking that so much evil emanates from Bitra," she added artlessly and was not the only one who caught the glitter in the prisoner's eye. "Though I rather suspect," she said on the end of sigh, "that Nerat's partly responsible this time." He gave an involuntary twitch before she added with a patient smile, "and Keroon." No one missed his nervous swallow. "They're so hidebound in Keroon!" She sat back, smiling with satisfaction. "Really, Sebell, you must increase your efforts there to show the hill folk how to improve the quality of their lives."

Sebell held up one hand in a rueful gesture. "We would if we could. Hill folk are the most hidebound of all."

Inadvertently Batim's face mirrored the Harper's opinion.

"That narrows it down, doesn't it?" the Lord Holder said, rubbing his hands together in satisfaction. "Take him away, Haligon."

"I have rights! Chartered rights! You're all so big about that blinding Charter of yours," Batim cried hoarsely as Haligon called the guard in. The prisoner made a frantic surge toward the table but was thwarted by the quick-footed Haligon. Struggling, Batim reached straining fingers toward the glasses. "Water. I've had no water all day."

"Actually," Lessa said in a cold voice, "the Charter does not cite water in the list of rights."

"But it has to!"

Haligon and the guard hauled him out of the room and they heard him demanding water as the door closed. Lessa gave a shudder of distaste. Master Crivellan continued to stare fixedly at the Benden Weyrleader.

"Crivellan," N'ton said, touching the Healer's arm, "F'lar only threatened the man, no more. You know that dragons won't hurt a human."

"The threat is usually sufficient," F'lar remarked, resuming his seat, "but the culprit has to believe the threat will be carried out. Batim would have ignored any physical coercion—apart from a one-way trip a-dragonback. So we put him off balance." He grinned at Lessa. "And elicited some interesting reactions."

"Oh!" was the Healer's relieved response. "My pardon for doubting your methods."

"Considering what harm the man did your Craft, you are remarkably forbearing," Lessa said, dropping her pose of indolence.

"I am dedicated to saving life, Weyrwoman," Crivellan replied with great dignity, "not taking it."

"And learning all you can from Aivas to improve your skills. Whereas the Abominators seem to want to stop progress in its tracks," she replied coldly. "We found out as much from what he didn't say, though the thought of trying to trace him in Keroon, where the hill folk won't even discuss the weather, is daunting." She caught Sebell's eye and held it.

"Shall we enlist Lord Kashman's help?" Jaxom asked. "I know he's new in his Holding but, if his people are in any way involved, he should be consulted."

Sebell cleared his throat. "None claimed Keroon as their hold."

"Did we expect them to?" Lessa asked scornfully.

"Did *you* learn anything else from Batim, Lessa?" F'lar asked.

His weyrmate gave a fastidious shudder. "Only what was foremost on his mind—denying where he came from. He reacted more strongly to 'Keroon' than anywhere else," she said, giving him a trenchant glare. "He was very annoyed that they'd been caught and was steeling himself against the abominations that would be practiced on him to make him speak."

"The very idea!" Master Crivellan was appalled.

"Someone like Batim would probably enjoy being tortured," Jaxom remarked.

"Jaxom!" Sharra exclaimed.

"He's right, you know," Lessa said. "Don't deny that you would have liked to help, considering how distressed Master Oldive was."

"*Then* I would have," Sharra replied candidly, "not now. I'm sorry they don't know better."

"They're a grudging lot," Jaxom reminded her. "Look how that woman reacted when Oldive offered to treat her and went to the trouble of explaining that he would be using traditional materials! She didn't want to hear the truth. Is it possible that we," he asked, indicating all the leaders, "have not taken into consideration how hold and hall will receive Aivas's innovations?"

Sebell cleared his throat. "We do hear things now and then that suggest that some people are dubious about 'progress.' Often because they doubt they'll ever be able to afford it."

"Or don't fully understand the benefits?" Lessa asked, thinking of her own quarters, warmed by an Aivas improvement. Cold seeped through the stone floor under the table and chilled her feet halfway up her shins.

"It'll take more than the few Turns we've had since Aivas died to explain to all who need to know," Sebell said.

"For that matter," Groghe remarked, "I've a significant number of small holders who won't believe dragonriders diverted the Red Star, because Thread is still falling."

"Some will never understand," Jaxom said wearily.

"We certainly make it as clear and to as many holds as possible," Sebell said, trying not to sound defensive. The burden of explanation was the Harper Hall's responsibility. "But the understanding of some is limited."

"And those are happy to believe easy lies rather than complicated truths," Jaxom said, shifting in his chair. "Most of my Hold has at least had basic lessons but even so, we are constantly having to dispel misconceptions."

Groghe brought both hands down on the arms of his chair. "That is not the question tonight. We have to decide what to do with this lot and, if at all possible," he added, nodding toward Sebell, "find out who planned such widespread raids. There had to be a central person or persons for so many to have acted as simultaneously as they did."

"And see what can be done to prevent any more," Jaxom said.

"Possibly we can find out more from the Keroonian," Sebell said, checking the pile of notes in front of him. "Tawer, by name. He's a tanner, judging by the calluses and dye stains on his hands."

"He could be a hide-binder, a bookbinder," Lessa muttered, "badly done as it was."

"Is Tawer the one who lost his family to fever?" Crivellan asked. "Our healer hall at Wide Bay keeps meticulous records."

"Good point," Sebell said. "I'll also find out what Tagetarl does with blurred or damaged pages."

"Unless Wide Bay healer hall is missing some of their medical texts," Sharra added.

"Yes, we must find out where and who issued that filth," Crivellan urged.

"I doubt we will," Sebell said. "But, if you'll pass the word of such things to your healers, we'll have harpers keep their eyes open. Runners, too." He glanced at Haligon, who nodded. Then he began to tick off more points on his fingers. "Right now we've enough to make some discreet inquiries in Keroon, trace the Crom runnerbeasts, see if anyone else saw them on the way here, or perhaps crossing Telgar and Keroon, find out where they got the fabric for their clothing, and pass around sketches of Batim, Scalp, and Itch."

"And suggest that all Halls keep guard at night," F'lar said.

"You're within your rights, Groghe," Jaxom said, pausing to smile ironically, "to keep them as long as they might be needed."

"Needed?" Groghe was offended. "I'll have them out of my Hold as soon as possible." Scowling, he glanced around the table, assessing all. "I know what I *want* to do with them. What I firmly believe should be done with all these dissenting Abominators." He brought his fist down again on the table. "Exile 'em!"

Crivellan jumped at the crack of fist on wood. "I thought that required a trial and jury," he said, surprised.

Groghe gestured to include those present. "Masters, Weyr-leaders, and Lord Holders. Adequate judges. The vandals were caught in the act. Plenty of people saw what they did. Destroyed valuable property, depriving others of medicines and services. And not just in Fort." He waved an encompassing arm. He focused narrowed eyes on the irresolute Healer. "Ordinarily, I'd send them to the mines. However, the notion of being exiled might make others think twice. I wouldn't want anyone to think the healer halls can be attacked with impunity. Right, Master Crivellan?"

"Yes," the man admitted hesitantly. "It will be hard enough to replace what was spoiled and broken today. Though stopping *that* sort of travesty," he added, pointing to the pamphlet, "is even more important!"

"I thought you'd see it our way," Groghe said. "We'll proceed accordingly."

Sebell rose. "I shall have many messages for Kimi."

"Meer and Talla can help if you wish," Sharra offered.

"Tris, too," N'ton said. He got to his feet, stretching stiffly.

"You know, exile is a just punishment for them," Lessa remarked. "They can't escape it or each other. Don't make it a large island, will you, N'ton." She took F'lar's hand to get to her feet and retrieved her heavy fur-lined riding jacket from the back of her chair. "We shall all keep our ears and eyes open during Fall two days from now."

"How soon can you get any information from the Runners, Haligon?" F'lar asked.

Haligon shrugged. "They've first to spread the word. When I explained the matter to Torlo at the Fort Station, he wrote messages for every pouch being forwarded."

"Pern has relied on the Runners for much," F'lar stated.

"It always will," Lessa added on her way to the door.

Sharra wondered if she was the only one to see Haligon's delighted reaction to Lessa's reassurance. She was as eager to get home as Lessa. It had been a very long and trying day.

"We'll sort this out," Groghe said at his heartiest. "Thank you one and all for assistance in this vexing matter. Let's hope the new Turn improves from here on out!"

"I'll second that!" Jaxom replied fervently.

FORT HOLD RUNNER STATION — 1.2.31

"We've no word from Crom yet," Torlo said the moment Haligon walked into the Runner Station. Torlo had just finished dispatching the day's runners, laden with Crafthall messages, resulting from a very busy Turnover. "Hard frost makes a hard trace."

"Weyr, Hold, and Hall are indebted to you, Torlo," Haligon said courteously, wondering now why he had proffered services last night that he might not be able to secure. Runners had unassailable ethics.

"No more than our duty to trace letters," the old man replied with a careless flick of his hand, "especially after all that dirty business at the Healer Hall." Then he cast a shrewd look at his early morning guest. "Too early, too, for you to be looking for Tenna, bearing in mind you should know by now how long it takes her to make a run back. You got to spend most of Turnover with her."

Haligon cleared his throat, not sure how to state his real business of the morning.

"Oh? Something else, is it?" Torlo, who was a perceptive man under a brusque manner, pointed to the corner of the empty hall of the Runner Station. "Fresh klah, Lord Haligon?"

Maybe this should have been done more informally, but Torlo had called the tone by using his title. Hiding his chagrin, Haligon accepted the hospitality and slid onto a settle seat at the end table while Torlo filled cups and brought a breadboard with some of the morning's bake on it. Everyone would have known about the meeting in the Hold's private dining room. That Batim had been questioned. Certainly the fire-lizard traffic out of the Harper Hall last night would have been noticed. The Runners had never objected—in so many words—to fire-lizards carrying messages. They appreciated that speed could be a critical factor that had not, yet, interfered with their craft. In the very early days, while clutches were still being found on the beaches of Boll, Ista, and Keroon, Runners had used fire-lizards, too.

The young Lord sipped the klah—it was always excellent here—and deliberated exactly how to approach Torlo. He had several very good reasons for not antagonizing either the man or the Runners and for carrying out last night's request, not the least of which was his firm regard, although his brother called it an obsession, for Tenna.

"The Abominator who led the vandals let drop some information," he began, choosing his words carefully.

"He's one of *them*?" Torlo's contempt was deep. "Same as who abused Master Robinton?"

"Similar but this time turning their spite on the Healer and Glass Halls."

"Glass Halls, too?" Torlo's spiky brows shot up on his lined forehead, his deep-set eyes fast on Haligon's face. He leaned forward slightly across the tables. "What about SmithCraftHalls?"

Something in Torlo's manner suggested to Haligon that *they* would have been legitimate targets. Haligon wondered why.

"SmithCraftHalls set up tighter safeguards after the first raids on their Halls ten or more Turns ago," he said.

"Hmm. Yes. Recollect now." Torlo rubbed his chin thoughtfully. "That Aivas guarded itself, didn't it?"

"A Hall shouldn't have to protect itself," Haligon said.

"True."

"Especially Healers, the one Craft that's benefited most from the knowledge Aivas left behind."

"Agreed." Torlo motioned for Haligon to help himself to the sweet rolls on the board. He broke a piece off himself, pushing the crumbs into his mouth.

Delaying, Haligon thought, so he continued.

"Stationmaster, didn't Master Oldive remove that growth from Grolly's leg? Couldn't have been able to do that before. I believe Grolly's running again. And the cataract film from Tuvor's eyes? He's got clear sight now. I heard they can keep guts from popping out of a man's belly. And they're not niggardly with their help. Didn't they show Beastmaster Frawly how to reduce the wobbles in that fine colt?"

"Aye? So what're you driving at, Lord Haligon?"

"Some are spreading evil untruths about the Healers, with vile pamphlets . . ."

"Runners burn the ones they're given."

"They've seen some?" Haligon was jolted so badly he spilled klah on his hand.

"Runners won't spread filth like that."

"But where? When? Does it happen often?" So Crivellan was right to fret over the matter.

Torlo gave him a long stare. "Runner business. We take care of it."

"But where? We must stop it. Do Runners know where it comes from?"

Torlo shrugged. "Runners stop it going further."

"Yes, but not all of it," Haligon said, becoming more agitated. "The vandals had a particularly grisly copy. Master Crivellan was distraught."

"He's not the only one."

Haligon stiffened at the satiric tone of Torlo's voice. "What quarrel do Runners have with the Healer Hall?" he asked in a low voice though there was no one else in the dining room just then.

"None." Torlo was surprised by Haligon's query.

"With whom then?"

Torlo paused, then a slight grin lifted the corner of his mouth and his eyes met Haligon's squarely. "You're not what you seem, Lord Haligon."

"Runners are as essential to us all as Healers, Stationmaster. What's the problem?"

Torlo considered that and then, making his decision, leaned forward.

"We've no objection to Healer Hall improvements: they benefit all. When 'improvements' threaten an entire Craft, now that's a different track altogether."

"Who would threaten Runners? Weyrwoman Lessa said last night that Runners would always be needed."

Torlo gave an ironic bark. "Did she? And who'll be need-ing the dragons *if* the truth is told about the Red Star?"

Haligon reassembled his thoughts. He'd never thought to step among so many verbal snakes.

"Red Star? You don't believe the Red Star was moved? But surely you saw it happen, here in the North?"

"Saw the light in the sky, but what did that mean to someone ground-tied?"

Haligon tried another tack.

"All right, usually a Pass is fifty years. This time Aivas definitely said it would be less. We know from our own Records that that has happened several times before. So there're sixteen more Turns to go till the end of this Pass. If it ends in sixteen Turns, then grant that Aivas knew more than we ever could: that when he gave a definite answer, it'll be proved truth. He said the dragonriders accomplished what he set them out to do—alter the Red Star's orbit so it can never come close enough to Pern to drop Thread on us again."

Haligon was rather surprised by his own intensity. He'd only been on the fringes of the massive effort that had occu-pied the planet for nearly five Turns. But, in his own heart, he'd believed in Aivas's solution to Pern's cyclical problem. He'd wanted—needed—to believe in it.

"I may live another sixteen Turns to the end of this Pass," Torlo replied. "So will you, but it'll take another two hundred to be sure that Aivas was right."

"The point is, Stationmaster, there are so many smaller miracles available to us right now to give Aivas credibility."

Torlo's cynical smile was lopsided. "Like making dragons—and Runners—unnecessary? If dragons won't be needed against Thread, they'll be looking for other things to do. Run-ners'll be unnecessary!"

"Runners unnecessary?" Haligon exclaimed, throwing up his hands in dismay. He knew the dragonriders were work-ing hard on their own future but Runners *had* an assured one. "Why, your Craft started serving a need before the dragons had their first Weyr. Right now, Runners're making traces and Stations in the south. Your Craft, like all the others, is expanding."

Torlo leaned forward across the table, his eyes sparking with anger. "Not when there are dragonriders taking messages and packing people and parcels."

Haligon countered quickly. "How many small halls and holds can afford to hire a dragon? Running a message costs only a thirty-second of a mark. There are currently six thousand two hundred and forty dragons, and half of them are brown, bronze, and gold who wouldn't consider running messages. You've that many Runner families working all the hours of a Turn and using youngsters on the short runs to keep up with the demand, not to mention what'll happen when the traces are laid in the south. The queens aren't flying to mate as often or clutching as many, scaling down now that the end of this Pass is in sight, so I don't really see greens and blues in competition with Runners. You've never been upset about fire-lizards."

Torlo snorted. "Only a few of them can be trusted to deliver messages."

"That's true enough," Haligon agreed, though his father's queen, Merga, having been exceedingly well trained by Menolly, had always proven reliable. "And no Runner has ever failed to bring messages through." His thought went to Tenna, out on the frozen traces at the moment.

Torlo regarded him thoughtfully. "Nor will we ever."

"So what is *really* bothering you, Stationmaster?"

"Those SmithCraftHall thingummies . . ." Torlo made a cradle of his fingers, scowling as he tried to find the exact word.

"The comm units?"

"Them! Seen one myself. People'll be able to 'talk' to anyone. Won't need Runners to take messages then."

Relief made Haligon laugh. "No, Torlo. Can't happen."

"Why not?" Torlo's sharp question was tinged with a belligerence he rarely displayed.

"Too expensive," Haligon blurted the words through his laughter. "Simple as that. Takes Master Bassage and his Hall months to make the things. Have to get the elements from several other Halls. And they have a short range here in the north because there isn't a satellite relay."

"A what?"

"Like the *Yoko* to relay the signal. Healer Hall has to put up the relay for this part of the west and one up at Tillek, possibly a third at Telgar. Two in the east, I heard. They'd work better on the southern continent because of the *Yoko*, but with so many starting out holds and halls down there, it'll be a long time before they have marks for that sort of gadget. My father will use Runners for a long time. He trusts you. For all he's forward looking on many issues, he trusts people more than machines. No, Stationmaster, Runners'll be necessary for as long—as long as they've legs to run with. They were the first Craft Fort Hold supported. Turns before the first Weyr was established. We'll never not need you, Master Torlo."

Torlo's expression had cleared as Haligon enumerated the problems to be surmounted by the new technology.

"Aivas is like that, isn't it? Shows how to do things better and that takes time all in itself. Perhaps that's the best way. No need to have things when we don't know we really need 'em." Torlo rose, tactfully bringing their dialogue to an end.

As he got to his feet, Haligon wasn't sure whether or not the Stationmaster had agreed to help the Hold.

"We support healers road and trace, Haligon," Torlo said with an emphatic nod of his head as he escorted the young Lord across the big long-ceilinged room. "Those as hears will give a word to the wise to them as is too badly informed to know what's what!"

"That's what's needed, Torlo."

"Myself, or Tenna, will tell you." The Stationmaster tipped two fingers in a salute, leaving Haligon no option but to leave.

How could the Runners think, for even a moment, Haligon wondered, as he made haste in the cold weather to tell his father of this conversation, that their services would ever be redundant? But the Weyrs would be. His step faltered as his eyes went instinctively toward the distant Weyr in the hills above Fort Hold. Weyrs, but not dragons! There would be a reason for dragons to remain in Pern's skies. Doing *something*! Why, it was ludicrous to think of Pern without dragons!

The air froze the hair in his nostrils. Was it warmer down near Boll where Tenna was running? He hoped so. His much-respected sire had been somewhat dubious about Haligon's keen interest in Tenna, but it was proving a very useful connection. Haligon wished he could persuade Tenna to make it a lasting commitment. There were enough children of the Fort Bloodline to carry on, short of another plague. Maybe she'd like to go south, once he'd been released from his filial duties to Lord Groghe.

He should also tell Sebell about his interview with Torlo. The Masterharper should know about their fears. And so much to be done. So much! He had all those petitions to sort through, to find those that did merit his father's particular attention. Well, today was a good one to stay inside and be warm. He took the steps to the Hold two at a time.

KEROON PRINTER HALL — 1.3.31

Tagetarl squeezed tired eyes shut and pinched the bridge of his long nose, wondering at the same time why he thought that would restore his eyesight. Sleep would help, but he had to get through the corrections to the dictionary; some old harpers with too little to do were challenging definitions and deploring the new technological ones, which were vital if young students were to understand the language in which manuals were written. Being able to print many copies of the same material was a vast improvement on hand copying. Any Harper apprentice who had had to do his hours in the Archives Hall blessed the introduction of printing presses, but there must be a trick to finding *all* the mistakes that could creep into typeset lines. In his apprenticeship, if he made a mistake, he was able to scratch it out with a knife blade and rewrite, preferably before Master Arnor caught him at it.

It wasn't as easy to correct a mistake *after* several hundred copies had been printed. So many printing runs were technical and had to be accurate: explanations and instructions crystal clear. Rosheen was particularly good at this, and her fast fingers could set up a page quicker than he could. But they were both learning how to manage the complexities of this new Hall, and Tagetarl was particularly determined to honor Master Robinton's faith in him by making this project the most successful of all that had been initiated by his Master and Aivas.

The slight creak of the office door sounded overloud in the still night. He jumped to his feet. Night? A glance at his eastern-facing window told him that it was nearly morning.

"It's me!" a whisper announced.

"The correct grammar is 'It is I,' or It's I,' " Tagetarl told Pinch wearily. "How did you get in? The gate's locked."

There had been no more Abominator attacks after the spate at Turn's End, but that didn't mean there weren't more being planned. Tagetarl had never figured out just how discards from the medical texts he'd printed a Turn ago had gotten into their hands. To be on the safe side, the Printer Hall now shredded all imperfect sheets.

"True, and it's a fine strong gate," Pinch said, coming forward into the pool of light from the desk lamp.

He was not tall and his angular face, blurred now with dirt and fatigue, had no distinguishing features. His present apparel was Keroon hill folk, and smelled it. His ability to blend into his surroundings, to imitate the accents and manners of speech in any quarter of Pern, north and south, along with his keen ears and sharp eyes, made him the ideal observer. His very active, cynical mind allowed him to interpret what he heard. Pinch cocked his foot around a stool and pulled it to him, sitting down as if he hadn't a care in the world. An engaging smile showed very even teeth, and there was a clever twinkle in his brown eyes.

"I didn't use the gate. Didn't really expect you to be up at this hour so I came in—"

"Across the roof again? One day you'll fall *through* the weaver's roof."

"Oh, it's safe enough. Rosheen's Ola came to investigate, by the bye, but when she saw it was me—"

"It was I," Tagetarl mercilessly corrected.

"—and Bista, she went back to bed." Pinch clicked his tongue. "Say hello to the MasterPrinter, Bista." The little gold creature, who looked like an extra scarf around the harper's neck, cocked her head and blinked her green gemstone eyes at the Printer. "So why are you up?"

Tagetarl jerked his thumb at the proofs he'd been correcting. "If you ever encounter someone in your travels who can spell and who recognizes proper sentence structure and syntax, I've a job for him, her, preferably them."

Pinch gave a sharp nod. "I'll keep my eyes open."

"I know you will. So what brings you over my roof at this time of night?"

"It's nearly day," Pinch corrected kindly. "I've been checking a few things, snooping about isolated holds and trader sites, sitting in Runner stations. Keroon has all sorts of hill folk, you know, the kind that don't want their kids Harper-taught or Healed. Then there're the ones who aren't really hill folk. Who get too many visitors and have had very interesting indoor occupations."

He reached into his jacket and removed a square of much-folded paper. Carefully he opened it to reveal small sketches: full face and profile.

"Mind you, I wasn't exactly an invited visitor, but I found me a spot to watch and make a few notes. I can flesh these out better with some decent paper and a carbon point." He looked inquiringly at Tagetarl. "Paper, Master? Pencils? Aivas's latest improvement on ink?"

"Hill folk?"

"No, people living in the hills. Paper? Pencil?" He hooked the stool closer to the desk.

Immediately, Tagetarl gathered up the pages he was working on, swiftly rearranging them into a neat stack out of Pinch's way. From a drawer, he pulled fresh paper, as well as a collection of different drawing tools. "Sit! Sit! D'you need klah, food, wine?"

Pinch grabbed a sharp carbon stick with one hand as he turned the sheaf of paper to his right—he was left-handed—and began sketching. "Thanks, yes, yes, and yes. And something for Bista. We came straight here without a stop, using Runner traces. They let me, you know. Give me tips. Good folk, Runners. Get me some food and drink, man, just don't stand there gawking."

When Tagetarl returned, lugging a heavy tray along with a bowl of fresh meat for Bista, Pinch continued speaking as if the Printer hadn't left the room.

"Told the Runners not to worry about mechanical things. Wouldn't want one of those things squawking about my person, I can tell you. It'd make folks notice me, and I don't need to be noticed. Anyway, I'll always trust legs over spare parts." He gave Tagetarl a sideways grin, full of malice. "Have a traditional outlook on life, you know." And when the Masterprinter snorted at such a remark from such a source, he added, "Well, I do. It's why I risk life and limb on Harper business."

Bista finished her meal and curled up on a shelf. By then, Pinch had completed one sketch and tossed it to the side, making the first line of the next sketch even before Tagetarl could pick up the first one.

Tagetarl examined the drawing. It was economically drawn, but it vividly depicted a big man, his right shoulder cocked up, a high forehead, black brows, a zigzag scar from his right temple and down the side of his nose to a gouge on his cheek, a thick, wide-bridged nose, gaunt cheeks, a thin mouth, a narrow chin, and a scrawny throat with a pronounced larynx. The left hand, which he was holding up as if to warm at a fire, was missing the first joint of the index finger. His clothes—the usual heavy leather tunic and trousers—were worn and patched. Thongs just under his knee in typical hill-style tied leggings, and his boots were long and thin, the leather cracked from wading through too many streams or bogs.

Using his right hand, Pinch pushed some bread and cheese into his mouth and washed that down with a long swallow of beer, while the left kept drawing. A real gift, Tagetarl thought, especially for someone involved in discreet surveillance. But then Master Robinton, the late MasterHarper, had had the ability to command the talents of many unusual men and women. Before the Present Pass and the awakening of Aivas, when dragonriders had been denigrated and even the Harper Hall in jeopardy, Master Robinton had made use of rare talents—harpers, men and women, who knew their way about most of the settled holds and halls, large and small. Tagetarl had met Nip, the first roving harper who had nonspecific assignments and rarely sang. What Nip's real name was, no one remembered now. Nip had trained Tuck, another nonconformist, and had taken Sebell along for some projects as Sebell, in turn, had made use of Piemur's unusually quick mind and abilities. Now Pinch had been added to the roster, along with two others Tagetarl knew about but was not sure that he had met.

Tagetarl concentrated on committing the first face to memory. Rather pugnacious all totaled, the Printer thought: the sort that would worry a crack in a cliff until it became a cave.

The next one Pinch finished was of a man who looked vaguely familiar. Younger than the first man, he was taller and well-fleshed, with a darker but not weathered skin and short fair hair. A pinched mouth suggested selfishness and obstinacy, and the eyes had a sly cast to them. His expression was both amused and supercilious.

A woman was the third: her stance—her left hand holding her right elbow—was awkward, her eyes wide and avid as if listening to instructions that she would strive to carry out. She, too, was clad as a hill woman, but the clothes did not fit either her body or her manner.

"These three were visitors, received with much fuss and fawned over. Stayed several days and talked most earnestly in low voices. Plotting probably. What, I couldn't hear, though I tried. I'd like these to get to Sebell as soon as possible. D'you think Ola would oblige? Bista's exhausted."

"Of course," Tagetarl said with gratification. Menolly had

helped Rosheen train her queen. This wouldn't be the first time Ola had flown discreet errands.

"I'll do the others when I've had a rest," Pinch said. He popped more bread and cheese into his mouth as he rose to his feet. His abrupt movement startled a chirp out of sleeping Bista. Absently, his left hand stroked her. "Can I indulge in a bath? I have to keep to these clothes." He held a fold away from his body with repugnance. "But I'd enjoy sleeping one night—or rather a full day—smelling clean."

"Yes, of course. I'll see no one goes banging about under you," Tagetarl said with a reassuring grin.

Pinch often made use of the loft above the outbuildings where paper and other supplies were stored. When the Print Hall expanded, as Tagetarl earnestly hoped it would, apprentices would sleep up there, but right now, it made a handy lair when Pinch wished to make inconspicuous visits.

"That would be appreciated." Pinch took another wedge of cheese and the last of the bread and left.

Tagetarl prepared a message cylinder for Ola, saw her off, and went to his own room. Rosheen sighed when he lay down beside her and, sleepily, she turned toward him for comfort.

BENDEN WEYR—MIDDAY—1.3.31

With the other Wingleaders, F'lessan attended a pre-Fall meeting in one corner of the Lower Caverns.

"It's the Ten pattern, so we meet it over the Eastern Sea and Igen joins us for the last hour over south Lemos," F'lar said, his eyes making a quick keen appraisal of each of the eighteen Wingleaders sitting around him. "Weather's cold and dull, but the visibility is good."

Out of the corner of his eye, F'lessan noticed that everyone was trying to look as alert as possible. The entire Weyr had been turned out to search for the four men involved in wrecking Benden's Healer Hall. The details the injured journeyman recalled about his attackers would have described half the male population of any hold; the only thing he was certain about was that they were not from Benden. Runners had agreed to spread word of the attack and ask isolated holds to report strangers. G'bol had scrupulously followed up one report, but the men had been honest traders.

Two of the oldest Wingleaders had not been called to fly this Fall, and F'lessan wished that F'lar would take a Fall or two off now and then. While he was more apt to listen to G'bol than anyone else, F'lar ignored the merest hint of letting anyone else lead his Weyr. No one would fault him, but the Weyrleader made no exceptions for himself, bar the very few occasions each Turn when Mnementh had taken a score or strained a wing.

F'lar assigned the levels and F'lessan jerked his attention back to the business at hand. His wing was high again: a measure of F'lar's trust in his leadership.

"Warn your younger riders that dull conditions can blur Thread in the higher reaches," F'lar continued. "Measure the wind as soon as you can. We'll know how the Thread falls, when it falls. We gather on the Rim in ten minutes. Good flying!"

As they filed out, closing their jackets, settling their helmets, and pulling on their gloves, F'lessan felt the air of anticipation that always gripped him, speeding his pulse, deepening his breath.

On the ledges of their weyrs, green and blue riders were already mounted, firestone sacks on either side of dragon necks; some brown and bronze riders were still collecting sacks, launching from the Bowl to the Weyr Rim. Wingleader bronzes were drifting down to meet their riders in an orderly confusion. Golanth hovered above the ground to his left. F'lessan, judging the distance neatly, ran and vaulted to his back.

Golanth pumped his wings skillfully and circled, dropping down to his position on the Rim, between the wingseconds and in front of the twenty-two strong wing.

The green reserves are ready and will bring us sacks when you call them, Golanth reported.

As he fastened his safety straps and pulled up the fur-lined tops of his boots—his knees were always cold by the end of a Fall—F'lessan thought of Tai, wondering what it would be like to have her in his wing.

Zaranth is bigger than any of the others, his dragon remarked, turning his head slightly so that the left many-faceted eye reflected a view of his rider in the mid-planes. *Firestone, please!* He twisted his head to his rider's leg and dutifully F'lessan supplied him from the bulging sack.

Deftly Golanth tipped his head back, positioning the rock on his thick grinders. Then, exercising great care not to bite the edge of his tongue, he began to chew—as did every other dragon on the Rim. Five pieces F'lessan fed his bronze, sufficient for Golanth to work up a proper flame.

From the bowl rose the four Benden queens. As they circled up, all eyes on the Rim turned to the Weyrleader and Mnementh. F'lar's arm was raised; F'lessan held his high. The queens completed their last circle up, above the Rim, heading north-northeast.

You know where to go? F'lessan formally asked his dragon.
We all know! Golanth answered.

Mnementh roared and sprang forward just as F'lar's arm came down in the command to take wing. As one, dragons leaped upward. Then, as every one of the four hundred and eighty-four Benden dragons was a-wing, they went *between*.

They came out again in an air almost as cold as *between*. It hadn't been bright at Benden, but here, above the Eastern Sea, the sky was grayer: a shade that would make the silvery strands of falling Thread more difficult to see. Benden Weyr faced the probable entry of Thread, glad to have the wind behind them as the wings sorted themselves to their assigned levels. Far below, F'lessan could make out the queens' wings, small dots against the gray of snowy land and pewter sea. Ahead of him, almost motionless, was F'lar, he and Mnementh as ever leading them by several dragon-lengths.

This was the worst part of a Fall, F'lessan felt, and, with a glove-thickened finger, he pushed the thick new scarf against his goggles. He tucked his left boot top against his inner leg, and then checked the firestone sacks dangling down Golanth's withers before peering at the sky for any trace of Thread. Sometimes blinking helped.

It comes! Golanth told him and stroked his wings forward.

Mnementh's flame spouted brilliant orange and accurately seared the first Thread to fall.

There was nothing wrong with the Weyrleader's eyesight, F'lessan thought as he squinted to see the first Threads slanting down. He felt a primitive surge of elation as he and his dragon once more attacked their ancient adversary.

MONACO BAY WEYR—FIVE DAYS LATER—1.8.31

Sunlight woke Tai—hot sunlight. She kept her eyes closed as her mind roused to awareness. If the sun was on her face, it was almost noon. She was in her hammock between two big frond trees whose great draping leaves usually shielded her very well. The sun must now be close to its zenith. As usual, her face was turned toward the wallow that Zaranth used as a weyr. The green dragon was in full sun—just as she liked it, head between her forelegs, wings slightly drooping from her backbone so that their folds would absorb the heat. Many dragonriders had pondered the question: did dragons store heat in their bodies for their forays into *between*? Zaranth had one eyelid open. By the gleam of the slit, she was watching something very carefully.

One of the disadvantages of living in the open was the insect population, in myriad forms: some scratched, even burrowed in flesh if possible; some merely moved in straight lines, like the trundlebugs that were the object of Zaranth's current inspection. A straight line for a trundlebug could also be perpendicular to the ground. They had been observed maneuvering up to the crown of a frond tree and down the other side. Right now, a very large trundlebug—the creatures could become quite large if no natural hazard ended their existence—was under intense draconic surveillance. This one had no fewer than five young still attached behind it, in various stages of maturation in the trundlebug's peculiar reproductive process. Their bodies collected pollen from low-growing shrubs and vines—also the occasional tree— and shed it in their progress to whatever unknowable goal trundlebugs had. What other purpose they served Tai did not know, but they were less of a nuisance than some crawlies and rather curious to watch. Single-mindedness was exemplified in the trundlebug. It had been suggested there was only a female of the species.

Trundlebugs were a good reason to sleep in a hammock. Humans used sticky-goo tapes around the trunks of hammock trees and the base of any living accommodation. Most buildings were on stilts as another deterrent to invading creepy-crawlies; in low-lying coastal areas, stilts also kept dwellings above high tide floods. Tai's little house was just beyond her hammock: all its shutters were open to let in what wind there was, the fine-net screens preventing the entry of airborne insects. The afternoon breeze generally wafted away those clinging to the material. The diurnal ones departed at dusk; the nocturnal ones were noisier but photosensitive. A tall spire of solar panel provided Tai with what power she needed: for lights, the warmer plate, the cold box, and for the occasional hot air during the worst of the cold weather— which, to her, was never as cold as it had once been in Keroon's foothills.

In the Southern hemisphere, some dragonriders preferred to live in companionable clusters or with their mates, but Tai loved seclusion. She had handcrafted such furnishings as she had, shelves, bedstead, worktop, hooks, and the chest where she kept her clothing.

Zaranth knew Tai was awake, but the green dragon was watching the trundlebug. Abruptly the inexorable path of the trundlebug—which would take it into Zaranth's left nostril— ended. Tai blinked. Had Zaranth exhaled from the victim nostril, tumbling the trundlebug and her offspring away from her? Movement out of the corner of her eye showed her that the trundlebug was now marching in an easterly direction, an exact forty-five degrees from its original course and at least a full dragon-length from its previous path.

How'd you do that? Tai asked, not sure she had seen what she had seen.

I did not care for it to crawl into my nose. I moved it.

Just like that?

Just like that.

Do you do it often?

Now and then. That ... and Zaranth moved her chin slightly toward the redirected trundlebug, *does not belong where it was going.* The dragon lost her pose of indolence; her eyes were wide open, and she was magically on her feet. *Felines! We're needed!*

Tai scrambled from the hammock, leaping into her quarters, pulling on trousers, stomping into boots, shrugging into her riding jacket—and bother a sleeved shirt—and carrying the dangling safety straps out to slip the harness over Zaranth's eager head. It was as dangerous to hunt felines as to fly Thread. Zaranth shrugged the leathers to the base of her broad neck and lifted her leg for Tai to clip them together.

Who sent for help?

Cardiff. Fire-lizard message. T'gellan's called half the wing.

Tai vaulted between the last two neck ridges, and clipped the safety harness onto her broad belt.

I know where, the green dragon said and took off so quickly Tai's head snapped. They were barely above the trees when Zaranth went *between.*

They were back in the moist southern air, a half dozen other dragons erupting nearby.

Cardiff herder spotted the pride. A big one.

They had come out low above the rolling highland plateau where the Ancients had turned loose their grazers and ruminators, unable to transport more than breeding stock to the north. The herds had multiplied over the centuries and mutated slightly from their northern relatives, affording them some protection against the local parasites and poisonous plants. The MasterHerder had found the alterations "fascinating." Right now, a huge herd of mixed varieties was stampeding from the edge of the jungle where the predators lurked to ambush the unwary.

As a relatively new southern Hold, Cardiff did its best to oversee its grasslands, but the hundred or so herders could not always protect the far-ranging stock. Watched by no more than three or four men or women, the beasts covered wide tracts in their search for edible grasses. Thunder, lightning, or the occasional jungle fire could send them into terror-stricken stampedes, which occasionally ended with masses of them falling over cliff edges or into ravines. Now they had been spooked by felines. The southern continent had a lot of problems with the big predators, the product of an ill-advised zoological experiment by one of the Charterers. Like the abandoned herdbeasts, they had flourished, too, and ranged freely through the jungles, grasslands, and up into the southern foothills. Humans avoided the felines whenever possible; dragons were thrilled by the challenge of hunting them.

Zaranth was gliding silently and speedily toward the nearest herdbeasts, which had obviously been split off from the main herd by the canny felines. The predators were as apt to injure beasts, rendering them lame enough to attack later, as to kill outright. Tai had seen the result of such tactics, a wide pasture dotted with bleating, moaning animals, awaiting the pleasure of the cubs that the felines hunted for.

There! A tawny spot, one of the fast ones, Zaranth cried.

Tai caught the merest glimpse of the yellowish-brown form, bounding after the terrified herdbeasts. She grabbed her straps instinctively as Zaranth turned on a wing tip that just cleared one of the stunted trees that dotted the grassland. A shape leaped from its shadow, barely missing Zaranth's wing, and in spectacular leaps, made for the cover of the jungle. To flush a feline was unusual. Neither dragon nor rider would have seen it lurking in the shade. Of course, neither would the herdbeasts who were obviously the intended prey.

Zaranth hissed at so close a swipe; a small flame, residue of the most recent Fall, escaped, spurting after the beast.

Watch it, love! The hide's worth more unsinged, Tai cried.

Despite being large for a green, Zaranth had lost none of the agility that was her color's most valuable characteristic. She dove, with a burst of speed that took the breath out of Tai's mouth. Matching the rhythm of the feline's bounds, she caught it mid-leap. Tai felt Zaranth's heavy shoulder muscles convulse, then relax. She had a glimpse over her shoulder of the limp spotted body stretched out on the plain, its back broken.

The other one! Zaranth cried, spinning obliquely to her left and heading back up the plateau toward the first predator they had seen, who was now closing in on a herdbeast and unaware that its hunting partner had just been taken down.

The most successful—and safest—tactic was to come up behind a feline as Zaranth was now doing, keeping their shadow from warning the carnivore of pursuit. Now, just as the feline swiped its front paws at the herdbeast's galloping hindquarters, Zaranth's claws made contact and snapped its neck in one clean jerk.

Not bad hunting, Tai said, well pleased with a bag of two, both prime specimens and, unless Zaranth had singed the first one, quite saleable. *Shall we continue?*

Monarth says it is all in hand. A big pride, but a half wing is sufficient, Zaranth said as she circled back with her second kill, depositing it with an almost disdainful negligence beside the first. *These,* and Zaranth's tone was possessive, *are mine!*

No one will dispute it, but I get the skins.

And skinning was hard work. Tai's brief elation departed.

I'll help, Zaranth said.

If you promise not to drool all over me or lick while I'm working, Tai replied with mock severity. In the heat of the day, in an open field, there was no shelter at all from the pests that would smell blood and come for their share. However, she told herself, two pelts would be worth the discomfort.

She debated throwing the bodies over Zaranth's neck and taking them up to the cooler, swarm-free foothills to skin.

Once she was on the ground beside them, she discarded that idea. They were big brutes. She was strong, but these dead weights would be impossible to shift onto her dragon. The first one was smaller, of a different mix, with a mottled hide; the other was a tawny yellow-brown, with striped markings on its legs. Both were females with engorged dugs, and Tai sighed at the thought of yet more of these monsters maturing to savage herds.

She removed her jacket and hung it on a low bush, taking a well-honed knife from her boot.

"Lift the first one up, please!" she said, "and remember, you get the carcass faster if you hold still—and don't salivate all over me."

I know, I know, but Zaranth's mouth was very wet as she lifted the feline by the head so Tai could make the first incision at the base of the thick throat. One zip down, slit the legs. Zaranth did drool as she helped. Tai quickly worked up a sweat. To distract herself, she pondered once again about meeting F'lessan and his interest in astronomy. Was he going to make that his career After? Maybe she'd meet him again. Then she reproved herself. He was a Benden Wingleader, son of Lessa and F'lar, and despite the fact that he had quite earnestly said that green dragons were essential for every wing, their paths were unlikely to cross again. She concentrated on her task. Helpfully, the green idly moved her wings to deflect the swarms of insects drawn to the smell of blood and raw flesh. The most persistent attacked between wingstrokes.

It was dry work, too, in this heat and Tai regretted that she hadn't grabbed up her water bottle in her haste to answer T'gellan's summons. She took a deep breath as Zaranth rotated the feline so Tai could strip the pelt from the limp body. A mass of flying insects covered skin and skinners as Zaranth, fanning furiously and growling, lifted the carcass a length away.

Without Zaranth's wings, clouds of insects attached themselves to the blood on Tai's arms. She broke a wide leaf off a low-growing shrub and, beating the air about her, walked up the slight incline to see how the rest of the wing was faring before she started the backbreaking task of skinning the second feline.

Shading her eyes, she saw that two dragons were still aloft, chasing felines away from the safety of the thick vegetation bordering the plateau. She counted eight dragons on the ground, waiting for their treats to be skinned. Three more were already eating. Dust settling off to the northeast indicated that the herdbeasts, stupid as they were, had stopped running. It was a good-sized herd. Then she caught sight of bright-colored shirts and galloping Runners streaming down toward them: the Cardiff herders catching up with the stampede. Brave of them, she thought, since they could still be attacked by any of the remaining pride. One of them hailed Tai on the hillock and turned his mount toward her. Slung across his back were a short bow and a weyrhide carrier full of the sort of barbed arrows that would be needed to bring down felines.

"Our thanks for such a prompt response," he said, halting beside her and swinging down. "Tai, isn't it? And Zaranth? We been following the herd since dawn. Got stampeded by last night's heat lightning, and with the smarts only such dumb critters possess, they headed right toward the thickest congregation of felines anywhere in Cardiff. We keep huntin' 'em, but they keep producing. And you got two. Big mothers!"

"You said it. Both were nursing cubs."

He cursed under his breath, wiping his forehead on his red sleeve. "More of the sharding killers to get. And getting smarter all the time."

"Dragons're even smarter," Tai said, grinning with pride. But quickly she shut her mouth tightly so as not to inhale any of the fresh insect clouds that zoomed in on both of them and the sweaty mount. She swept her frond in a wider arc to discourage the swarm.

"Miserable things, ain't they?" he commented with a rueful smile, using his broad-brimmed hat as a fan and tugging a big, dirty cloth from a leg pocket to mop his sweaty, sun-weathered face. She didn't recognize him, but she wasn't surprised that he knew who she was; Cardiff holders were punctilious about knowing the riders who weyred at Monaco Bay.

"I'm Rency, Cardiff Hold Journeyman," he said, squinting against the sun glare. "Ain't easy to bring down two," he added, impressed.

"We flushed the first by chance," she said easily. "Zaranth's fast."

"Obviously."

"The other didn't see its partner go down and we came up behind her."

He chuckled appreciatively, but her disclaimer did not lessen his respect for her double kill.

"Heard tell you're as good bringing down vandals," he said, touching his own face to indicate he had noticed her healing cheek. He untied the water bottle from the back of his saddle and handed it to her. As she drank, he kept fanning.

"Thanks," she said, refreshed by the cool water. His canteen must have been one of the new thermal types. She coveted one for herself. They were expensive, and the waiting list was long. Still, the price of the two pelts would bring that wish closer.

"Drink up, Tai. We're not far now from water. Can I help you skin the second one?" He gave her a broad smile. "Won't take two of us long."

She nodded, her smile appreciative. As he divested himself of the bow and arrow sheath, she took a second, longer drink, carefully replaced the plug, and handed it back to him.

"Would you know yet how many the dragons brought down?" he asked as she led the way down to the second feline. Zaranth didn't raise her head from her meal.

"I saw eleven dragons on the ground. T'gellan brought half the wing, and a couple are still hunting."

"And you accounted for two!" he said again.

She skinned up the front leg as he deftly did the hind one.

"We'd been trying to catch up with this part of the herd," he explained in a rueful tone through clenched teeth. "Wanted to get 'em turned before they got this close to the jungle. Felines don't usually hunt so late in the day, but if there were two with litters, they'd be hungry and more apt to attack when they saw so much food on the hoof."

He gave a resigned sigh, swiveling to look at the dense forest with its multiple shades of green leaves, fronds, and spikes that bordered the plateau, the light breeze ruffling the taller, more flexible branches. He mopped his forehead and cheeks and shook his head. "Wal, if we didn't have so much on the hoof nearby, it'd save us to track down and finish the cubs before they start hunting." He paused. "As it is, they'll have to take their chances like the rest of us."

"Can we help you turn the herd back out of immediate danger?" Tai asked as they flipped the hide from the legs and wrestled the carcass over. Rency was almost as good as Zaranth as a helper.

"We'd sure appreciate it," Rency said.

Herdbeasts were as terrified of dragons in the air as felines on the ground, so herding them merely required the dragons to keep their shadows on the beasts.

"Sure. Dragons have to fly straight with full stomachs, you know," she said. "No reason we can't help you spook the herd in the right direction for now." Today's feed would last Zaranth a sevenday.

"Just need to set them in the right direction, Tai," he said. "There's a ravine"—he pointed in a northwesterly direction—"and water. Whooshing 'em that way is all we'd need."

"No problem," Tai said. *If you'll be kind enough to stop eating long enough to tell Monarth what's needed,* she said to her dragon.

He just told me, Zaranth said, sucking the tail into her mouth and licking her lips.

"Makes short work of it, doesn't she?" Rency remarked approvingly.

Tai grinned. "Monarth says we'll be glad to help. Half the wing has fed today."

I am the only one who has two. Zaranth, her faceted eyes

flickering with orange pleasure, strolled indolently over to them to await her second course.

Rency and Tai pulled the skin cleanly off the flesh. Once they had rolled it up, he went back to his mount, which stood far enough away from the dragon to feel safe. Tai, letting Zaranth move in on her bloody kill, followed him, hoping to get away from the worst of the insect swarms. Rency handed her the water bottle and a towel.

"Take a good swig and then we can wash off some of the gore. Like I said, I'm not that far from water," he said and Tai was grateful to be able to rinse herself.

Feeling somewhat less sticky, they walked to the top of the incline. Though they had washed off most of the blood, the swarms began a renewed assault in waves so that they clenched their teeth and kept their eyes narrowed. Fanning vigorously with his hat, Rency watched with satisfaction as they could see other riders heaving pelts to their dragons' backs. Suddenly the mass was whisked away. Zaranth had finished eating and was sweeping her wings broadly, scattering the insect cloud.

I'm ready to leave when you are, Zaranth announced with a final lick of her lips.

"D'you need the loan of my rope?" Rency asked.

"That'd be real welcome," Tai agreed. Her riding harness would secure one . . . but two?

"Be sure to check no nits burrowed into your skin," he said.

"I most assuredly will," she told him through clenched teeth.

Deftly the two humans roped the pelts on either side of Zaranth's second neck ridge. Flying straight was time-consuming, but Zaranth could fly high enough—once they'd helped move the herd—to be cool and escape the insects. Tai held out her hand to Rency to thank him for his help and the loan of his rope, and swung onto Zaranth's back.

"My pleasure, dragonrider," Rency said, stepping back, fanning with his hat as swarms tried to settle to the hides.

Get us out of here before I eat bug, Zaranth, Tai said, windmilling her hands in front of her face.

I ate very well, Zaranth said smugly and Tai could feel a satisfied belch rumbling from her chest, to her throat and out.

Inelegant, Tai muttered with mock severity as Zaranth leaped skyward.

Courteously, Zaranth dipped her wings, causing Rency's mount to back away from him in sudden panic.

Out of here. The man doesn't need to be chasing his Runner. Then they were out of range of bloodsuckers and into cooler air. Zaranth circled, looking for Monarth and the rest of the dragons.

Monarth is aloft, and so is Path, Zaranth told her and headed in their direction. *We are to swing wide behind the beasts,* she added.

It's not the first time we've herded, Tai said grumpily. She wished she had more in her belly than cold water; she'd had no lunch.

At this altitude, she had a good view of the bright-shirted herders, stringing out over the grassy plain, starting the beasts back the way they had stampeded.

It would be good to have a swim when the herd is turned.

It most certainly would. There were plenty of hospitable coves on the way back to Monaco Weyr, and trees full of ripe fruit.

Altogether, Tai thought, apart from the insects, the day had been profitable. It would take time to clean and stretch the pelts, but once word got around to the traders of today's kill, she might even get to sell them raw. One day she might keep a particularly fine one—she fancied a clouded fur with ghost stripes—but in the meantime, northerners prized whatever was taken.

PART 2

Disaster (Throughout the Same Day)

RUATHA HOLD —
LOCAL TIME 12:04 IN THE
MORNING — 1.9.31

STEPPING OUT of the cothold, Sharra wrapped her cloak tightly around her. It was very cold, but the wind, which could cut like a knife down the broad avenue back to Ruatha Hold, had died out. She was tired from a long nursing, but relieved that the weaver would recover from his accident. She silently thanked Aivas once more for the medical information he had left. She had been able to repair the tendon in Possil's hand—something she could not have done five Turns earlier—and to stitch shut the jagged wound. She could honestly tell him that he would have the use of his hand and be as skillful as ever in two months' time.

A light caught her eye. To the east! Startled, because it was automatic to be fearful of anything coming from the east, she saw shooting stars, long straight slashes in the dark sky. She stopped in her tracks. These were not like the Ghosts of Turnover, for all they'd been bright this year. Ghosts lasted a second or two. These were visibly longer, almost ribbons in the night sky. One bright spot seemed to linger, then exploded.

She blinked. This could not be the result of fatigue after a delicate surgery. Certainly not Thread! She told herself firmly. Thread isn't due to fall anywhere tomorrow, and Thread came down silver-gray, like rain, in daylight, not like a streak of fire at midnight.

She didn't realize she was running until she was halfway up Ruatha's broad causeway and could hear the fretful whine of the watchwher.

"Mickulin!" she called, remembering from the duty roster who was on guard that night.

"I'm not seeing things, am I, Lady Sharra?" Mickulin's hoarse whisper sounded scared as he leaned over the top of the smaller tower.

"If you're seeing long white streamers, you're seeing the same thing I am!" She raced up the stairs. "I'm calling Jaxom. Go rouse Brand. But it's not Thread, Mickulin, and it's not Turnover Ghosts either." *Ruth! Ruth! Wake up.* She felt the very reassuring presence of the white dragon—a sleepy one—in her mind. *Wake Jaxom. Tell him to bring his binoculars. There's something he must see. Hurry! And it's cold.*

Mickulin rushed past her to open the great Hold door just wide enough to slip through it on his way to wake Steward Brand. Sharra stood with her back to the door, facing east, hoping that this amazing display would continue long enough for Jaxom to see it.

There! Another long streamer, shading to a yellow tinge in the trail—the Ghosts never had colors—and another! A long drop and then nothing.

"What's the matter?" Jaxom hauled the door open, the sound echoed by the opening of a second door in the lower, inner courtyard as Ruth poked his head out of his quarters in the old kitchen. The white dragon's eyes began to whirl as he stared at the splashings in the sky. "Shards!" his rider cried, and lifted his binoculars to focus on the display.

"What are they? What are they?"

"That isn't Thread," Jaxom said decisively, "and they're too bright for Ghosts—besides which, according to Wansor and Erragon, that cometary shower is long past us. And they seem to be coming from one place in the sky. I think. Hard to focus." He propped himself against the door frame and held his breath. "A little better. Here! Brace yourself before you look!" He handed the binoculars to her.

It took her a moment to alter the focus of double-eye; they were a relatively new acquisition, an instrument that Jancis had recently developed.

"Oh, they are beautiful! And they are radiating from one spot." She said the last in a fearful tone.

Jaxom pulled her toward him, moving oddly from one foot to another until she saw his feet were bare.

"I said it was cold!" she exclaimed.

"If you're not going to look, I will," he said, taking the binoculars she had lowered from her face. "Oh, Wansor and Erragon are going to want to know about this. How many sparks did you see?"

"I wasn't counting," she said tersely. She undid her scarf and put it down. "Stand on this. I'm not nursing you again."

Without looking down, Jaxom stepped onto the scarf. "Eight, nine, ten." He counted off another five rapidly, swinging round as he followed the path of whatever was burning so bright. "Possibly just another cometary tail."

"Has Thread ever fallen at night?" Sharra asked in a whisper.

Jaxom shrugged. "Too bad there's no way I can reach Tippel at Crom. He's nearly as dedicated a sky-watcher as Master Idarolan, and he's got binoculars, too. Maybe he did see it." Jaxom took another long look. "Think I'd better have Ruth bespeak D'ram's Tiroth. Cove Hold should be informed. It's early morning dawn there."

He was talking to Ruth when the door behind them opened and Brand came out. The steward saw the long streaks in the sky and stood as transfixed by the sight as everyone else.

"How beautiful!" he said.

"Is, isn't it?" Mickulin said, looking up as five separate glowing spikes flared out at once. With a jaunty set to his shoulders, he moved past the three in the doorway and returned to his post.

"Yes, it is," Sharra agreed, by now overcoming her initial concern. She eased against Jaxom, who tightened his affectionate hold as he offered the binoculars to Brand.

"Did you note the time, Brand?"

"In passing, Jaxom," the steward said, his attention on the sky. "Whatever it is . . ."

"Meteors, I suspect, if I remember my astronomy lessons from Aivas," Jaxom said.

"They seem to be flying from east to west but—" Brand swiveled to follow another shower. "—are they likely to strike the ground?"

"Probably burn up in the atmosphere," Jaxom said, almost regretfully.

Pretty, Ruth said from the courtyard. *I have told Tiroth. He will tell D'ram, who is running around and very excited.*

"Could be this is more widespread than it would seem," Jaxom said. "Brand, keep an eye on it, will you? I think I'll get dressed."

"You can't have been undressed," Sharra said somewhat caustically, because she could see his legs encased in the same trousers that he had worn all day.

"Not completely." He flicked his tunic away so she could see his bare chest. "I was waiting for you to get back. Were you able to repair Possil's hand?"

"Thanks to Aivas, I was."

"I may go on to Landing, love," Jaxom said, "but you'd better get some sleep."

"And you can do without?" she asked reproachfully as he guided her into the main Hall.

"You know me. I'll rest when I find out what this is all about. If D'ram is running around at Cove Hold, then what we're seeing is more than pretty shooting stars."

TELGAR WEYR—LOCAL TIME 4:04 IN THE MORNING—1.9.31

H'nor and old brown Ranneth were on night duty on Telgar's Rim when the rider saw the tiny sparkles of light low on the horizon in the southeast. He blinked and turned away. Couldn't be the Red Star, he knew too well how that looked. Besides which, it couldn't *be* in the east: it had been nor-nor-west when it had been skewed out of its old orbit. It wouldn't be in a position to drop sharding Thread on Pern ever again. No way that sharding thing could bounce back east.

He took up the binoculars—now required watchrider equipment—and focused carefully on the sparkles. They were like a shower; could they be coming from one place before disappearing? That wasn't what the Turn's End Ghosts looked like: they were pale and strung out across the sky. Furthermore, the Ghosts were much farther north, nearer the ice regions. He had an uneasy feeling.

H'nor rose from his comfortable position on the upper arm of his brown Ranneth, eyeglass still focused on the brilliant showers. There was another long one. Definitely not Ghosts. Burned too long.

What is it? Ranneth demanded, coming out of his doze. A brown of many Turns, he slept when and where he could, but his rider's alarm was palpable. He turned his head in the direction H'nor faced and was equally startled, rearing back on his haunches. *It is fire but what could stay alight so high above Pern?*

H'nor gulped. *I don't know.*

Sometimes metal fell from the sky, large enough to cause damage. Like the big hole at Circle Runner Station.

Knowing that the Dawn Sisters had been the ships that had brought the Ancients to Pern had not been easy for H'nor to assimilate. Learning about Aivas had also been unsettling. He was too old for such complications. He wanted no flaming things falling down before he and Ranneth could retire to a warm and comfortable weyr on the Southern continent.

As watchrider, he did have a duty to sound an alarm for any unusual occurrence and this ranked in that category.

Tell Willerth, H'nor told Ranneth. The old brown rider was glad that the Weyrleadership of Telgar had changed recently, to a younger bronze rider, J'fery. Old R'mart had become quite difficult before he'd gone to the Southern Weyr for less onerous duties. Bedella and her queen, who hadn't risen to mate in three Turns, had gone with him. *Tell Ramoth while you're at it. Benden's supposed to know.*

I will also tell Tiroth at Cove Hold.

Yes, yes, tell them, too. They should know all about such things.

BENDEN WEYR—LOCAL TIME 6:04 IN THE MORNING—1.9.31

The watchdragon reared back on his haunches and bugled a warning, as bright sparks appeared almost directly overhead in the sky.

Since it was nearly dawn in Benden, a good number of weyrfolk already breakfasting in the Lower Cavern were startled by the bugled alert. It coincided with Ramoth giving Lessa Willerth's message from Telgar, so Lessa was on her feet, grabbing at F'lar's tunic to drag him with her. Everyone else present scrambled to the Bowl after the Weyrleaders to see what was happening.

"Those aren't Ghosts," Lessa cried, coming to a stop so abruptly that F'lar had to sidestep. She could see what had alarmed the watchdragon: long flaring ribbons in the sky, almost directly above Benden. One large burst startled everyone, as if some smaller piece had broken off the bigger ball.

"No, they aren't!" F'lar agreed, gazing up, his hands on his weyrmate's arms, rubbing them to warm her.

Willerth didn't say they were, Ramoth reminded her rider.

Then she added, surprised, *Ruth says there is something above Ruatha that Jaxom doesn't think are Ghosts either*.

By now every dragon in the Weyr was peering up at the manifestation, their eyes beginning to whirl with agitation, creating the effect of rings of vivid color around Benden's inner walls. F'nor and F'lessan joined their Weyrleaders, peering up at the phenomenon just as more flares burst from it.

"All the shooting arrows"—Lessa gestured with her hands—"seem to come from the same source."

"I'd like to know *what* source," F'lessan said, scrubbing at his thick hair, an uncharacteristic frown on his face.

"You're the one who studied astronomy," F'lar remarked, turning his head slightly toward his son but not taking his eyes off the sprays of brilliant lights.

"Not something like that," F'lessan said. "Though it could be a meteor coming through the atmosphere. We do get them."

"Yes, Circle Runner Station never lets us forget!" F'nor murmured wryly.

"Do we have to worry about it falling on us?" Brekke asked, curling her hand over F'nor's arm.

"Shouldn't it be moving?" Lessa said, becoming a little nervous. "It seems to be hanging right over us."

"I'd say that's an illusion," F'lessan replied, trying to sound reassuring. He caught F'lar's cocked eyebrow and shrugged. "It'll probably disappear in a few moments. Though the Ghosts usually travel from west to east. Noticeably."

"They're also paler," Lessa said. "This one is getting brighter!" She shivered.

F'lar dropped his arms across her to provide more warmth in the wintry early morning light.

It is very high above us, Ramoth said, *and it* is *getting brighter.* She blinked the first protective lid across her eyes.

I agree. The winter Ghosts are higher still, bronze Mnementh added.

"Would the *Yoko* see it, do you think?" Lessa asked. "Or is it too far north for the sensors?"

Tiroth says that he takes four to Landing to see, Ramoth said, sounding surprised.

Lessa echoed that surprise when she repeated the message to the other riders grouped around her. "Well, Master Wansor certainly should be there, and that journeyman of his—what's his name?"

"Erragon," F'lessan said.

"Erragon, to see what the *Yoko* reports," Lessa finished.

"I'll go, too, for Benden's sake," F'lessan offered gallantly. "Sellie—" He caught the arm of his second son, Sellessan— technically he should call him S'lan, as the boy'd Impressed a brown two Turns ago—who had sneaked out to see what was causing the commotion. The boy was as curious as F'lessan had been as a youngster. "Run get my flying gear. First table on the left." The boy raced to obey.

"Erragon has that big telescope," F'nor said.

"He'd've been off watch at dawn," F'lessan said with a grimace. "Two hours ago at least."

"Wouldn't he have seen such a phenomenon?" Lessa asked, gesturing overhead. Just as it seemed the splashings were gone, a fresh burst exploded into the predawn sky. "It just couldn't appear out of nowhere, could it?"

"There have been reports of other such things," F'nor said, dismissively enough to reassure Brekke, who was shivering beside him. "Let's go back inside."

"It'll go away because it isn't being watched?" Brekke asked, regarding him with an affectionate smile, but she went with him.

"Well, I'll find out what *Yoko* thinks it is," F'lessan said. Summoning Golanth from his ledge, he didn't take his eyes off the long ribbons in the sky as he shrugged into the riding gear S'lan had brought him and crammed on his helmet. "Thanks, son."

"It's not going to fall on the Weyr," S'lan asked, gulping nervously, "is it?"

"Mnementh says not." F'lar gave his grandson a reassuring look. "Go finish your breakfast, young S'lan."

Obediently the brown rider moved away.

"I'd like to see what *Yoko* reports, F'lar," F'lessan murmured. "It may just be skimming the atmosphere, which is what's causing all the bright trails."

"But you're not sure," Lessa said, craning her head around to look at her tall son's face.

"No, but there's a great deal about the skies of Pern that I don't know," he admitted with one of his ingenuous smiles.

"I thought you were using those fancy new binoculars you got from Jancis," she said.

"So I am, Lessa, so I am," he agreed as Golanth dropped elegantly to the floor of the Bowl just beyond the riders, "but they're at Honshu! So we'll go to Landing, where I can learn what this is all about." With an agile leap, he vaulted to the back of his bronze.

Lessa blinked. "Oh! Talina's Arwith says that T'gellan is going to Landing, too."

"I'm away. Golanth will inform Ramoth!" He raised his hand in farewell and the big bronze ran a few steps to launch himself and abruptly disappeared.

"You must have a word with him," Lessa said under her breath to her weyrmate, scowling.

"Why?"

"He shouldn't take off that quickly and scarcely a wing's span above the ground. He's setting a bad example for young riders."

F'lar grinned, surreptitiously looking around. "No young riders nearby and it's still too dark for him to have been seen."

Lessa glared up at him. "I doubt he checked. For all we know, S'lan may have seen. You know how he tries to be like his father."

"Let's finish our breakfast. Now, while we've a chance."

"With that thing still glowering overhead?"

"Why not? We've seen the displays. If it starts to drop on us, we're safer in the Lower Cavern than out here. And it's cold."

With that, Lessa agreed and, with one last look at yet another trio of bright flarings, she huddled close against his warmth on their way back inside.

HARPER HALL—LOCAL TIME 1:00
IN THE MORNING—1.9.31

Drum messages from Telgar Hold had roused Sebell. Beside him, Menolly groaned.

"Now what?"

" 'Shooting stars, unexpected, confirm.' Confirm what?" Sebell said, hauling his heavy robe from the chair.

"At this hour? Couldn't it wait until morning?" Menolly complained sleepily.

"Probably," Sebell replied, tying the belt tightly to keep out the cold. "But Larad's not generally nervous." He went to the window of their bedroom. He couldn't see anything in the east, as the cliffs around Fort Hold occluded his view. He did see a light come on up at the Hold.

Groghe! He said the name to himself. The old Lord did not sleep well at night, so he'd hear any drum message and want a full report. Sebell sighed.

"Go back to sleep, Menolly," he said softly and watched her, with the deep and abiding affection he had for his extraordinarily talented mate, as she cuddled into the warm spot he had just left. He picked up the hand light, found his fleece-lined house shoes, and made his way through their apartment, down the stairs. Ronchin, who was on duty in the Hall, was turning on more lights. He pointed out the window and Sebell saw a figure running down the steps of the Hold, toward the short tunnel that linked the Hold with the Hall. Haligon, probably, Groghe's usual messenger. He was not particularly surprised to see a dragon settle in the big forecourt of the Harper Hall. He gestured for Ronchin to throw up the bar on the heavy door and open one leaf for their visitors.

"Ruth and Jaxom called me to Ruatha," N'ton said urgently. "There's a meteor or a comet in the east, showering stuff. Had a look at it through those binoculars of Jaxom's. It isn't a late Ghost and, for all it's in the east, it most certainly is not a return of the Red Star."

"Red Star?" Haligon, just entering the Hall, repeated that with scornful incredulity. "Couldn't be. Father thinks the Abominators are up to something."

"Not this," N'ton said, shaking his head. "I spoke with Sharra, as Jaxom and Ruth had gone straight to Landing. There are reports of seeing these shooting flares from Telgar, Benden, Cove, and Landing. There'll be more messages in, Sebell, so I thought you ought to be aware."

"Then what is it?" Haligon asked, straightening hurriedly donned clothes and trying to look more alert than cold and sleepy.

"That's what we'll have to find out," Sebell said. He motioned them to go into his office. "Bring us some klah, Ronchin, will you? I'm sure the Harper Hall will be the first to know what's going to keep us up all night." He stirred up the fire and threw more black stone on it.

"It has nothing to do with Abominators, does it?" Haligon asked. "I told Father it couldn't have."

"How?" N'ton asked with some exasperation. Lord Groghe had been seeing Abominators in anything unusual. He strode to the big map of Pern hanging on the wall and pointed as he explained. "Watchrider at Telgar saw it and at the same time it appeared to be directly overhead at Benden, visible from Cove Hold and Landing. That would make it very high up, probably above the atmosphere. I doubt even Aivas could have rigged such a display over such an immense distance. So tell Lord Groghe to discard any notion of an Abominator scheme. Ramoth said Golanth and F'lessan have gone to Landing. They'll report directly to her. We'll know as soon as she does."

Haligon's face was thoughtful, obviously trying to figure out what to say to allay his father's alarm when Menolly, well wrapped in a robe, arrived with a tray of steaming cups of klah.

"I didn't mean to wake you," Sebell said.

"You didn't but Haligon's boots did," and she gave the Holder a mock-angry scowl as she passed cups around.

"You're very good to Lord Groghe, you know," she added in quiet approval.

"Then it has to have come from beyond Pern," Sebell said. "Abominators cannot have contrived that."

"Whatever it is," Menolly said cheerfully, handing Haligon his cup of klah, "the Abominators will be sure that somehow Aivas arranged it Turns ago."

"How?" demanded the three men in chorus.

She shrugged. "Or maybe the Red Star is on its way back? You know how many people feel that we should never have tampered with it in the first place."

LANDING—LOCAL TIME 10:12 MID-MORNING—1.9.31

Fairs of fire-lizards blanketed the air above Landing as F'lessan arrived. They were volatile at any time, and, on this morning, were exceedingly raucous and flying in intricate acrobatic displays, screaming in cacophonous descants. Their antics did not, however, obscure the next burst from the object in the sky. It amazed F'lessan that the phenomenon of a fireball, which could seem directly above Benden, could be visible in almost the same position here at Landing. It was brighter, which meant, he thought, that it was very bright indeed to be seen in daylight over Landing. And casting odd shadows, coming from the west, which was eerier. He hoped that *Yoko* would have noted the increase in its magnitude. Could it be a comet, swooping down so close to Pern? Hopefully, he thought, on a hyperbolic orbit that would give everyone a beautiful display, a bad fright, and then disappear, still shedding part of its mass. Unusual! Most unusual! Exhilarating, too, in a scary way!

He saw more dragons emerge from *between* and recognized Monarth, with green Path on his right. So Monaco Bay was curious, too. A host more of dragons appeared. These were occluding his view of the fireball, clearly visible on the

northeastern horizon. He shouldn't waste any time getting
to the Interface office and *Yoko*'s screens. He wondered how
long the old ship's telemetry had been monitoring it. This
would be much more interesting than astronomy accounts of
things that had happened a long time in the past.

Put me down, Golly.

There're too many people. Golanth said, backwinging
strongly as he was unable to find enough space in the dense
swarm of people in front of Admin, nervous fire-lizards dipping and flitting above them.

They'll move. F'lessan *had* to see the thing, the fireball,
whatever it was, land.

They've nowhere to move to, Golanth told him.

Cursing under his breath, F'lessan examined the mass of
heads and bodies, the ring of guards around the door preventing entry. It would take time to push through that crowd
and he was boiling with eagerness to see *Yoko*'s telemetry
reports.

Land on the roof, he told his dragon.

But I'm heavy.

Just get me close enough to drop on it. F'lessan swung his
right leg over the last neck ridge, slightly swaying with
Golanth's maneuvering to get directly over the roof. Golanth
raised his foreleg. This was an exercise rider and dragon had
perfected in drill for use when the dragon couldn't land and
the rider had to reach the ground. F'lessan smoothly dropped
to the sturdy forearm, his feet dangling in the air as he let his
hands slide down to Golanth's paw, hanging on to the talons.

Right over the entrance, F'lessan added. *I'll just drop to the
ground. Someone'll break my fall.*

His right foot connected with something solid. He dropped
to all fours on the roof, sliding down backward until his feet
caught on the drain. Slipped on that and slithered until his
knees lodged briefly in the rain gully.

"Drop, dragonrider," someone below him shouted. "We'll
catch you."

Hands tugged at the toes of his boot. He went limp, committed to the downward fall. Instantly his ankles were caught,

then hands fastened on his knees, letting him down, supporting his thighs. In the next moment he was on his feet, being congratulated and enthusiastically thumped for the success of his daring stunt.

Made it, he said somewhat smugly to Golanth who was hovering above.

"Thanks! Thanks, thanks!" he said, skewing around to those behind him and then turned to the door. "Benden Weyr's orders," he said to the two guards who were preventing anyone from entering. The crowd behind was bombarding him with a babble of questions. "I'm F'lessan. Lemme in," he shouted above the tumult.

They did, immediately resuming their defensive postures. F'lessan strode forward, wondering how much time that stunt had taken, opening his jacket and peeling the helmet off.

She's here, Golanth said.

Which she? F'lessan's tone was amused.

Both of them. She studies stars, you know, Golanth added. *She's shared night watches at Cove Hold.*

Then please inform Zaranth that F'lessan requires her rider's assistance in the Interface office.

F'lessan turned back to the door guards. "The Monaco Weyrleader's on his way in." He had to shout to be heard above the babble outside. "See that green rider Tai comes in, too, as quickly as possible." Then to all the others shouting questions, he smiled and waved, saying "We'll sort it all out and report to you shortly."

Monarth said he saw how you got in, F'lessan, and Golanth rumbled with amusement. *They'll try it.*

Maybe Mirrim will break a leg, F'lessan muttered, feeling uncharitable toward her. As he continued, he nodded in a blithe, unconcerned manner to a knot of anxious men and women at the other end of the reception area and hurried down the right-hand hall to the *Yokohama* Interface offices.

At the end of that hall, the door to the Aivas chamber was open. He felt the usual grab at his throat when he saw the blank screen that had once given humans access to the most amazing intelligence on Pern. He swallowed the lump and turned left into the room where, seven Turns ago, he had learned how to build a computer.

There had been significant additions to the original office, of course, to deal with all the data sent down from the *Yokohama*, the one remaining colony ship. Ordinarily the office was pleasantly busy, people at the four banks of workstations that were arranged back-to-back in the center of the large room. Now an odd anticipatory silence dominated the room as all eyes were trained on the wall monitor, which F'lessan couldn't see from the door.

"You can't come—" began the burly door guard, whom F'lessan recognized as Tunge, one of the regular men. He skipped aside and explained with soft intensity. "Sorry, bronze rider, but everyone and his fire-lizard's been trying to get in here since that thing in the sky was spotted." Tunge was impressed, and scared.

F'lessan made a quick survey of those in the room; where was Wansor? Surely Lytol and D'ram had got him here so the phenomenon could be described to him?

"Master Wansor?" he murmured to Tunge.

"Oh, him." With a quick grin, Tunge jerked his head back down the corridor. "Him 'n' Lord Lytol 'n' bronze rider D'ram are in the conference room. There's a big screen there, too, you know, so they could tell him what information's being processed."

Directly across the room, one of the smaller monitors was blinking the legend PHO. F'lessan shook his head, trying to remember what the initials stood for—possibly hazardous object? Why had he assumed that the bright light was a comet? Below the title "Encounter Analysis" were eight columns, headed ESTIMATED TIME TO PERIGEE, DISTANCE, VELOCITY, PROBABILITY, ATMOSPHERE BREAKUP, IMPACT ERROR, LATITUDE, and LONGITUDE. These were showing numbers that altered rapidly, either decreasing or, in the case of longitude, increasing. As F'lessan watched, the Estimated Time to Perigee ticked over to 5800.

That display gave him another frisson of apprehension. When had that clock started ticking down? He'd come as fast as he could without timing it. But then, he hadn't anticipated that this could be a real crisis.

He inched carefully along the wall, moving people who were almost unaware of being manipulated, so intent were they upon the monitor's reports. He recognized several as off-duty technicians. Being tall, he eased into a spot in the corner and still had a clear view of the monitor. In front of him, Stinar, the duty officer, was standing with the barrel-chested man of medium height, dark-haired, with a handsome hooked nose, whom F'lessan recognized as Erragon, Wansor's assistant. Shouldn't he have been in the conference room? F'lessan chided himself. Lytol and D'ram could explain adequately to Wansor but Erragon was needed in here, interpreting the *Yoko*'s telemetry. When this was over, he'd undoubtedly report to Master Wansor the more technical details of this unusual occurrence. The two were intent on the visual transmitted to Landing by *Yoko*.

At maximum magnification, *Yoko* showed a small image of the nucleus, embedded in clouds of dust. *Yoko* added another window, attempting to trace it back to its original orbit. Details came up as:

Semi-Major Axis = 33.712
Period = 195.734
Eccentricity = 0.971
Perihelion = 0.953 AU
Inclination = 103.95 degrees.

But F'lessan, knowing all these figures would be available later, concentrated on the comet, now resolving jets and debris. Yes, it must be a comet. That would explain its slowing with respect to the stars. Outgassing can push a comet about, making an estimate of its orbit even harder. Furthermore, with the long axis running from the northwest to the southeast, who could tell? It may skid across our atmosphere and disappear south, thought F'lessan hopefully.

Yet another working window opened, labeled SEARCHING. Images of what F'lessan knew to be Pernese space flashed past, the streaking orbits of some of the minor planets against the background of northern hemisphere stars.

"What's all that about?" Stinar asked Erragon who was blinking at the rapidly altering display.

"I'd hazard the guess that it's searching for any old images of the comet. It is possible, you know," Erragon went on, frowning at the speed of the search pattern, "that the comet originated in the Oort cloud." His grin was forced. "It might even have been seen by our Ancestors."

"Really?"

Erragon sighed, flicking his attention to some of the other sidebars. "We have a lot of material to review, you know. Just for our home system. Ah, yes," and he pointed back to the search. "The material we're seeing was released from the comet two to three weeks ago. Here we go," he added, intent on the newest sidebar readings.

Encounter Analysis
Estimated Perigee in 1800 seconds
Projected Perigee Distance 16km, error + −296km
Encounter Velocity 58.48kmsec + −0.18km/sec
Probability of Impact 48.9%
Probability of Atmospheric Breakup (Airburst) 1.3%
Impact Error Ellipse 3698 times 592km
Location and Orientation of Ellipse 9° north, 18° east,
  Major Axis bearing 130°

At that point, Erragon visibly tensed, leaning slightly forward on the balls of his feet in an attitude that confirmed F'lessan's bad feelings about the alteration in probability of impact. He wasn't certain that the error ellipse of impact was reassuring. Unless the comet suddenly pulled itself up in an escape parabola. Estimate to Perigee decreasing: 1500 seconds, or 25 minutes, F'lessan told himself. He also didn't like standing around, watching, in a room full of people who didn't seem to realize what could happen. The tension was palpable but everyone was so focused on the screen, too scared to ask questions or to break into the concentration of Stinar or Erragon.

New figures at 1200 seconds, from the *Yoko*'s synchronic orbit over Pern, gave coordinates of Range 71377km, *Yoko* latitude 45.IN, *Yoko* longitude 118.4m. The magnitude was −5, which was bright enough and getting brighter and the fireball was suddenly moving a degree every minute. He stepped right beside Stinar and Erragon.

"Where will it impact?" F'lessan murmured for their ears only.

"We still don't know that it will," Stinar said softly, restlessly shifting his feet, turning his head sideways so that his words just reached F'lessan.

"There's a three-hundred-kilometer range error," Erragon said as if that was significant.

"Where?" Stinar demanded.

"Right now, the range extends along the farther Eastern Island Ring."

"On the islands themselves, or in the sea?"

Stinar took the hand-control unit from his pocket and punched in a command. The monitor opened a small window in the right corner, while the Probability Impact percentage rose steadily into the 50's and the error ellipse—that narrow band along the far islands to which the fireball was inexorably aimed—got smaller. The new window showed the Eastern Sea as it must be seen from *Yoko*, and the scattered islands of both Eastern Rings. A wide band was superimposed over the upper islands.

"Looks more like the islands," Stinar said with a little shrug.

F'lessan knew that the islands were uninhabited, too far out in the Eastern Ring Sea to be attractive for anyone, even Toric, to hold; except whichever island currently housed the Abominator exiles—and no one but N'ton knew where that was.

"I don't like that," Erragon said, stiffening.

"Why?"

"Those islands are all volcanic. An impact on them might trigger eruptions all along that chain," he said, pointing.

"Then we'll just hope it falls in the sea," Stinar said with a slightly nervous laugh.

"That will produce other hazards," Erragon said solemnly.

F'lessan caught his breath. He'd seen volcanoes erupt; the one Piemur had discovered off the westernmost tip of Southern Hold blew up periodically, sending clouds of gray ash to blot the sun and stifle even the rich tropical vegetation. The one in the near Eastern Ring, which the Ancients had called Young Mountain, liked to send immense boulders skyward and great lava flows down its side, spinning burning chunks onto its neighbors. The islands that the comet was heading for were much larger and he shuddered at the thought of all of them becoming active. They would cause tidal waves, which could have a disastrous effect on coastal areas—like Monaco.

"It could *still* just graze," Erragon murmured to Stinar, in a tone that gave F'lessan no confidence in that possibility at all.

He glanced up at the legend, numbers whirring into new configurations all the time, as *Yoko* telemetry updated them.

"It's only got a few minutes to change course," F'lessan said.

Erragon glanced at him, blinking, as if he'd forgotten the bronze rider's presence. "Did you know your Weyrleaders are in the conference room with Master Wansor?"

Lessa and F'lar were also here? When—and why—had they arrived? Obscurely he was glad they had, especially the way this event was proceeding.

"No, but I'd rather be in here and know the worst," F'lessan said, watching Erragon's shoulders twitch in startled reaction to the last word. "Where will it hit us?"

"We don't know yet," but F'lessan saw Erragon's eye flick to the Impact Probability, which flickered onto 60 percent.

All three men caught their breath as the percentage jumped in a matter of seconds to 100 percent.

"That's still a consequence of the grazing impact,"

Erragon said but F'lessan didn't think he believed that. "The ellipse is shrinking. Can you adjust *Yoko*'s visuals?"

On the map in the right-hand corner, the figures flickered in latitude and longitude, following the last downward plunge of the comet. Filling that screen at maximum magnification, the tuberlike shape of the comet nucleus showed geysers and jets blowing into space; chunks breaking off, floating slowly away. F'lessan was amazed since he knew the speed at which the comet was traveling and that eerie, almost dignified, breakup of its parts was like a Gather dance.

"It's going to miss . . ." Stinar whispered, unconsciously pushing both hands in a deflecting motion.

"Just a few more degrees . . ." Erragon, too, was taut as if, by exerting sufficient willpower, he could shift the plummeting fireball south and east.

"It's got to be far enough away . . ." F'lessan was adding his tension in an unconscious effort to affect a descent that no effort could now alter.

F'lessan found himself squinting at the sudden brightness of the picture—the brightness of sunlit sea or the comet. The magnitude of its dust trail now registered an eye-blinding intensity of −9!

A new message imposed itself prominently: *120 seconds to perigee—105 seconds to impact.*

The monitor altered abruptly, darkening, and F'lessan saw the line on the sidebar that indicated *Yoko* was displaying a constructed image, made up of the optical, infrared, microwave, and other print capabilities that Erragon had once tried to describe to F'lessan. The nucleus of the comet looked suddenly darker but the reduction of the glare relieved his eyes. Ominously the message now read *60 seconds to atmosphere.*

Another read *20 seconds to impact, Angle 12° : magnitude of dust trail −9.*

People splayed fingers in front of their eyes. The glare-reduced optical version saved them from the splintering whiteness that erupted, which the monitor hastily continued to reduce. A screen flicked to a new image—identified as "synthetic radar"—as *Yoko* attempted to see through the clouds.

Twenty seconds couldn't have elapsed, F'lessan thought and then realized that *Yoko* was slightly behind in its reporting. Where had it impacted? The island chain or the sea?

No one spoke. All seemed to be holding their breath. The silence was broken by printers churning out reams of hard copy that fell unnoticed into baskets or spilled to the floor. As the comet was spilling its substance onto the sea? Flaming molten debris down on the nearest Ring islands?

Even the image on the screen seemed to recoil from the incredible brightness. Squinting through his fingers, F'lessan saw the radar image showing the surface topography—and a series of rings on the ocean. Waves traveled outward from the impact point, immediately followed by a much higher fountain of water as the sea fell back into the impact crater. Then he had the distinct impression of a wall moving out with astonishing speed and saw a column of red-brown steam spreading down to the sea, with black bits whirling up and out, and then vast billows rushing out from it across the sea.

Still the silence in the Interface office was broken only by machines doing what they were programmed to do: disgorge columns of figures. The human observers struggled to absorb what they had just seen, were still witnessing as retinal afterimages: the creation of a storm of staggering proportions, blossoming up and outward. Steam, gas vapor, and whatever the head of the fireball had been composed of were part of the storm. The fireball had extinguished itself and then hit the sea, F'lessan repeated, making his mind believe what his eyes had seen: it made a hole that made a wave, which fell back, and sent up a fountain of water. Abruptly the data on the screen changed.

Impactor Summary
Probable cometary origin
Impact velocity 58.51km/sec
Dimensions 597 times 361 times 452 meter ellipsoid
Volume 51 million cubic meters

Average Density 0.33 (+ −0.11)
Total Mass 17 million tons
Derived Impact Energy 29.7 Exajoules
Explosive Equivalent 7.4 gigatons
15° northern latitude, 12° east longitude.

"It came down in the sea!" Stinar's sigh of relief held a triumphant note.

Ramoth saw this, too, Golanth told his rider in a muted tone. That's when F'lessan recalled that Erragon had said that the Benden Weyrleaders and Wansor had been watching this on the conference room screen.

They weren't all that lucky, after all, that the comet had missed the volcanic islands. A huge mass like that hitting open sea would cause a great deal of trouble. There'd be a shock wave, wouldn't there? In how many more minutes? How much damage would that cause? Was Landing far enough away? Monaco Bay was at sea level. It'd be flooded to the hills and they were a long way up the sloping beachfront.

He tried to calm these thoughts, to resurrect the necessary information from lessons long past. He started to recall sentences, paragraphs, and irrelevant details.

A cold fear in his guts increasing with every second, F'lessan peered at the screen as the cloud boiled, red-brown, to occlude what was actually happening. They ought to *know* what was happening at sea level, the bronze rider thought; there was something—. Everyone in the office had now recovered their wits and their tongues. If everyone around him would only stop babbling excitedly about this spectacular event, he could think. Where was Tai? She might know. She should be here. So should T'gellan. The coast of the southern continent was not going to escape the effects of something so big dropping at that speed!

Suddenly the view on the screen altered, not only dropping the infrared screen but also presenting a new perspective, well back from the impact site. A discernible wave, a darkness of water, was moving outward, just faster than the flat-topped clouds boiling up and out. More data was being presented in margins. F'lessan blinked, unable to decipher the critical messages given.

F'lessan kept his eyes on the screen. The *Yoko* adjusted its viewpoint by pulling back at speed, back beyond the hump of one of the big rainforest islands just north of the impact point. It was burning! Burning? Oh, yes, memory informed F'lessan, the thermal flare of the comet would cause flash fires with the heat of its passing.

"We're very, very lucky," someone muttered. "It didn't hit any landmass."

"No, we're not lucky," F'lessan said savagely, watching the dark watery circle expand. "That island's on fire!" Then he pointed to the map in the right-hand corner. "The one due south will be burning, too. And look at that gap between them! There'll be sea pouring through that gap, circling out, spreading, and coming straight down to the southern coastline in a wall of water . . ." He paused, uncertainly, trying to recall the specific term.

"Tsunami!"

Tai's soft shocked voice behind him in the silence of the Interface office gave F'lessan the word he had been trying to remember. She stood with T'gellan and Mirrim against the wall. He hadn't even seen them arrive. She stared with awed fear and fascination at what the monitor depicted.

The distant cloud expanded sideways and skyward, and the surface of sea was reacting in its depths and sending ominous black undulations out in all directions. And something swirled up and over the rainforest island. Then the view retreated to show a new aspect; the island had been subsumed! And a thick line of debris: the lush huge trees, some thirty meters tall, were now just sea wrack, bobbing until finally they would be tossed up on beaches as jetsam. The dark circle continued to spread outward, westward. East, too, F'lessan now realized, though the cloud obscured that fact. He checked with the radar screen and yes, the rings were heading east and south, right at unprotected lowlands, possibly as far as the Hook Islands, and certainly speeding right toward the lovely little bays that dotted the Monaco coast, and Monaco Bay itself, the Harbor, the busy boatyard with sheds, pier, and cotholds. And Cove Hold? Would the Kahrain Cape protect it?

"That's what a tsunami does to what's in its way," F'lessan said, pointing to the wreckage, the shocking disappearance of two substantial islands. A shaft of cold, deep fear engulfed his bones. He urgently signaled Tai to join him.

"Tsunami?" Mirrim echoed in a surprise tinged with denial, fear, and resentment. She lifted her hand to stop Tai but F'lessan scowled at her as he waved the green rider to his side.

"I thought tsunami occurred with sea or earthquakes," T'gellan said, stunned.

"Tsunami can also occur when something very hot and heavy falls out of the sky," Erragon said in the tone of someone who wishes he did not have to announce such news. "And a comet just did!" He pointed to the grim Impactor Summary figures.

F'lessan shook his head, unable to deal with such incredible quantities as a mass of 17 million tons and a derived impact energy of 29.7 exajoules. Now *that* was a typically esoteric Aivas word. He was almost relieved to see Erragon and Stinar were also struggling to put such terms into Pernese contexts.

"What does all that mean?" Mirrim asked, her tanned skin pale. In all the Turns he had known her, F'lessan had never seen this confident woman so scared.

Erragon swiveled on his heel, giving her such a piercing look that she recoiled slightly against T'gellan. He gave his head a final shake, took a deep breath, and regarded the Monaco Weyrleader.

"I don't know how big the tsunami will be. That depends on the shoreline and what might deflect or diffract it, but Monaco—" He pointed to the map still up in the right-hand corner of the big screen. "—will be inundated, flooded." He gestured with his fingers, west, north, and east. "The force of the impact will send the tsunami in every direction." He shook his head again as much in denial as emphasis. Then he took F'lessan by the sleeve with one hand as he reached out for T'gellan with the other, giving the Weyrleader's shoulder a resolute shake, his expression filled with compassion. "You must evacuate the coastal holds to the hills, to high ground. The harbor, too!" He put a hand to his forehead, obviously marshalling his thoughts. "Stinar, are there maps of the coastlines we can access?"

"There are," said a gruff new voice, rising above the stutter of printers and the low anxious murmuring of frightened people in the office, "and I have them." Master Idarolan stood in the doorway.

Mirrim wasn't the only one to stare blankly at him. F'lessan felt a sense of relief. They'd need the retired Masterfishman more right now than at any time in his resourceful life. Fleetingly he realized that the captain had probably been taking his usual morning weather scan: the deck of his hold in Nerat was above the sea, facing east, and he might well have seen the comet. If it had been visible at Benden Weyr, it had probably been visible to anyone looking in the right direction. Master Idarolan could have seen it from Nerat's Ankle.

"But how . . ." F'lessan stammered.

"The Weyrleaders required my presence," and Idarolan winked at F'lessan before turning to T'gellan. "You've a lot to do, Weyrleader, and we won't stand in your way. You, bronze riders—." He paused significantly. "You will need to make good *time*," and he stressed that word, "to get all accomplished or so the Benden Weyrleaders inform me and you!" He made a sweeping gesture for the dragonriders to make their exits. As they started to move, he added, "Warn Portmaster Zewe to ring the Dolphin Bell and get any ships in harbor out to sea. It won't be as dangerous offshore."

They were out the door by then, hearing his gruff voice saying, "And I need your best mathematician and the use of a computer that isn't talking to the *Yokohama*!"

"Does that mean we're to time it?" Mirrim asked T'gellan in a hushed tone as soon as they were past Tunge, who had not recovered from the multiple shocks.

"What else?" F'lessan asked, right behind her, hauling Tai along beside him.

"How else could we do what is to be done?" T'gellan added as he dragged his weyrmate into a near run. "Yes, Ramoth just confirmed it to Monarth."

"But what do we do first?" Mirrim demanded in a scared voice.

"Monarth's bespeaking Talina's Arwith. I've told her to take four wings at once to Monaco Bay, to warn Portmaster Zewe and to start moving people to safety."

"The dolphins will be safe?" Tai asked.

Mirrim shot her a furious look. "We have to think about the Weyr. It's spread out all over!" Despair made her flush. "So many people."

"The dolphins will know what to do," F'lessan said, taking a firmer grip on Tai's arm, hurrying her along. "If we can time it," and he couldn't resist grinning at the permission, "we will *make* the time we need."

"But our Weyr's no more than fifty meters from the sea," and Mirrim's voice rose with anxiety, her face pale under her tan. "On low-lying ground."

"Weyrfolk are a lot better at taking orders than holders or crafters," Tai said, for once the one to reassure.

"And all those seaholders?" Mirrim gasped at the enormity of the task ahead of them.

"I've maps in my office of every holding that looks to Monaco," T'gellan said as they strode, ever faster under the impetus of their anxieties, toward the back door. The guards at the front entrance were now shouting that there was an emergency: specialists to stand right, other volunteers muster to the left. Landing itself was completely safe here in the foothills. Except from the shock wave. When would that be hitting them? "We'll warn them all."

"How long ago did you leave?" F'lessan asked as T'gellan straight-armed the door open, holding it for the others to exit. "We can go back as soon as you've left. Get a bit of a head start."

"I don't know," T'gellan said, startled. "When we finally

made it into the office, Time Remaining stood at 4870. I remember that!"

"An hour and a half ago? As well as the time we wasted talking," F'lessan said. Had so little time elapsed? And yet it had seemed so long—watching the stunning visuals as mere curiosity in a bright point in Benden's morning sky turned into a planetary disaster at midday in Landing.

Ramoth says only bronze riders are to manage the timings, Golanth said, his tone awed.

T'gellan gave a sharp bark of laughter, glancing over his shoulder at the Benden Wingleader. "So which of us has more experience timing?"

"Not a point to argue," F'lessan said. "Let's do it. All we need are our dragons."

There wasn't enough room for four dragons, even if two were green, to land on the area outside the rear door, and the guard was goggle-eyed at the flurry of so many wings.

Next avenue over, F'lessan told his bronze. *Tell Zaranth.* "This way, Tai, between the buildings. Meetcha there!" He raised his voice so T'gellan would hear over the noise of Monarth's descent. Path crammed herself against one wall to drop as close as she could to Mirrim. He glanced at his watch before he drove his fist into the sleeve of his flying jacket. "Golanth! See the comet as we saw it coming in to land."

F'lessan and Tai ran through the space between buildings that had become classrooms for the many youngsters studying at Landing. Golanth was in the act of putting his feet down when F'lessan leaped to his forearm and vaulted astride. As the bronze immediately began to ascend, F'lessan caught sight of Tai astride Zaranth's back.

Golanth, tell Zaranth to take her coordinates from you, F'lessan said, not even bothering to close his flying jacket or jam his helmet on his head. Maybe the seconds *between* would cool him down from the heat that he hadn't even noticed in the Interface office. He concentrated on timing it and Golanth took them *between.*

IN THE CONFERENCE ROOM
AT LANDING — 1.9.31

Once again Landing had become a command center, Lessa
thought. Though she could wish it otherwise, she would be
happier, as well as more useful, here than at Benden Weyr. It
had been Ruth's query to her through Ramoth that made her
wonder if perhaps that bright spark in the sky, still hanging
overhead at Benden, was dangerous. Tiroth had already
brought Wansor, Lytol, and D'ram to Landing. Maybe the
Benden Weyrleaders should join them, if only to see what the
old Star Master had to say about this intruder. Stinar was
quite willing to turn on the screen in the conference room so
that Lytol and D'ram could describe what was happening to
Wansor. He could still distinguish light from dark but no details. Despite his blindness, he had cultivated an uncanny
ability to locate other people in the same room with him,
sometimes calling them by name when they came near.

His round face with its opaque eyes had lit up with an extraordinary smile when Lessa and F'lar entered. "Lessa!"

"How did you know?" Lessa asked, swiftly moving to take
both his hands in hers. She had half a mind to give him a kiss
for his unqualified welcome.

"My dear Lessa, wherever you go there is a vibrancy that is
unmistakable. And then," he chuckled, "you wear a fragrance
that is unique." He held out his right hand toward F'lar and returned the strong grip.

Craggy-faced Lytol and D'ram, whose weathered skin was
nearly the color of his bronze's hide, had risen at their entry
and now Lytol was holding a chair for her, one facing the
screen with its view of what the *Yoko* was seeing.

"Is all this serious?" Lessa asked, taking the seat and
noting a bewildering amount of information scrolling down
one side of the monitor. The fireball that had seemed almost
directly overhead was now coming straight at them, even
from *Yoko*'s altitude above the surface.

"It could be," Wansor said. "Erragon is watching with Stinar—and, of course, we now have you here." He smiled. "Do go on, Lytol. Any new information on that error ellipse?"

"Some of this will be very technical, Lessa," Lytol said courteously, reseating himself before he leaned close to Wansor to describe the scene and recite the numbers that were flowing down the side of the monitor.

Beside her, F'lar gave it his attention, though he, too, she noticed, scowled subtly; the complicated astronomical data was beyond him. Someone brought in a tray of klah and meatrolls and, eyeing the screen warily, departed as quickly as possible. There was a degree of fear in the girl's manner that troubled Lessa. She was accustomed to listening to her instincts. As she served D'ram a cup of klah, she bent close to his ear.

"What would happen if that fireball came down anywhere?"

Clearly that possibility had occurred to the old bronze rider.

"It could be a miss," he whispered softly.

"A near one?" Lessa said, hazarding her opinion.

"We can hope so," he replied, shifting his position in his chair. "*Yoko* hasn't displayed any information about its size, but it's clearly a large object."

"Flaming," she said sardonically. "So it will make a large hole and shake the surface."

D'ram gave her a startled glance. "We don't know that it will impact, Lady Lessa."

"Let's think of the worst that could happen and then we can be pleasantly surprised."

"Fortunately there's a lot of sea for it to cross," he murmured.

"Then it's best if it falls into water and does no harm."

His eyes widened. "It will cause harm! If it falls, there will be tidal waves of tremendous force, flooding all low coastal areas and surging inland. You remember the high waves caused by the last eruption of Piemur's volcano?"

"Indeed, but the hurricane of two Turns ago caused a great deal more havoc."

D'ram thinned his lips. "This would cause more wide-spread damage, believe me. That is," he amended hastily, "if the worst should happen." He paused, frowning and twisting his lower lip between two fingers. Looking her full in the eyes, he added. "But if we *know* about it, we could prepare, evacuate."

"We—meaning dragonriders?"

He nodded quickly. "People could be lifted to higher ground *before* the wall of waves reaches them."

Maps hung on the conference room walls behind them. She skewed herself around and saw the big map that Aivas had called a Mercator projection. "Faulty," she remembered him saying, "in that the polar areas are larger than their actual size but it gives you a coherent grasp of the disposition of land and sea masses." She wished with all her being that somehow Aivas's deep quiet voice would issue from the speakers, informing them how to deal with this crisis. But Aivas was gone! Whatever problem this fireball presented was theirs and D'ram had suggested a way in which they could—in an emergency—reduce the potential damage. Master Idarolan had once told her about seeing a huge wall of water drowning an island; a tsunami, he called it.

"If it's coastline we need to protect, we will need Master Idarolan's experience and knowledge," she murmured to D'ram. "He still has his charts of deep harbors and shallow moorings."

"What are you two whispering about, Lessa?" F'lar asked as quiet-spoken as they.

"If that thing,"—she gestured to the fireball and it suddenly looked a lot less amusing—"falls on us, we need to be prepared."

"But . . ." F'lar began.

"Besides," she went on, intensifying her glance at him and giving an indolent shrug, "even if it misses, this is a phenomenon that would fascinate Idarolan. He'll see it better from here than from his deck at Nerat's Ankle."

"You say," and Wansor's light voice turned excited, "that the probability reads fifty-eight percent?"

"Go, F'lar. And give Idarolan enough *time*," she said, stressing the word, "to bring all the records he might need."

"I'll be—" F'lar grinned at her, "right back."

Lessa glanced over at the wall clock: 11:35!

"Is he going to—" D'ram began, stopping in surprise. "But you don't encourage—"

"No, I don't, but, as I said, if we prepare for the worst, we can be pleasantly—rather than unpleasantly—surprised. Something about that—." She regarded the fireball. "When a dragon's eyes are that color, she's at her most dangerous."

D'ram looked at the screen. "Yes, you're right."

Seven elapsed minutes later, when the clock registered 11:42, F'lar and Idarolan swung into the conference room. Both of them were laden with bags of chart rolls and looked as if they had been running. Idarolan's eyes swept those gathered, then were held by the monitor as he swung his burden to the tabletop.

"I see that I am in *time*,"—his roughened seaman's voice caressed the word—"to be of use."

"Oh, yes, Idarolan, yes, I'm glad you're here," Wansor said excitedly. "I don't think the cometary fragment is going to miss us." He sounded as if this were an achievement to be relished. "What's the object's magnitude right now?"

"It's sending a brightness of minus eight," Idarolan exclaimed and sat down heavily, ignoring his paraphernalia. "I'm glad I did some calculations before I came." He swung about. "Where's Erragon?"

"Interface office," Lytol said as repressively as he could, trying to concentrate on giving Wansor at least some of the readings.

"It will hit us then, won't it?" Lessa murmured.

"Yes, I fear so," Wansor said, all his initial enthusiasm and excitement lost in acceptance of that reality.

They were all silent as the screen depicted the catastrophe that was on its way to them.

Master Idarolan was the first to recover his wits. "I will need the help of your best mathematicians," he said, hunting through the bundles on the table and selecting a tightly wrapped tube of papers. "Monaco must be evacuated first. I don't know how long they will have—two, maybe three hours."

Lessa stood also and clasped the hand holding the papers. "Tell the dragonriders there that I want them to *make*—" She paused to impress that on him; his eyes twinkled as he took her meaning. "—time to accomplish what needs to be done."

MONACO WEYR—10:22 IN THE MORNING—TIMING IT

Golanth and Zaranth were hovering at tree level above the wide clearing that surrounded the large long building that was Monaco Bay Weyr. The space was big enough to accommodate many dragons, F'lessan thought. Then he winced. So much time was consumed by doing "safe" landings and take-offs. They had no time to waste right now. As Golanth sank to the ground in front of the Weyr center, F'lessan caught one glimpse of the sea, tranquil and pale green, and a bright streak slightly north and east of Monaco Bay.

As much as I wanted to see that comet, I may wish I never had, F'lessan remarked ironically.

Zaranth's rider said that, too.

Well, tell Zaranth to remember the position. We can use it as a handy time-mark today.

Monarth arrived, too, inches above ground. Without waiting for the bronze to touch ground, T'gellan was sliding off and racing up the steps to the wide porch, shouting orders, banging on doors as he went down the wide porch that surrounded the Weyrhold. Path landed even closer to the steps, Mirrim dropping right onto the porch and scrambling to the nearest wide door.

"But you just left!" a woman exclaimed, coming out of the Weyr's main building.

"Well, we're back and there's an emergency, Dilla," Mirrim said, going to the bell and rigorously pulling its rope. "C'mon,

Tai, we can start evacuating the children. You can help, too, F'lessan, while 'Gell gets the maps." She raced inside and F'lessan heard her announcing the crisis to all within.

Typical Mirrim, he thought, but at least she was over the panic that had seized her in the Interface office. Immediately there were screams, sobs, shouts, and general confusion. The loudest complaint was "There's bread to be baked . . ."

"How far inland is safe?" F'lessan cried, catching Tai before she could follow Mirrim indoors.

"They can get high enough in twenty minutes fast-walking." Tai pointed toward a well-used path that led around one corner. "Not much time for packing but we'll need some things."

She wavered for a moment on the threshold, looking beyond the clearing, then sighed and shrugged her shoulders, hurrying on inside.

Mirrim's shrill voice was organizing the weyrfolk inside, while others, alarmed by the tolling bell, were racing in on the various paths, to find out what was wrong. Just then a crowd of half-grown boys and girls came swarming to the end of the porch, joining the other worried weyrfolk.

"The Weyr must be evacuated," he told them.

"I told you that fireball was bad luck," one of the older boys told the others.

"How could it make the sea burn?" a girl demanded, looking to the bronze rider for an answer.

"It won't," F'lessan said authoritatively. "Don't make guesses. Right now you need to do what you're told." He gave them his best reassuring grin. "This is going to be an adventure! You've got to get to your own weyrs. Pack as much as you can as quickly as you can. No more than you can carry. Tell everyone to make for the heights." He pointed the path Tai had indicated. "You need to be at least two hundred meters from the shore, up into the grove of fellis trees." He gave the bell another clanging to reinforce the urgency and those who had heard what he had to tell them dispersed in seconds, running in all directions.

Mirrim came out, herding little ones in front of her, helped by her sturdy son, Gellim, while other weyrwomen followed her, some carrying sacks and bundles. Tai had one arm burdened with packs and the other around a screaming toddler.

"Tai, get aboard Zaranth and I'll hand the babies up to you. F'lessan, use the safety straps to tie them to her. Oh, do stop screaming, Vessa," Mirrim said to the hysterical child behind her. "F'lessan, get her aboard Golanth. She can hold another once she's on his back. He can follow Zaranth to the heights with this lot. Then come back for another. It's too far for them to make it on their own."

Mirrim's bossy streak was in full operation, F'lessan thought as he hoisted an hysterical mother up to Golanth and started passing up sacks and bundles. Tai placed the screaming toddler on Zaranth's neck, an action that instantly silenced it. She leaped astride and took the others Mirrim lifted up to her.

"I'm ready," Tai cried.

Follow Zaranth, Golly!

Of course!

"I know we're responsible for all of Monaco but I can work better if I know our folk are safe," Mirrim said, excusing her actions. "While Golanth's gone, you can help me organize the others inside. We have cradlers to take, too. Will Golanth mind?"

"Not likely," F'lessan said; even his dragon would not thwart Mirrim in this mood or under these circumstances. Fortunately Mirrim was already on her way back inside the room and did not see how close to the ground both green and bronze had been when they went *between*. Think of the time they saved, he told himself.

"You, you can go on Path," he heard her saying and she nearly ran him down on her return with three older women, barely able to move for the things they were clutching. "F'lessan, we'll need rope to tie the cradles to Golanth. Over in that closet."

"We have some time to spare, Mirrim," he told her as he complied. *Golanth! Carry cradles? Well, who better?*

"I'll send these off on my Path. She knows where to

go. F'lessan, when you've got the ropes, put them on the porch. The tanner journeyman needs your help with his materials. And we've rolls of fabric in the loft we simply must save."

"There's Monarth doing nothing," F'lessan muttered under his breath, but he got the ropes, put them on the porch, and went to the assistance of the crafter who was trying to carry too many hides as well as various tools, and dropping things. And where was T'gellan with his maps?

By the time much of the Weyr's most urgent household items had been shoved or bundled into packs, brown, blue, and green dragons had arrived to be loaded and sent off. Three other blues took the cradled children. Browns were draped with fabric rolls and sleeping furs, and bulky items were tied to willing backs.

It was as well that dragons had an innate instinct for avoiding each other on the ground as well as in the air, for the traffic in and out of the main Weyr clearing was amazing. With Zaranth, Golanth had made three more trips *between* without his rider, conveying the healer and half a dozen patients.

T'gellan finally came to F'lessan's end of the porch, lugging one end of a heavy chest as two brown riders held the other. Tucked under his belt were maps. While the brown riders lifted the chest to Monarth's back, T'gellan beckoned to F'lessan, who was beginning to worry about how much time this was all taking.

The Weyrcook, arms full of bundles, nearly fell down the steps, followed by weyrfolk struggling with sacksful of clicking pots and leaking supplies just as Golanth touched down again. T'gellan rolled his eyes significantly at the younger rider and F'lessan offered Golanth's services. The cook mounted first, securing as many things as she could to Golanth's ridges. When no more could fit on his back, he raised just high enough above the ground to go *between* yet again.

Then T'gellan was at F'lessan's side, unrolling one of the maps just as three bronze dragons deposited their riders on the recently cleared space. Two riderless brown dragons hovered above the trees, waiting to land.

"I suspect you're more adept at timing than that trio, my friend," T'gellan said, admirably cool in manner, "so you get to go the farthest. Take St'ven on Mealth and C'reel and Galuth to help." The Weyrleader gestured to the browns. He unrolled the map to F'lessan who took one edge as he recognized a copy of the aerial maps that Aivas had supplied to all the Weyrs. "We were out over this area last time you flew with us. You'll remember this orange cliff!" T'gellan tapped at the recognizable landmark. "Long wide bay, long, sloping sands to the sea." He grimaced at the thought of the clear path that would give the incoming tsunami. "Granite cliff. White sands stand out against it. Bay looks like the sea took a toothless bite out of the coastline." He gave the younger rider a reassuring grin. "Don't let them talk you into conveying their boats. Those are replaceable. Lives are not!"

With that philosophy F'lessan agreed, but he also knew how difficult it was to make holders abandon whatever treasures they might own.

"Holds're mostly near this stream, but that would provide the tsunami with a channel to flood badly way inland. Be sure everyone is well back on the summit. We can't estimate how high the tsunami crest will be. Reaching the heights will be a climb for some but there're switchback steps cut in the lower levels. But among the three of you, you ought to be able to evacuate them all. Somehow or other." T'gellan's expression was grim again as he thrust the map at F'lessan. "You're a good rider." He gave F'lessan a supportive clout on the shoulder. "Secure that chest on Monarth, will you, C'reel, St'ven? Then F'lessan's your Wingleader."

"I've called in as many riders as can be spared to clear Monaco Harbor and Cove Hold," T'gellan said, his forehead furrowed with worry. "Sweep riders are warning inland holders but we can't take time to figure out how far above sea level they are. They'll just have to get as high as they can. But all have got to be warned." In a final aside, before the Weyrleader mounted, he leaned into F'lessan. "Don't shave time too close! Lessa would kill me if you got time-lost."

Then he was astride his dragon and Monarth leaped skyward and was gone *between* before the upper sail of his wings cleared the rooftree on the Weyr building.

"C'reel, St'ven, mount up! Golanth? *Golanth?*" He felt the sudden air pressure on his body and didn't need to look to know that his bronze had landed on the ground beside him. He couldn't resist a proud grin at such accuracy. "We're going to the Sunrise Cliff Seahold. Take your directions from me," he added, stuffing the aerial map into a thigh pocket. *Remember where the fireball was when we got here first, Golanth?*

Of course.

Put it in the same place above Sunrise Cliff Seahold and let's go then! F'lessan vividly imagined the grass-topped rock face with white sands for contrast.

Golanth sprang upward, once again going *between* a leg-length above the ground. In the cold *between*, F'lessan had just time enough to wonder if the dragons were all embarked on something like Moreta's Ride. What had she used for a time-mark? Or had its absence caused her death?

IN THE CONFERENCE ROOM AT LANDING — LOCAL TIME 1:10 — 1.9.31

After seeing Master Wansor leave with D'ram and Lytol to return to Cove Hold to organize its evacuation, Lessa's mind raced with all the details that had already been sorted out. She'd need time, of another sort, to organize her thoughts. How F'lessan must be loving this license, she thought sardonically. Erragon or Idarolan would be here soon enough to explain how bad this tsunami-tidal wave-wall of water phenomenon might be. She turned off the monitor. She'd had enough of its depressing show of figures for the time being. She felt the klah pot and decided its contents were still warm enough to be drinkable. Who knew when she might have time to eat or drink in the time-tossed turmoil that had just been set into motion? She sipped as she reviewed the last hectic half hour. She thought they'd done rather well, leaping into action after the initial shock.

F'lar had gone to muster Benden Weyr, sending sweep-riders to warn the most obviously vulnerable holdings along the Nerat and Benden coastline. Few on the rest of the planet would have any idea what had just happened in the Eastern Sea. It was Monaco that would suffer the first huge wave. T'gellan had thirty-four experienced older bronze riders to manage evacuations. F'lar would ask J'fery at Telgar and G'dened at Ista to send more bronzes to assist. Manora and Brekke would organize supplies, food, medicines, and healers. She would organize Landing. She had before. Ramoth had called Benden's junior queens to help with dragons coming and going. Jaxom and Sharra would bring Sebell. They'd have to call a conference with Lord Holders and Craftmasters— that is, as soon as she had enough details.

She finished the last of her klah and turned as she heard the door click open. Erragon stood there, his face expressively conveying that his "details" were not going to be good news. Resolutely, he closed the door and strode over to the Mercator projection, fumbling to extract a red marker from his pocket.

"I'm afraid," he said, "that while Monaco Bay is in the direct line of only one main wave, it will also be inundated by several waves, diffracted by the inner Ring islands." He put his red marker on the islands and made a rapid downward stroke, ending at the coastline. "I figure the first wave—"

"First wave?" Lessa exclaimed.

"Um, yes, first wave of five, to be accurate." While Lessa was speechless, he hurried on. "The first will strike at Monaco Bay at four hours fifteen minutes, local time—three hours and twenty five minutes after impact—and hit the Jordan River mouth an hour and a half later. Rather spectacularly, in fact." He paused. "I can't help it, Lady Lessa."

"That's just the first wave?" she asked grimly.

"Stinar's trying to do a diagram so you—so we all—can

see how the waves will be spaced and reflect against the shore. One comes in a straight line from the impact site. The others won't be as strong, of course, as the unimpeded tsunami." He tapped the headland that jutted out into the sea east of Monaco Bay. "The cape may provide some protection, but the harbor facility . . ." He shrugged with regret. "I'm confident that the dolphins will warn ships at sea. We know they do. They will surely have *felt* the impact. They are so tuned in to their medium. Ships may not experience more turbulence or be much the worse for it. It's when a tsunami meets the shore, or shoals or shallows, that it crests and runs in. As to Cove Hold, Lady Lessa, it's shielded by the point east of the coast and the islands between—" He tapped it by way of demonstration. "—from some of the waves that Monaco Bay will experience. Additionally, the underwater extension of the eastern point at the Upwelling will break incoming waves. Spectacular breakers but much less actual wave height until fairly far west along the coast. Most of what the Cove will see is a splash wave as a result of the secondary wave breaks." He gave her a swift ingratiating smile.

Lessa shifted restlessly in her chair. Devastated by Erragon's talk of *five* tsunamis striking Monaco Bay, she felt perversely irritated by the fact that they had only recently restored the Hold to its pre-hurricane elegance.

"I suppose the news about Cove Hold provides a little relief." Instantly aware of how bitter she sounded, she held up her hand, "Which is none of your fault, to be sure." She nodded at him to continue. Better to hear the worst and clear her mind to plan how to proceed.

"Now, there will be flooding west of Cove Hold." His pen crossed the open area to the out-jutting of Southern. "These two coastlines will also be flooded," his pen moved again, "possibly with less force."

"The new Dolphin Hall?" she asked, hoping that young Readis's new project would survive.

"I believe it's on the west side so this headland," and he marked the spot to the right of the mouth of the Rubicon river, "will protect it. There might be a very high tide but the dolphins will surely have spread the warning."

"That's their bargain with humans," Lessa said drolly.

"However, to go on west," Erragon continued, almost as inexorably as that wretched tsunami, Lessa thought to herself, "Macedonia will experience four different waves, but I understand that coastline is not well settled."

"Then Monaco has not been singled out?" Lessa asked caustically. She had to find some balance in this calamity; her mind roiled with all they would have to do. At least this time they would be able to rescue those most vulnerable, unlike the hurricane that had taken them by surprise. She had to keep that thought foremost in her mind.

"Oh, no," Erragon assured her. "The most direct wave will arrive in Macedonia about nine hours after impact, about four in the afternoon local time. Then a direct tsunami will strike Southern Hold about eleven hours after impact—four in the afternoon local time. The second will arrive about fifteen minutes later and the third at about four fifty, local time."

"Toric is going to be furious," Lessa commented, but that caused her none of the heartache that she had felt on hearing about Monaco Bay.

"On the Northern continent," Erragon went on as he shifted his all too busy red marker upward, "a tsunami will strike the Foot of Nerat, and all the way up the shore." Lessa sat straight up as she saw him reddening the entire eastern coastline.

"But there's time," Erragon assured her. "Three to four hours *after* impacting on the southern shores, the other section of the waves will reach High Shoal in front of Loscar and demolish it—which, I understand from seamen, might reduce the dangerous currents the Shoal produces. Loscar will definitely need to be evacuated but there's time enough to get people to foothills. Even a good portion of their belongings and herdbeasts. You see, there's not much to stop the straight line of the tsunami as it radiates due west from the impact site."

Lessa stared, disbelieving the extent of a "wave."

"Ista," Erragon continued, producing a tentative smile, "will only get ripples produced by reflection off Nerat's Toe. They did suffer far more damage during the hurricane." He paused briefly, and turned to the other side of the Mercator projection. Lessa gasped.

"The Western Ring of islands will absorb much of the tsunami's force, though, from the tip of Tillek and south to the end of Southern Boll, they can expect to experience tsunami about sixteen hours after impact, or four-thirty in the morning their local time. It will reach the west coast of Fort, much of which is rocky, about twenty-one hours after impact, seven in the morning their time. Tomorrow."

"Tomorrow?" Lessa echoed.

"Yes, it takes time even for something as violent as a tsunami to cross that much sea. The farther away from the impact point or the secondary points, the less the expected effect of the incoming wave. It will spread out and reduce amplitude until it encounters an obstacle."

"Like Monaco Bay," Lessa murmured bitterly.

"For instance," Erragon said, trying to interject a positive note, "the west coast of Southern, from Ierne Island to the tip on the east side of Great Bay, will feel only a small effect from the eastward wave." Now he looked closely at the map and, checking longitude and latitude, made a little X. "The two waves, what's left of them after losing much of their energy, will intersect in the open sea at about Longitude two degrees at Latitude fifteen degrees, but I don't think that'll be notable."

Lessa regarded him blankly. Erragon continued.

"The worst of all this should be over in about sixteen to seventeen hours," he said in an attitude of encouragement.

"I hope you'll be able to repeat this, Erragon," she said wearily. "We are obliged to inform those Lord Holders most affected. Now that we know who they are."

He bowed his willingness. She closed her eyes briefly while she contacted Ramoth to bespeak the dragons at the various Holds. It saved some time, at least, that Benden had the right to convene an emergency meeting and expect those invited to respond speedily. Even as speedily as that sharding wave was going to smash along both coasts.

When she opened her eyes, Erragon's expression showed deep concern. He was rather a good man, she thought, and not like some who could thoroughly enjoy spreading bad news.

"Sit down, man, and I'll get us something more to eat. We'll need to fortify ourselves." She left the room, giving him a few moments alone.

Twenty minutes later, Master Idarolan and Erragon had contrived to red mark the vulnerable portions of coastline along both continents, including some quick estimates of how deep inland the flood would surge. To Lessa's intense sorrow, they had intricately marked the projected paths of the five different assaults on Monaco. F'lar had returned with F'nor. No sooner had the two Benden riders started to eat a hasty luncheon from the food Lessa had found than Lords Ciparis and Toronas arrived. Close behind them came Haligon, representing Lord Groghe, Jaxom, and Sharra; Lord Ranrel of Tillek with the new Masterfishman Curran; Fortine of Ista; Langrell of Igen; Kashman of Keroon; Janissian from Southern Boll as Lord Sangel was too old to travel anywhere, even a-dragonback, and the other six Weyrleaders.

"What's this about some sharding wave going to destroy the coast?" demanded Fortine. "Surely it can't reach from the Ring Sea all the way to my coast?"

"Come, come," Master Idarolan said, gesturing impatiently to the newcomers. "All of you be seated." He waved at Haligon to distribute chairs from those stacked in one corner.

"It had better be good," Toronas of Benden said, "getting us up and down here so precipitously."

"Oh, it is, I assure you," Lessa said in such a caustic tone that no one else spoke as they hurried to get settled around the table.

"At least it was already morning for you, Toronas," Jaxom said, seating Sharra, who was blinking to clear her eyes from what little sleep she had had. "Not the middle of the night and yet you see Ranrel, Haligon, and Janissian wide awake and with us."

Lord Toronas clearly wanted to object to the presence of Janissian, who looked younger than she was, even if she had been sent to represent her grandfather, Lord Sangel.

"Sit by me, Toronas," Lessa said, smiling encouragingly at Janissian who remained close to Sharra and Jaxom. The Southern Boll girl composed herself to listen but her eyes were darting to the red-streaked maps and then back to the other members of this emergency meeting. Ranrel nodded a greeting to her and Kashman stared boldly.

"If you will begin again, Journeyman Erragon," Lessa said formally, "then everyone will have a better understanding of why this meeting is so vital. Some of us have less time than others and none of us have time to waste."

Just as Erragon was about to explain how the multiple waves would inundate the southern coastline, a rumbling *boom* made him stagger. Lessa clutched at the arm of her chair as the awesome noise vibrated through the soles of her feet.

"What was that?" she cried. They could both hear the shouts and screams from the hallway.

"That," Erragon said on his way to the door, "was the ground shock wave from the fireball impact." He glanced at the clock. "Right on time! Excuse me!" He hauled open the door. "It's all right! That's the shock wave reaching us!" He shouted to those milling in fright in the hall and closed the door behind him, leaving Lessa to contemplate the multiple disasters of the day.

SUNRISE CLIFF SEAHOLD — TIMED-BACK

The three dragons arrived at Sunrise Cliff Seahold circumspectly, above the first rank of dunes that marked high tides. The dunes would no doubt be wiped away, dragged back by the tsunami, F'lessan thought. The dragons glided along the shore to where the granite escarpment had been broken during an earthquake, tumbling boulders, creating the wide shallow bay and a defile along which a stream now found its way to the sea. Beyond the stream, the escarpment began to rise again, ending in another height on the eastern arm. Along the white sand beach, they could see small fishing craft pulled up. Don't let them talk you into rescuing their boats, T'gellan had said, but maybe they could somehow sling . . .

Not before people, Golanth told him sternly. *People we save today.*

It looked like the entire population of the Seahold was out, standing on the dunes, gazing northward. White sands sloped down to the little waves lapping serenely up the wide beach with a picturesqueness that would shortly be devastated. They had barely two hours to evacuate. F'lessan sensed that was not going to be easy. Who would believe his tale of catastrophe in the making? Everyone was so intent on the fiery ball inclining now toward its impact. The air was so crystalline clear!

There were twelve holds leaning up against the orange cliffs where the granite began to rise from the sands. These seaholders had done well in the fifteen or so Turns since they'd settled here, F'lessan thought. They wouldn't abandon their prosperity so easily. Babes were being held up to see the fireball, and a scatter of children, in various states of dress, had followed their parents to behold the wonder! Near to a hundred people in all, F'lessan estimated quickly. Some of the older folk would have a hard time scrambling up the switchback way to the safety of the cliff height.

Dolphins! Golanth said. Startled, F'lessan switched his gaze to the sea. Scarcely fifty meters offshore, where the shallows sloped into deeper, bluer water, the curving bodies of eight or ten dolphins dove in and out: but not idly. He could hear their high-pitched screeing. He was accustomed enough to their graceful movements to realize that their antics today were frantic. Three rose, tail-walking, then splashed heavily back into the water, their dorsal fins cutting the waves they made. Their squeeing was shrill though he couldn't hear what they might be saying.

So they know! Relief diminished at least that worry from F'lessan's mind. Natua and her calf, all the Monaco Bay pod, would be somewhere safe. *I can't hear them but it's obvious this pod is trying to warn the seaholders!*

If they are, no one's watching them, Golanth said, gliding in to a landing. *We will be more noticeable.*

"Look!" One of the youngsters had noticed the dolphins. "Da, da, the dolphins! They're squeaking their warning calls. But there's no storm! What's wrong with them?" So the boy was the first to see the dragons out of the corner of his eye, heard the grunts as dragon feet made contact and skidded in the soft sand, backwinging adroitly to a halt.

"They are warning you," F'lessan shouted, hands cupped about his mouth. *"That fireball in the sky. It will land in the sea and cause tidal waves. Worse than the worst storm you've ever been in."*

"We can hear you, dragonrider," said one of the men, turning slightly toward F'lessan without taking his eyes off the fascinating orange ball that was far more of a spectacle than three dragons.

"They've gone!" cried the youngster with keen disappointment. He whirled at the dragonriders as if their appearance had frightened the dolphins.

F'lessan was intensely relieved that not a single dorsal fin remained visible. They might be cutting it fine to reach safe depths, but they'd kept their pact with humans once again in giving an alarm.

"The dolphins . . . the shipfish," he continued in a voice loud enough to reach those still mesmerized by the vision, "are warning you. Surely you know they consider that their duty to all sea folk." He pointed at the man who had challenged him.

"Yeyah, they let us know where fish schools, when squalls're coming, but never seen 'em act like that before." The man preferred to watch the sinking fireball than attend the dragonrider.

"Look, man, it's not just Thread that falls from the skies!"

F'lessan said. "We're here to move you to the cliffs, up there, high enough to be away from the wave."

"Wave?" Another man walked toward F'lessan, his expression patronizingly amiable. "We're well above the high tide . . ."

"Not this one," F'lessan said.

"Ah, now, bronze rider, I can see you ain't even wearing Monaco's badge. What call have you to—"

"We're Monaco!" C'reel said and St'ven nodded emphatically. "Listen to F'lessan, Golanth's rider!"

"We're evacuating you," St'ven added. "All the coastal holds. Every Weyr is helping!"

F'lessan swung his leg over and slid down, gesturing for the brown riders to dismount. Maybe face-to-face, not perched on a bronze dragon, he could instill some urgency for the present crisis.

"Who's Seaholder?" he asked, striding as fast as he could across the soft sand to the crowd.

"Me!" The first man jerked a thick, scarred thumb at his tanned chest. He wore the customary sleeveless top and shorts. He had strong hairy legs and was barefoot, toes splayed in the sand. "Binness, Journeyman, FishCrafthall!"

"Journeyman Binness, we are acting under orders from T'gellan, your Weyrleader and—" F'lessan had a sudden surge of inspiration—"MasterFishman Curran, to evacuate all your people to high ground." He gestured broadly to the western arm of the cliff, higher by a half dragon-length than the eastern one.

Binness chortled. "Don't try that one on me, bronze rider. The Master's way east at Tillek as he should be."

"It makes no difference where he *should* be, Journeyman," C'reel said, losing patience. "He *is* at Landing, meeting with everyone trying to save lives."

"Binness, wake up and listen!" F'lessan said. "When that thing hits the ocean," and he pointed to the bit of the fireball still visible on the horizon, "the biggest wave you ever had nightmares about is going to come straight to this bay. There's no Ring island in its way to break its crest and this holding is going to be *drowned*!" He scissored both hands together to indicate the totality of the disaster. He caught sight of his watch, visible as his jacket cuff pulled up. "In one minute, that fireball hits the ocean. You might be able to see the cloud of steam that the impact creates!" Again he pointed northward.

"It's gone!" a woman cried, flagging her hand in a pathetic farewell to the novelty the fireball had presented to an isolated community.

F'lessan closed his eyes at the waste of time. Two hours to move over a hundred people, and whatever possessions they could grab, and he hadn't even managed to get them to see the gravity of their peril.

"You've a far-seer," he shouted, abruptly noticing the one slung in a holster at Binness's side. "Take a *good* look!"

Binness did use the glass, more as an accommodation to the dragonrider's whim than because he expected to see anything. It took him more precious time to focus the instrument. Only because F'lessan knew exactly in which direction to look did he see the top of the rising cloud.

"Sompin's there, Binness," one of the net-bearers said. "He's right about that. You know my far-sight's good."

"Yeyah," Binness grudgingly admitted. "Probably a storm." He collapsed the telescope and returned it to its keeper.

"Dolphins was warning us then," another fisherman put in his opinion.

"Why . . . will . . . you . . . not . . . believe . . . me?" F'lessan demanded, spacing his words as he sensed the passage of such valuable time. "Pack your belongings! We'll convey children, your aunties and uncles first."

The reaction of the women was to hug their children to their legs, suddenly frightened of his presence. F'lessan struggled to control his aggravation. Didn't they trust dragonriders? T'gellan was a good Weyrleader.

"Look, spread out that fishnet," he said, pointing to the nearest man with one draped across his shoulder. "That will carry a lot."

"Ever had a ride a-dragonback?" C'reel asked, hunkering down by the youngster who had seen the dolphins.

F'lessan kept checking his watch. Maybe he'd just have to wait for the shock wave to hit to prove that an emergency existed. Being nearer the point of impact, this Seahold would feel it a lot sooner and harder here. It'd be seismic, wouldn't it, traveling ten times faster than sound along the rock of the seabed. They'd feel it, then hear it!

Right up through his boots—and the bare feet of most of the seaholders—came the shake! A *boom* that beat eardrums with its intensity. Several people fell to the sands; even the dragons were unbalanced, raising wings to steady themselves.

"D'you believe me now, Binness?" F'lessan demanded, brushing sand off his leathers.

Two of the women began to keen, nearly as unnerving a sound as dragons made when one of their kind died.

"Believe you, dragonrider!" The Journeyman could also see the disturbed ripple of the waves in the bay. "*Go! Go!* Pack!" Wide gestures of his arms sent the women scattering. "Lias, spread that net. Lads, go with your mothers. Collect everything you can carry. Petan, get the other nets. You sure your dragons are strong, bronze rider?"

"As strong as they need to be, Journeyman," F'lessan replied, grinning. He gestured for C'reel and St'ven to help spread nets. "We'll need rope . . ."

"Line . . ." C'reel corrected him when Lias looked puzzled.

"Line, then, in the corners, to make a knot for the dragons to lift the nets with. Where's the most sheltered place up on those cliffs, Binness? Are there woods? You'll need shelter. There will be winds and rain, not to mention the high seas."

"Plenty shelter a-top," Binness said, deftly flipping another net wide on the sands.

A lad came running up with a rocking chair.

"No, no, furniture will come last," F'lessan cried, waving the boy and the chair to one side. "Bring pots, pans, food, necessities," he called as the scared boy dropped the chair and sprinted back to the largest cothold.

"That's my old dam's chair," Binness said, pausing to prop

his fists challengingly against the wide belt, which had knife sheaths as well as the telescope holster.

"Where is she?" F'lessan demanded.

"Coming. Lady Medda's coming." Binness pointed to the largest cothold. Two women, their hands making a seat, were hurrying out with an old woman, white braids bouncing. "Joint-ail but she runs us right well!"

"She can be the first to go." If the woman managed the hold, then F'lessan would station her where she could do some good.

"She'll show you where!" Binness shouted back, grinning maliciously before he grabbed a piece of line and tied it to the back of the rocking chair. "Where?" he asked F'lessan.

Shards! But it wasted time to argue with him. F'lessan swung his arm in Golanth's direction. "Loop it on the third neck ridge. I'll take her myself and the two carrying her."

He ended up with far more draped on his bronze than the delighted Lady Medda, whose wrinkled face suggested nine or ten decades of living. She was in high spirits as she settled on Golanth's back, shouting orders to those who jumped to obey.

"Use tablecloths for the food and loose things. Bring the water skins. Stuff each pot with what comes to hand. Dragon-riders don't haul empty space when you can fill it with something useful."

C'reel's brown Galuth had two younger women on his back, with two children apiece, and rough packs hung from the neck ridges and trailed down his backbone. St'ven was leaning over Mealth's side at a dangerous angle to be sure nothing was spilling out of the first of the packed nets the dragon lifted from the sand.

It took much more time to disencumber the dragons on the summit. To his disgust, F'lessan found the knots with which Binness had tied the rocking chair were hard to undo. Awaiting her usual seat, Lady Medda was upright on the trunk of a fallen tree and continued her stream of succinct orders, using a frond to keep the biting insects from her. Beyond her, Mealth carefully maneuvered his net to the ground,

and landed beyond it to let his passengers off. The old lady
gave a whoop of a cheer for such precise flying. F'lessan
struggled with the knot until the youngster who'd seen the
dolphins came running over. With a pitying look and a flip of
one trailing end, the boy released the knot and the rocking
chair was loose.

"You should know how!" he accused F'lessan and ran the
chair to his grandmother.

F'lessan rued not his ignorance of sea knots but the time
consumed fussing with them. Time! Time! He vaulted—
not as effortlessly as usual—astride Golanth. The bronze ran
toward the precipice, wings wide, and fell off the edge. When
F'lessan heard shocked cries of alarm from behind him at
Golanth's timesaving exit, he grinned.

Binness and the other men had filled two more nets and
held up the knots for the browns to grab. F'lessan managed
five children, two more women, and a string of sacks down
Golanth's back on the next trip. He could see women and
girls filing up the uneven steps zigzagging up the cliffside,
everyone laden with so many bundles he wondered how they
moved.

On his way back down to the sands, he saw that one of the
fishing dories had been manhandled up over the dune high-
tide barrier. Four men were racing seaward, obviously to get a
second one. "Don't let them talk you into conveying their
boats," T'gellan had warned him.

"We can't handle *that*!" F'lessan cried, leaping off Golanth's
back to confront a belligerent Binness. Beside him was Lias,
equally determined.

"No boats, no fish, we starve."

"We sailed 'em all the way down from Big Bay, dragonrider," Lias put in, his wizened face fierce. "Days of sailing.
We can't abandon them."

Gasping for breath, the other four arrived with a second dory.

"The masts're unstepped," Binness said, as if that made
transport feasible. It would make them less unwieldy. "We

can rig the hulls to be lifted like you did the nets. We got the line."

F'lessan delayed his answer, wiping sweat off his face and neck. Did they have the time? He glanced at the two small craft, then at his watch. These seaholders were about to lose their cotholds, and neither of the dories was longer than a dragon's body. He saw they were clap-sided, only the sharp V of the transom covered. They couldn't weigh that much. Lias grabbed a cleat, slung a line quickly about it as if this proof would be sufficient to sway F'lessan's doubt.

"You said dragons're as strong as they need be! Be they strong enough, dragonrider?" Binness's eyes were wide and fierce with an entreaty and a challenge that F'lessan could not resist.

F'lessan swallowed.

"Rope 'em, then. We'll give it a try. Be quick about it."

"Three dragons? Three sma' little dories?" Binness cried, eyes suddenly full of hope again. "Outta the nine boats we got?"

F'lessan groaned. He couldn't believe he was agreeing.

"Quick, a-fore he changes his mind," Binness cried, sending off the four who were still gasping for breath. They turned to stagger back down the dune. He and Lias began to secure lines. He paused, tossed a coil of rope at F'lessan. "Start on the second one. Be sure the lines are the same length."

And F'lessan found himself wrapping lines around cleats on the second dory.

"Everyone out of the holds? Everything you need?" F'lessan cried as the exhausted fishmen arrived with the third hull, collapsing against it, wheezing, their sweating bodies covered with sand where they'd stumbled.

"You, go check!" Binness ordered and the man crawled gamely to his feet and staggered toward the nearest cot. "Lias, tighten that line. You, rig the portside. You, do a running bowline through the anchor bracket. Make it *real* tight!"

When C'reel and Galuth arrived to find the first ship rigged to be conveyed, the brown rider obviously thought F'lessan was asking too much of them. All sorts of odds and ends, buckets, rakes, hand nets, a pair of sandals, more nets, fish spears, small buoys, floats, light anchors, and even some folded sails had been dumped in the dories.

"Nothing really heavy," F'lessan said, peering over the new cargo as he wondered how all that had been stashed in when he was looking elsewhere.

"We can do it, C'reel. Galuth can do it! *Up* you go, Galuth!" And he gave the Wingleader's signal to lift.

Golanth added a roar and Galuth was aloft so fast C'reel's head snapped, but the brown dragon had the knot in his claws and the dory was rising, swinging erratically in the air. Galuth waited until its swaying lessened and slowly rose, leading the sway slightly. If he didn't get the height, the ship could be dashed to bits on the cliff. It just cleared the edge. The fishmen cheered and then Mealth positioned himself to receive the knot for the second.

F'lessan nervously eyed the still-calm surface of the wide bay until a spray of sand announced the return of the man who had gone to check the cotholds.

"Everyone's out, Binness."

"Then we're for the steps, dragonrider. Mount and I'll give the knot to your bronze."

Just then the sea seemed to creep up the sands, leaving behind a wide lacy border. Binness stared at it.

F'lessan swept his eyes across the sea but he could see nothing that looked like the crest of a tsunami. The shoals were at least fifty meters out, where the dolphins had been swimming. And shoals were bad when a tsunami was rolling shoreward.

"Lift, dragonrider," cried Binness, knot in one hand, waving urgently with the other.

F'lessan obeyed, Golanth rising and craning his head down, trying to look between his front legs. F'lessan felt Golanth catch the knot and take up the slack in the lines. They had barely risen a few feet from the sands when they saw Binness, arms and legs pumping as the fishman raced toward the steps.

It isn't that heavy, Golanth reassured his rider, but it took him time to lift so as not to unbalance his load or lose his grip on the rope cradle. The summit was alive with people and goods, leaving no clear spot for the dory. Shouting orders from her rocking chair, the old woman solved the problem. It was with great relief that F'lessan felt the tension ease in the bronze shoulders as Golanth succeeded in getting the third dory landed. Golanth soared up, bugling with his success. Well, it wouldn't be their problem to get the dories back down to the shore.

Not today!

Golanth tilted northward, dipping low around the granite outcrop, so that they could see the last of the seaholders reach the top of the rough stairs, crawling a little farther from the cliff edge. Rider and dragon could see Binness still racing for the first step. The man stumbled, obviously winded, and re-gained his balance with difficulty.

That's when F'lessan saw the water being sucked back, away from the beach, all along the shoreline.

He will not make it!

Golanth did not wait for an order but dove sideways toward the man who was straining with effort, head up, arms car-ried tight to his chest, elbows flaring to suck air into his la-bored lungs, knees pumping.

The bronze intercepted him, dipping to secure the man in his front paws.

Binness looked up at the outstretched claws, panic con-torting his face. Out of the corner of his eye, F'lessan could see the wall of water that was rising higher, higher, higher and coming straight at them. He saw the cliff looming up: if the tsunami didn't drown them, they'd smash against the cliff. Having slowed to catch Binness, Golanth did not have enough air speed to gain altitude!

Between had never been so cold or so comforting. Eight seconds, four deep gasping breaths, and then a watery deluge all but drowning them.

The wave is nearly as high as this cliff, Golanth said, sounding amused. He had changed position to bring them out of *between* not far from the point where they had first entered over Sunrise Cliff Seahold.

The bronze had also *timed* that rescue! On his own initiative!

Dazed, F'lessan stared down at the tremendous tsunami wave that should, by any rights, have drowned them. Water splashed high, its topmost point lapping the summit. Behind the first, a second tsunami roared ashore, battering the land, taking with it the steps that had so recently led the way to safety.

I will put him down near the others, Golanth said, backwinging, hovering in front of the terrified seaholders who were clutching at each other, watching as the crest of the second wave just missed the summit. Mealth and Galuth had spread their wings high, providing some cover from the windblown spray for the ancient woman sitting very upright in her chair that was rocking in the wind. *I hope my claws did not scratch him badly.*

He's lucky to be alive to be scratched, F'lessan responded weakly. He couldn't quite believe they had survived the double peril. One more second and the three of them would have been pasted on the cliff face!

I knew you wouldn't mind getting here before that happened. Golanth turned his huge head to his left as the tsunami flooded inland, boiling up the streambed. Almost daintily, Golanth turned on his forequarters and paused midair, lowering Binness safely to the damp ground.

F'lessan stared down at the man, supine on the thick drenched ground cover. There were indeed red marks on Binness's bare arms, where the dragon had clutched him. The bronze rider sagged across Golanth's neck ridge. He was aware of a booming noise, not like the shock wave but frightening in its intensity. Water splashed high on the cliff again, as if seeking to regain a victim that only the initiative and quickness of his dragon had rescued. He did feel Golanth land; he was aware of Golanth tucking his wings loosely along his back, of the darkness that had replaced the bright sun, of the cries of those who had seen the tsunami curl and nearly inundate their summit refuge. These were dim, background noises to the rush of blood pounding in his body, the dryness in his throat, the extreme weariness he felt.

Breathe deep, said his dragon with proud affection. *We're all safe now.*

"Who has the wineskin?" The rasping voice cut through his self-absorption. "Help him down. Can't you see he's wore hisself out saving us. Give him a drink. Cona, go help your man. He thinks he's dead of drowning."

"It was real close, Granddam," a young voice said.

A hand tugged at his sleeve. "Dragonrider, here's the wineskin."

St'ven and C'reel had to help him down, Golanth crouching as low as possible to make that easier. The brown riders propped him up against his dragon and put the spout of the wineskin against his lips. He opened his mouth to accept a sip of wine. It was a rough sort, but its effect was more important than its quality.

"Get a cup, someone!" Lady Medda ordered. "Can't have a dragonrider who saved our lives drink like a sot right from the skin!"

"Get several cups . . ." St'ven yelled over his shoulder.

"Could only find one," said a woman, a moment later extending it to the brown rider. "Everything's mixed up."

"But it's here," said Lady Medda. "Lias, Petan, haul Binness back outta all that splashing. Then come back and carry me to shelter. Don't aim to sit in all this wet any longer'n I have to. You fixing to stay longer, dragonriders, you'd better get under cover, too. Never saw a storm blow up so fast."

"It'll pass," F'lessan whispered to C'reel who repeated his words loud enough to be heard.

The wine revived F'lessan sufficiently to get to his feet, propping himself against Golanth, hoping no one but his bronze noticed his trembling.

Ramoth says to come back to Landing, Golanth said. Evidently an order which Mealth and Galuth heard because the brown riders straightened up at the same time.

"We are ordered to return to Landing . . ." F'lessan began.

"Can ye get that far?"

F'lessan turned himself toward the sound of her anxious voice.

"Yes!"

Lady Medda had pushed herself to her feet—she had a cane on which she leaned heavily—as she extended her right arm in a gesture that still retained a vestige of youthful grace.

"We owe you, dragonriders. We owe you much." Behind her, the wet and bedraggled seaholders paused in transferring their belongings and, as one, bowed!

"We owe you much, dragonriders."

The dignified simplicity of their tribute rewarded all three riders for the effort they had made to save the ships. Then Lias and Petan waited until Binness's dam had reseated herself before they carried her into the shelter of the forest.

"Send the lads out to see what fruit's on the ground. Find enough dry wood to build a fire . . ." Lady Medda was saying as she went.

"Thought you were dead, F'lessan," C'reel murmured, his face wet. "Here, get your arms in your jacket or you'll freeze solid *between*."

When St'ven saw F'lessan's hands trembling, he did the jacket fastenings, then found F'lessan's helmet and put that on, too. Then he and C'reel heaved the bronze rider astride Golanth. "You're some Wingleader, F'lessan. Proud to fly with you!"

"I, too, bronze rider," C'reel said and saluted before he ran to his waiting brown.

IN THE CONFERENCE ROOM—LOCAL TIME 2:12 AT LANDING—1.9.31

"*I've* got to break the news to Toric?" F'nor demanded, staring first at his half brother, then at Idarolan who nodded emphatically.

"You and K'van are the logical messengers," F'lar said.

"I'd send G'bol as my emissary but he's . . ." He quirked one eyebrow expressively. ". . . making time."

K'van shrugged, raising both hands in reluctant acceptance. The expression on his angular, tanned face did not suggest great enthusiasm for the task. "We could take Sintary with us. He's used to dealing with Toric."

"He respects me," Idarolan said with one of his fierce growls. "Get him organized and we can proceed on to assist at Southern Boll," he added with a quick sideways glance at young Janissian. He'd heard good things about her, taking hold with her grandmother ever since old Sangel became so erratic. This might be an excellent time for the girl to show her leadership qualities. She was the best of Sangel's blood. "Unless, of course, Master Curran," and he deferred amiably to the successor of his rank, "you have need of me."

"I have need of you, Master Idarolan," Ciparis of Nerat put in quickly, almost apologetically. "Nerat has more coastline to be affected." He glanced at F'lar. "We'll need so much help."

"Sweepriders are already out informing holders," F'lar said, "but, Master Idarolan, if you will share those invaluable charts of yours?"

"They can be copied, indeed, they can." Idarolan slid out the relevant sheets.

Idarolan was, F'lar thought, the only one who had come at all prepared to this meeting. An early riser by nature, he was in the habit of scanning the morning skies for weather signs, so he had seen the fireball. He was also aware of the phenomenon of tsunami and had immediately consulted his charts and logbooks. As Erragon had done, he had used red for the most vulnerable seacoast, orange for danger, and blue for easily accessible highlands. Before the Benden Weyrleader appeared to ask for his help, he had a pretty good idea how serious the situation was.

"Here!" With a deft finger Idarolan extracted an open sheet and flicked it toward F'nor. "Toric likes charts and maps and details. This'll give you what he needs to know. He'd have— let's see . . ." Idarolan turned his eyes up, mentally figuring.

"Eleven hours, minus the time of this meeting," Erragon said with an apologetic nod to the old MasterFishman for giving the answer, "before the tsunamis meet the shoreline of his hold."

"At that he'll get off lightly. And consider himself ill-used to be assaulted from east and west," Lessa said, her expression inscrutable. F'nor gave her a long wide-eyed look. She responded with a smirk as Erragon agreed with her.

"But not entirely. He has many seaside holdings."

"Southern Boll will be hit harder," Idarolan said, nodding solemnly at Janissian. "And Tillek."

"More rock face than shallows along that south-facing coast of ours," Ranrel said, speaking almost for the first time; he'd been taking copious notes. "We are very lucky that there has been such advance warning."

"The *Yokohama* has more than justified her continued existence," Idarolan said with a slightly sanctimonious air, glancing sideways at Kashman of Keroon.

"I wonder what the Abominators will say about this," Jaxom remarked in a deliberately languid tone.

Into the dismayed silence that greeted that comment, F'nor noisily pushed back his chair, reached across the table for the sheets Idarolan had sent in his direction and finished the last of the klah in his cup.

"C'mon, then! We can send a fire-lizard to apprise Sintary of our arrival." He looked to Lessa and F'lar.

"Might as well," Idarolan said, also rising to his feet. "I shan't be long, Lord Ciparis, and then I'm yours to command. But I'll point out that the Keys, and Long Beach at the head of Nerat River, will reduce the violence of the tsunami there. The Tip of Nerat, Bent Ridge, Grethel, Saluda, and Berea will be affected and the river may flood all the way up to Waneta. I'll be back."

"I'll return Janissian to Southern Boll," Jaxom said, "once we've copies of all this for you and Curran, Ranrel, and for us."

BACK AT LANDING—LOCAL TIME—3:40

The instinct that saved dragons from colliding during Threadfall kept Golanth and his rider from disaster as they came out of *between* over a Landing that, at first, seemed covered by dragon wings, like a vast multicolored sunshade.

Ramoth says to land on the square. We are to rest! And, without waiting for F'lessan's comment, Golanth pivoted wearily on one wing tip, gliding over to the edge of the wide Gather square. F'lessan had time enough in that spin to see Ramoth, perched behind and above Admin, wings half open as she constantly swung her head from side to side across the area below her. Two more queens—the juniors from Benden who were accustomed to working with Ramoth—sat on either side, slightly below her position. They also were watching and, quite likely, directing dragon traffic in and out of Landing.

Golanth was making his way toward the roasting pits and the nearest open space.

She is here.

Wearily F'lessan blinked his eyes at the several green dragons immediately below him.

Both shes? F'lessan asked, trying to inject some humor into his voice. His body felt as battered as if they had been rolled by a tsunami.

Both. I land. Should you see a healer?

I'll be fine when I've had some rest.

Golanth's thought rumbled with disbelief but he landed, flicking his wings up so that the tips and claws touched over his head and he didn't touch the greens on either side of his chosen landing site. Zaranth was on his right, several shades lighter than she had been that morning. The other green had curled her head under one wing and was asleep, her rider's head pillowed on her wrist. With narrowed, blurry eyes, Zaranth watched Golanth settle. When the green extended her head to nuzzle the bronze's shoulder, F'lessan, tired as he was, felt a spurt of surprise. The touch was more caress than acknowledgment.

She likes me, Golanth said.

F'lessan saw that the green cradled Tai on her forelegs, the girl's sprawled figure covered by two beautifully marked feline pelts.

So, F'lessan thought, she did save them.

"F'lessan?" Someone pulled at his leg. He looked down at S'lan, amazed to see his son in the south. The boy and his brown Norenth were only just out of the weyrling barracks.

"What are you doing here?"

Grinning proudly, S'lan held up a small cup.

"All of us were brought down to help. Healer says to drink this down and then dismount and eat."

He climbed onto Golanth's foreleg to hand the cup to the bronze rider and F'lessan tossed back the liquid. Just as well, he never would have sipped the beverage if he had sampled the taste of it. What a taste! Worse than the seaholder's wine! It did revive him enough to dismount, if only to eat something to get rid of the taste of it in his mouth. Golanth groaned as he sank to his belly, stretching out as much as he could without interfering with the tired dragons on either side of him. Using Golanth's shoulder as a prop, F'lessan slid down to a sitting position against his dragon.

"Help me out of my jacket, Sellie." I must remember to call him S'lan now, F'lessan thought. "Hang it on Golanth to dry, will you?"

That done, he took the breadroll the boy offered.

"You have to rest," S'lan said, scowling at his father and looking, at that moment, like his grandmother. He unslung the two canteens looped over his shoulder. "One's water. Don't drink the klah in the other one yet. It'll keep warm. Ramoth says every dragon and rider has time to rest."

"Ramoth says we have time? Good. Do I get back what time I lost?" F'lessan murmured facetiously, more to himself than for his son's ears. "Thanks, S'lan," he added.

F'lessan glanced slowly across the panorama of so many dragons sprawled in or near the square. Sticking the breadroll between his teeth, he put the canteens on the ground beside him. Was Lessa aware of how much his son looked like her? Dark haired, dark eyed, with a certain familiar tilt to the chin? Scamp!

"No one argues with Ramoth, you know," the boy said. "Gotta go! I'll be back."

It seemed to F'lessan more like a threat but he chewed a huge bite of the roll—the bread was crusty and still slightly warm. With his free hand, he slipped the sweat-soaked helmet off his head and spread it where it could dry. Shards! That tsunami shed a lot of water! Wearily, he looked over at Tai but she was sound asleep. She was lucky. Would he see that damned wave hovering over him if he slept? Or himself, Golanth, and Binness plastered like insects on the cliff? A vision out of a nightmare sure to become one! Golanth really was the best dragon on all Pern.

Of course I am, murmured the bronze immodestly.

F'lessan chuckled around the last piece of the breadroll that he barely tasted, he was so tired. He swallowed the last of it with a sip from the water canteen. He could hardly keep his eyes open. Had there been a dash of fellis in that healer's cup? He took a long swallow of water.

Golanth groaned and dropped his muzzle to one foreleg. F'lessan reached up to pat the right eye ridge, nuzzled himself into a comfortable spot against Golanth's shoulder, and immediately fell asleep.

HARPER HALL—5:00 IN THE MORNING, AND SOUTHERN HOLD—2:00 IN THE MORNING—1.9.31

At wintry Fort, F'nor and Idarolan informed Sebell of the dangers and the details. Idarolan had acquired sufficient extra copies of the projected tsunami path through the Southern and Western Seas to give a set to the MasterHarper. The Interface office had the only automatic copier, another of the many technological wonders that were coming in so very useful. Considering the panic of drum messages into the Harper Hall from those minor holds and halls that had drummers, Sebell needed accurate information to give them. It was still night in the west but the constant drums had interrupted the sleep of many and lights were on in cotholds as well as in Fort's great façade. A messenger came running up from the Healer Hall with queries from Master Oldive as to where he was to send healers to help in this emergency of which he'd like pertinent details so he could organize his craftsmen and -women.

"Have you time for something to eat and drink?" Sebell asked when the core of the emergency had been explained to him.

"No, it's earlier at Southern Hold and we'd best not delay explaining it all to Toric," F'nor said, grimacing.

"He'll demand to know why he's had to wait to learn about the fireball," Sebell added. Then he chuckled, his eyes bright in the gleam of the Hall's night lamps.

"I could use a laugh," F'nor said.

"I think he may regret having so many—ah, shall we say *undisclosed*—coastal holdings?" Sebell snorted, his expression amused. "Truth will out. K'van probably knows."

"We'd best go. He and Sintary will be waiting for us at the old Weyr site."

"We will try to defuse rumor with fact," Sebell said.

A task that F'nor did not envy him.

Idarolan gave a malicious smile. "Keep ears open for what those seaworm Abominators spread."

"It's a natural disaster, isn't it?" F'nor remarked.

"Reported by the *Yokohama*," Sebell demurred.

"And sharding fortunate we are to have at least one eye on the skies above," Idarolan said in his caustic fashion.

F'nor thought about timing it; there was no question in F'nor's mind that Toric's informers would eventually mention the exact minute and hour Landing had recognized the fireball as a threat, but he decided against making the effort just as Canth spoke.

*Ramoth said not to! We do not know what else we will have
to do today.*

All right, Canth. I'm chastised.

You are not! his dragon replied in mild protest.

You know me too well.

Another drum message rolled in and with a backward
wave, Sebell trotted up the steps to deal with it. Once sure
that Idarolan was seated comfortably again behind him,
F'nor gave Canth a vivid view of Southern Hold's rocky
cliffs—at night.

Ruth is not the only dragon who knows when he is, was
Canth's exit remark.

F'nor experienced an odd dislocation as they arrived over
Southern Hold; the peaceful sight of the riding lights of four
coastal ships anchored in the harbor and night glows up
the harbor steps: all serene here. Landing had been chaotic!
Fort Hold had been alive with activity and tension. Silently
and, F'nor hoped, unseen by anyone watching below, Canth
glided through the warm air over the sleeping Hold and on
to the original Southern Weyr site. He was painfully aware
that right now, on the other side of the planet, Monaco Bay
Weyr would be experiencing the tsunami. There had been
enough dragons to rescue every man, woman, and child,
hadn't there?

The news he brought Toric was not as dire, though the
Southern Holder might not agree. Idarolan was reasonably
sure that Southern Hold's cliffs were high enough to with-
stand the diffraction effect of the tsunami, compressed between Ista Island and the Southern headland. Unfortunately,
Toric would be experiencing the event on both sides of his
Holding. Idarolan's chart, and Erragon's calculations, indicated a direct line of westbound tsunami, which might—
just—lose significant energy. Either way, there were coastal
holds that must be evacuated and herdbeasts moved inland
from the low-lying pastures. However, during the bad, bad,
bad blow of which the dolphins had warned Toric, he had not

moved quickly enough to reduce the devastation of the horrific gale winds of that hurricane.

K'van, with his Weyrwoman, Adrea; Master Sintary; and four of the Southern Wingleaders, moved out of the shadows as Canth landed in the flower-scented night. Five pairs of blue-green eyes shone as the brown dragon crooned a greeting and went to join them. K'van distributed hand lights.

"Neither moon's out tonight," the young Weyrleader said, his white grin visible in the reflection of the light he carried. "R'mart wanted to come but we convinced him that retired means no more responsibility."

F'nor bowed to Adrea, nodded to the other bronze riders, and finished stripping off his flying gear. He was grateful for the fresh breeze on the plateau.

"I have my own light," Sintary said, turning his beam on the well-worn track from the old open Weyr to the Hold.

"Of course, Toric could just ignore all this," F'nor remarked in a low tone as the eight of them carefully proceeded to the Hold.

Before they reached the first bend, a fierce challenge stopped them.

"Who's out there?"

"F'nor, Canth's rider," and F'nor tilted the light to his face.

"K'van, Adrea, M'ling, N'bil, S'dra, H'redan," the Weyrleader said, also lighting his face and flashing it at his companions as he named them.

"Idarolan and Sintary," the Harper said in turn.

"Bringing an urgent message to Lord Toric from Landing," F'nor said.

"A very urgent and very important message," Idarolan said, stepping forward in a purposeful manner, "and you had best guide us to him immediately."

"It's the middle of the night!" was the protest.

"Since when has the middle of the night been free of trouble!" Idarolan did not pause in his stride and the guard gave ground.

"You sound like Idarolan," he said dubiously.

"If you don't know your Weyrleader by sight," Sintary remarked acidly, "you're in a lot of trouble."

"This way, Master Harper, Weyrleader K'van. This way." They were going past the large square when he made one more remark. "You've got to wake him, not me!"

F'nor wasn't the only one who chuckled.

Luckily, it was Ramala who answered their summons, holding up a glowbasket to identify the visitors.

"Bad news?" she asked, leading them to the main hall.

"Perhaps not as bad for Southern as it is for others," Idarolan remarked which made her stop and regard him speculatively in the dimly lit hall. "If you would be good enough to wake Toric?"

"Yes, it had better be me," she said and waved them to chairs as she opened the nearest glowbaskets.

She disappeared on her errand and, because they were listening, they heard Toric's muffled shout of protest. Then she came back, nodded at them and said, if they wouldn't mind opening more lights, she would get fresh klah.

"Or wine, if you feel that would suit better."

"Both," F'nor said bluntly. He could use a glass of wine right now. Breakfast at Benden seemed to have been a long time ago despite the food that had been served during the emergency meeting at Landing.

Sintary and two of the bronze riders opened only sufficient glowbaskets to light the front part of the big hall. They had taken seats at one end of the long table when they heard the scrape of sandals on stone. Idarolan grinned, arranging his papers on the table, preparatory to an argument with Toric.

Shirt open, drawstring shorts rucked at one hip, the Lord Holder swung into the room, scowling, and the scowl deepened as he paused on the threshold, regarding those awaiting him.

"What the shards is the matter now? This can't constitute a Council!"

"A fireball impacted in the Eastern sea at approximately twelve hours twenty minutes Landing time," F'nor said bluntly.

"The impact of what we believe is a cometary fragment has created tsunamis," Idarolan said. "You will remember what happened when that volcano Piemur discovered erupted."

Toric's eyes rounded, thick sun-bleached eyebrows turning his scowl into an expression of unpleasant surprise.

"Some of your Hold is in the path of the tsunamis—two sets of them, one with three different waves from the east and the other from the west," Idarolan went on relentlessly. He used the map in front of him to point them out. "Journeyman Erragon and Master Wansor confirmed the phenomenon." He paused for a moment and then rushed on, as a man who regretted what he had to say. "Even as we speak, Monaco Bay is probably being drowned!"

Adrea gasped, and S'dra and N'bil inhaled sharply.

Toric stared at the retired MasterFishman and then glared at K'van. "Then what are you dragonriders doing here instead of being there to help them?" He waved his arms furiously to indicate the different sites. He dropped his eyes to study the chart, pulling it toward him.

"Every Weyr has sent wings to help," F'nor said, "We're here to tell you what to expect in roughly eleven hours from now."

Toric blinked.

"I will have riders in the sky rousing the coastal holders as soon as Adrea's queen gives them the orders," said K'van with a stiff bow to Toric. "We know you prefer to be informed of the Weyr's movements. I have just returned from the emergency meeting at Landing."

"I'll rouse your portmaster myself," Idarolan volunteered, "to warn the ships at anchor. They'll be safe enough at sea. Able to ride the tsunami swell, if they notice it at all. It's the land that's vulnerable."

Ramala came in with a tray of cups and food, followed by a very sleepy and resentful pair of holder women, one bearing a big klah pot, the other a wineskin. "You all need something in your stomachs to organize the evacuations!" she said.

F'nor wondered how she knew what they had come to

organize. Ramala was a good woman to have subtly on your side.

"Then, leaving you in good hands, Lord Toric," F'nor said courteous, "I will return to Landing."

"Good hands? I'll . . ." Toric lurched at F'nor.

Instantly, before Toric had a chance to complete his lunge at the brown rider, Idarolan stood between then. With a well-calculated blow of his fist to Toric's shoulder, he spun him off balance.

"If we're to save any of your coastal holds, Lord Toric, you'd best pay attention to *me*," Master Idarolan said in a loud harsh voice that had quelled argument before and made the infuriated Lord Holder think.

F'nor? Canth's mental tone was alarmed.

F'nor saw Sintary move to Idarolan's side as the stern MasterFishman held Toric motionless with his stony glare.

The Southern Lord Holder seemed to shake himself. With teeth clamped shut behind his bared lips, he gave a long hiss of breath and pivoted back to the table, spread with maps of his holding.

He's under control now, Canth, F'nor said, turning as casually as he could, trying to calm himself and his dragon. *Sharding idiot!* He could feel the anger of the other dragonriders as he left the hall in measured strides. Thank the First Egg that Idarolan had been right that Toric respected him. Slowly his fists unclenched. He took his time walking back in the night to the old Southern Weyr to regain full control of himself. And to face the other disasters this day seemed to be so full of. As much as he dreaded what he must see of a flooded Monaco, he was needed there, or at Benden. He could get back to his duties in time. After all, at the very beginning of this Pass, thirty Turns ago, Lessa had sent him a full ten Turns back, to raise weyrlings. Timing it was far more wearing on the rider than the dragon. He wondered if he could make time to see Brekke at Benden. She'd undoubtedly be extremely busy organizing the mass evacuations along the Benden Hold coast. She might even be annoyed with him for interrupting her at whatever she was doing. He knew that he took strength from her slight person, strength and comfort, and he did so need to be comforted—however briefly—for the terrible reality of a drowned Monaco.

She is at Loscar. The High Shoals should protect it, Canth told him, eyes a brilliant blue as he stepped from the shadows. Other bright eyes watched the brown rider.

"Your riders will be here shortly," F'nor told the other dragons, trying to strike a cheerful note. "Lord Toric had no immediate argument with the news we brought him." He shrugged into his jacket, secured his helmet, and climbed to Canth's back, affectionately slapping him on the shoulder.

Where do we go now?

Where else, good friend? Landing.

Sometimes it was as well to do the hardest thing first, F'nor thought as they went *between* to Landing.

And some hard things, F'nor realized, tears blurring his eyes, his chest painful, were harder than others. Canth had come out above Landing, facing north, so he had too good a view of the watery plain that had been forested Monaco, sparkling in the afternoon sun. He had given Canth a time *after* the waves hit Monaco, but before they pounded the Jordan River mouth. Involuntarily F'nor covered his face, but he could block out neither the gleaming expanse of water that had boiled inland on the crest of the tsunami nor the smaller seiche waves that were sloshing back and forth in perpendicular movement across what had been Monaco's crescent bay.

The water will not stay. It will drain back. His dragon's voice was so full of sympathy and understanding of the pain in his rider's heart that F'nor dropped his hands, the wind in his face drying the tears on his cheeks. He forced himself to think of the red indentations on Idarolan's chart and hoped that the tsunami had not penetrated as far as initial estimates. For partial reassurance, he could see blobs of green on the western side of Monaco Cape where stands of the big trees had survived the assault. And more, farther inland, on other hills.

A rumble penetrated his grief for the stricken coast and he felt Canth tilt and turn. There were other dragons in the sky, all facing west, all carrying at least two passengers: he easily recognized Ramoth, Mnementh, and the other Benden queens with nine more bronzes, ten browns, and some greens in attendance. They hovered above the Jordan River inlet.

Join them! Might as well twist the knife a little, F'nor thought with rare masochism.

They were not in time to witness the initial heaving of the sea, like the shoulders of a great, headless, pewter-colored beast. They did see the white spume, outlining the leading edge. And they did see the gigantic wave—dragon-lengths of it—crash against the Jordan cliff, and the way the spray tried to curl over the massive basaltic precipice, the wind blowing back the sound of that assault! They saw the second wave lurching against the bulwark. They could see old Oslo Landing inundated, see the tsunami streaming along the sloping coastline to attack the stones of Kahrain Cape. Out of the corner of his left eye, F'nor saw that part of the tsunami now seemed to swell and race along the basalt walls lining the Jordan River, pushing it in its wake, back up the length of the deep chasm. At his altitude, he could see the tsunami race—it seemed to flow over the natural seaward current—splashing against the rocky sides, but powerless to rise to the forest above.

The tightness in his chest eased as he understood that, powerful though the tsunami was, the land could survive.

The other watchers suddenly disappeared, going *between.* F'nor had seen enough. He asked Canth to spiral down to Landing. Hard work was a good way to blunt difficult emotions.

LANDING—LATE AFTERNOON—1.9.31

F'lessan felt the tentative prod on his shoulder. Felt a second, harder one. Felt Golanth's groan in the dragon's deep chest. Smelled klah and an appetizing odor of something roasted, held under his nose.

He opened one eye and saw a figure hunkered down in front of him, holding out a cup and a small plate, heaped with bite-sized food. He pushed himself against Golanth and straightened. He nearly fell back because his right arm was half asleep.

"F'lessan? Drink! You need the liquid."

That sounded like Tai's voice. He opened both eyes. She didn't look any better than he felt; her face was dirty and haggard. Oddly, her hands were clean. She sat down cross-legged in front of him, without spilling the klah or scattering the food from the plate.

"They let us sleep longer. I don't know why, but I'm grateful."

"So am I!" F'lessan yawned mightily, holding the klah out in front lest it spill on himself or Tai.

Then he realized that it was cloudy. Landing's usually bright sun was visible as a hazy yellow orb in the forbidding sky.

"Dust in the air, someone told me," Tai said with no expression in her voice. She wasn't a volatile personality, like Mirrim or Lessa, F'lessan thought. More like Brekke, quiet, self-contained; definitely reserved.

"What's happening now?" The bronze rider jerked his thumb to the three Benden queens, still on duty.

"The tsunami keeps going," she said, her head averted.

"Did it destroy Cove Hold?" F'lessan blurted the question out. He could endure almost any other destruction but that.

"Oh, no," she said quickly, with a sudden magically reassuring smile. "Cove Hold has only a little bit of flooding in the gardens. They had nearly four hours to pack up everything portable, but the water never reached MasterHarper's porch."

He felt tension in his midriff snap with relief. He closed his eyes, thinking of Cove Hold as he had last seen it. Gardens could be replaced. Whatever other things had been destroyed by the tsunami, he was deeply grateful Robinton's last home had come through this disaster relatively unscathed. But Tai did not look happy. She paused, her eyes unfocused and her shoulders sagged again. The smile disappeared and she seemed sunk in depression. He caught her hand, thinking he knew what would trouble her more than Cove Hold.

"The observatory?"

"Not as badly damaged as it could have been. That dome is watertight. Kahrain Cape above it caught the brunt. There was a spectacularly high crest at Jordan Cliffs." F'lessan shuddered, remembering the one he had so narrowly escaped. "I'm told a lot of people watched."

The brief animation in her face faded quickly.

"I'm sorry, Tai. Not much of Monaco would have survived," he murmured, squeezing her hand hard in sympathy.

"There were five waves, you know," she said flatly. "One after another. They sort of bounced off the nearer Ring island and then plowed into Monaco." She raised one hand and smacked it slowly, five times, into the palm of the other, then her shoulders sagged and her hands dropped. "Pier went in the first one and all the cotholds on the beach. People saved a lot of the tools and supplies from the boatyard. The careening cradles are just splinters after the seiche waves. T'lion said those are the perpendicular waves, when the main ones subside. I don't know how he could go and look except that he was trying to find the dolphin bell pylon. He said it's made of an indestructible material." She gave a heavy sigh as if she doubted anything could have survived the surge of five tsunami waves. "Portmaster Zewe took down the dolphin bell, you know. T'lion said he'd been out far enough to sea for Gadareth to land on the water and call Report. It was pretty choppy and cloudy but the dolphins reported." That seemed to cheer her a bit. "No pods suffered casualties and they warned all the land people."

F'lessan stroked her hand soothingly. "I know. They warned Sunrise Cliff." He hesitated. "Is Readis all right? At his Dolphin Hall?"

"Yes." She managed a weak grin. "T'lion checked. Readis was high on Rubicon Cliff."

He didn't know what else to say. He knew that Monaco Weyr Center was probably bobbing with the splinters of the pier and the vegetation. Wherever she and Zaranth had weyred was deep under water.

"Eat," F'lessan said gently and held a bit to her lips because he hadn't seen her take any of the roasted meat.

She put a piece in her mouth, chewing it slowly, automatically, not tasting anything, and not looking at him, distraught. Why wouldn't she be? he thought.

"What news of other shoreline holds? Was everyone lifted to safety?" Would he always see the panic on Binness's face when he realized he was trapped between a wave and a rock?

Irritation made her flush. She stopped her chewing and looked up at him, a small outraged frown knotting her eyebrows. "I heard there were some who didn't believe the dragonriders and . . ."

"Crept back to get something they couldn't live without and drowned," he finished for her. "The Weyrs are not responsible for arrant stupidity!"

"But they'd been brought to where it was safe!" She gripped her fingers so hard her knuckles were white.

"Like the dolphins, we can't help it if people don't listen to our warnings." F'lessan caught both her hands in his and tugged them to get her to look at him. "Tai, how much *time* did you spend today warning, rescuing?"

She blinked furiously, tears spattering onto his hand. "I . . . I can't remember. The fireball was always there," and she cast a frantic glance to her right, to the north.

He massaged her taut hands and fingers, doing his best to soothe her, to relieve her inexpressible grief.

"Every dragon here did what he or she could do. I'll wager there're hundreds of exhausted dragons here. We did *all* we could!" He thought of his son, barely fifteen Turns, taking his dragon on the longest trip *between* they'd yet made, to serve food and drink. "We didn't lose a dragon, did we?" No, he would have known. Dragons made a terrible noise when one of them died.

She shook her head. He continued to stroke her hands as he

looked out over the resting dragons, most of them Monacan, though he recognized a few from Telgar and High Reaches Weyrs.

"How much more do they expect of us?"

"The fireball fell. And made tsunami," she said, her tone utterly bereft. Zaranth crooned sympathetically, encouragingly.

F'lessan reached out and pulled the dejected green rider into his arms. Her skin was cold beneath his hands. He snagged one of the feline pelts from the ground by Zaranth.

"How in the name of the First Egg could dragons have stopped the fireball dropping or the tsunami from starting?" he demanded bitterly. "We did what we could!" Once again he used Golanth's shoulder as a backrest and made Tai as comfortable against him as he could. He felt Golanth's sympathetic rumbling and Zaranth shoved her nose over to give Tai's arm a brief lick. F'lessan felt the reassurances of both dragons humming through him. Tai lay motionless, her breathing gradually easing from despairingly ragged to a calmer rhythm.

"You'll see, Tai. We'll be more famous than Moreta and her ride. There were thousands of us doing it."

We mustn't say that we timed it, F'lessan, Golanth whispered.

"We're not to say we timed it, F'lessan," murmured Tai in the same breath.

"Another little miracle of the day covered up, huh?" F'lessan felt rancor building in him. What did it matter if half the population of Pern knew dragons could go *between* time as well as place? It's not as if people could learn how. On the other hand, he'd had enough timing it these last few hours—felt more like days—with that damned fireball hanging over his shoulder.

Tai, who had begun to relax against him, now tensed again and struggled to sit upright.

"Did you save these?" She held up one leg of spotted pelt.

"Me? No. Are these the ones you skinned in Cardiff? Beauties."

"How did they get here?"

Tai's eyes widened, her mouth dropped open and she stared at Zaranth who now looked very uncomfortable and dropped her head from her rider's arm, hiding her eyes.

Zaranth said to Tai that she wanted them so much and there was no time to go get them, Golanth said very softly to F'lessan.

"What does she mean by that?" F'lessan asked, seeing an unreadable expression on Tai's face.

SAME TIME AT KEROON PRINTER HALL—LOCAL TIME 11:15—1.9.31

"Sir, Masterprinter, sir," an uncertain young voice said at Tagetarl's elbow.

"Just a minute." Annoyed, Tagetarl held up his hand so he could listen to the last of the drum message being passed. He didn't want to miss a vital one; most had been seeking information. Telgar and Lemos had confirmed a fireball visible in their sky. Benden drums confirmed that it had fallen into the Eastern Sea.

Roused from his bed early that morning, Tagetarl had gone to his office to find what reassurance he could from his maps. The Eastern Sea was a long way from Keroon. But he was awake so he went down to the kitchen level to make fresh klah. He had a hunch he'd need it before this day was done. Several hours later, when the shock wave rumbled over Wide Bay, he blithely told everyone that this was natural enough. Most believed Harpers, but not all. His spouse, Rosheen, gave him a skeptical stare.

Drums rolling a message on to Keroon Hold informed him, and anyone else who could interpret drum messages, that "everything was under control." A tag to it—that only a harper would know—was an urgent invitation for Lord Kashman to be conveyed to Landing.

Nor was what "was now under control" explained. Situated in an old warehouse that had been converted to its new purpose, Tagetarl's Printing Hall was on the north side of Wide Bay. He had a good view of ships entering and leaving the harbor but the Hall was not conveniently situated to see if a dragon had taken off from Keroon Hold. With his good long-range vision, he could make out frantic activity on the wharves as goods waiting to be shipped were taken back into warehouses. He didn't need his prized collapsible far-seer to see colored sails being hoisted on the dozen or so ships, some of which he knew were waiting for cargo. All through the morning, a tension seemed to pulse in on every wave that splashed the seawalls. Gales whipping either east or west of Nerat's tip often blustered up past Igen's headland and up wide Keroon Bay. Tagetarl frequently found reasons to stop in his office for a few minutes and check what was happening in the bay. The ships were sailing south on a wide port tack, evidently heading up Keroon Bay. For safety.

A shuffling reminded him that he'd nearly forgotten the messenger.

"Sorry . . ." he caught back "son" because the person in front of him was a young girl. He was still not accustomed to girls as green riders. She looked very uncertain of herself, but somehow proud; he'd seen that combination when a young student managed to play a complicated score correctly. She had her riding helmet crushed in one hand and a thin message packet in the other. Hesitantly she held it out for him to take. She wore Monaco colors and a green weyrling's knot on her flying jacket. "Sorry, green rider. Is all well at Monaco?"

She stammered. "Very wet, Master. I am to deliver you this." His polite inquiry produced fear and anxiety in her face. "For your *urgent* attention, Masterprinter. I must wait until you've done it."

"You must, must you?" Tagetarl smiled reassuringly. She couldn't be more than sixteen Turns and he wondered if this was her first long journey as a weyrling. She also looked very tired. However, any news from Monaco might clarify and en-lighten the tense situation—and explain why Lord Kashman had been called to Landing. Of course, the new Lord Holder may not be quite sure of procedure in what appeared to be a widespread emergency.

"Yes, sir, and where may I wait?"

"Sit, before you fall, girl," Tagetarl said, pointing to a stool before he opened the message. "From F'lar?" he exclaimed, recognizing the handwriting—bad enough under any circumstances, though the bronze rider had obviously tried to be legible.

"Tag, urgent notice to publish facts. Should get inland where sweepriders have not already given warnings. Runners have been asked to distribute. Give the messenger a hundred to take to Nerat. Please ask Keroon Stationmaster to distribute another hundred. Riders will be sent for the rest. Rush." This last was underscored several times.

Any irritation Tagetarl felt for the peremptory tone was discarded when he read the copy for printing. The body of the message was in another handwriting altogether, much easier to read.

"Rosheen! Turn on the big press," he shouted down the hall. He heard her answering *"What?"* and continued to call orders at what his spouse called his "harper volume," audible inside and outside the hall. "Apprentices! I'll need the big notice sheets. Check the toner cartridges." He turned back to the green rider. "Where's your dragon?"

"Ptath's in the court. F'lar told me we'd fit. That's why I was chosen to bring the message. The Printer Hall wasn't hard to find once I got to Wide Bay. I'm Danegga. No one here seems to mind a dragon dropping in on them," she added with a charming naïveté.

"The Printer Hall is accustomed to visitors, Danegga, but you look tired and you may want to get something hot to eat. *Between* is cold." He gave her an encouraging smile. "Your first assignment out of Monaco, Danegga? Good ride. Much damage at Monaco Weyr?"

Her face twisted and tears came to her eyes but she pulled her shoulders up proudly. "They say the water will recede. We'll rebuild, Masterprinter. We saved everybody and as much else as the dragons could carry."

"Then you did very well, Danegga. Very well indeed. Now, run down to the kitchen—just follow your nose. There's always soup on the stove and there was fresh bread this morning. Might just be time for you to get a short nap while I print these. Monaco will be proud of you."

"Thank you, sir, thank you," and as she turned to leave, she nearly ran Rosheen down, bobbing again to excuse herself.

As Rosheen reached Tagetarl, he flourished F'lar's message at her, not allowing her time to read it.

"We'll both need to set copy. Headline in the boldest print face we have, biggest letters," he muttered, pulling her down the hall to the Print Hall proper.

"FIREBALL WILL CAUSE COASTAL FLOODING!" he said, making a big bracket with his hands. Good time to try that 26-point they'd just added.

She grabbed the message from his hand.

"So this is what's got the ships sailing away. A fireball? What's that? Oh, the text explains. And they got Master Esselin to sign this, too?"

She nearly tripped in surprise and Tagetarl grinned at her. They'd both done their stints of copying under his critical eye.

"Makes it more official, though, doesn't it?" Tagetarl grinned. "Apprentices, front and center! We'll need to wrap in hundred-copy packets."

"Did I see Monaco colors on the girl?" Rosheen asked as they took the last few steps to the Hall floor.

"You did and you know as much as I do. Let's get this job done as fast as possible. Rumors of course will spread faster, but if the Runners distribute a written message, people are more likely to believe the printed word."

"Considering how scarce they are . . ." was Rosheen's whimsical remark as she followed him.

The results were not bad for a rush job: the new toner dried fast so the copies didn't smear. He gave Danegga the first packet; he'd be on up the hill to deliver the second one as soon as he saw her off. Over his shoulder, he saw Ptath lift from the ground, but only high enough to safely go *between*. It didn't take him long to reach the Wide Bay Runner Station, situated as it was on the wide main road. He paused on the threshold since the entrance was full of men and women, a few dressed as Runners. When the very air buzzed with excitement, Stations were good places to garner news.

"Stationmaster," Tagetarl said, effortlessly projecting his voice through the babble. To his right, inside the main room, Arminet stood on tiptoe to see him.

"Let the MasterPrinter pass. He's just the man to explain all this," cried Arminet in his equally loud deep bass voice.

People stepped on each other to get out of Tagetarl's way but almost everyone asked "The fireball? Do you know about the fireball?" as he passed them.

Tagetarl held the package over his head, waving it. "It's all in here." He almost stumbled when he saw Pinch duck to one side. Trust that one to be in the thick of things. "Stationmaster Arminet, I've been asked by the signatories of this message to request Runners to pass these along inland. Sweepriders are warning coastal areas. I'll pay any charges you think fair."

"Ha! You know we carry community messages free, Master Tagetarl," Arminet said, his bass voice rumbling with sardonic amusement. "What does it say?"

Tagetarl began to recite the text of the message as he eased through the crowded room to hand the packet to Arminet. The Stationmaster was besieged by those who wanted their own copy. Tagetarl stopped talking, so as not to interrupt the concentration of those who had difficulty reading the smaller print below the banner headline.

"Then Aivas *prevented* disaster?" Someone in the crowd said, doubtless Pinch, Tagetarl suspected, though the voice was muffled.

"And what are the Abominators saying?" Tagetarl demanded, hands on his belt, glaring around.

"That Aivas caused it, with all its meddling with the Red Star. And dragonriders let it pass. It was seen from Telgar, y'know," a man shouted.

"And Benden!" a soprano cried.

"Benden and Landing acted!" Tagetarl responded sharply.

"More than any Abominator did. I expect I'll have more news later. I'll publish as I receive. I stopped here first to start spreading truth."

"I'll see these go out with every packet," Arminet had to raise his voice again above the cries for copies.

Pinch did not follow Tagetarl out but he would probably be one of the first to spread the news where it would do the most good. Or thwart rumor quickest!

When Tagetarl got back to the Hall, he was surprised to see a crowd of people, all wanting their own copy of the newssheet. Rosheen and the two apprentices were handing them out as fast as they could. Tagetarl saw some far too curious folk circling by the shelves where he kept galley pages of work waiting for approval.

"You, there, wait your turn. Come up front," he called, gesturing authoritatively for them to stop wandering about the print shop. "You've no business back there." He went to supervise their departure and decided maybe he could do a second run of the sheet. Get people to rely on the printed word and he'd get new customers for the books and manuals he kept in stock.

LATER, ON AN UNUSUALLY BRIGHT EVENING AT LANDING, SUNRISE CLIFF, AND HONSHU HOLD—1.9.31

F'lessan and Tai had finished eating when the word passed among the dragonriders that the emergency supplies were ready to be collected. Riders had been told to return to those holdings they had visited earlier that day. They were to check on injuries and determine if it was necessary to convey anyone *between* to Landing's Healer Hall. Enough healers had been sent by Master Oldive to assist those locally assigned. There were Healer kits of bandages, numbweed, fellis juice, and fortified wine for riders to bring with them. The riders were to make their own judgments about staying overnight at holdings if critical situations had developed.

"What could be critical after this morning?" F'lessan remarked facetiously.

Tai gave him a hard stare. "I suppose we can bed down here tonight." She gave a shrug. "There's nothing left of our Weyr."

He knew that she, and a few other riders, had had the courage to overfly the flood that had drowned Monaco Bay Weyr.

"You can stay at Honshu," and before she could refuse, F'lessan extended the invitation to C'reel and St'ven nearby. "Have you been to Honshu?" he asked the brown riders.

"Hunted nearby once or twice," C'reel said but his grim expression lightened at the invitation.

"There's plenty of space," F'lessan said expansively. "Though I'm not sure about having enough food. Bring some with you, but there's a whole cliff of space for dragons."

"How many can you accommodate?" Tai asked.

F'lessan raised his arms. "Well, not all of Monaco Weyr but two, three wings of riders and dragons. And any weyrfolk attached to them." As Tai turned away to spread his invitation, he added, "And tell 'em to bring blankets. It's cooler up there."

He and C'reel fitted Zaranth's load to her back before Tai returned.

"Everyone's grateful," she said and he knew that she was, too. "T'gellan and Mirrim may have to remain here at Landing and there're others promised to help the weyrfolk on the hills. They thank you, F'lessan. Landing's facilities are overtaxed."

"There're always the Catherine Caves," F'lessan said, trying for some levity.

"Too small for *our* dragons," C'reel said, with good-natured condescension.

"Move on there, if you're loaded up," someone yelled at them.

They did. Zaranth following F'lessan, C'reel, and St'ven out of the line.

"Have you ever been to Honshu?" F'lessan asked Tai.

"Got taken there once. Oh, Zaranth says Golanth just made sure she knows the landmark. I'll see you!"

Zaranth trotted away, sacks bouncing on her back, until she had enough clear space to launch herself.

Tell her good flying, Golanth. F'lessan experienced an unusual sense of apprehension for the green rider.

She is strong. Zaranth is strong. The sooner we go, the quicker we get to Honshu. Honshu is quiet, his bronze told him and F'lessan couldn't agree more.

St'ven and C'reel mounted over the supplies. He wondered if they were as uncomfortable as he felt, perched on sacks with hard things prodding into his legs. He latched his helmet, made sure his jacket was closed and, raising his arm high, pumped it to direct his companions upward.

Let's not make shallow jumps a habit, brown riders, he said, waiting until they were well above the surface. Then he extended his arm southward to their destinations. *We all know where we're going?*

Riders and dragons acknowledged.

Let's go.

Coming out above an almost obscenely quiet sea front where Sunrise Cliff Seahold had been was as much a shock to F'lessan as to the other riders: he could hear their exclamations above the sad noises all three dragons made.

There might never have been human habitation here. Waves splashed idly against granite cliffs instead of wide white sands in grassy dunes, waters draining muddily back from the break in the cliff face that had been a streambed. From the flotsam deposited, piled in places, they could see how far inland the tsunami had coursed. It had not yet pulled back far enough to show what might be left of the cotholds. Whole tree trunks floated on the waves, idly being pushed in by the high water. It was logical to assume that these had been swept from the islands just off the coast. Most were craggy, with no place for a holding of any sort, except near the summits, but they had supported the same variety of fruit and timber trees that grew on this part of the continent. And the fish would return to an area rich in feed.

Mealth sees smoke, Golanth told his rider and turned his head.

F'lessan let out his breath. He hadn't known he'd been holding it. His throat ached. He hadn't a doubt that Lady Medda had organized everything to her satisfaction. Odd that there was still light in the sky—a strange sort of luminescence, possibly something to do with that sharding fragment. After today he was going to review his old astronomy lessons and he doubted he'd be the only one.

Let's see where the fire is.

Someone is waving a banner near the forest, Golanth said, and picked up the beat of his wings, angling slightly over the summit.

Why were his binoculars in Benden when he needed them here? But he could make out quite a few figures, several waving what were probably the shirts from their backs. He hoped they'd saved more clothing when he remembered the full nets that had been conveyed to the cliff top.

She is there! Golanth said and F'lessan looked about for a green dragon and her rider. *The old one. In her chair.*

And so she was, looking dry, her hair carefully plaited, her rocking motion reflective. It stopped at the sight of the incoming trio of dragons. They were cheered as they landed and would have been welcomed, but a barked command from Binness kept all at their chores. A circle of stones accommodated a brisk hot fire over which two huge kettles had been set on tripods. One was already steaming. At the forest edge, two men were skinning a herdbeast, fallen fruit had been gathered and lay in nets to one side, and wood was stacked under an oilskin.

Binness, his arms bandaged where Golanth had seized him, came to meet them, limping a bit. He was still barefoot, curling his toes up from the coarse ground cover.

"Didn't expect you back, dragonrider," Lady Medda said.

"You didn't think we'd check to be sure you'd survived, Lady Medda?" F'lessan asked, grinning.

Binness shrugged. "Mostly the only time we see dragonriders is Threadfall but you saved us from far worse today. And three boats." He nodded solemnly to where the dories had been propped up on stout branches to provide shelter for sleeping children.

"Landing has sent water, bread, klah, glowbaskets, hand lights, medical supplies, and canvas for tenting," F'lessan said cheerfully.

"It's warm enough these nights," Binness said, tilting his head back.

"I believe there're wineskins, too, which we thought you might be in need of," St'ven added, grinning.

"Did I hear him say 'wine,' Binness?" shouted Lady Medda.

"Grand dam you have, Binness," F'lessan said.

"Bring him and the wine here, Binness. We've only herbal leaves to serve but it's my own recipe. Puts heart in man or beast. Wine'll increase its medicinal value."

"Anyone wounded? Sick?" F'lessan asked Binness when he had dismounted with one wineskin in his free hand.

"More shocky than hurt. May I have your name, dragonrider?" Binness asked with a respectful bow. "I thought I was dead, between that wave and the cliff."

"F'lessan, Golanth's rider, Benden Wingleader."

They had reached her in her chair which, F'lessan could now see, rocked on a square of worn rug, with a footstool to prop her swollen feet. The dragonrider bowed respectfully to the indomitable old woman.

"Lady Medda!"

"I'm no lady," she replied with vigor but she smiled at him coquettishly. "Not but what I haven't had a dragonrider or two warm my bed at night."

"Granddam!" Binness was shocked. "That's no way to speak to the man who saved us."

"Did you thank him for saving you?" Her sharp blue eyes

pinned her son before she turned on F'lessan. "He thanked you proper?"

"He did and Golanth and I were glad to be—in time."

"In time?" She gave him a long startled glare. "Closest run thing I ever saw. An' only a foolish dragonrider would've risked his neck and his dragon's for my son. Though I'm glad you did. He's my eldest." Then she flicked her hand, dismissing Binness, and peered shrewdly up at F'lessan. "How'd they fare at Monaco? I remember it's flattish there. Someone bring a cup for the dragonrider. For the others, too."

"Monaco is flooded," F'lessan said, quickly, sparing C'reel and St'ven the need to answer such a painful query. He waved away the cup that a girl offered. "There is much to do. We can't stay long. I'm to ask what supplies you'll need to rebuild."

"Ach!" Lady Medda flipped her hand. "We'll see what's left us. There'll be stone enough to rebuild. You saved some of the dories. S'all we need."

F'lessan gave her another respectful bow.

"We'll be back in a day or so," C'reel said. St'ven reinforced the promise with a quick nod.

"And you, young F'lessan?" the old lady asked, pointing her stick at him and rocking her chair forward so that it nearly touched him.

"Would that I could match you, Lady Medda," he said with his most charming smile and backed away. As he strode to Golanth and vaulted astride, he could hear her laughter, a genuine rippling laugh, not an auntie's cackle. He gave a final wave to all before asking Golanth to launch. *Properly, not over the cliff edge,* he added.

They reported the particulars of Sunrise Cliff Seahold to a harried archivist who had set up a temporary office in a tent on the edge of Landing's Gather square. When they were done, the archivist waved them in the direction of the tables on the other side where food was being served and remarked that they would doubtless hear from their Weyr queen when and where they would be needed.

"You wouldn't happen to know where what's left of Monaco Weyr is being accommodated?" C'reel asked.

"No, no, over there. She'll know." The man waved his pen vaguely.

"Well, I could use clean clothes," C'reel said, noticing that clothing was being stacked at the north side of the square.

"Me, too," St'ven said. Although F'lessan kept extra clothing at Honshu, he wouldn't be able to supply more than a few.

All at once, the heat of the square, the noise of those thronging about, the day's exigencies seemed too much to endure a moment longer.

"You get clothing, C'reel, St'ven," he said. "Find out where the rest of your Weyr is quartered. I'll get to Honshu and make ready for you."

To F'lessan's dismay, Mirrim was already there, and had organized the couples who were holding a little north of the Weyrhold. He had thought her safely stuck at Landing. He should have known better. He should also be grateful to her—or try to act as if he were—though she still tended to give orders to him. Very soon after his arrival, he was genuinely glad she had come. She was the one who had organized food and there was succulent meat grilling on the main terrace for the many Monaco Weyr riders who had taken up his invitation. Tai was one of them. He would have liked to be able to show her around Honshu, especially the observatory and the telescope . . . one of his most treasured possessions.

He had found it when he and Golanth had been repairing solar panels on the Cliffside and discovered the thin, straight seams on what appeared to be solid rock, but were instead halves of an observatory dome. Getting in had been another problem, but the telescope, covered in that thin film that the Ancients had used—vacuum packing, Aivas had called it—was still on its U-shaped mounting. Wansor and Erragon had been excited about its existence but warned F'lessan that awakening the scope would require a great deal of preparation: it required a computer to direct and focus it, and a screen to show what it observed.

Tonight he didn't have the energy to climb that long spiral staircase and he was reasonably certain Tai didn't either.

Honshu's sprawling precipice, its two terraces and ledges, were so covered with dragons that soon others had to find space on the rocky terraces down by the river. Their numbers would be sufficient to keep away the herdbeasts who often came for shelter in the lower cave as well as the felines who hunted them. Even in the early days of its discovery, Honshu had never had so many human guests.

Sitting on one of the few chairs on the main terrace, F'lessan airily advised each new arrival to dump his or her flying gear on any unoccupied space and come back for food. T'gellan had brought four wineskins and St'ven and C'reel added two kegs of the light beer Landing brewed. From Honshu's deep cellars, F'lessan sacrificed some of the good Benden he had put aside for a special occasion; surviving this day could be considered in that category. There was enough for everyone to have at least a cup of beer or wine. That would be sufficient for men and women who had served double the hours a day usually spanned.

Unaccustomed to having "his" space at Honshu so overly populated, F'lessan took his wine up to the second terrace and was delighted to find Tai there.

"I suppose we'll need time to wind down," he said, coming up behind her. "Sorry," he added as she whirled around, spilling some of her wine. "Don't waste it."

"You startled me."

"So I see. Again, my apologies."

She flicked her hand in dismissal and seemed hesitant.

"So you noticed it, too," he said, gesturing to the northeast where a silvery glow arched in the general direction of Monaco.

She sighed and then looked up, where the light from other stars was undiminished.

"Yes, but Rigel's still there." She pointed at the first magnitude star above them.

"Hard to miss," he said, laughing softly. "And Betelgeuse,"

he said, subtly testing her knowledge of the southern night sky. She looked in the appropriate direction and he chuckled.

"Also Acrux, and Becrux," she quickly added, taking up his challenge. "The one forty degrees away is Gacrux. Erragon said there was a fourth star in what the Ancients called the Southern Cross but you can't find it with the naked eye."

"I'll match those with Shaula and Antares," and he lightly touched her shoulder to turn her toward Adhara.

"I am glad that you retained Honshu's old name," she said softly, her voice rough with fatigue. "I think it is honorable that we use the names the Ancients had for their places, and their stars."

"Why not? They brought the names with them. The stars haven't moved that much and there are bright ones in our skies that the Ancients saw from old Earth only as dim ones."

"It isn't the stars we have to worry about," Tai said, her voice as weary as the sudden slump in her shoulders.

"No, it isn't," he agreed tiredly, "but it's good to see they don't change. I've a pair of binoculars, you know, if you'd like to use them tomorrow night."

"You do?" Excitement briefly sparkled in tired eyes and then she sighed. "Tomorrow, if you'd trust me with them. They're . . . hard to come by."

F'lessan managed a wry grin. "I've known Piemur and Jancis a long time, you see, so I snuck to the top of the list. Besides, they're very keen to get the Honshu instrument working. A bit of extortion!"

"Extortion?" That startled her.

"It's all friendly. A dare and challenge situation," he assured her. "Tomorrow night then. We both need the sleep tonight." He put his hand lightly on the small of her back and gave a push.

Quietly they left the upper terrace and separated in the hall inside. For this one night, fire-lizards would stand watch. F'lessan shared his room with the last to arrive: T'lion, bronze Gadareth's rider, and his brother, K'drin, brown Buleth's rider. Fortunately, neither snored.

PART 3

Aftermath

HONSHU — 1.10.31

F'LESSAN FOUND himself awake at Benden's usual dawn hour though night lingered at Honshu.

Ramoth says we must come back to Benden, Golanth told him. *The brown riders will visit your seaholders. They are Monaco's people, not Benden's.*

F'lessan quietly gathered his clothing, hoping to have a chance to bathe and change, and left his room without waking the others. He took a quick shower; there'd be many people wanting one. He was glad he'd fixed the cisterns. As he padded down the stairs, past many sleepers, the pungent and irresistible odor of fresh klah told him someone else was awake. He heard voices, arguing quietly but intensely. Well, that was their problem, whoever it was. He needed klah.

He slid open the panel into the kitchen and nearly ducked out again when he saw that it was Mirrim and Tai who were bickering. Or rather, Mirrim was ranting at Tai, who kept saying "No, I didn't," "No, the children came first," and "I don't know how."

Zaranth says, Golanth told him, *that Mirrim thinks Tai deserted the Weyr's children to save her skins.*

Skins?

Her pelts from the Cardiff felines.

She saved the children. I sent you with her.

Zaranth says she got the skins.

225

How could she? F'lessan looked from Mirrim's angry face to Tai's pale one. *You were with her. She came and went with you.*

"Golanth says Zaranth was with him all the time, transporting children," F'lessan said and strode across the counter to the huge urn of klah. He'd have a cup no matter what the argument was.

Mirrim whirled toward him. "She didn't have the skins when she got to the Weyr. She did have them when she left."

"I didn't get them."

She's telling the truth, Golanth said.

"Golanth says Tai's telling the truth, Mirrim, so leave her alone."

"Then how did she get them?" Mirrim demanded.

"I didn't!" Tai was taut with anger and frustration. "If I'd had time to get to my place, I'd've saved my books and notes. Not sharding pelts."

"Pelts like that would have given you enough credit to *buy* new books," Mirrim countered.

"Ahha, but not her notes, Mirrim. Golanth says she's telling the truth. Now leave it!" F'lessan rarely spoke in such a tone. Mirrim gulped, and swallowed whatever she had been about to say. F'lessan used her silence to drink as much hot klah as he could. "Thanks, whoever brewed the klah." He looked toward the pale, tense Tai and smiled, indicating he was certain she'd made the klah.

"I couldn't sleep," she murmured.

"And, if that doesn't—" Mirrim began.

"I told you to leave it, Mirrim!" F'lessan took a menacing step toward Mirrim who unexpectedly gave ground. He saw the meatrolls on the counter behind Tai and, stepping around her, grabbed a handful. "Thanks, Tai. Besides which, Mirrim, I didn't see the pelts on Zaranth's saddle until Landing."

As he hurriedly slid the door open to leave, he heard Mirrim sputtering behind him. He bumped into T'gellan who looked thin and haggard despite a night's sleep.

"No matter what Mirrim says, 'Gell, Golanth says Tai's not lying. Good flying today."

He raced down the stairs and out the wide door to the main terrace before he sat down to put on boots and jacket, allowing Golanth time to arrive from wherever he had weyred that night. Slits of blue and green dragon eyes on the terraces above watched him mount but closed again before Golanth tilted off the ledge and made his first wingstroke. Far to the east was the brightening of the sky on a new day.

And what does it have in store for us? F'lessan wondered.

Tai was telling the truth.

I know.

Zaranth saved the pelts.

I suppose, F'lessan said facetiously, *because she didn't know which books and notes to save.*

Quite likely. Ramoth calls me.

With that, the bronze went *between*.

Considering what filled the day, it was not at all surprising F'lessan did not dwell on that exchange. He and Golanth conveyed people and necessities to various Benden coastal holdings, reporting on how the flooded areas were draining, occasionally using dragon strength to shift wave-driven debris, and everywhere he had to explain that the dragons could not have stopped the Fireball from hitting nor held back the tsunami. He was repeatedly asked why Thread was still falling now that the Red Star was supposed to be gone. Few understood that the Red Star had only shepherded Thread close to Pern and what was falling now was what the Red Star had dragged in behind it.

At first he'd used diagrams on the sand, in the dirt, or on a piece of paper: a big circle for the Sun, a much smaller one for Pern, tiny ones for the two moons. He'd draw the orbit of the Red Star, and show how it swooped down and around Pern, then out, carrying with it the cloud of Thread.

"Why does it take so long?" he was asked.

"Thread's been on its way and it takes between forty-five and fifty of our Turns to get past it again."

Then he'd be asked why the Fireball had dropped. He answered that by saying it had been a leftover fragment from the Turnover Ghosts, lost trying to follow the others. (That might not be exactly the truth; Masters Wansor, Idarolan, and the newly promoted Master Erragon still had to deliver an official verdict, but at least most people had seen Ghosts and could accept the little fiction.) He'd drop another stone—the Fireball—into the water and show them how the tsunami was like the ripples. It was, he knew, an explanation, not an answer. He didn't know what the answer was, especially for those who'd lost a lot to "ripples."

Back at Benden Weyr, no one had the energy or the wish to settle on a better explanation. Or an answer. The next day Benden was flying Thread so, after eating quickly and checking on S'lan to be sure the lad was holding up well, he retired to his weyr, checking his safety harness and wondering if he could afford new leather pants to replace the ones the last few days had split, torn, and scraped. F'lessan remembered Tai's fine pelts. Well, there were plenty of felines to be hunted near Honshu. He could probably trade such pelts for wher-hide pants from the Weyr's tanner. It'd be fun to hunt with Tai and Zaranth. Golanth agreed. So F'lessan gave the drowsing bronze an affectionate rub and went out to the ledge of his weyr. He clasped his arms with his hands against the chill. During those earlier lessons with Aivas, he had made himself familiar with the names of the brightest stars to be seen in Benden's wintry skies. Canopus was low on the horizon, Girtab outshining her.

He really ought to get to work now; to make Honshu a viable part of what dragonriders could "do" to protect the planet. That was at least obvious to him. He had no idea how a dragon, or all the dragons of Pern, could stop another fireball—they didn't have any more antimatter engines to drop on them, he thought wryly—but it made a lot of good sense to find out if anything else was likely to impact any time soon. From some scrap of those nearly disregarded astronomy lessons, he remembered that hazardous impacts were infrequent. There were a few documented, like the Circle Runner Station and the most recent meteorite that had rammed into the prison yard at Crom Minehold.

Wansor, old Lytol, and D'ram were certainly working all

out on updating orbits with Erragon down at Cove Hold. The skies currently above Pern had altered within Rukbat's system since the colonists had first surveyed it twenty-five hundred and fifty-three Turns ago. Asteroids had collided, broken up into different pieces, spinning into new orbits. Perhaps one of them had been the Fireball. Others, like the erratic wanderer inaccurately called the Red Star had entered the system as comets or fragments. In the spare moments F'lessan had had, he'd reviewed his old astronomy notes from his classes with Aivas. A long-forgotten lesson reminded him that the *Yoko* got its information from what the Ancients had called "a southern array of satellites." Aivas had once mentioned the absence of a northern array, which would have given a much clearer picture of minor planets, comets, and other orbiting bodies. He remembered that there were more telescopes stored in the Catherine Caves, which probably would have been set up in observatories to keep track of such objects. Old Earth certainly had known exactly what was in its solar system. But no one had anticipated the Red Star and Thread falling on Pern.

Thread must have sharded a lot of the colonists' plans, F'lessan thought to himself.

To identify what now circled in Pern's spatially near vicinity would need more than however many apprentices and journeymen currently worked at Cove Hold. The telescope in the ingenious observatory that old Kenjo had contrived was the type that required a computer and a screen to display what it saw. The 10x50mm binoculars he had wheedled out of Jancis worked well enough. With these he had been able to spot what were marked in the Aivas charts as minor planets and the larger objects in the asteroid belt. But to have an instrument that would produce images that one could study in detail! That would help enormously in charting the skies. He grinned, rubbing his cold arms. And maybe he'd get Tai to help him. Ah!

When the entire furor over the Flood had eased down, he was sure he could now get authorization from Master Wansor to withdraw the appropriate boards and crystals out of storage at Admin to be able to focus the primary mirror. Aivas had taught him how to assemble a computer. Benelek, another of his old friends and now Master of the Computer Hall, could probably be talked into helping him. Screens were harder to come by, but he might just cajole Stinar into giving him a spare one, if he promised regular reports of what the ancient Schmidt-type telescope detected.

Enough stargazing. He had a tiring day ahead of him. He hadn't had a chance to show Tai where he kept the binoculars or the stand. Much less the glory of the Honshu observatory. As he turned on his heels and walked quickly back into his weyr, out of the cold, he smiled to himself: she'd like that!

CIRCLE RUNNER STATION — 1.18.31

"Not the first time things have fallen on Pern that weren't Thread!" Chesmic, Circle's garrulous Stationmaster, said to the two men who had asked for a night's shelter. Since it was extremely cold and there was enough in the stew pot for two more, Chesmic allowed them in. Besides, he could use a new audience. Every other Runner gathered for a warm meal before continuing their runs had already heard his usual tale.

"Why d'you think we call this place Circle?" he went on, glancing first at one and then the other.

"Do tell us," the younger man said, his tone so close to downright rudeness that Chesmic almost didn't continue.

"Do tell us." The older man with the scarred face spoke more courteously, in a deep, oddly muffled voice. When he broke off a piece of bread from the big loaf in the center of the table, Chesmic noticed that he was minus the top joint of the first finger on his left hand.

"Not because it's built round." As he took up his tale again, Chesmic's penetrating glare included everyone at his table and their quiet conversations stopped. "Which it ain't. But, 'cos o' that great hole out there!" He pointed in the appropriate direction. "Twenty good paces from the front door and twice as deep as the tallest man ever growed. 'Cos that's where *that*—" and now he pointed to the twisted black fragment displayed in a niche in the stone wall, "—landed!"

Of the two guests, only the older man looked at it. His companion assumed a supercilious smile as he continued to spoon stew into his face. At least, Chesmic thought, they won't complain they hadn't been well fed at Circle.

"Nothing compared to what the Fireball did," the younger man said, openly contemptuous. "Never should have messed with the Red Star."

"That—" Chesmic waggled his hand toward the crater, "fell over a thousand Turns ago before Aivas had the dragonriders push the Red Star out of harm's way." He rushed on before the arrogant young man could do more than open his mouth. "So it stands to reason there ain't no connection twixt it and the thing what plowed through Crom Minehold. Both of them are meteorites." He pronounced each syllable. "Ain't the first that have fallen. Fireball was a different thing altogether. Right?" he asked the Runners.

They murmured agreement with him.

"Does Crom Minehold display its meteorite as you do?" asked the older man in his odd speech.

Chesmic couldn't quite place the man's accent. He was certainly not from Keroon; Keroonians drawled—that is, when they spoke at all. Nor was he from the eastern coast. Runners bred there spoke in crisp tones. West coasters did, too, though they accented some words differently. That was it. The man had no accent, no tone to his words: he just spoke them and sometimes blurred the *t*'s and *d*'s and *n*'s.

"Naw, sold it to the Smithcrafthall for more marks than the mines've earned in Turns." Chesmic did not wholly approve of that sale but it had been their meteorite. Not that he couldn't have sold his to the Smithcrafthall, if he felt like it, but you couldn't sell something that had been in his family so long. Wouldn't be right!

"I heard that they think it's part of the Red Star," the young man said, a sly gleam in his eyes.

"That's a bundle of snake wallop," Chesmic replied contemptuously. He pointed skyward. "Iffen the Red Star had

broke up—which Masters Erragon and Stinar and Wansor
has seen through Cove Hold that it hasn't—we'd have rocks
falling down all over the planet. And we don't."

"That Fireball made enough trouble for us," one of the
Runners said.

"It was wrong to move the Red Star," the older man said,
his face somber and his voice forbidding. "It has circled Pern
for centuries and to alter its course is a bad deed."

"Oh, it's still to circle Pern," Chesmic agreed. "Just not
close enough to drop Thread on us again."

"Thread, and the dragonriders flaming it out of our skies,
is tradition. So many have been broken. So much has Aivas
corrupted our way of life, our traditions."

There was something about the man's toneless voice that
caught you up in his words but Chesmic knew about traditions. Runners followed ones that belonged to the first Crafthall to be formed at Fort Hold.

"There isn't a Runner on any trace on Pern, north or south,
that does not follow tradition. And since you've both finished
eating, you'd best make use of the beds that tradition—"
Chesmic paused to be sure these strangers understood what
he meant. "—requires us to offer travelers during winter." He
rose and gestured toward the loft steps.

The older one rose and bowed. So did the younger man, but
his expression was sullen as they both made their way to the
sleeping loft.

Mulling over the unease he had felt about that pair, Chesmic recalled the description that Prilla had given of the man
who'd stopped her on the trace to carry a message onward.
Definitely it had been the older fellow, for Prilla had mentioned his odd deep voice. He'd've been wearing a hat, possibly, so the scar wouldn't've been so noticeable. Of course
he'd paid his mark piece for the service or Prilla wouldn't
have carried it a stride farther. But why'd a fellow waylay a
Runner when he could have easily brought it to the Station
and had it logged on and all in the proper manner?

HARPER HALL

Well into the next month, as the flooded coasts drained and, in most cases, resumed their previous contours, food and materials were sent by almost every inland hold, minor or major on both continents, to sustain and rebuild drowned holds. Messages bulged Runner pouches and fire-lizards carried more, finding out who needed what and where. Shipmasters volunteered free cargo space and, on the days between Threadfalls, riders offered the services of their dragons and themselves. In the atmosphere of renewed friendships and mutual assistance, the unfortunate occurrences at Turn's End faded in the press of other priorities. The general movement of matériel and people included some of those in whom Pinch had an interest. He did know that messages were sent, but not to whom or their content. None of the people he watched so assiduously had fire-lizards, which proved that fire-lizards wouldn't come to just anyone who fed them. He could never quite get close enough to hear their discreet conferences. He'd come back to Harper Hall to report, get some new clothes and marks.

He found Sebell in his office, piles of odd-sized papers on his desk, held down by rocks.

"Well, come to do your share of petitions?" Sebell asked, gesturing to the mess.

Pinch groaned and looked away. "Bad timing on my part."

Traditionally all petitions presented at Turnover were forwarded to the Harper Hall and read by a special group of journeymen and masters who determined which were urgent enough to be submitted to the Council at Telgar on the first of the Third month. Some of the petitions should have been handled at Hold level. However, if there were sufficient complaints brought against major or minor Holders, the Council was the best place to decide if the matter should be investigated further. Pinch was often assigned to get specific information.

"I'll do my share. I always do. I'll look at any in Keroon, Igen, or Bitra—I know most of the troublemakers there anyhow."

Sebell gave a little smile. "Not much from Bitra so far. Sousmal seems to be taking such good hold that everyone's happy with him."

Pinch widened his eyes, moved one pile of papers to hitch his hip up onto the desk. "For now! How about those sketches I sent you? Any of that trio known?"

"Woman's from Tillek, rather a sour contentious sort, apprenticed to local healer hall but released prior to her third term as unsuitable to the Craft. Petitioned Lord Ranrel to be given her father's hold in preference to the younger brother who had been named by their father, evidently with a specific instruction that she was not to be considered. She and the brother had a huge dispute and she left. Hasn't been seen since Tillek's autumn Gather last Turn."

"So she's holdless?"

Sebell shrugged, searching briefly in the wide drawer under his desk and finding the three sketches. "One of the Traders through here—a Lilcamp—recognized this fellow." He tapped the one with the missing index finger. "Travels a lot. Does his share when asked, can put his hand to a lot of jobs, has a habit of asking questions. Funny sort of voice, too." He paused. "Young Sev mentioned the questions were— how do I put it—provocative."

"Provocative? And he asked Traders?" Pinch was mildly surprised by such gall.

"They see a lot of people and are smart enough to know what's going on where and how folks are reacting. Better than Runners who can't stay long anywhere."

"They're helping though," Pinch said. "Chesmic up at Circle Hold says he's had strangers in, sending messages, and others leaving them at a Runner Halt, a half mark left to pay carriage."

Sebell raised his eyebrows. "Overpaying? Bribing?"

"Not when Chesmic tells me."

"Does he know you're Harper?"

"Doesn't ask." Pinch's eyes danced with amusement. "By the bye," he added, his grin turning malicious, "did you know that the window glass that broke during the shock wave was all made by Master Norist? None of Master Morilton's shattered! Another point for our new technology." Then he cocked his head. "Do we know, officially or unofficially, if the—ah—exiles survived the Flood?"

Sebell pursed his lips and regarded his companion. "Has there been a question about that?"

"Not in so many words but it might be handy to know."

"And you're curious?"

"Part of it." Pinch's shrug was noncommittal.

"As I understand it, one of the natural attributes of a proper exile is that no one, searching in a ship for dissidents, would find a beach to land on. Many of such islands are sheer-faced cliffs. The relevant ones were drenched but not drowned. What's the other part of it?"

"A snippet of conversation I overheard—misinformation, actually—that I'd like to honestly—" He put his hand over his heart. "—genuinely, sincerely, trustworthily repudiate. As I was saying, I suspect our plotters, and perhaps the *ingenious* scum who assembled the pamphlets, that so distressed Master Crivellan, lurk in the foothills of Keroon where dwell many with insufficient teachering to argue, and no interest in what happens to the rest of the planet. Did you identify that third chap?"

"He looks slightly familiar but I can't place him."

"Nor can I. He *resembles* half a dozen men I know, same age, same height, same general features, but he seems to have no morals or ethics. He does have some responsibilities that he has to attend to from time to time or a person he makes reports to. He may be a younger Holder son, not likely to succeed; he holds his nose a lot. You've seen the type, though he adapts to his surroundings better than Third and Fifth do."

"Third and Fifth?"

Pinch made a face. "They go by the numbers. The one woman's referred to as Fourth. I think the original second is dead. I got the distinct impression that they're glad he is since he objected to some of their plans. Third's the big one, Fourth the female. Seven in all or at least seven who come to the hill retreat from time to time. I'd suspected Sixth was from Tillek, with that flat nasal twang. Third's traveled—as we know—and Fourth's been in so many places I can't tell where she came from. Definitely Third is in it for money and sport. I think Third is genuinely concerned about too much technology. Fourth uses Tradition as a reason to exist. Her thinking's skewed. She wants to lead and she hasn't got the personality for it. She's too concerned about doing things the old way, the right way, the way she was taught that ought to be the way *everyone* does it." Pinch paused. "Too hidebound to know the color of her pelt."

"Are they planning something?" Sebell asked.

"They act like it, all this leaving of messages at Runner Halts so the sender can't be identified."

"How do they collect messages, then?"

"I suspect one of their docile hill folk do. I asked at Wide Bay—Stationmaster Arminet knows me—and he remarked, casual like, that a lot of hill folk were getting messages."

Sebell rubbed his chin thoughtfully. "They must know that now most healer halls lock away their stores—and use Master Morilton's glass." He gave Pinch a telling look. "The Glass Halls have shifted healer-hall work to more secure places, the SmithCraftHalls have started using digital lock systems . . ."

"And Aivas scores another posthumous victory over vandalism," Pinch said with customary impertinence, raising his hand in triumphant gesture. "Never know what we'll need next because of them."

"Benelek's delighted. The units are easy to build and attach to alarms. I've sent some handy apprentices down for a few weeks' training with him."

"You're not worried about them breaking in here, are you?" Pinch was genuinely alarmed.

Sebell laughed, lightening his generally serious manner. "Not with the Fort Hold watch dragon!"

"Who didn't hear the vandals in the Healer Hall . . ."

"Because they entered quietly and wearing healer green.

Then there're all the fire-lizards that live here—not just Menolly's." Sebell pointed a finger at the roving Harper. "You hear anything of their plans, even a whisper . . ."

"My hearing's excellent and Bista's is better."

"Send word." Sebell frowned a little, thinking. "Odd, isn't it, that those who dislike the advantages Aivas gave us should force us to use his technology to thwart them!"

"Ironic, too." Pinch rose from his perch on the desk corner. "I've read enough in Aivas's historical files to feel that Pern will never be in danger of becoming over-technical. Takes too long to develop the skills needed, except in special instances like the digital locks, and we certainly don't have the production systems the Ancients had. As a population, we have been conditioned to this slower, more methodical rhythm of living and only a very small portion will ever feel the urge to aspire to Aivasian heights."

"A Pinch of philosophy, too, huh?" Sebell said, grinning. "I wonder would such reassurance suffice to content the dissenters."

"We all have a choice," Pinch said and rubbed his hands together with an air of anticipation. "What petitions d'you want me to go over? I'm here overnight at least."

Just as Sebell was deciding which pile, the latch of the Master's office door was being pulled down. Both men heard a child's delighted laughter and then the door was pushed inward.

"Da, I learnt 'nother tune. Perfect!"

The child—and Pinch had no difficulty in identifying him by his tangle of dark curly hair as Menolly's oldest son, Robse—swung in on the door handle, waving his wooden recorder over his head. "Ooops, sorry. Dint know anyone was here."

"No, come in, come in," Pinch said, wondering if he could escape being lumbered with petitions.

"Is by Aivas!" Robse announced as if the source made all the difference.

"By Aivas, is it?" Pinch could not resist echoing the phrase.

"By Aivas!" Robse affirmed with a nod that made the curls on his head bounce and his expression turn very stern indeed.

"If it's by Aivas, then it's all right," Pinch said.

"These, Master Mekelroy, are for your perusal," Sebell said, bowing as he held out one of the larger piles to Pinch.

"Thank you, Master Sebell, thank you. You are always so generous to me. I can't thank you enough for giving me something to busy myself with while I'm here," and with such effusions, and a wink at the mystified Robse, Pinch backed out of the room. "A perfect tune really must be heard as soon as it's learnt," and he closed the door on that remark.

He'd given Sebell the most important news, though he still had to discuss the problem of far too many people wanting to know "What were the dragonriders going to do about things that fell from the sky?"

BENDEN WEYR—

The watch dragon trilled the note that Weyrleaders were flying into Benden and Mnementh and Ramoth on their ledges rose to bugle a welcome, which informed Lessa and F'lar of important, if unscheduled, visitors.

Tileth and Segrith, Ramoth said, raising her head from her front legs.

"Really?" Lessa was as surprised as F'lar. "Did you forget they were coming?"

"I wouldn't forget something as unusual as that," he chided her as he quickly slipped off the soft, fleece-lined ankle-boots he was wearing and pulled on leather ones warming near the heating unit, shrugged off the wool vest, and rose to his feet, straightening his collar and settling the deep cuffs of his wool shirt.

With an air of not noticing his rearrangements, she wrapped her long braid into a more formal coronet and smoothed the creases out of her woolen trouser-skirt.

"We have wines, don't we? And perhaps Manora will send

someone with fresh klah and whatever is freshly baked," she said. "I wonder why they're here!" she added.

"No doubt they'll inform us!" he said as he opened the thick curtain that kept cold air from leaking into their comfortable quarters. He frowned as he looked out. "They should have checked our weather first. It's turned into a miserable day."

Did they ask, Ramoth?

No, or I would have told you. I, too, do not forget anything. Ramoth turned lightly, whirling reproachful eyes on her rider.

"Of course not."

She heard voices on the ledge and stepped around the curve of the wall to see Pilgra slipping, putting one hand firmly out to the stone to get her balance.

"My dear Pilgra, you should have checked the weather," she said solicitously. Pilgra was not her favorite of the Old-timer Weyrwomen but anyone venturing out today would receive her concern. "Come to the heat. Let me take your coat. Ah, you've one of the new long ones! Is it warmer, d'you think?"

"On a better day, it might be enough but I didn't expect it to be so miserable here. It's cold enough in High Reaches, but at least the sun's out."

Holding the wet coat, Lessa noticed that Pilgra's wool trousers were baggy at the knees and unattractively creased at the thigh.

"Oh, how warm you've made your weyr," the older woman said, her eyes taking in the heating units. "Good day to you, Ramoth," she added, nodding formally to the queen who was observing the visitor with tranquil green eyes. Then she walked rapidly to the nearest source of warmth, giving a mock shiver. "How marvelous! We have heat now, too, but nothing seems to penetrate the cold in High Reaches."

Suddenly Lessa had an idea why the two Weyrleaders had come.

The sun may shine on High Reaches, but it never warms, Ramoth remarked. *I have told Tileth and Segrith to warm*

*themselves on our Hatching Sands. It would be better than
waiting on the ledge in this weather.*

How thoughtful! Lessa responded.

Then she turned to greet M'rand and saw the pinched look
on his face. Yes, definitely, they were here about stepping
down. Not that they *had* to discuss such a decision with
Benden since the Weyrs were autonomous, but M'rand was
punctilious about such fine points.

"Wine? Or some of Master Oldive's liqueur?" she asked
him.

"That'd do fine, Lessa," M'rand said, and a spasm of coughing shook him.

Why hadn't she noticed that M'rand was aging? When
was the last time the Weyrleaders had seen each other? The
queens exchanged messages from time to time but the riders
had not visited. The mental image she had of the High
Reaches leader, hearty, vigorous, straight, underwent a distressing revision: he was slightly stooped in the shoulder; his
solid features—once handsome—were thinned and dry, his
cheeks a network of red lines; the tip of his nose was mottled
and the flesh sagged slightly under his chin and neck. Pilgra's
dark hair showed no glint of white but the density of the color
suggested to Lessa that the woman made use of some of the
personal products that had become available from Aivas's
files. There'd always been a red dye available from Pernese
roots but the result was not as natural-looking as the new ones
that had many shades to choose from.

F'lar served the liqueur to all, and Lessa asked after friends
in the Weyr and Lord Bargen who, she was informed, was
still annoyed that three of his sons had abandoned him to find
holdings in the south.

"Hosbon's done quite well," Pilgra said. "Has a pier, a
drum tower, and a sloop at Seminole."

"He got that much out of Toric?" Lessa said, exchanging
surprised looks with F'lar who chuckled.

"Must be a chip off the old block if he can wheedle amenities out of Toric," he said.

M'rand nodded enthusiastic agreement. "Well, Bargen

brought 'em all up to work hard so that he'd have a choice when it comes time for him to quit holding."

"Which is why we're here, Lessa, F'lar," Pilgra said, sitting forward on the edge of her seat. "We want to step down."

"Four good Wingleaders who know every bit as much as I do about Threadfall," M'rand added in a rush. "Weyr'll follow any one of them. Three good strong queens and a young one not yet old enough to mate. So we want to go south. Found a place down there in Cathay, when we were helping after the Flood. Small bay, protected east and west, not a big holding but don't want a big one. Got four to five weyrfolk want to warm their bones along with us. Wanted to ask you, can we?"

"Can you?" F'lar regarded him with surprise. "Of course you can. You and Pilgra have done more than your share of flying, in this Turn and the old one."

"You don't think we're deserting?" Pilgra directed her question to Lessa, her face screwed with anxiety.

"By the Egg, no." Lessa leaned across the space between them and patted Pilgra's hand, noticing the brown spots and the puffiness of her fingers holding the glass.

"Segrith hasn't had any of the old urgings to fly," Pilgra went on, adding, "though she's clutched every two Turns since we got here."

"With at least fifteen eggs and all living to fly. I wonder you've any space left in the Weyr."

"Well, it's space another queen can fill from now on," Pilgra said with a touch of asperity. "M'rand wants to see the Pass out but . . ." and she raised one hand in a helpless gesture.

M'rand cleared his throat, leaned forward, elbows on his knees. "Did hope to, F'lar, not many get the chance, you know." His grin was a brief echo of his former vitality and charm. "But, after seeing the place in Cathay, what with R'mart stepping down, I thought maybe, with three queens available and I've got some fine bronze riders, we might . . . well . . . go south and get warm!"

"You don't have to ask our permission, you know," Lessa

said gently, smiling with genuine gratitude. "You didn't have to come Forward from your own time to help F'lar and me during this Pass."

" 'That was twice decided,' " M'rand murmured softly, quoting the old Question Song. "We came because that was what we'd done, had to do, did."

"And, for thirty-one Turns, we've been grateful for your splendid generosity," Lessa said.

M'rand demurred with a chuckle. "Wasn't having as much fun in the Interval. I was young enough to accept the challenge. Now I'm old enough to think R'mart was right. We got you started and now we can retire in good faith. Of course, he still wants to be *in* a Weyr. Ourselves, we've been in one too long and Pilgra and I'd like to be by ourselves. Not," and he held up a hasty hand, "that you can't call on us and our dragons whenever you need to!"

"Now, if you're trying to get us to argue you into staying in that cold Weyr of yours, you've come to the wrong ledge," F'lar said, with an amused tilt to his mouth. He flicked one hand at M'rand. "Go, rider, and enjoy a well-deserved rest. May it take you into the next Interval."

"You mean that?" Pilgra turned to Lessa, eyes wide.

"Who thinks this is wrong?" Lessa wanted to know. And when both exchanged uncertain glances, she went on. "Let me guess: G'dened."

"Well, he's the oldest of us," Pilgra said.

M'rand cleared his throat. "Stubborn, too, won't let go at Ista because he's been at that Weyr—" He paused to guffaw. "—a half a hundred Turns and he knows all there is to know about leadership and Fall."

"One can appreciate such a sense of loyalty," Lessa said after a moment, and smiled. "Tenacity, too, and dedication, sense of purpose, perfectionism."

F'lar dropped his head, looking away from Lessa who was being outrageous and sounding so sincere.

Pilgra caught it first, blinking with astonishment as Lessa found a few more similar adjectives. Then M'rand roared with laughter, which turned into the hacking cough.

"Go before you die of the cough and get done out of your ease," Lessa said sternly.

"But—but—"

"Four good bronze Wingleaders? Let each one lead in turn during the next Falls until a queen rises," F'lar said pragmatically. "You'll be available for any problems. In fact, it'll take you time to step down even after you have. Now where's this splendid cove in Cathay? Did you think to get—ah, you did," he went on as M'rand withdrew a folded paper.

"Got Master Idarolan to do the map work for me. He's good at that." M'rand offered it to F'lar, once again the decisive leader, and a very relieved man. "I don't know which is better to have, map readings or your dragon knowing where to go."

Lessa had had a woodsmith make a cabinet with long, deep drawers where they could store the documents and charts that displayed chosen sites in the southern continent. The fact that the Weyrleaders controlled such dispositions rankled with many but, after heated debate in the Council, that had been agreed. What had also been stipulated was that each new holding had to be self-sufficient and had to have instructions about the dangers, as well as the advantages, of life in the south.

F'lar found the chart, flipped it to the worktop, angled M'rand's map, and found the coordinates.

"You're not asking for very much."

"Don't need much, and it's one in the eye for Toric," M'rand said.

Pilgra and Lessa came over as F'lar was outlining the new hold with a silver marker, reserved for dragonriders.

"A hundred square meters?" Lessa exclaimed. "A patch!"

"The nicest patch you could imagine," Pilgra assured her stolidly and started to describe the amenities. "There might even have been an Original Settlement there. Stones piled, like they finally fell, and just where you'd get a marvelous view of the sea below. All kinds of trees and it was so warm for First Month."

"There really aren't that many holdings allotted there yet, are there?" M'rand said, surprised.

"More than there were," Lessa said, "and far fewer than there will be when certain folk can make up their minds." She favored her mate with a dour look.

"More than I expected," Pilgra said with a sweeping glance of the chart. "That isn't all of Southern there is."

"No, it's not," F'lar said, tapping the drawer. "That's just the Cathay area, eight degrees to ten degrees longitude, fifty to twenty latitude. From the aerial photos on the Aivas scale, so they're big enough to delineate holds. I'll send the official register down to Admin." He opened another drawer and took out the register documents, which he tossed back inside. Opened a third, smaller one and took out a form. "This'll be your Deed." He riffled the side to show there were several pages. "I'll just fill it in, Lessa and I will sign it, and get it witnessed by the Weyr harper and perhaps Manora or G'bol and the holding's yours."

M'rand blinked. "Just like that?"

F'lar grinned. "You're Weyrleaders. You're entitled to your choice and require no further Council authorization." He leaned over the worktop, filling in the form, printing quickly but legibly, M'rand watching him.

"But it takes other people so much longer?" Pilgra asked, cocking her head to one side, her expression concerned.

"Other people take only as long as fulfilling the requirements of emigrating do," Lessa said. "Proof of being reliable people from hold or hall, with sufficient skills to survive in what can be hazardous terrain—where predators are bigger than the largest tunnel snakes they'd encounter here in the north—and a definite area where they will establish a new hall or hold. It's no more than was required by the original Charter, and that's another reason why it's important that everyone *knows* what's in the Charter."

"I did remind you of that, Pilgra," M'rand said, regarding his weyrmate with a jaundiced look. "People can get some ridiculous notions, listening to drunken Gather talk."

F'lar accorded that a grumble, checking from map to form

to be sure he had the longitude and latitude correct to minutes and seconds. "That's why the harpers keep—you'll excuse the pun—harping on the subject of reading and understanding the Charter."

M'rand started to chuckle; it turned into a hard coughing spasm. Anxiously Pilgra handed him the rest of his liqueur and Lessa rushed into her room, coming back with a dark brown bottle and a spoon.

"Here! Take a dose of this. It's reinforced with something Oldive found in the Aivas files to reduce just the sort of hacking cough you have." She measured and gave him the dose. "Not that getting into the sun won't correct it in short order."

F'lar finished the official Deed, separated the copies, and shoved one with M'rand's original little map into a plastic sleeve. While M'rand was recovering his breath, the Benden Weyrleader presented the Deed to Pilgra with a bow. "Take him there today."

"Today?" Pilgra was as breathless as M'rand, Deed clutched in her hand.

"Certainly. What else were you going to do on such a miserable day? Get your weyrfolk to pack up what you need for a few days: plan there, 'in the warm,' " and Lessa pointed southward, "what else you'll need."

"Go? Today?"

"Think what a pleasant surprise it'll be to your Wing-leaders and the junior queens," Lessa said, eyes bright and wide and far too innocent. When Pilgra looked unhappy, she added more solicitously, "Oh, they'll miss you because you're both good-hearted and fair. But who would fault you?" She shook her as Pilgra took a breath. "And don't say old leatherface G'dened. Cosira has her work cut out soothing his injured feelings. D'ram's not likely to gripe. Living in Cove Hold has put Turns on his life. You're both popular leaders but I cannot imagine anyone faulting you for going, and making the break quick."

F'lar says if we go with them, Mnementh told Lessa, *it will stifle any complaints G'dened might make. He adds, don't think you'll get him to retire so easily.*

Not when he's twenty Turns younger than M'rand and G'dened. I expect your rider to finish the Pass with me! Lessa replied stoutly.

And me! Ramoth said.

"We'll come with you," Lessa said out loud, brightly, as if she had just thought of it.

"That's a better way to spend a miserable evening than anything you've come up with, Lessa," F'lar remarked, knowing perfectly well he would pay her a forfeit later for such a remark.

Taking into consideration the difference of time between western High Reaches and eastern Ruatha, the Benden Weyrleaders had plenty of time to assist M'rand and Pilgra in their hurried departure south and get back to Benden for a late supper. In the interval, they had supported M'rand and Pilgra in his explanations to their Wingleaders and queen riders, organized the men and women who were to accompany them south, and allowed M'rand a hurried conference with his Wingleaders, some of whom had trouble concealing relief and anticipation. Pilgra, too, spoke to her queen riders (the youngest one obviously upset and the older three eyeing each other speculatively, since the first one to fly to mate would be the new Weyrwoman). For Lessa, that was great fun and for F'lar a chance to assess the bronze riders.

M'rand is right. F'lar agrees that there are four well-experienced men who can take over immediately, Mnementh told Lessa.

Which queen? she asked the bronze.

Yasith, Ramoth said so firmly that if Mnementh had a different candidate, he did not now mention her.

Lessa kept her opinion to herself. Yasith's rider was Neldama, weyrborn in High Reaches twenty-five Turns before, and twelve Turns younger than the oldest of the queenriders. So she was of this Pass, which, in Lessa's estimation, meant fewer problems. Not exactly a pretty girl—attractive enough to rate a long look from F'lar—with green eyes that looked right at a speaker and a considerate, sensible manner as she set about collecting the items that Pilgra said she'd want to pack.

M'rand fretted over how to inform three main Lord Holders and the most prominent minor ones of his sudden departure.

"It would be courteous, but it's only a formality. 'Due to continued ill health, in the best interests of the Weyr and the Holds that look to High Reaches for protection from Thread-fall during a Pass.' " F'lar rattled off the phrases. "A change of Weyrleadership is *our*—" he rocked his hand to indicate the four of them, "—business."

"It's not as if the whole Weyr is retiring," Lessa said just as Neldama and Curella, the oldest queen rider, brought in mulled wine and small hot savories to be served in the Weyr-woman's quarters. "And it's not as if you haven't traveled between both continents before. Be easy, Pilgra, M'rand. This time you're doing what's best for you!"

Of the other two Oldtimer Weyrleaders remaining in control, G'narish of Igen was flexible enough in his mind to accept suggestions while G'dened of Ista was nearly as contrary as R'gul had been. All the Weyrs needed to look ahead to After. G'dened gave her the impression that he didn't even consider After. He certainly wasn't suggesting to any of his riders that they would have to look to their own support once this Threadfall was over and the traditional tithing of Hold and Hall no longer appeared on a regular basis.

BENINI HOLD—EAST MONACO AND HONSHU—1.20.31

"If one more person asks me 'what are dragonriders going to do about things that fall out of the sky on us' or 'how we're going to keep the sky from falling on them,' " F'lessan said with a great deal of bitterness to Tai, "I'll—I'll tell Golanth to drop him, *or* her, *between*."

He stood up, stretching to ease his back muscles from bending over to plant saplings around Benini's cothold. The dwelling, a sprawling extended family site, had lost its roofs from the tsunami winds. Mud, sand, and debris had been dug out of hold and beasthold; the structures had been soundly built twelve Turns before and could be repaired. The large family—by craft, herders, Benini himself a Journeyman—were out early and late, hunting strays that had been scattered inland ahead of the wave. Redfruit trees and the giant fronds, which had amazing vitality and could be trimmed to provide windbreak, had once shaded the hold. Paradise River had offered new starts of both, as well as young fellis saplings.

Planting was not work most riders would volunteer to do but, when F'lessan saw Tai's was the only name on that list, he added his. He had done very well getting on work teams with Tai, mostly jobs as backbreaking and thankless as this, waiting until he saw where she was going to spend her spare hours before he signed up. She was willing enough—even eager—to discuss their mutual interest in astronomy. They were sometimes the only dragonriders on such sites. She seemed to know many of the more isolated cotholders and was welcomed warmly. The two dragonriders had been shown where to find tools, where fresh water could now be obtained, and what was available for their lunch. All the Benini holders had ridden out on their runnerbeasts for another long hot search.

When the two dragonriders had collected the plants at sunrise, rootballs wrapped and secured on wooden flats, Jayge had greeted F'lessan with surprise and gravely shook hands with Tai, remarking on what a fine green she rode.

"Didn't think to see you again so soon, F'lessan," the Paradise River Holder said, grinning at the bronze rider.

"And will do as long as Paradise River is intent on reforesting Monaco," F'lessan responded. He waggled his finger at Jayge. "You and Aramina have been exceedingly generous. T'gellan told me."

"The least we can be," Jayge said. "We were very lucky here, protected from the tsunami by the Kahrain cape." He gestured first over his shoulder and then down the river. "We can find as many young trees and bushes as are needed. You two look tired. Have you eaten?"

F'lessan dismissed that with a wave of his hand. "Yes, yes, thank you. We can get untired when things are more or less back in order." He examined the thick lift knot on the flat, the net that secured the young saplings to it, and the corner ropes. All the dragons were now deft at lifting such carriers. One trick was to keep the ropes taut and lift vertically very slowly to keep the load from swaying; dragons were perfecting the maneuver. The other step was going *between* very close to the ground, again to prevent swaying. After being root-pruned several days before, the young bushes and saplings were wrapped in balls early on the morning they were to be re-planted. Dragon transport meant they could be in the ground, watered, and staked within hours.

It also meant that the transplanters could finish before the sun started baking gardeners and plants. F'lessan checked the angle of the shadows; his watch was in his jacket. It was just midmorning and they were nearly finished. He wasn't sure how much longer he could keep up this pace, even if they had both stripped down to sleeveless tops and shorts.

"You're getting pretty good at this," Tai said, pushing her hands up to her knees until she was upright, too. She removed the sweatband from her forehead, mopped her brow, and retied the kerchief.

"I like restoring things," he said, looking at the zigzag line they had been working on, a windbreak on the eastern edge. The holding was actually on a rise, which had saved it from more damage. Redfruit on the inside, handy to the hold, a curving line of fellis, and then the fronds. Some untagged saplings, which didn't resemble either redfruit or fellis, they decided to plant in the rich loam here and there. Someone had started a garden patch. Luckily this was midsummer and they'd have fresh vegetables in a few weeks. With just a little husbandry, there'd be good growth in the windbreak plants before winter's winds.

"Like Honshu?" she asked, leaning down for the canteen. Benini's spouse had left cool juice to slake their thirst.

"Yes, like Honshu." F'lessan grinned, sweeping sweaty hair back from his forehead. He gave her a quirky grin. "Place fascinates me. There're still levels of it I haven't had a chance to show you."

They had spent several evenings on the upper terrace, sharing the use of his binoculars, held steady on the stand. He'd let her have more time using them because he liked watching the intent expression on her face as she observed, jotting down time and references. She was quite circumspect, taking down notes—but then she'd been training with Erragon—marking degrees carefully, asking him to verify the objects she viewed. He even teased her—she had to *know* that he was teasing her or she got quite upset—about minutes and seconds in the degree readings of the fifth planet out from Rukbat, currently visible at right ascension 19 hours, 32 minutes, 53.7 seconds; declination 27 degrees, 16 minutes, 25 seconds, just below Acrux. She said it was a habit she'd got into, sky-watching at Cove Hold, to keep a record. Erragon was collecting such information from other sky-watchers. F'lessan had wanted to take her high on Honshu's eastern face for a panoramic view of the forest and foothills below where sometimes he'd used the binoculars to spot felines, hunting at dawn, but the long spiral staircase was not a climb he could face with equanimity and she was as tired as he was.

"I would really like to see this mysterious observatory of yours, F'lessan," she said shyly as she passed him the canteen.

"Oh, I'll take you, never fear—one night when we aren't dragging tired. It's a steep climb."

"Well, whenever," she agreed amiably as she reached for the next plant from the nearly empty flat. "We're about done here. Let's just put these untagged ones near the garden," she added with a sigh and glanced over at their dragons, lounging on the ridge behind the hold, in the thick ground cover that not even the tsunami had been able to scrape away.

F'lessan took note, but did not mention, that the dragons were, unusually for dragons, so close they were touching. He'd had a few ideas of his own but with a personality as reserved as Tai's, he deliberately kept his manner as casual as possible. The excuse of sky-watching had reduced tensions and given both F'lessan and Tai a respite. Not that he had been able to join her every evening. F'lessan was only too willing to give Tai the chance to replace the notes that had been swept away. He had several reasons for rediscovering an interest in astronomy.

Most of the weyrfolk had left whatever temporary accommodations they'd been in; riders had cleared space for their dragons and built personal shelters. A new Monaco Center was being constructed on a height, well back from the shoreline. Today, certainly tomorrow, the very last displaced riders would be gone to new quarters. As far as he knew, Tai had not found any. She might have, when he was at Benden; he hadn't wanted to appear to be keeping a watch on her. And Zaranth.

He watched now as Tai gravely considered where to dig holes for the unidentifiable plants. He picked up an armload and carried them over to her. Out of the corner of his right eye, he caught movement in the thick grass cover just beyond Zaranth. He looked more closely and muttered in surprise.

"Trundlebugs," he said. He deposited the plants within her reach. "I'd thought most of them got swept out to sea."

"They can, and have, tread water," Tai said, grinning at him as she pushed the spade into the ground.

"Really?" F'lessan regarded their relentless progress. "How long?"

"I don't know. But I have watched them cross streams." She dug deeper.

"Hmmm."

She handed him the spade and knelt to take the wrapping off the balled plant, deftly spreading its roots before she put it in the prepared hole.

"Big mother," F'lessan said, commenting on the size of the

lead bug. "Four offspring. If she's not careful, she'll lose the biggest."

Tai shot a glance at the trundlebugs, then quickly knuckled loam around the plant, tamping it down well. For some reason, she was smiling.

"Coming right at Zaranth. Shall I . . ." He hefted the spade and took a step forward to intercept the trundlers. One had to swat the wretched mother bug out of her line of march but, at the same time, be careful not to break off her largest offspring at the end of the reproductive line, lest she retaliate with some of the stink-spray to defend her offspring.

"No, no! Wait."

"They're heading right for her. I don't know about Zaranth but Golanth hates 'em crawling on him. If he wakes, he'll squash them." F'lessan did not add that Golanth was showing more and more of a proprietary interest in the green's well-being, one of the subtler reasons why he was glad Tai preferred to work away from projects with other dragonriders. He wasn't ready for others to notice the growing relationship between Golanth and Zaranth.

"Watch," she said, her eyes sparkling green as she rose from her knees.

F'lessan dropped to the ground, narrowing his eyes in the bright sun to check the angle of the trundlebug approach.

Tai held up her hand, grinning. "Just a moment!"

"They're heading right for her nose. Doesn't she sense them? Golanth usually does."

"Wait!" Putting up her hand to stay his attack, Tai grinned widely, her look almost mischievous.

The trundlebug parade marched relentlessly in its unswerving path, oblivious to what was in its way. Zaranth's nose twitched but she didn't open so much as a slit of one eye. The parade was abruptly at right angles to its original path, heading back into the scrubland.

"There!" Tai beamed at her dragon.

"She blew them away?" F'lessan exclaimed.

"No. She didn't. They can only get so close to her and they

go off in another direction, any direction so long as it is away from her."

She reclaimed her spade from him and began to dig another hole. "There're two spades, you know."

"Yes, yes, of course, my dear green," he said, making a play of diligence, going for the second one. Anything to keep her from noticing the brilliant green of the sleeping Zaranth, lounging so gracefully in the sun by the sleeping bronze. How long would Golanth continue to fake sleep? F'lessan wondered.

"Tai, a question," he began, digging busily. "I was watching and Zaranth didn't move. She only twitched her nose. How could she make a trundlebug detour doing that?"

Tai dabbed at a drop of sweat rolling down her nose and, picking up the next to last plant, removed the wrapping and dropped it in place.

"I don't know. But, if they get close to her, they are suddenly perpendicular to the original line of progress. You know trundlebugs: they never deviate from their chosen path."

"Amazing!" He blotted the sweat from his face, then unwrapped the last plant, placed it firmly in the ground, and tamped dirt around it. "That's that. We're supposed to water them now, aren't we?"

Probably the first thing Benini had done after the flooding receded was to sink a new well and provide a long watering trough from which they could easily fill buckets for that last garden chore.

"Didn't Benini say they'd rigged a shower over by the beasthold?" he asked, when they had finished.

"Yes, with a big enough cistern above to wash all of them," she said, looking eagerly around to point to the freshly painted enclosure. "Or so his spouse said. We'll get clean much quicker showering than having to wash in a bucket," she added, dropping hers on the shadowed side of the well.

"Leave enough warm water for me," he said, waving her to go first. "I'll return the tools." He gathered them up and started for the shed, calling after her. "I plan to hunt Golanth this afternoon at Honshu. How's Zaranth's appetite?" Well, he thought privately, "appetite" was one word for it.

Tai cast a look over her shoulder at her sleeping dragon. "She isn't the least bit off-color."

F'lessan blinked and then, with an engaging grin that Mirrim would have identified as "devious," added, "We could hunt felines. Saw some a little closer than they should be to the Honshu herds. Get us some good pelts."

Since the Flood, most green riders had been giving all their customary courier services free of charge. But there'd be a Gather in Telgar in two sevendays, when the Council met, and that was time enough to cure hides for sale and give her book-money.

"Fine by me!" Tai called back. He caught just a glimpse of her back and long tanned legs as she entered the shower enclosure.

He gathered their riding gear and packs and walked slowly up to the shower, giving her time for a good wash and rinse.

"Hey, leave me some," he said, speaking above the sound of vigorous splashings. He slipped off his muddy sandals. Well, cleaning them could wait till he got back to Honshu, but he smacked them against the side of the wall to remove as much mud as he could.

"You'll find it warm enough," she assured him. "Can you hand me my towel?"

He opened her pack and dragged it, and her fresh clothes, out.

"Where is it?" she asked.

He saw her bare arm extending from the shower wall and accurately lobbed the towel to her searching fingers. There were shiny new hooks screwed to the wall and he hung her fresh clothes on one, his own on another. Riders were not as bothered by nudity as holders or crafthall folk so he stripped down, glad to be out of the sweaty, dirty shorts. As she emerged, toweling her body dry, she gave him a fleeting glimpse. He stepped courteously past her, into the shower, and looked around for sweetsand.

When he had had a good scrub, especially his feet, he

rinsed off well and, vigorously drying himself, sauntered across the changing area to his clean clothes. Dressed in her leathers, with her jacket still open, she leaned against the wall, in what shade there was, looking out at the scene of their morning's hard work, feeling pleased.

Summoning their dragons, they took off before heat brought fresh sweat.

As they came out of *between* above Honshu, F'lessan first noted that there were no dragons lounging on the summit or the main terrace.

Will you hunt today, Golanth?

I will hunt well today, Golanth replied, watching Zaranth as she glided past him to land on Honshu's main terrace.

Startled by the odd note in his dragon's tone, for a moment F'lessan worried that he hadn't been as sensitive to Golanth's needs as he should be. When was the last time he'd hunted Golanth?

I will hunt very well today!

The bronze was coming in slowly—almost stealthily—to land so that Zaranth was directly in front of them, her rider stripping the safety harness, which was never used when dragons went after a meal. F'lessan could not miss Zaranth's condition. She was gleaming with more than health. Why hadn't Tai noticed that the green was coming into heat? He tried to think which dragons had been at Honshu early this morning. Most had gone well before dawn, as they had, to begin whatever work was slated for that day in the reconstruction of Monaco's Weyr building. In a traditional Weyr, with dragons basking on their ledges, her readiness would have been noticed long before the green herself might be aware of her form. Honshu had been guesting dragons since the Flood. True, both riders and dragons arrived tired: riders eating quickly and seeking their beds, dragons finding a spot on sun-warmed terraces and rousing only when their riders called them the next morning. He and Tai had gone directly to Paradise River and from there to Benini Hold, their dragons sprawling in full sun; several hours in the sun. Heat was known to trigger a dragon's mating instinct. He swore, wondering if any of the other dragons had been awake to the nearness of Zaranth's cycle? Riders were known to remember when greens were likely to come into heat. Most of those staying at Honshu were Monaco Weyr riders. Would they come storming in from all over now Zaranth was active? Was this a delayed reaction in Zaranth? Overdue? But he was a Wingleader and he shouldn't have missed the signs. Well, Tai had!

I didn't.

For once, Golanth jolted gracelessly onto the terrace, throwing his rider forward in an unexpected assist in dismounting. F'lessan was lucky to keep on his feet, running a few steps to restore his balance. Did Golanth sense other male dragons near enough to challenge him? Certainly the bronze demonstrated his eagerness by arching his neck, tucking his head into his chest, proudly male. Sweeping the skies for the appearance of more dragons, F'lessan quickly stripped off safety straps, shucking the pile to the nearest bench, as he began to shed his flying gear. Golanth moved carefully toward Zaranth, his eyes beginning to whirl in anticipation.

Tai was standing there, the harness folded over her arms, gazing fatuously at her dragon.

"Good to see her looking so well. She'd gone quite dull there for a while after the Flood," she remarked as F'lessan strode up to her. "How near are the felines?"

"Looking so well?" F'lessan paused, astonished by her choice of words. Then he pointed dramatically at Zaranth. "By the Egg, *look* at her, Tai!"

Her eyes gleaming orangey-red, Zaranth angled her head coquettishly back at Golanth who was displaying, moving cautiously nearer, his faceted eyes sparking more redly.

Tai gasped, eyes widening with an expression of such fear and intense loathing that F'lessan wondered just what had happened during Zaranth's other mating flights.

"But there's just us!" she cried defensively, the harness slipping off her arms as she spread them wide in a gesture of panic and confusion.

How had she thought there was safety in that? Of course there had been other dragons and riders around, in and out of Honshu. Until right now! But, with a green in heat, there was no safety in numbers. Her hands turned, palms toward him in flat rejection. And, of course, he thought in fury, when Zaranth had gone proddy before, every blue, brown, and needy bronze had appeared: their riders had corralled her rider, waiting to see which dragon would win the green. He closed his eyes; he knew very well how intense the mood would be. But the green rider would choose!

"Tai, did you never choose?" he cried, outraged for her as he started to close the distance between them. And halted. He mustn't crowd her. The others had. How much time could he give her? *How* could he soothe her?

She was trembling violently, her eyes wide—not in an answer to her dragon's sensuality, but in sheer terror. She seemed to draw into herself, denying what was about to happen. Crossing her arms in a defensive position! Shards! Had previous riders raped her as their dragons twined? He tried to remember which blues and browns weyred at Monaco.

Tai continued backing away from him, looking about wildly for some refuge.

"They were all the same," she muttered. "There's no escape from them. From their . . ." She swallowed, trying to lick dry lips, white-faced with revulsion: her green eyes stark.

"Tai, were you forced?" With those words Tai shot F'lessan a look of such fear laced with guilt that he felt his belly fall flat. "You didn't choose?" He spoke very gently, appalled. This should be the most wonderful experience: a doubled ecstasy as both dragon and rider exalted in the union. He'd thought he'd made it so for those he'd partnered. The queen riders had always *known*: they had *chosen* him. With the state she was in, there was no way Tai had ever chosen. "It shouldn't be a violation. It should be a celebration for you and your dragon. The most glorious union!"

"Union?" She snarled the word, the panic in her eyes telling him that mating had been far from that.

How many times had Zaranth mated? How many times had she been . . . he struggled to find the appropriate word . . . violated? He knew hold and hall girls often were; it was one reason so many sought sanctuary in a Weyr. Dragonriders, except at this one time in their dragon's cycle, were known to be considerate, and ardent, lovers. Without conceit, he knew that he enjoyed a certain reputation. Is that why Tai had been so chary of his company? He'd thought she was just naturally reticent. Now he realized she had been motivated more by fear than reserve. He'd have a few well-chosen words for Mirrim after this—if he could only reach the girl now, when it was vital to soothe her.

With the stunning warble of a lustful green, Zaranth issued her challenge to Golanth and launched herself, straight up. Unlike the queens who needed to blood a kill to give them extra strength for longer mating flights, greens required little preparation beyond the onset of their cycle. Golanth did not hesitate for a moment, the bugle of his acceptance echoing back to their riders.

Tai screamed in anguish, reaching out futilely as if she could have stopped her green.

"Tai, listen to me," he said, keeping his voice light. "Let me explain how it should be." Carefully, slowly, he held out one hand but she backed away along the terrace.

Eyeing his hand as if even his touch would sully her, she cowered away, her green eyes frantic.

"Oh, Tai, my friend, if I could, I'd stop Golanth," and he would have given anything to have been able to prepare her more. If he hadn't been so callous as to ignore what he'd thought was a natural reserve rather than sexual fear. "I can't, not now when Zaranth wants *him* so badly."

"How can she *want him*? I don't want you! Not *that* way!"

That admission was at least something in his favor, F'lessan thought, struggling to find a way through companionship to solving the intensely immediate problem of their situation. All too soon the rider would be consumed by the dragon in a bonding neither could escape. He had to reach

Tai, the human being, before her mind was locked into her mating dragon.

"But you see, she does. She just challenged him," he said softly, infusing as much gentle persuasion into his voice as he could. "He answered. He has been admiring her in so many ways. Just as I admire you, Tai."

She blinked, confused.

That was good, F'lessan thought, somewhat frantic himself. If he couldn't reach her, she'd never realize that it needn't *be* rape. He knew he could control his human self, no matter how he might wish to revel in orgasm with his Golanth.

"Haven't you learned anything of me?" he cried in soft desperation. "Have I offended you? Slighted you as friend, Tai?" She blinked again, shaking her head, more confused than ever as the hold of her dragon increased. "In this let me *be* your friend—and lover, too. Challenge me, Tai, as your dragon challenged mine. Challenge me to make love to you, to you, Tai, not to Tai-rider. Choose me!" He spread his hands across his chest. "Choose *me*, Tai!"

"I have no choice," she said, whimpering. She collapsed inwardly.

"Oh, Tai, love," he pleaded, holding out his hands but careful not to crowd her. She was so near the edge of the terrace. She was suddenly so dear to him, he was surprised to realize. This was not all Golanth's yearning: F'lessan the man was yearning, too. "Please, Tai, please choose me!"

Whether it was Tai who reached slowly out to her friend for support, or the dazed rider, he wasn't then sure but she did reach. Was there enough of the human there to have made a choice?

"Please, Tai, come with me now," he said, taking her hand in a light grasp and gently turning her back, toward the nearest door. "My friend, we must go in."

He tried not to startle her, slowly guiding her steps—she couldn't see the arm he held behind her, just in case she might still bolt. Her eyes were glazing: she wouldn't know how close the edge of the terrace was if she should suddenly feel trapped and try to escape.

Murmuring encouragement, he got her inside the weyr-hold. With equal care, he closed the door behind them, grateful that the hinges were oiled and hoping she didn't hear the slight noise as it shut. Her fingers were slack on his, her gaze distant: she was half in rider trance. He wanted to settle her before she was completely submerged by Zaranth's sensuality. That would have been frightening enough the first time it happened if no one had explained it in full detail. Tai's reserve should have warned him; he cursed himself for insensitivity. How long had he been a rider?

Abruptly Tai tensed. He glanced at her eyes, pupils enlarged against the dark in the hallway. He kept his hand relaxed while hers tightened convulsively. He put his other hand on the small of her back, lightly, offering no threat, just guidance.

"I'm honored you chose me, Tai," he said. She must believe that. "I didn't believe you would, you know. I admired you for how calmly you got the children out at Monaco." He'd better be careful what he said now. "Be calm now, Tai. Be calm and let me help you now."

As deftly as he could, he turned her into the nearest sleeping room. He could feel Golanth's desire mounting. He had to control his. He had to remain human as long as he could. And that was becoming an effort. He couldn't just push her on the bed—that would frighten her—but he also didn't want to turn dragon and have her endure rougher handling.

Gently, he put his arms around her. "You have chosen me, F'lessan, and I will love you well!"

He kissed her forehead and slowly tightened his arms about her. If she weren't completely thralled by Zaranth . . . but had she ever been lovingly kissed? He bent his head, his mouth tender on hers. Let her still be human enough to feel this! He had not expected the flare of passion that passed between them in a kiss he had intended to be delicate. She trembled violently. Instinctively he tightened his embrace.

"You chose me, Tai. You chose me," he cried but her body went stiff in his arms. Rocking her, he kissed her face, her cheeks, her mouth, her neck. "Choose me, Tai!" he begged as he felt the rigidity that was dragon-frenzy, not human.

And *he* was abruptly Golanth.

She had launched herself well, and then ducked sideways, streaming away from him with unusually strong sweeps of her wings. She was big for a green and he liked that in her. He did prefer greens to golds. The golds always felt as if they were conferring great honor on a bronze by permitting them to mate. But greens could be grateful. They were certainly lustier than queens. Perhaps because they mated more often. She dodged to the right and he followed lazily. Let her wear herself out a while. He could wait. He would wait. This one was worth it. He had been so careful, not being too possessive of her company but he had let the others know that he intended this green to be his. He had been marshaling his strength whenever possible, knowing how tired other dragons were. But he was Golanth! Of Benden Weyr! Sired by Mnementh! Hatched of Ramoth! Worthy of that noble pairing!

She tucked her wings along her back, diving obliquely. He followed quickly. Did she realize how close she was to the ground? Oh, she did and swooped up again, proudly, head reaching for the low clouds that scudded over the foothills.

She'd play that game, would she? With one quick glance around him to see if any challengers had entered the chase, he swept after her. Sun sparkled off her brilliant skin between clouds and he pursued her, wondering if she knew that he could see her so clearly.

She turned on one wing tip and, knowing these skies better than she did, he did the same and soared through the narrow pass. If she thought he'd fall for that wily trick, she hadn't his measure. Soon she would.

She rose above the filmy cloudbank, heading toward the thinner air, then almost tumbled back down. He followed this maneuver effortlessly. She raced forward, rolling slowly as if caressed by the chill air. He nearly overshot her but didn't, so she failed with that ploy. She ducked, dodged, and fell surface-ward again, pulling up with the most graceful and powerful of movements he had yet seen in a green. Oh, she was a prize, this one! How he loved her! And she had chosen him!

Clouds again and he shadowed her progress through them by the glow of her reddened eyes. Then, just as she let him get very close, to evade him at the last moment, he gave his wings a sudden massive stroke and reached for her, making the catch, pulling her to him, connecting. Wings entwined and beating together, they flew suspended and, because he was a bronze and cleverer than she had thought him, their flight was horizontal to the ground and he could extend this passion for a long, long time. He did, sweeping them both carefully over the great inland sea where the thermals caressed their gleaming hides.

F'lessan was back in his body and Tai's was his. They were both panting from the exertion of a marvelously extended flight. He felt both triumphant and drained. He hadn't felt such repletion in a long while. She lay limply beneath him, eyes closed, head to one side, curls of sweaty hair concealing her face. He hadn't the strength—nor, to be candid, the wish—to release her, to leave her body. Considerate of her, he shifted. For all the pleasure he had enjoyed with other women, this encounter really was different. He couldn't think of anything appropriate to say and he had prided himself on knowing exactly the right words to use in any situation.

"Oh, Tai, you did choose me," he murmured, propping himself on his elbows, looking down at her with a feeling close to awe. "You did!"

His words took him as much by surprise as they did her. She turned her head slightly, her eyes wide and human again. Her lips were swollen from kisses he had been unable to control, and her eyes filled with tears.

"Please say you did?" The human in him needed to be reassured but he was also aware that their meeting had been incredibly intense, even for a dragon-generated mating. That could only be achieved with the enthusiastic cooperation of both partners. He couldn't be feeling the way he did right now if rape had been involved.

"I didn't know it was supposed to be—like that!" she admitted softly and she turned her head, embarrassed.

"My very dear green," he said tenderly, stroking her face with his thumbs, feeling slightly superior because he was no stranger to the "that." "It is assuredly the most intense emotional and sexual experience. We know exactly what our dragons are feeling, and they mirror ours. It can be stunning enough when humans love, but magnified by our emotional bond with our dragons . . ." He spread his hands, unable to quantify it and smiled tenderly at her. "Well, it—" he hesitated, "should have happened to you before, Tai." He couldn't help making fists and driving them into the rumpled furs of the bed. "I'm appalled and concerned that you were so abused. That's *not* the way dragonriders should behave even when the dragon's in control. I'm . . ."

"Sssh," she said, reaching up to lay her palm against his cheek, her face calm, the hint of a smile on her kiss-roughened lips.

He wished he could see her eyes but there was so little light filtering through from the hall.

"I'm glad it was you I could choose," she said.

"I—" He started to protest, stunned that, despite his best efforts, she had somehow sensed his wile.

"I know me well enough, F'lessan," she said, putting both hands on his face now. "I am so very grateful to you."

"Gratitude in a snake's arse," he said, incensed. He wrapped his arms around her, wanting very much to take her again, and with human lust. "It's not bloody gratitude I want from you, my dear Tai!" He loosened his hold when he felt her resist with a hint of the panic she had shown on the terrace. He made his body relax beside hers, looked down into her eyes, wishing he could see the expression in them, the color they were right now. "I *liked* you when we first met. In the Archives. I know you knew who I was, that Mirrim had probably prejudiced you against me. Had probably said I was—reckless. I'm not. I'm a good Wingleader. Riders trust me. So do their dragons. I want you to choose me, of your own free will, Tai. I'd like to—choose you, too, as a person I want to know better, not just because your green went into heat and Golanth was the only dragon available."

She looked up at him for a long time and then, tentatively, curled one hand around his bare shoulder.

"How did you manage it?" Her voice was low, even.

"How did I manage—?" His voice broke in surprise. She meant Zaranth challenging Golanth. "Believe me, it is not something even I could manage!" A laugh burst from him. "Your dragon wanting mine!"

And then he wondered. Dragons could be very cunning.

"Wasn't there *one* dragon in Monaco Zaranth liked?" he asked quickly. "Didn't Mirrim tell you to decide which rider *you* preferred and latch on to him?"

Her eyes slid from his and she swallowed hard. "Don't go after Mirrim, F'lessan. She said—something like that. But I didn't—didn't prefer any of them."

"He didn't have to be Monacan, you know."

"You're angry with me again." Her body was stiff beneath him.

"With you? Again? When have I been angry with you, Tai?"

"When you got back from Fort."

He blinked.

"When you found me swimming after—after—"

"When you were injured," and he stressed that word, "trying to stop those sharding vandals." He got angry just thinking about that attack.

"You're angry with me again."

"No, I'm—" He closed his lips on "not" and saw that, unaccountably, she was smiling a little; that her body had relaxed, that both her hands were lying loosely on his back. He took a deep breath and made taut muscles loosen. "I'm not angry with you, my dear Tai, I'm angry *for* you."

"I'll have to get accustomed to the difference."

"Will you, my very dear green?" he asked very gently.

"Will I what?"

"*Want* to get accustomed to the difference? To me?" He searched her face, rubbing his thumbs gently from her temples to her cheeks. "I do so very much want to know you better." He kissed her lightly at the corner of her mouth, felt her lips twitch under his. Then, carefully, he moved to one side of her long body and pulled her against him, pressing her head against his chest.

"They're lying just like this, you know," she murmured.

He smoothed her hair back and settled his cheek against it. "Hmm. I know. On the ledge. But they're almost asleep."

"Aren't we?"

"We." He liked the sound of that and especially the idea of sleep. Of sleeping with her in his arms.

I told you I would hunt well, he thought he heard his dragon say. Had Golanth been planning a very subtle courtship after all? Just as his rider had?

HARPER HALL—1.28.31

"You wanted to see me?"

Sebell gave a start. Pinch closed the door that he had opened so quietly that his Masterharper had not even heard it. He grinned.

"Losing the old skills, are you, Sebell?"

"So long as you don't," Sebell said and flipped a piece of paper across the table, nodding for Pinch to read it. "From Crom's harper."

"Serubil? Sensible man. Knows endless verses to that dreadful 'Down the Shafts.' " Pinch gave a revolted shudder as he stepped forward to take the note. His eyes brightened as he scanned it. "So if the body was never found, even if the trackers were delayed looking, Serubil says the man must have escaped. Possibly taken the river down to the plains."

"Read on. There's bad news, too."

"Oh. The prisoner did have a missing finger joint. No facial scar though." Pinch sighed. "Well, he could have got the scar on one of those early forays the Abominators made. Or even during or after his escape, you know," and Pinch eased his butt to the edge of Sebell's desk, not quite disturbing the piles of papers as he continued to read. "Didn't we send every harper a copy of the sketch I made?"

"Thought we had."

"Ah!" Pinch's somewhat sleepy expression brightened as he read further. "The prisoner—did the man have no name at all?—was sentenced for life to the Crom mines with several others for attacking Aivas."

"While I was waiting for you to arrive," and Sebell adroitly teased Pinch though, indeed, Master Mekelroy must have hurried to the Masterharper's door before pausing to slip inside in a stealthy fashion. That was often how Pinch entered this office, in stealth and at night or other inconvenient hours. "I had time to review Master Robinton's report of that incident."

Sebell stroked the blue leather cover of the journal and opened it with gentle fingers to the place where he had left a slip of paper. "Aivas thwarted the attack with what he called a 'sonic barrage'—a noise so fierce and penetrating that it rendered the intruders unconscious. Aivas said that some aural damage might be permanent. When we expressed amazement that he would retaliate, he remarked that, and I quote him, 'These units are programmed with industrially and politically valuable information. Unauthorized access and/or destructive actions must, therefore, be actively discouraged, and this has always been a minor function of an Aivas facility.' "

Sebell looked up from the open pages to regard Pinch.

"Well, yes." Pinch scratched the back of his head. " 'Some aural damage might be permanent.' According to Serubil—" and Pinch rattled the message in his hand, "—this prisoner was deaf. Maybe he recovered his hearing? Convenient and useful to pretend not to hear if someone wanted to escape."

"Yes, in the next paragraph, Serubil says this wasn't the man's first attempt. However—" Sebell held up a finger, "neither this one or the others ever gave their names."

"If they were deaf, how would they hear even that question?" Pinch asked.

Sebell grimaced. "Usually there are ways to get across as simple a question as that. Me," and he punched his chest with his thumb, "Sebell. You?" He widened his eyes, assumed an interrogatory expression, and pointed at Pinch.

"Having failed to crash or crush Aivas, the last thing I would want to tell was my name."

"Good point, but—" And Sebell looked down the closely written, beautifully inscribed handwriting to the paragraph he wanted, planting his finger on the margin. "—while the men carried no identification whatever in their clothes, one of them had been a glassblower, judging by the pipe calluses on his hands and burn scars on his arms." He regarded Pinch with an anticipatory expression.

"And Master Norist was one of the most outspoken adversaries of Aivas and his new techniques. He was also exiled for his part in the abduction of our Master Robinton." Pinch's face went as bleak as Sebell's at that reminder of the man both had respected, admired, and loved.

"Three of Master Norist's sons were journeymen in the Glasscrafthall. All were very much under their father's control."

Pinch considered this. "Mind you, after thirteen Turns in a mine, pipe calluses might not last but burn scars made by hot glass do not fade." He cocked his head at his Craftmaster. "So I should take a sketch of our good friend up to Serubil and maybe question some of the prison guards about those burn scars. Someone must have noticed them in thirteen Turns."

"And if he regained his hearing."

Pinch gave a snort. "He'd have to be able to talk if he's been plotting raids and selective booty."

"Find out, too, will you, Pinch, in your delightfully subtle way, how long it was before they went after the escaped prisoner? I'd heard tell the Smithcraft gave them twenty marks for that meteorite."

Pinch gave an appreciative whistle. "No wonder the latest ones have made such a stir."

Sebell shifted uneasily, his mouth pursed with annoyance.

"No matter how much they're worth, they're causing more trouble than they could possibly be worth to the Smithcraft."

"Oh?"

Sebell gave him a sharp look. "The one on the Keroon plains has the hillmen certain they'll have a fireball next and aren't the dragonriders going to blast it out of the sky before it falls on them and burns up all the fodder."

"I thought the one in Paradise River Hold only fell through a roof?"

"It harmed nothing and Jayge got fifteen Smith marks for it. He also said," and the expression on Sebell's face suggested to Pinch that the Masterharper wished that Jayge had not been so garrulous, "that the dolphins had seen several 'hissy hot' objects sink into the sea and they'd be happy to dive for them."

Pinch gave an indifferent shrug. "From what I remember, meteorites are more often apt to come down at sea than on land since we have so much more water on Pern."

"That's not the problem. Even people who should know better are demanding that the Weyrs send out more sweepriders to prevent more objects falling out of the sky."

Pinch gave a bark of laughter. "Dragons can move fast but not as fast as a meteorite. And meteorites are so hot when they hit the atmosphere that however hot dragon flame is, it couldn't stop a meteorite—even if a dragon could match its speed."

"I know, I know." Sebell sighed gustily.

"Now—" Pinch rattled Serubil's message. "Why don't I do something useful, like go to Crom Minehold?"

"I've asked N'ton to have you conveyed. You've about time to get your sketch of that Abominator and change into riding gear."

"Good. Bista loves going a-dragonback." Pinch neatly folded Serubil's message and put it in a thigh pocket. "I shan't be long."

"I hope not."

*　　　*　　　*

He was back by late evening. This time he knocked discreetly at Sebell's office door and entered, carrying a tray with a klah pot, cups, and a plate of sweet biscuits.

"I do not come empty-handed," he said and strode to set the tray down on Sebell's desk. He gave the piles of papers a quick appraisal: Sebell seemed to have made little headway with the stacks. "Did you do nothing today about all those petitions?"

"I put them in different piles. What's your news?"

Pinch poured klah for them both before he made himself comfortable on the edge of the desk again.

"The prisoner did not have a scar on his face when he left. He lost the top joint of the first finger on his left hand in a mining accident. He had tried to escape before but was easily caught. The trackers were sure he couldn't hear them coming. That's one reason they delayed going after him."

"When were those attempts made?"

Pinch consulted notes he had made in the margin of Serubil's message. "In the first couple of Turns he was there—" His eyes widened and he pointed at the MasterHarper just as Sebell reached the same conclusion.

"So he got enough hearing back to try again!" They spoke in unison and then both grinned.

"And he waited for the right time—" Sebell said.

"What better time than when a meteorite has knocked out holes to escape through!" Pinch jumped to his feet again. "Right. The prison bathroom has partitions in its stalls so no one there remembers any scars on his arms."

"And no name?"

"They called him Glass because of the pipe calluses."

"So he could be Norist's journeyman?" Sebell asked.

"That's likely."

"So he'd have plenty of reason to hate Aivas. Norist thought of Aivas as the Abomination. There's enough circumstantial evidence to believe that the escaped prisoner is the new leader."

"My man, Fifth," Pinch put in. With a sigh, he sat back down on the edge of the desk. "Now all we have to do is find

him and see if he can hear our questions clearly enough to answer them."

"I suggest we set our minds first to finding out what he
and his fellow Abominators plan to do next," Sebell said
gloomily.

Pinch watched his Master for a long thoughtful moment.
Then, with an artificially bright expression, he asked, "Did
you hear that M'rand and Pilgra are retiring to Cathay?"

"Yes," Sebell said. "And I'm glad. For their sakes—
they've fought Thread long enough—and because the new
Weyrleaders are young and will balance old G'dened who's
so conservative you wonder where he got the courage to
make the trip Forward thirty-odd Turns ago."

HONSHU HOLD — 2.1.31

F'lessan and Tai still reported to their respective Weyrs for
Threadfall but F'lessan was in Benden as infrequently as possible, returning to Honshu and his continued maintenance of
the weyrhold. Though he knew that most of the Monaco
riders were now settled in new quarters, Tai kept returning to
Honshu—and him. He also got her to talk to him, about her
childhood in Keroon, her schooling with Master Samvel, her
work at Landing, and her apprenticeship with Master Wansor
and Erragon. In the bright evenings, they would take turns
identifying more and more of the stars in the southern skies.

"You know, I've often wondered why there are four more
telescopes in the Catherine Caves," F'lessan said one night on
the terrace as they lay comfortably beside each other on a
wide mattress.

"I didn't know you knew that," she exclaimed, lowering
the binoculars to her chest and looking at him.

He chuckled. "You forget, I was in Landing almost from
the beginning and I certainly took every opportunity I could
to poke about in those Caves. I even made up outrageous treasures for the sealed cartons—that is, before I learned to read
the bar codes and ancient invoice words. Speaking of outra-

geous, how *does* Zaranth move trundlebugs? And for that matter, how did she rescue those hides of yours? The ones Mirrim got so upset about the day after the Fireball."

F'lessan silently berated himself for startling her with those questions. Hurriedly he went on, "I mean, I don't doubt it was Zaranth who saved them, but how? All the while I was there helping clear Monaco Weyr, you were too busy loading Zaranth with personal things, you couldn't even have timed it to your place." He rose to one elbow, turning his body against hers, and running a caressing finger down her face, which had turned all stiff and uncommunicative. "Zaranth told me she got them. I know her. I know you."

Tai's taut body relaxed and she turned her face, inviting his touch.

"All I know is she got them. Sometime before we had to leave Monaco ahead of the first tsunami wave and before we got to Landing." She shook her head back and forth on the mattress, vaguely waving one hand. "I was so tired by then. I don't know how long T'lion kept us timing it, back and forth—" Her voice trailed off.

He kissed the side of her mouth and nibbled at her lips. "Did you ever ask her? I mean, later, when all the furor had died down and we could start thinking again?"

"No."

"Could we ask her now?"

"I don't think she knows. But I'll ask her." Her eyes took on the unfocused look of a rider speaking to a dragon. She blinked and gave a little laugh. "She says she knew I'd want them before they floated away so she just brought them to me."

F'lessan thought that over, not much the wiser.

"Well, does she know how she moves the trundlebugs? The ones at Benini Hold?"

"Oh," Tai said, her voice less taut, "she does that with any that get close to her. She just points them in another direction."

"How?"

This time Tai closed her eyes to speak to Zaranth. "She

says she used to do it to tunnel snakes who got close to my weyr, too."

"What could she do it to here? Now! Tonight!"

"There aren't that many trundlebugs around here and snakes would all be holed up."

F'lessan sat up and looked around the terrace. "Ask her to move that bench," and he pointed to one against the wall, "here." He patted the ground beside him.

"The bench is not threatening you and it won't climb into your nose or your bed."

"So, something has to be harmful for her to shift it?" F'lessan asked, a little vexed with Zaranth's lack of comprehension. Then he remembered how patient Aivas had been when trying to get the fire-lizard, Farli, to go to the *Yoko*'s bridge, so far above Landing.

"No, just aggravating. The bench is not aggravating her."

Swiftly, F'lessan took a bowl from the tray of refreshments they had brought out to eat while stargazing. He aimed it at Zaranth, lounging beside Golanth on the upper terrace.

"What—" was all Tai had time to say before the bowl reappeared on the tray.

Glaring at him, her fists clenched, Tai turned on her lover with more anger than he had ever seen her display.

"You may *not* throw things at my dragon!"

"It *was* aggravating of me but look how she reacted!"

It took him time and much coaxing to calm Tai down, a pleasurable enough activity since her body responded to his deft caresses even if she did not wish it to. When she did see what he had been trying to prove, she herself made a suggestion: a cover from their bed since the night wind was proving chill.

"Maybe Golanth could bring us some wine?" she proposed.

Golanth peered down from the terrace above, his eyes whirling with some anxiety. *I don't know how Zaranth brings things you want.*

"Maybe we should try him with trundlebugs in his way," Tai said, giving her lover a sly grin. "If he does it Zaranth's way, they don't get upset and spread that stink of theirs."

We don't have trundlebugs in Benden, Golanth told his rider but he was plainly curious about how Zaranth had managed to move things around. Dragons moved themselves and their riders across great distances all the time; and recently Golanth had moved between times, but this moving something *else* was another matter altogether—one he had never attempted and could not do.

"We'll find some then," F'lessan said aloud as well as mentally to his bemused bronze. Some stray memory— associated with the time Farli and Ruth had gone to the *Yoko*—hovered at the back of his mind. "Will you have time tomorrow to help us locate some?" he asked Tai.

"In the afternoon, perhaps, but I did volunteer to help Erragon calculate orbits."

"Well, if you should see any trundlebugs at Cove Hold, give us a shout."

"Why not come help me calculate orbits?"

"A splendid notion since you know very well that I need the practice. Speaking of practice—" Carefully he lifted the thong of the binoculars from her neck and put them to one side and practiced making love to her. That was the most important reason he had brought the mattress out to the terrace and suggested they lie down and challenge each other at identifying stars.

When they met the next afternoon on the west side of Cove Hold where Tai had already spotted trundlebugs, they landed. Golanth was still dubious about arranging himself in the direct path of a mother trundlebug and two offspring, and Zaranth crouched behind a nearby thicket to encourage him. F'lessan and Tai stood in the shadow of a large frond tree as spectators.

Sublimely unaware of the obstacle set in its path, the trundlebug continued.

"Zaranth is telling Golanth that it's just a matter of turning it."

With a wide and mischievous grin, F'lessan closed his fingers around Tai's hand.

"My very dear green, I can hear everything she says."

"Can you?" Tai shot him a surprised glance. She knew that Ramoth and Mnementh, even Monarth and Path, spoke to each other's people.

The unmistakable stink of trundlebug interrupted this revelation.

What did you do? both riders cried, holding their noses as they ran for their dragons to mount and leave the clearing before they were actively ill.

I turned it, Golanth said as he leaped into the air, hoping *between* would absorb the awful reek.

Into mush, Zaranth said with some disgust.

They came out, so high above Cove Hold that they could see the whole of it spread out before them and the observatory sitting on its hill.

I can't smell me, Golanth said in an unusually meek voice.

I hope no one visits that clearing in the next day or two, F'lessan told Zaranth.

Tai says she sees another clearing and that Golanth must try again. I think I know what he didn't do, Zaranth said.

Riding at Golanth's right wing tip, Tai grinned across at his rider and gestured down. F'lessan nodded vigorously. Zaranth and Tai veered left and let the following wind ease them down until both dragons circled the new clearing of the thick young growth that was springing up after the tsunami flooding.

Again Golanth sat himself down in the path of the trundlebug, one with five offspring, the last nearly big enough to go off by itself.

Now, you want to turn them just enough so they go in another direction, Zaranth was saying calmly. *Not grind them into the sand at the same time. Just point to the east and give them a gentle* . . . I SAID GENTLE . . . *Where'd you send them?*

East, Golanth said very softly.

The green dragon and both riders looked to the east. There was a noticeable passage, trundlebug-wide, in a straight line through the grasses as far as they could see to the very waters of Cove Hold.

"Didn't you say they can tread water?" F'lessan asked, almost as chagrined as his dragon.

"If they don't already, they'll learn today," Tai replied. "Trundlebugs are survivors."

He does understand what to do, Zaranth said. *He was— well, maybe, too enthusiastic?*

"I think," F'lessan said, making good use of a chance to put his arm around Tai, "that more practice will determine exactly how much—energy? enthusiasm?—is enough to do the trick."

FORT HOLD—2.13.31

When Tenna came in from her run and handed Torlo her packet of letters from the Southern Boll stations, he leaned close, on the pretext of making a notation of her arrival on his schedule pad.

"Need to see your friend—" The old man paused so that Tenna would appreciate which friend. "—tonight. You, too. Side bench. Ten-thirty."

Tenna was becoming accustomed now to arranging meetings with Haligon for Torlo.

"You've a run uphill tomorrow, Tenna," he said more audibly.

She made an amused grimace. "Then I'm for the baths and a good long soak."

"As well, things considered," was his reply and she went off, pausing first in the dormitory she shared with other girls. It faced the main street and she pulled the curtain across to the exact center of the window. Haligon, who knew she was back at the Station, would now realize that she wished to see him. She didn't know which hold child ran his messages but they always got to him. She gathered up clean clothes, and then had a long soak and a brisk leg massage before the evening meal.

It was a fair evening, if cold, and a wind always blew down the main road from the hills so she had her lined jacket ready

when Haligon appeared at the door. Everyone expected the
two to be together when she was in Station so she smiled him
a welcome and was glad to see his expression lighten at the
sight of her. He'd had a lot of responsibility laid on him by
Lord Groghe this Turn, being what Haligon privately described as "the Lord Holder's Runner," and had remained
cheerful and accommodating. Or such was the impression she had from Torlo, as much because of what the Station-
manager *didn't* say as what he did.

"Walk, Tenna?" Haligon asked, nodding courteously to
Torlo and his wife, and extending the acknowledgment to the
others in the main room.

The usual jibes of "a walk will do her good after the run"
and "don't walk her legs off " followed them out. Such impu-
dent comments were better than disapproving silence.

The new electric lights, fashioned like glowbaskets, were
positioned on poles up and down the main road so, despite
the chill, they weren't the only ones taking an evening stroll.
They walked beyond the fixed lights and off to the side, near a
shed by the beastholds. In the shadows there, she and Haligon
could embrace without being overseen and with considerable
enthusiasm. She'd been away a sevenday and she had missed
him. Considering the ardor with which he kissed and nuzzled
her, the feeling was mutual.

They had not *really*—not in so many precise words—
discussed their association. She knew that he knew she felt
that she wasn't good enough for a son of one of the oldest
Bloodlines on Pern. He felt she would miss the freedom of
her profession and did not wish to constrain her. He had
other, older brothers so his father might not be so particular
about whom he espoused. With the problems caused by the
Fireball—which Haligon called the Comet—and Flood, they
had both been extremely busy. Fort Hold had taken no
damage but Lord Groghe had sent Haligon to arrange assistance in Southern Boll, which had had bad flooding. Tenna
wondered if perhaps that was Lord Groghe's way of suggesting that Haligon favor Lady Janissian. *That* would have been
an acceptable alliance to Tenna's way of thinking. Haligon's

only comment was that the young woman would make a good Holder and he liked her.

They were both conscious, though no one in Fort mentioned the fact, that Lord Groghe was losing some measure of his phenomenal vigor. Not surprising, considering he was eighty-nine. The vandalism at Turn's End had so shocked the old Lord that he was determined to prevent a repetition in *his* Hold and to identify who was behind this "resurgence of all that Abomination nonsense." He had managed to enlist the support of Torlo and many other Stationmasters, but not all Runners; there were those who still did not understand that it would be many, many Turns before the "abominable" hand units significantly affected their profession. Nevertheless, most would follow Station policy: they abhorred the violence displayed by the Abominators and their callous attack on the Healer Halls. Tenna might be one voice but she did her part, when she could, repeating what Lady Lessa had said—that Runners had long served Pern and would continue to do so.

Held passionately in Haligon's arms, she could forget duty, responsibility, and anything but the sensual contact she was enjoying. Tenna did nothing by halves and neither did Haligon.

With the innate sense of time that most Runners possessed, she reluctantly wriggled out of his arms and started pulling her clothing straight. She smiled when she heard his deep exasperated sigh.

He finger-combed his hair—which he hadn't had time to have trimmed—into a neat club at the back of his neck, fixed the collar of his jacket and lengthened his stride to match hers. Tenna certainly could set a brisk pace.

Torlo, or rather a shadow that could be a man, was already seated on the side bench, where the corner of the Station jutted out from the line of its neighbors. Tenna and Haligon often sat there, out of sight. Without a word, they sat on either side of him.

"Runners finally traced all those messages to Keroon," Torlo said without preamble. "Wide Bay and two inland holds, both isolated. Another reason it took so long to confirm Lord Groghe's request was because sometimes the messages were handed to Runners already on the trace."

"They were?" Tenna was astonished.

"Runners were paid, so it was permissible. 'Cept it happened quite a few times in Keroon, and Chesmic got suspicious and asked Runners and other Stationmasters, sort of quiet-like, how often that happened. That's why we got a network for Runners—never too far for someone to bring a message, proper-like, to the Station and have it logged in from source. Then it took time to catch up with the Runners who logged in such messages at their next Station. Seems odd to have it happen in sort of bunches, like in twelfth and thirteen month last Turn."

He paused. "Then I got confirmation that sort of thing had happened elsewhere, too. Same time. Only *now*—" and he paused again, "same thing's happening and all down Keroon way. Three times in the past two sevendays, man twice and woman t'other, stopped Runners to take on messages. Chesmic may be old, but he doesn't forget a face. Seen one too often, in different clothes, garbling words, too, saying he was picking up for Apprentice-this or Holder-that. Sent some off, too. Recently. We're still tracing where they were collected. *We,*" and putting his thumb to his chest indicated he was referring to all other Stationmasters, "think it's how those Abominator fellows are passing messages. Make sure that Pinch fellow knows, too."

Only the dark prevented Haligon from betraying surprise that Torlo would know Pinch by name and could hint at his discreet function within the Hall. Since Turn's End, Haligon had developed a healthy respect for Torlo's discretion and judgment. Son of a Lord Holder though he was, and allowed into many conferences his father held, he was surprised at how much more Torlo knew and understood about matters in Fort Hold and all across the two continents.

"Tell that MasterPrinter to be especially on his guard. It was his Hall printed that paper that's got folks so worried. I'd send a fire-lizard soon as I could, Lord Haligon."

"I will."

"Like right now," Torlo added at his driest. "See Tenna back. She's got a hard run tomorrow."

So dismissed, both rose. As they strolled around the corner to the Station door, Haligon circled her shoulders with one arm, wishing they didn't have to separate quite so soon. In front of the Station, Haligon gave her a quick hug and let her go. He didn't know how many eyes followed him up the steps to the Court, but no one would have seen that he made for a narrow side staircase on the far left of the Court that led to the Harper Hall. Later, on that moonless night, the departure of a fire-lizard, from an upper window in the Hall, was seen only by the vigilant watch dragon who wished Menolly's Beauty a safe flight.

PRINTER HALL AT WIDE BAY—SAME NIGHT

If Beauty woke the Masterprinter by picking delicately at his ear, he had the good sense not to thrash about in surprise. In fact, the fire-lizard's unexpected arrival merely confirmed the presentiment of trouble that Rosheen had confided in him three days ago. To cap her uneasiness, Stationmaster Arminet had sauntered into the Hall the day before, ostensibly to get a fresh notice of Runner fees printed. He had seemed far more interested in prowling the big Print Hall, asking if the glass were Morilton-made or the original. It was now a joke that the impact from the Comet had smashed glass that had come from old Norist's Hall while Morilton's remained intact.

"Morilton, of course," Tagetarl had replied with a grin.

"Good locks on the windows," Arminet had closed one eye with slow significance. "Sky-broom wood in gates and the Hall doors, too."

Tagetarl raised his eyebrows but Arminet had gone straight on to discuss his printing needs. That night Tagetarl had checked the gates, Hall doors, and windows himself, and slid into the brackets of the outer gate the heavy bar of sky-broom tree wood, which the former owner of the warehouse had used to dissuade pilferage. At both ends, the bar had ingenious fastenings that made removing it difficult if one didn't know how to release the latches. Sky-broom wood was too dense to break or chip so he felt safe enough.

No matter, on top of Rosheen's uneasiness and Arminet's odd remarks, a late-night message from the Harper Hall, and from Beauty, Menolly's gold, was alarming. Tagetarl wondered why Ola, Rosheen's fire-lizard queen, did not instantly appear to "supervise" the visitor. Ola wasn't usually absent when needed.

He held out his hand and Beauty stepped onto it. He could see the message holder on her left foreleg but it was too dark to read it. Rising carefully so as not to disturb Rosheen unnecessarily, he slipped yesterday's shirt and pants from the clothing rack and left the room. He pushed his hand for Beauty to leave it and motioned her down the stairs. He pulled on his clothes, her annoyed chirp hurrying the process. The thin carpet on the hall was cold under his bare feet, another incentive to move quickly.

As he descended the stairs, he peered out the windows into the court, silent and shadowed. Maybe that's where Ola was, lurking on the rooftop. The weaver's roof abutted the Hall's outbuildings. Pinch had made use of that entry. But Ola knew him. Tagetarl paused on the landing, listening for any sound from the hall that led to the upper story of the Print Hall. Nothing moved in that direction. He heard an admonitory chirp in the other and continued on to the spacious kitchen that was also their main living room.

Then Tagetarl berated himself for assuming that the message dealt with the Print Hall. There were any number of reasons—all equally worrying—that could have prompted Menolly to send Beauty in the middle of the night. It wasn't that late at the Harper Hall. Maybe she was merely inquiring about the musical scores she had recently sent him to be printed. Even with Beauty impatient, Tagetarl took the few steps to the porch door. It had a fine lock, strong, well-cast metal with another cunning catch that you'd have to know about to open the door once it was set. And the glass was Morilton-made, not easily shattered.

Tagetarl turned right into the big, dark kitchen, warm enough from the banked fires in the big range. Orange light from the ash grate made an eerie glow on the flagstones: not bright enough to read by. The shutters were closed against the winter's cold so he flicked on a small light and saw Beauty perched on a chair back, ruffling her wings shut. She held up her left foreleg for him to remove the message tube, cocking her head at him as if reproving his slowness. Taking a deep breath, Tagetarl unrolled the thin sheet of the message.

"Runners confirm trouble at Wide Bay. Guard the Hall. Assistance planned."

Rosheen had been right. Had Arminet been just passing on suspicions? Which now the Harper Hall was confirming? Trouble? From whom? Instantly the Abominators came to mind. But there hadn't been any more activity from that source since Turn's End. Of course, the Fireball Flood had kept everyone busy.

"Trouble? What sort of trouble?" Out of habit, he filled the kettle, put it on the range, and stoked the fire with blackstone. Then he stared at the range. "Fire trouble?" He swallowed hard. Paper burned just as easily as dried herbs or powdered medicines. And he had all those books displayed in the Hall, more packed to be shipped north and south. The presses could be smashed just as easily as medicine bottles and equipment, toner and ink could be spilled, and the sheds where he stored paper had wooden doors, because he hadn't been able to afford steel doors.

The note didn't mention Abominators. What made him think they would attack his Hall? What made him think they wouldn't? He was using a process that Aivas had provided, encouraged. Was the use of "Aivas procedures" all that was needed to agitate them?

"What sort of assistance?"

Perhaps he should ask some of his male apprentices to sleep in the Hall, or in the sheds. And Ola. Which reminded him. Where was she? Menolly had helped train her and she was certainly most responsible when Rosheen sent her with messages, going and returning as quickly as anyone could expect.

"Shouldn't you be getting back to Menolly?" he asked, a little sharp with worry.

She blinked her green eyes. Well, *she* wasn't worried if her eyes were green.

A whir of wings and into the kitchen flew Rosheen's gold queen, Ola. She may have landed on his shoulder but the warble of her message was for the Harper Hall queen. For a brief second, Tagetarl was amused at Ola's proprietary perch. Beauty's eyes whirled and, with a very definite air of command, she trilled several long musical phrases at the younger fire-lizard.

Ola straightened on Tagetarl's shoulder, sending her claws into shirt and flesh.

"Easy there, Ola!" She stroked his cheek with her head in apology.

Beauty trilled again briefly and disappeared.

"So she was waiting to speak to you, eh, Ola? Just what did she say?"

Closing the first lids over her eyes, Ola regarded him in what Rosheen called her "you-don't-need-to-know" response. But, under the lids, her eyes were picking up speed, with little flecks of yellow. Tagetarl was not as good as Rosheen at reading fire-lizard eye colors but he knew the color was edging toward alarm. Orange or red meant danger. She pushed against his shoulder, digging her talons into his flesh deep enough to make him wince, and then she, too, disappeared.

Tagetarl went to the window and put back the shutters, wondering if Beauty had ordered her to guard the Hall. It wasn't quite dawn—the brightest of the northern stars just fading—so he could distinguish the uneven roofs against the dark blue sky. All of a sudden, he saw the silhouette of one fire-lizard, wings cupped high, head extended and the wink of a yellow-green eye. He liked to think his harper hearing sharp enough to catch the call she was obviously sending. Her summons brought immediate results: it was rather heartening for him to see the mass of fire-lizards that congregated along the rooftops.

"Assistance planned" the note had said. He knew that fire-lizards could be fierce in protection of their human friends but Ola was only one and, while Wide Bay had several large fairs of wild fire-lizards, the creatures were notoriously short of memory. Surely Menolly meant more substantial assistance than a watch maintained by fire-lizards?

The kettle began to steam so he measured klah into the big pot and poured in hot water to the top. Hadn't Benelek told him at the last Gather that he was experimenting with an electrically heated kettle? His stomach grumbled so he looked in the bread cupboard and cut himself several slices to toast on the reawakened range. He was looking for sweetening to spread on it when he detected just the barest sound, a scuff. Had he been stupid enough to unlock the outside door when he examined it? He picked up the full klah pot; moved toward the hall, ready to fling the hot contents on anyone who appeared.

"It's me," a familiar voice whispered.

"It is I, please, Pinch," Tagetarl corrected irritably, lowering the klah pot.

One step brought Pinch to the doorway, his gold Bista clinging to his jacket.

"How did you get in? No, don't tell me. Over the roof."

Pinch made an apologetic face.

"How'd you get in the hold?" Tagetarl was really startled now, having spent so much on a difficult lock for the hold door.

Pinch held up a slender key. "You told me how to release the safety catch when you gave me this. I didn't want to wake you up." He dropped the key back into an inner pocket where it gave a muffled *clink* as it settled and Tagetarl wondered how many other keys the Harper had collected.

"But Ola's on the roof with fairs of fire-lizards." What good *would* fire-lizards do in his defense?

"For one, she knows me. And two, Bista vouched for me. I'll give her this, she was ready to call her fairs down on me." Then Pinch sniffed, noticing the klah pot still in Tagetarl's hand. "You knew I was coming?" he asked, faintly surprised.

"Beauty brought me a message. Are you and Bista my 'assistance'?"

Pinch's weary face was wreathed in a smile. "Part of it, but I'm glad to know that the warning got through to the Harper Hall, too." He looked over his shoulder and said in a louder voice, "It's safe to come in now. There's fresh klah. And," he went on to the startled Tagetarl, "by the way, I suspect that when they decide to enter these premises for their subversive activities, they, too, will use the weaver's roof. He's listened to loom clacking so long he's deafer than a shuttle."

Pinch moved confidently to the wall cabinet and started hooking cup handles on the fingers of his left hand, gathering four more together with a clink in his right fingers. He placed all on the table as his companions solemnly entered one by one.

"Still, it's wiser to *let* them use a known vulnerability and prepare. Oh, by the way, these are more of the promised 'assistance.' Don't gawk, Tag. Pour the klah while I introduce them."

Five young men and three girls filed in, packs on their shoulders, covered buckets in their hands, giving him a nod or a shy smile.

"Oh, leave the stuff on the landing or there won't be anywhere to stand," Pinch said, gesturing them to do so before he handed out the cups. Then he named them as he poured klah. Macy, Chenoa, Egara, Magalia, Fromelin, Torjus, Garrel, and Niness.

"Much obliged, Master."

"Thank you, Master Tagetarl."

"You're very kind, Master."

"Appreciate this."

"Eight, Pinch?" Tagetarl said, automatically steadying cups as he filled them; trying to absorb the presence of the

Harper and the assistance. Would there be enough klah left for him?

"Yes, that's the number we figured it would take to paint all the wood you've got," Pinch said with a weary sigh. He snagged a stool to set his backside on, gesturing for his followers to be easy. "For all that most of your Hall is made of good fieldstone, you've wood in your doors and floors and window frames. They'd burn just as easily as paper will." Pinch raised his hand to soothe Tagetarl's explosion. "So we have thoughtfully brought a fire-retardant. A coat of that's to go on all your wooden surfaces between now and full daylight. Doesn't smell either. Or won't with all the stinks this close to the wharves. The stuff dries quickly, Piemur assures me, and since our Abominators would scarcely have delved that far into Aivas's files to know such useful substances exist, it'll help foil their plans."

"It is the Abominators? You know what they plan?" Tagetarl exclaimed, nearly sloshing hot klah over Macy's hand.

"We can make some pretty good guesses, based on what they've done before," Pinch said condescendingly. Then his lips thinned with distaste.

"But why should they attack the Print Hall? We're supporting the teaching program after all and . . ."

"Well, you printed a concise report of the Fireball and the true extent of the Flooding," Pinch said, grinning at the outraged Tagetarl. "We've surmised that the Abominators wanted to set about the rumor that Aivas had meddled with the very rhythm of Pern and that this Fireball was a direct result. Therefore anything that Aivas had suggested, recommended, dispensed the plans of, offered solutions to should be suspect, avoided, discarded, and forgotten so we can go back to the pure days when all we had to do was worry about Threadfall every two hundred and fifty Turns—give or take a few."

"Is that what they were going to say? After the good that's been done by the Healers since they learned how to rectify so many ailments and provide cures for maladies that used to *kill* people by the hundreds? Not to mention being able to refer to books that provide explanations and—and—"

Tagetarl was stunned. Pinch poured a cup of klah and put it in his hand.

"Drink. You're not awake yet. But that gives them more reason to try and put a stop to the Hall."

"More reason? Stop the Hall?"

"The written word has a power all its own, that rumor can never replace. So you publish truth. The Abominators circulate rumor. A person can reread words and reestablish truth. Rumor can't be caught, can't be traced. It may be more fun to pass along but a book, a sheet of printed paper, that's tangible and the sense of it doesn't change when it's passed from hand to hand. Drink the klah, Tagetarl," Pinch said very gently, raising Tagetarl's hand to bring his cup to his mouth.

The MasterPrinter managed one sip of the hot liquid. "What do I do? I'll need guards. My apprentices aren't going to be enough!"

Pinch raised hands to silence him. "Of course they aren't. Nice enough lads but not trained, though I suspect Marley's a good man in a brawl, but my reinforcements here—" He gestured broadly at the young people who were quietly sipping klah. "—have a few tricks and they know one end of a brush from another. We've arrived timely, too, since Beauty was here and my suspicions have been confirmed by the Runners." He grinned brightly at Tagetarl. "Dragonriders aren't the only ones who can be where they're needed when they're needed."

Tagetarl's jaw dropped at what was almost a profane remark from a harper.

"Now you've finished your klah, boys and girls, we've a lot to do before daylight. Smear the retardant on anything wooden. The gloves may be clumsy but they'll save your skin. Work quietly, if you please. I don't want even to hear the slap of brushes on the wood. You've all had practice."

While two of the group gathered the cups and set them in the sink, the others went out, collecting their supplies and quietly leaving by the kitchen porch. Tagetarl glanced out the window and, in the dim predawn light, could barely see the other side of the wide court.

"Stuff's dark going on, dries transparent. Don't worry," Pinch said, rising to refill the kettle from the tap at the sink and put it back on the stove. As he swung his leg over the stool, he took a sheet from a pocket and smoothed it on the table in front of Tagetarl. "Seen him around here lately?"

Tagetarl frowned. "That's the same man you drew the last time you were here. I thought he looked familiar. I thought it odd of him to ask for a copy of Teaching Ballads. I'd actually filled an order for Lord Kashman and had none in stock. Told him to come back in a sevenday."

Pinch nodded as if that wasn't news to him. "Tomorrow."

"You mean, he plans to just walk in here . . ." Tagetarl was appalled when he remembered the incident. "I showed him through the Hall. It seemed only courteous."

Pinch's smile was sardonic. "I hope you limited it to the Hall."

"I did, but I also mentioned how many apprentices I'm training." Tagetarl slammed his forehead with his hand. How naïve of him! Had he lost all his Harper-trained acuity? He had seven lads, none of them fully grown except Marley, and three girls, who were all of them light-boned, hired for their quick fingers. Add in the eight Pinch had brought—

"Don't fret," Pinch said soothingly. "You'd no cause—then— to suspect anything. No reason not to be courteous. You are, after all, offering a special service. Even if the Abominators don't like it."

Tagetarl swallowed, the hot klah cooling too rapidly in his belly to give him the comfort it usually did. "How many were there in that attack on the Healer Hall? Ten? No, fifteen."

"I'd say there'd have to be at least ten for the job here," Pinch said casually, as if that made no difference. "Had any other 'curious' visitors lately?"

Tagetarl buried his face in his hands, rubbing it and then scrubbing his scalp with his knuckles. "Quite likely and all of them seemed perfectly reasonable folk."

"They may well be," Pinch remarked amiably, "except

those who get a notion that you're a wicked tool of the Abominator because you can turn out whole books in days instead of months."

Tagetarl groaned.

Pinch reached over and patted Tagetarl on the shoulder. "But we've warning and I know who—and what—to be looking for."

"The three sketches you showed me?"

"I'm hoping all three will come to this party." Pinch's expression turned enigmatic.

"Party?" Tagetarl was livid.

"Evening exercise, if you prefer. Since they expect to surprise you, we'll just prepare a few of our own." He rose and Bista glided from her perch on the windowsill to his shoulder. "I'll go give them a hand." When Tagetarl started to rise, throwing off the last of this infamous shock, Pinch motioned to the kettle. "We'll need a lot more klah. And don't notice me walking about today, will you? The others'll hide in the loft. Just don't send anyone up there, will you? Fine. We brought food and water with us. No one will know we're here."

He started to leave, and then stopped, putting up a hand to steady his gold fire-lizard on his shoulder.

"There's one more thing, Tag," he went on. "You might just get an unexpected gift, like a skin of good wine. Don't even sample it out of courtesy. Or any provisions offered in kind for books received."

"What?" Tagetarl bristled at that. They did take fresh fruit or meat in return for printing. Would an Abominator stoop to poison? Then he remembered that Master Robinton had been drugged at the Ruatha Gather and abducted right in front of hundreds of people. "How many are involved?"

Pinch gave an indolent shrug. "Don't know, but Abominators seem to work in groups. Since they intend to damage the Hall, they'll bring enough brawn to smash stuff around. There are still persons," and he heaved a sigh for those so misguided, "who'll do any job that drops marks in their pockets."

Tagetarl shuddered; he had a vivid picture of the Hall,

paper burning, toner powder splotching the whitewashed walls, hammers smashing his presses, even if Pinch seemed certain that fire could be prevented.

"You are *not* reassuring me, Pinch!" he said in a caustic tone.

"While we want them to get *in*," Pinch said, "to show that they had evil intentions, we want to keep them from getting out." His grin was malicious. "That'll be easier to do, you know."

"No, I don't know, but this is just the sort of adventure you enjoy!"

"You used to, too, in your younger days, Tag," the Harper said with an unrepentant grin. "Until you got your Mastery and started a new Hall." He rose before Tagetarl could marshal a stern rebuttal. "By the way, if you should hear someone whistling," and he provided a trill, "that's me. If you hear this one," and the intervals of the five notes in the next warble were very odd indeed, like some of the quartet music Menolly liked to write for very experienced players, "that means someone suspicious close. Got 'em?"

"Of course," Tagetarl replied with some heat. "I'm a MasterHarper. Which reminds me: where did you so handily assemble that crew of yours? One of the Halls?" There was something familiar about them that Tagetarl couldn't place.

"Here and there," Pinch replied enigmatically but added with uncharacteristic candor, "Runners, a few of 'em are seafolk waiting for a ship, useful types. All vouched for, I assure you. Ran me ragged getting here in time. Quick over the roof, too." He glanced outside. "Experienced with brushes . . . of all sorts."

Then he and Bista were out of the kitchen before Tagetarl could ask anything else. Bewildered by Pinch and the imminent threat to his Hall, Tagetarl looked around, wondering how he was going to break this news to Rosheen. Well, if he washed the cups and put them away, she wouldn't know at first glance that there had been early morning visitors.

HONSHU HOLD—2.9.31

"Come, my dear Tai," F'lessan said as she entered the kitchen area at Honshu, "we will eat—and get down to business." He rose and came to meet her.

She gave him a wary smile. He had a tendency to jump in different directions, as if he enjoyed catching her off balance. He probably did. She'd thought that, once Golanth had flown Zaranth, F'lessan would disengage from her, perhaps more kindly than others had. On the contrary, he had insisted that she remain at Honshu, that she choose a room as her own— though they mainly shared the large one he preferred, and had shown her every part of an installation that must have originally been designed to support a large population. She hadn't known there were so many levels in the stone mountain. She loved the well-equipped machine and tool room, just off the ground level where the covered hulk of an Ancient's sled was stored. The night of the Fireball, when so many displaced Monacans had found shelter at Honshu, had probably been the first time in centuries the Weyrhold had been even half full.

He encouraged her to talk about her interest in astronomy and managed to bring texts from the Archives that she was certain Master Esselin did not realize he had borrowed. He was very conscientious about returning them.

"We've put it off long enough, I think!"

A sparkle in his eye was all the warning she had before he swung her up in his arms and twirled around. She clung to his shoulders, not fearing that he would drop her, but so she had this excuse to touch him. She wasn't yet accustomed to either his spontaneity or his preference for touching but she was learning to welcome them. His gray eyes echoed his smile. If she weren't so familiar with the weather and worry lines on his face, she'd've thought him much younger than she knew him to be when he smiled like that. Such an open, merry smile!

"Put what off?" she said, humoring his mood. He wanted to surprise her, that was certain.

"It's a beautiful clear night." He paused tantalizingly, and then she knew what he meant and could not suppress a gasp of excitement. "Yes, tonight, my dear green, we can hook up the scope."

Tai couldn't suppress her crow of delight. "You got a monitor!"

"And the operating disks. Erragon copied them for us and supplied fresh blanks for the imager. He's given us a search pattern to follow. As if we'd ever get enough exposures to do a thorough job." His eyes flashed with determination. "All we need is the *right* one at the *right* time of night or piece of sky."

He was right, of course, she knew, but with his merry grin and wide-open eyes, it was as if he was somehow going to succeed despite the odds against it. His was a personality of great contrast. She was fascinated by it and rebuked herself that she had ever considered him shallow. Over the last few sevendays, she had seen how seriously he took responsibilities, exuding an optimism that could fire those around him, and how he never shirked tasks, like the Benini Hold planting, which he could have delegated to another rider. He was certainly not the casual reckless weyrbred lad Mirrim had described.

"I can certainly help with the search patterns," she said, noticing how easily he involved her in his schemes. "Erragon trusted me with comparisons and scannings."

"I'd prefer scanning just you, Tai m'dear," he said, kissing the hollow in her throat; his teasing lips were warm against flesh still chilled from her trip *between*. "But we'll have to show Erragon results from Honshu or he'll insist on dragging you back to Cove Hold."

Slowly he let her down. She liked the feel of his body against hers; F'lessan was so vital, so energetic, so—alive! He did not release her entirely, affectionately looping one arm across her shoulders.

"I also spent my day doing what Aivas used to call a refresher course," he added with one of his mischievous grins.

"I don't think I paid as much attention to him the first time as I should have."

She noticed how his eyes darkened with the knowledge of wasted opportunity. She touched his cheek in a brief caress. "If only we all knew then what we know now."

"Ah, yes," and his lips curved with a touch of bitterness.

Once again she was amazed that F'lessan was willing to show his regrets. He always appeared so self-confident. Still feeling a little embarrassed by such intimacy, she caught sight of the steaming pot on the range.

"You cooked?" And looked again. "That isn't a Honshu pot."

"No," and he chuckled, giving her a hug as he guided her to the range. "I stopped off at Sagassy's hold on the way back. I'd some nails for them from Landing's Smithcrafthall. She insisted that I take this as a delivery fee." He shrugged. "Remind me to return the pot."

"I will," she replied. "After I'm sure you've washed it properly." She couldn't resist teasing him as she picked up the wooden spoon to stir the stew. "Oh, you've nearly let it scorch!"

"Then it's hot enough to eat."

F'lessan pushed her out of the way, gesturing her to sit at the end of the table that she saw had been set for two, and began ladling the stew into the wide, deep bowls. Mirrim would never believe that F'lessan could be so useful. She pinched the bread loaf and it was fresh; there was a salad, too, as greens were beginning to flourish again along the coast. She poured wine from the skin into glasses while F'lessan brought heaped plates to the table.

"Sagassy said that Riller, Jubb, and Sparling have all seen signs of felines creeping back into the valley," he said. "They haven't run a check for missing stock but the herds have been spooky lately." He blew on his spoon to cool the gravy-soaked meat. "Those sharding creatures may be hunting on this side of the ridge again."

Eight families, gradually clearing enough land to grow essential crops as well as round up wild herdbeasts, had settled the valley that spread out north of Honshu. They protected their cluster of buildings and beastholds with dragon dung and firestone mash, the best deterrents for any pests in the south, apart from trundlebugs. Visiting dragons—and those staying at Honshu after the Fireball had added considerably to the perimeter—were encouraged to donate. Once the residues dried, there was little smell to aggravate human sensitivities, but what there was was sufficient to put off all but the hungriest predators.

She and F'lessan had hunted there during their first week together. She and Zaranth had just missed catching one of the cloudy-coats that wore such valuable pelts. There was so much else to do that they hadn't been able to take time to hunt felines again.

"We'll have to plan to swing round the holds' borders and re-discourage the carnivores," he said, breaking off a piece of bread and offering it to her before taking some for himself. "You've about finished curing the last pelts we got, haven't you?"

"Just about. Someone else must have pegged skins on the wall I'm using," she said.

"Probably. Hold records suggest they were self-sufficient." He shook his head. "I've never understood what happened to the people who were doing so well here. Why they simply . . ." he spread out his hands in bewilderment, ". . . left?"

She felt gravy on the corner of her mouth and used a bit of the bread to remove it, right past her lips. "Plague?" Disease had wiped out so many holdings it was always the first guess.

He shook his head. "No, no skeletons."

"Vermin would have scavenged the remains."

"Their effects were all neatly put away."

"As if they meant to return?" she asked, surprised, but then F'lessan had been researching the history of this weyrhold of his.

"No, as if that was the way they took care of tools and equipment." He gestured to the kitchen and the utensils visible on the work surfaces.

"As they did in the workshop." All the shelves and drawers

fascinated Tai, the contents neatly packed away in oil or grease and the airless plastic envelopes that the Ancients had had. Even the flying machine—a sled, F'lessan called it—had been cocooned. She'd never had the opportunity to visit the Catherine Caves as F'lessan had, but he'd said that these weren't thoroughly explored or emptied of treasures. Samples of the things the Ancients had used were on display at Landing, some still encased in the packing used for the voyage to the Rukbat system. She—and others—had puzzled over the use of some items. "Why would they leave such a beautiful place?"

"Once this Pass is over, you may be sure I won't leave," he said resolutely. "As it is, I'm here more than I should be," he added with that irrepressibly engaging grin she so enjoyed. "Eat up, my dear green."

"Shouldn't have eaten so much," he remarked twenty minutes later as she trudged behind him up the steep stairs to the observation room. He was panting, too, she noticed. "As well we don't have to lug things all the way up these stairs. Only down one level when we get where we're going."

F'lessan had explained the almost secretive design of Honshu's observatory; not all the secrets, he'd said, grinning with a boyish delight, but Kenjo had made sure it was not readily accessible. The first challenge was the stairs that went up six levels inside Honshu's cliff.

"Does Golanth watch stars with you, too?" she asked. Zaranth affected to and never objected when Tai spent long hours on her green back, studying the night sky.

"He pretends to be interested," F'lessan said in a mock-soft voice, turning to grin down the metal spiral at her.

I hope I will not hurt these things when I bring them to you so high up, Golanth said facetiously.

"Golanth, you will carry them as carefully as fire-lizard eggs," F'lessan said, his voice stern as he winked down at Tai. "When I found the place, it was a mess and outside most of the solar panels were fouled or missing. Worse than the Admin building." He took a deep breath before the next step. "Golanth was very good about helping me repair and reinstall them. He doesn't fit in the observatory, of course, but he's good at encouraging me to work hard." He chuckled as he plodded up several more steps, boots clanking on the metal. She could feel the climb pulling at her muscles. He went on. "Good thing the cylinder had been vacuum-wrapped—another point in my theory that they intended to come back!" She could see that he was using the handrail to pull him upward. Good idea! She followed his example. "So we cleaned and repaired the vents and solar panels, and let power build up. I'd the finder scope to use to see if the instrument still worked. It did." He gave a deep sigh of satisfaction. "We'll have to run a pointing recalibration but I've got the files for the stars we use. Once we've hooked up the computer and are sure it's pointing accurately, we can proceed to search whatever part of the sky Erragon wants us to scan. The program makes it possible to shift the primary mirror. We'll get pictures on the monitor and decide what to save."

He paused, taking in deep breaths before he started upward again. She wondered that he didn't save his breath for the climb but F'lessan loved to talk and, since his voice was very pleasant to listen to, she didn't mind. She didn't usually have much to say.

"Got the generator working, too, so we don't have to limit solar panel use." He had breath enough for a chuckle. "Mighty clever those Ancients were in harnessing renewable energy. When we told Aivas that we'd found the old machinery, I swear he almost laughed."

"Laughed?" It would never have occurred to Tai that Aivas had been endowed with a sense of humor. She nearly stumbled on the steps but caught herself on the handrail.

"Oh, Aivas had a powerful sense of humor. You know the kind of pause that means someone's laughing inside? Well, Aivas would pause, wait a beat, and go on with what he was saying. Piemur was sure Aivas laughed to himself in such beats, but Jancis was horrified by the mere suggestion of a machine that could laugh."

Tai couldn't see his face but, though sometimes he made jokes about his Turns under Aivas's supervision, his voice was tinged with a respect that he didn't accord even his Weyr-leaders. She'd been so young, fresh from Keroonian hills when her mother and father had come south to work at Landing, and painfully naïve. Told over and over what a splendid chance she was getting in a Landing education, she had concentrated on learning as much as she could to avoid disappointing anyone, including Aivas. She had never questioned anything *then*. Now, and in the presence of F'lessan, she felt able to ask.

"Why would Aivas be amused that you had discovered this valuable instrument and a power generator?"

"I suspect," and F'lessan climbed a few more steps before answering, "because Kenjo had been very clever about so many things. Like saving fuel in sacks each trip down from the *Yoko* so he could fly the little plane he built. And using the stone-cutters far more extensively than any other colonist. Yet what a beautiful place he designed—although, come to think of it, his wife, Ita, was artistic and it's likely she did the murals in the Hall and some of the tapestries."

"Here we are," he said and she could hear the relief in his voice. Dragonriders were more accustomed to flying heights than climbing them.

She didn't mind showing that the narrow winding stairs had winded her. Her thighs felt heavy, and she had an ache in the calf of her left leg. She gave it a quick massage as he fiddled a key into the locked door they had climbed so high to reach.

At first, Tai saw nothing but the smooth sides of the vertical shaft's creamy rock, eerily lit from small guide lights. She could feel a light breeze sweeping upward, cooling legs, body, and even the sweat on her forehead, and then a door opened just above her eye level. F'lessan lifted himself through, for a moment blocking her view. He moved to one side and, in the light from the shaft, she saw more creamy rock. She clattered up the last few steps and walked into such a splendid space that she just stood, looking around in amazement. A large dark brooding mass dominated the center of a wooden floor.

F'lessan pressed plates on one side of the door and lights blinked on, one by one, girdling the room about F'lessan's height from the floor. She could also feel more fresh air circulating.

As the lights came up, she saw the long barrel of Honshu's telescope, thicker in circumference than she could have put her arms about, longer than F'lessan was tall. A U-shaped fork structure held the barrel and, as she got closer, she could see that the fork was itself supported by a heavy metal plate, attached to a metal turntable. This tilted arrangement was an equatorial mount entirely different from the up-down, left-right, alt-azimuth mounting that was appropriate for Cove Hold's larger, skeletal type scope and its position near the equator. Honshu's scope was a dull cream of a composite material, slightly longer at the front, with a blunt rear end that she knew sleekly enclosed the 620millimeter reflecting mirror. Unlike the Cove Hold scope, where the mirror was clearly visible inside the supporting skeleton, this mirror was hidden within the opaque cylinder. Only the services connecting to the telescope revealed what else was inside. She could see cooling pipes and electrical cables feeding through the cylinder at its midpoint, which she knew led to the camera at the heart of the telescope. What she could identify as the finder scope was attached to the upper surface beside two other anonymous cylinders. The Cove's instrument—one of the Ancients' classical Cassegrains— was half again as long as this one, having a one-meter lens, its optics based entirely around mirrors and enclosed in a light gray composite of some ancient material. Here, too, was a raised wooden floor, to keep vibrations from being transmitted to the telescope and to allow people to walk safely around while observing. Not that the sheer cliff to which the scope was attached would move: Cove Hold had a cement base on its rocky promontory, high above the sea.

Tentatively, she approached the cylinder, saw the cover at the top and controlled her impatience to see it. She did, however, appreciate F'lessan's proprietary feeling for the scope.

That he was willing to share it with her was yet one more un-expected boon.

"Now watch!" he said, holding up his left hand, grinning with anticipation. With the fingers of his right, he pressed more plates, diverting her from a closer inspection of tele-scope and mounting.

She was startled when a crack appeared in the ceiling. She stepped back, close to him, as what had seemed to be solid rock shifted. Gears whirred and the halves dropped and spread slowly apart, continuing to sink down, out of the way, against the observatory dome, stopping just above the girdle of lights.

"Full range," F'lessan cried in a proud tone, gesturing to the opening created by the sliding roof. "Golly found the seam in the rock when we were repairing the solar panels. No rock has straight seams," he said with a snort. "Took Jancis, Piemur, and me days to oil, repair, and get this working again."

Tai knew that she was gawking idiotically at the superb view of the southern night sky now visible. She gasped then, when two dark shadows stealthily loomed down into the opening.

Us, said Zaranth and gave an audible chirp, well pleased with herself for scaring her rider. She had kept her eyes shut and now opened them, happily whirling green.

You meant to scare me, she accused her dragon, hand still at her throat.

Golanth thought it would be all right, Zaranth said in a meek tone, cocking her head slightly at her rider, eliciting pardon.

Golanth made amused sounds of his own, showing his white teeth.

"They're a right pair of Gather fools," F'lessan said, giving her a reassuring squeeze before he walked over to where Golanth was peering down. Then, in one of those abrupt changes of his, F'lessan turned almost brusque. "Golly, take care not to step on those solar panels when you swing those controls down. Tai, can you manage the one Zaranth has for you? I'd like to get this system up and running before dawn."

He reached up, tall enough to grasp the boxes that Golanth dutifully lowered one by one to him through the open roof. Tai shook off the moment of panic—too astonished by the open sky to feel her dragon's presence—and took hold of the well-padded square that Zaranth dangled down to her.

"We'll unpack up here, Tai. More space. The control room's just down that short staircase." He pointed to the far wall where she now saw the well of the other stairs.

Did I really scare you, Tai? Zaranth asked penitently, drawing one set of her eyelids across in apology.

"Of course you did," Tai replied and then relented. *Is Golanth teaching you bad habits?*

None I don't like, her dragon answered with a flirt of her eyelids.

Tai cleared her throat. "What do I have here, F'lessan?" she asked, changing the subject.

He spared a look from what he was unpacking. "The monitor!" he replied and he sprang toward her. "I'll just turn the lights up down there," he said and strode to the stairwell, tapping the keypad. "Kenjo must have been a security freak the way he designed this observatory. As if someone could steal this or the stars."

With lighting, Tai had no trouble taking the ten straight steps down into the control room. The worktops had been cleaned recently and the shelving above them fitted with jacks for the controls. Two wheeled half-chairs had been pushed back under the stairs. An enclosed panel ran slantwise from the jack in the direction of the base of the telescope on the floor above. She settled the flat-screened monitor on a mounting that was an exact fit. Well, no doubt the long-dead Kenjo had used a similar unit to view the images she devoutly hoped the scope would still mirror.

F'lessan clattered down with the keypad, decoder box, and storage disks. His eyes gleamed with anticipation. With no wasted effort he arranged his burdens on the worktop and put the storage disks on the shelf where he could read the labels. He hauled connectors out of his thigh pocket and began plugging them in, murmuring as he did so, reminding himself which went where until he had the system connected. Standing with his hands on his belt, he let out a long breath. Then he reached toward the rank of storage disks, found the one he needed for the calibration, and slipped it into the operating slot.

"Shall we see if it'll light up? Ooops," and he was halfway up the stairs, "got to uncover its eye, first."

She heard the thump of his footsteps on the wooden flooring and his admonition to the two dragons to find themselves comfortable places to stay and not to step on the solar panels.

He ran back down, rubbing his hands, grabbed both seating units from under the stairs, swinging one over to her while he planted himself on the second and, for one long moment, poised his hands over the controls.

"Now," he announced, grinning at her, his eyes glittering with high spirits, "let there be light!" He tapped out several sequences, inhaled deeply when the monitor came to life, entered another series of commands, and then folded his arms on his chest. "Remember to breathe, Tai!"

She did, smiling because she hadn't realized she'd been holding her breath.

The monitor cleared and they had an image of the skyscape of the northern horizon, the direction in which the telescope had pointed, covered, for centuries. "So," and F'lessan rubbed his hands together, "let's run the pointing calibration. I'll use Acrux as the first check." His eyes crinkled in a smile as he reminded her of the stars she had pointed out to him the first evening she was at Honshu.

Tai caught her breath, for this was another example of how he endeared himself to her without really trying.

"I'll allow for the time elapsed since we last checked positions." He went on and she rose to stand behind him as he tapped in the commands, daring to put her hands lightly on his shoulders. "Good ones to start with." While waiting for the system to respond, he lifted her right hand to his lips and kissed the palm, his eyes never leaving the screen as the scope began to shift in obedience to the coordinates for Acrux. "When we have a chance, we can automate this procedure but I can't resist the temptation to show off a little. You've had so much more time on a working scope than I have."

He put her hand back on his shoulder, giving it a final pat. "Ah, here we are!" He flourished his hand as the winking pulse of Acrux appeared on the monitor, centered. He leaned forward as the calibration came up to one side, confirming the focus. "And no optical aberrations noticeable."

He grinned up at her, his gray eyes sparkling, infecting her with his exuberant enthusiasm. He was so boyishly pleased with Honshu's performance—as if it were all his doing—that she couldn't resist rumpling his thick hair. He laughed softly, pleased by her spontaneous caress.

"Now Becrux," he said, tapping in its position and obediently the focus altered. "Sudden idea!" And he turned to her, his expression one of recklessness, "Once we've done enough calibrations to be sure the focus is accurate, let's dispense with the rest of Honshu's catalogue and focus on whatever strikes our fancy. Some of those globular clusters I was just studying about. Or the spiral nebulas. Or something that isn't anywhere close to Pern!"

She gawped at him, unaccountably thrilled at such a suggestion. She'd often wanted to just "look" beyond this dark corner: to the cloudy canyons with dark holes, the cartwheels in various orientations, ghostly circular shapes of planetary nebulae, wisps of gas lit up by newborn stars. She did so want to see the eternal and changing magic of the universe.

"And we'll take some images of the ones we like best, shall we?"

She grinned back at him. But, before he did anything else, he kissed the dimples in her cheeks.

NIGHT AT WIDE BAY—2.9.31

Tagetarl spent a terrible day, trying to conduct himself as he would any normal day in front of apprentices and clients alike, all the while wondering what "normal" should look like. For instance, on a normal day, he wouldn't have made so many pots of klah before dawn nor washed so many cups. He did have a fresh pot ready at the usual time that he opened the outer gates for his apprentices and unlocked the double doors of the Hall. He noticed that there was a slight shine to the wood but, though he sniffed deeply—causing his oldest apprentice, Marley, to regard his Master oddly—the smell was composed more of the prevalent odor of fish and toner than paint. He regained some of his usual composure by assigning the day's tasks.

He heard the whistle, had to think for a moment, and then saw two grimy fellows rolling in two big barrels.

"Just as you ordered 'em, Master Tawgurtall," the older man said, chewing his words as he deftly shifted his cask into a corner by the right-hand door. How like Pinch to mangle his name, so Tagetarl merely nodded at the shabbily dressed drudge. His equally scruffy associate rolled a second barrel into the opposite side. "As required." Then, with that cryptic statement, they both left.

"As I was saying, Marley," Tagetarl went on, tapping the copy to get Marley's full attention.

He tried to concentrate on the usual tasks of a day, making up a new order for different weights of paper from Master Bendarek—well, he could delay that for today. He checked the two girls stitching bindings, made sure Delart was cutting the leather economically, that Wil was trimming only the paper edges neatly and not his fingertips with the extremely sharp edge of the wide blade. Idly Tagetarl wondered if he could detach that broad knife and use it against the Abominators tonight, or whenever they attacked his Hall.

On brief trips across the court, he did notice that Ola

seemed to make a great many short dashes from roof to kitchen window, checking on Rosheen wherever she was. He hadn't told Rosheen yet because she seemed happy today, and had possibly forgotten her uneasy presentiments. She also had a complicated Smithcrafthall manual to proofread. He didn't recognize Bista's pale gold hide among those coming and going on the roofs, but she was as sly as Pinch. There seemed to be no more than the usual wild ones, sunning on the slates. Or were they wild? Tagetarl couldn't tell and decided it didn't make any difference. Fire-lizards were volatile creatures.

He had no appetite for lunch and fretted over how Rosheen would scold him for not letting her know the danger the Hall was in. He usually told her *everything*. But why should she spend the day worrying, too? She had to keep her mind on the manual; that was one task he could *not* handle today! He did not see any of Pinch's helpers, nor did he see Pinch again in any guise. He didn't know whether to transfer paper from storage to the Hall as he usually did at the end of a day. But then would anyone be watching to see that he kept to his usual routine? He kept running a hand over the wood of doors and frames but couldn't really feel any difference, much less recognize a substance that could retard flame.

He was anxious because no one came to his office with new work, but also relieved. How did you tell an Abominator from any other ordinary man or woman? It was the set of their minds: their self-appointed mission to deny choice to others, to neutralize all the useful things that were already in operation. Aivas had made available a great deal of knowledge, some of it information miscopied over the Turns that only needed careful research in the Archives and invaluable to all the Crafts to rectify. Any thinking person would examine what was sensible to add to what Pern already had—like printing, but he required no one to read or buy his books: that was their decision. For all the amazing diversity of processes and products that the Ancients had known and used, just learning how to faithfully execute some of the designs was enough to discourage making the unnecessary. As Master

Menolly said—and he knew Sebell basically agreed with her—not everything and anything new meant an improvement. But people should make that decision themselves, not have it arbitrarily denied.

The five-note whistle that Pinch said was a warning startled Tagetarl: it seemed to float across the court from nowhere. He wrenched around to face the outer gate, trying to compose himself. He, Master Tagetarl, who had never flubbed an entrance or forgot tune or words, felt himself unnaturally stiff with fear and apprehension. What should he say? What could he say to someone who had decided to destroy his livelihood? People were passing by the Hall on the road outside. Then in walked the man of Pinch's sketch: there was the missing joint of the left index finger and the zigzag scar on the forehead, all but hidden under the black knit cap. The man stood for a moment looking across the court with narrowed eyes, his expression disdainful and his lips twisted scornfully—as if, Tagetarl thought, he was anticipating the changes that might shortly be made to the order and serenity of the Printer Hall.

"Good evening," Tagetarl said as affably as his wariness permitted. He reached for the book he had placed on one of the barrels.

"Come for the book. You said a sevenday," the man said as if he had no faith in that promise. He spoke tonelessly, as if coming for a book was only an excuse.

He kept his lips over his teeth as if hiding them. Pinch's drawing had not included that detail or the smell of the man: stale sweat, campfires, and beast dung. Nor was he wearing hill-style clothing. In fact, the black leather jacket and trousers looked barely used, his boots were definitely new, if road-stained. The man sauntered deeper into the yard; Tagetarl following him, trying to give him the book and get him out of his Hall.

"That'll be three marks," Tagetarl said, amazed at how even his voice sounded in his ears. Was this Scar-face the leader? The man seemed determined to make a final close assessment. Tagetarl intercepted his circuit, pushing the book at him and holding out an open hand. "Three marks."

Digging in one pocket of his jacket he wore, Scar-face dropped two full marks and two half marks, all weaver stamped, into Tagetarl's hand.

"Weaver marks good enough for you, Master Harper?" he asked without the usual inflection of a question.

"MasterPrinter," Tagetarl corrected automatically. "Weaver marks are well guaranteed!" Shards, did the man want to provoke a fight? Or spread word that the Print Hall disdained weaver marks?

Scar-face took the Ballads from Tagetarl's hand much as one would cautiously grasp something dirty or repulsive. Tagetarl, loving the books he published so that at times it was hard to sell them on, had to grip hard on the worn marks to prevent himself from grabbing the volume back. The man shoved it roughly into a pocket of his jacket.

"MasterPrinter," the man said with a queer grin. "You're kept busy?" He kept darting glances to the Hall and around the courtyard where the genuine apprentices were sweeping the cobbles and tidying up in the Hall. Then his eyes settled briefly at the heavy leaves of the outer gate and his lips twitched across his teeth.

"Busy enough," Tagetarl admitted, wondering how he could get the man to go. He heard the rumbling of a cart on the road outside, and then saw one being pushed through the outer gate, dropping wisps of the straw that cushioned the wine-skins inside. Tagetarl knew very well that he hadn't ordered anything from his local supplier and was about to protest when he remembered what Pinch had said and turned casually about.

In the moment he had looked away, Scar-face departed.

"Shipment for Master Harper?" the wineman announced, lifting his hand for attention.

"MasterPrinter," Tagetarl corrected for the second time in a few minutes and wondered why no one could give him his proper rank today.

"Ahem, sorry, sir, MasterPrinter Tagetarl?"

"I am he." And Tagetarl hoped that Pinch was listening somewhere.

"Promised to deliver this myself," the stout man said with a hearty air.

"Indeed, and who might have required extra service from a busy man like yourself?" Tagetarl asked, noting the second set of new black leather jacket, pants, and boots of the day. The reek from this man was sour wine but no improvement. He did wear the proper journeyman's Craft knot. Tagetarl admonished himself that he hadn't noticed which knot, if any, Scar-face sported.

"You had no message to expect this delivery?" The man looked shocked and pulled up his paunch as if the waistband of the pants needed easing. "Runners are getting lazy."

Tagetarl heard a muted oath and spotted the shabby drudge collecting the straw wisps.

"As you can see, it's a fine Benden red," and the wineman turned the tag for Tagetarl to read.

"Yes, indeed, it is," and Tagetarl was impressed. "A 'forty-two! Excellent vintage. I shall enjoy that. Whose health do I drink tonight since the donor's message is overdue?"

"Why, the Lord Holder's, of course," the man replied easily.

Tagetarl beckoned for the drudge to put his broom down. "You there, take this into the kitchen and we'll all drink the health of the Lord Holder tonight. I expect he must be pleased with my latest publications," he added mendaciously.

"Cellar to cellar is our boast. I'll take it in myself. Wine needs to be handled carefully." The wineman held an arm up to discourage assistance.

"Very good of you, I'm sure," Tagetarl said, sternly motioning the drudge to obey, ensuring that the wineman wouldn't enter the hold. "I see you've other skins. Would you happen to have a Benden white among them, of a good vintage?" He stepped forward to look at the labels hung from the neck of the skins in the cart.

"No," and now the false wineman intercepted Tagetarl—every bit as good as a Gather play, Tagetarl thought, experiencing a flash of amusement and stepping back. "Nothing as good as what I'm delivering to you now."

With unexpected agility, the drudge had deftly got under the wineskin to slip it to his shoulder in a way that would not muddle the wine unnecessarily and, straightening, carried it to the steps and up into the Hall. There was an unmistakable air of disappointment on the wineman's face. Wanted to have a good look inside, had he? Tagetarl thought.

"Too bad," Tagetarl said heartily. "Had some marks to spend." He gripped the weaver circles tightly in his hand. "Do stop by again if you should have a good white 'forty-five," and maliciously Tagetarl named what he knew had been an inferior year.

"Good choice, Master-ah-Printer."

Tagetarl escorted him to the outer gate in firm dismissal and watched him push his cart away, up the hill. He sprinted back to the hold then, to see what Pinch—if that had been him under the rags—had done with the wineskin. He was not in the kitchen, which was as well since he could see that Rosheen was busy getting supper. She'd've wanted to know where they had acquired a dirty drudge as well as a wineskin. Hearing footsteps echo on the steps down to the under-cellar, Tagetarl followed. When he reached that level, the wineskin had been deposited into one of the flint laundry sinks and the drudge was unwinding his holey tunic and reaching into a belt pouch.

"Carefully pour out a measure, Tag," Pinch said, drawing out a small vial which Tagetarl knew contained one of those invaluable powders that most long-distance travelers carried to check the potability of stream water.

Taking down an old glass, Tagetarl unstoppered the skin and poured a sample. Pinch carefully tapped a few grains of the powder into the glass. The wine slowly began to froth.

"You'd have been dead asleep—or maybe even dead," Pinch said. He replaced the bung in the wineskin. "Definitely a malicious attempt to render you incapable of defending your Hall. Where can we hide it?" He looked around the room.

"Underneath the sink, behind the laundry soaps," Tagetarl

suggested and helped Pinch bestow it, with a final glance to be sure the bung was in tight. "And we were supposed to drink a whole skin tonight?"

"You usually drink with your evening meal."

"Cider," Tagetarl said in protest. "Wine only on special occasions. And how do they know we drink at dinner?"

"Probably watching. Your kitchen faces the road. You don't close the shutters until you go to bed." Pinch shrugged. "Then, too, most people'll drink freely of free wine, you know. And you did say you'd drink the Lord Holder's health."

"It couldn't possibly be Lord Kashman he meant?" Tagetarl asked.

Pinch twisted his chin sideways and shrugged. "He wasn't specific, was he? Or do they intend to impugn Lord Toronas since it's a Benden wine? Or implicate Lord Kashman? Interesting." Then he gave a delicate sniff of the savory odors drifting down from the kitchen level. "When did you say dinner is? I mean to join you. All that free wine!"

Rosheen came into the cellar. "I thought I saw someone strange. Pinch?" she added, staring at the Harper as he discarded the outer layer of rags. "What are you doing here?"

"I perceive you haven't told her," Pinch said with a long-suffering sigh.

"Told me what?" She glared at both of them.

"You were right, Rosheen," Tagetarl said with a sad grimace. "There is trouble coming our way."

"Abominators?" she exclaimed when, between them, Tagetarl and Pinch disclosed all they knew.

As ever, Rosheen did not react the way Tagetarl thought she would.

"You mean, you didn't tell me to cook enough to feed your friends a decent supper, Pinch? You left them waiting up there in that awful loft all day long?"

"They brought food and they've slept most of the day," Pinch added as if that was occupation enough. "Couldn't let anyone know they were here."

Abruptly she sat down on the stairs, her face suddenly white as she absorbed the danger the Hall was in.

"You mean," and now her white skin was flushed with angry spots on her cheeks, "you let me go through the *entire* day oblivious to all this?"

"Now, now, Rosheen, one of us had to act natural," Tagetarl said.

"Well, now, I've a thing or two to say to *that*, MasterPrinter Tagetarl—"

"Later, Rosheen," Pinch said. "You can say anything you want to him *when* we've got all this behind us."

She paused, one hand raised to point accusingly at her spouse. "When?" she repeated in a very scared, small voice.

"Tonight, if we're lucky," Pinch replied.

"That's lucky?" She blinked. "Is that why Ola hasn't let me out of her sight all day?"

"Quite likely," Pinch agreed amiably. "Now, we'll eat dinner, and drink merrily from whatever you have in the hold that's safe to drink. Some of your good cider?" he asked ingenuously.

Rosheen took a deep breath, started to say something, changed her mind and pointed down the cellar hallway. "Harper, you know exactly where I store the cider!" She turned and started up the stairs, slamming each foot down hard on the riser to disperse her anger.

"I think she took it rather well," Pinch said to Tagetarl. He rewrapped his rags. "Now, this drudge will hobble out and disappear in the lanes and byways. And shortly a very respectably dressed gentleman will arrive from the direction of the wharf with a commission for the MasterPrinter that will be discussed while his hosts visibly toast the Lord Holder's health."

And that was exactly what happened as dusk settled over Wide Bay. Then, with a great show of having enjoyed the wine, Tagetarl and Pinch went to close the outer gates for the night. The heavy sky-broom wood bar took considerable heaving to get into place. Tagetarl clipped over the unusual fastenings at both ends.

"Now don't worry, my good friend," Pinch said as they

walked back to the kitchen porch, giving him a reassuring shake on the shoulder. "They may get in, but I assure you, they won't find it so easy to get out. Nor a chance to do any harm. Now we go inside, like the innocents we are, and lock the door."

Though Pinch had explained the various precautions he had taken during the day and where his helpers were now hiding, Tagetarl was realist enough to know that Thread could fall in unexpected tangles.

"Try to relax, Tag," Pinch advised him. "I think every fire-lizard in the town is ready to come when Ola warbles."

"If they remember," Tagetarl muttered to himself, shivering a little. The night air was chilly.

Pinch gave a soft, wry chuckle, "Bista's there, too, you know, and she'll remember. Now, I've one more trick to see to." He clapped him once more on the shoulder and took the short interior corridor to the Hall.

"Relax?" Tagetarl repeated under his breath.

"How *could* you leave me in ignorance all day, Tag?" Rosheen demanded, coming out of the kitchen.

"Now you know, would you rather have known earlier?" he replied more bitingly than he meant and put his arms about her in a tight, apologetic embrace. He could feel her trembling.

"No, I guess not, but you've been very brave, Tag."

"I'm scared stiff. If only we could have put in steel doors!"

"Steel doors didn't keep the Abominators out of the Healer Hall, now did they? They just walked themselves in. Well, at least they can't just walk in here!"

He reached over to turn out the kitchen lights.

"Shall I giggle drunkenly or something? Having enjoyed the Lord Holder's wine? Or s-s-should we reel up the s-s-stairs?" She spoiled her casual manner by stammering.

"A waste of effort, dear," he said, trying not to sound grim. "Now the gates are closed, no one can see in."

He transferred one arm to her waist as they climbed to their sleeping room, dowsing the lights as they went up. Then they crept back down the stairs. Fully dressed, they made themselves as comfortable as possible on the long kitchen bench. Rosheen had padded it with pillows to ease a long wait.

"Is Ola on watch?" he asked Rosheen softly.

"If she were more on watch, she'd give her vigilance away." She gestured to a long shadow on the wide sill.

Even the pillows could not make the upright design of the bench comfortable. After the very long tense day he had spent, Tagetarl found waiting in the dark for the expected attack the worst part. He could have used the time to edit the copy to be printed the next day—if his presses still worked. Surely, with most of Pinch's folk hidden in the Hall, his presses would be untouched? He tried to remember the latest verses Menolly had sent him for setting and found he remembered her new tunes better. Then he was aware of a sleepy murmur from his spouse and realized that Rosheen, her head pillowed on his shoulder, had actually managed to fall asleep. He was further distracted by the many soft noises the building could make. He had to identify each one as normal. And inside the hold. Not outside.

He was struggling to keep awake when Ola's soft hiss roused him. He shook Rosheen and she mumbled before she realized that she shouldn't make any sound. He felt her body tense.

Then the fire-lizard disappeared. What had she heard that he hadn't? Could he risk looking out the window? His ears hurt with the strain of listening.

A noise! Outside. The muted thud of the sky-broom bar rattled in its slots. He grinned. They'd have trouble just finding the safety catches. A sudden flare of light: a match? Hunching down, he got to the kitchen door, crammed his body to one side so he had a partial view of the outer gates but wouldn't be seen. Since his eyes were accustomed to the night, he made out two dark burly figures struggling to lift the sky-broom bar. Then another black shadow, visible crossing the pale cobbles, joined them. Three? That was the number Pinch reckoned would come over the weaver's roof. Their initial job would be to open the outer gates and let the others in. He heard once again the muted thud as the sky-broom bar refused to lift from its brackets. He suppressed a malicious delight in their frustration. Suddenly, outlined against the lighter building across the road, three shadows—heads and shoulders—loomed over the top of the gate. The figures disappeared back the way they had come. Had he heard muted cries? The three inside huddled together briefly and once again tried to lift the bar.

Another flare of light, carefully shielded, but then held against one end of the stubborn bar. Tagetarl chuckled. They'd need full daylight to puzzle the mechanics: an old, old device. Another huddle; one was left examining the catch. A match was struck and he saw it passing from the head of one torch to another. In that light, he followed the progress of the arsonist across the court, saw him jam one torch under the edge of the first shed door, the second under the farther one. They burned merrily and Tagetarl held his breath. Maybe that paint wasn't a retardant. Fearfully he watched but, although the flame leaped up along the lower edge of the door, all that was really burning was the torch, its light reflecting back from whatever covered the wood. The man who had placed the torches didn't seem to notice, returning to the stubborn bar securing the outer gates.

Movement there caught Tagetarl's eye. He caught a glimpse of someone scraping the arch in an effort to avoid the top of the gates. That was a very awkward method of clearing a height, wasn't it? One of Pinch's surprises? When had Pinch had a chance to trick out the gates? Not that Tagetarl had noticed since the heavy leaves reached a good half meter above his head. There was some kind of argument, carried on in emphatic gestures, some indicating the gates and another undeniably made to the person's crotch. Whatever that had been about, now they were concentrating on both ends of the restraining bar. He counted those now inside and came up with at least ten different shadows. The attempts to shift the bar were abandoned and the group moved toward the Print Hall. Tagetarl wondered if they were falling behind their schedule.

What had been in those barrels? He couldn't see the Hall doors as easily as the outer gate but he did hear the scuff of heavy soles on the stone steps leading to the kitchen porch. A dark figure, a big man, was silhouetted against the useless torches across the court.

Pinch had given Tagetarl the task of preventing anyone from entering the link from the hold to the Hall. He took a firm grip on his cudgel, wishing he had chosen a thicker one. The man looked huge in the shadows. Not since his journeyman's days had Tagetarl been in a brawl. He heard the clink of something against the pane and smiled to himself. It took a smashing blow to break glass of Master Morilton's manufacture. And would make a lot of noise, too.

But it didn't, because the intruder held something over the pane as he hit it again. The glass made a tinkling sound as the splinters fell on the inside carpet. Another dull sound and the door lock was broken. If he and Rosheen had been drugged and asleep, they would not have heard those sounds. Then he had no time to think because the man pushed open the door and crouched, listening. Tagetarl pulled back his arm and just as the man moved forward, so did he. But the man suddenly tripped, swearing as he fell. Tagetarl aimed at his head and brought down his cudgel, numbing his arm to the shoulder when his cudgel connected with something else, much harder.

"Got 'ya," Rosheen said in a low and very smug voice and then saw Tagetarl's cudgel lying across the heavy iron pan with which she had clouted the intruder. "I didn't see you, Tag!"

Tagetarl was reeling somewhat with the shock that was still coursing up his arm, his hand numb from forceful contact with an iron skillet. A whirr and Ola arrived, hissing down at the intruder. Three more fire-lizards neatly zipped in through the broken pane.

"How'd you drop him?" he whispered.

"Tripped him with the broom," she said. "I heard the glass go. Where were you?"

Tagetarl jerked his head over his shoulder.

"Let's throw him down the cellar steps, out of the way," she said so coolly that Tagetarl regarded his spouse with surprise.

She was generally the kindest of women. "Ola will make sure her friends don't let him go anywhere."

"If you haven't killed him."

"If I killed him, what was he doing where I could do so?" she demanded in a hoarse whisper.

He was still alive when they took him by the shoulders, dragged him the short distance to the top of the cellar stairs and then tipped him down, the hissing fire-lizards following him into the darkness below.

Crouching, they moved back to the open kitchen door.

Rosheen gasped as she jiggled her hand at the flaming torches across the cobbles. He caught her before she could move. "Look carefully," he whispered in her ear. "It's only the torches burning."

"Yes, but what happens when they see the fire hasn't taken?" she shot back at him.

Where *was* Pinch?

Suddenly he heard a loud, creaking rasp of wood, the odd, squeaking, popping sound of screws being wrenched forcibly out of their seating, a mutter of triumph, and, in the light of the torches, he saw the double doors of the Hall being flattened to the cobbles. The intruders, audibly pleased with this success, started trampling across the broken leaves of the door. In the next moment, Tagetarl's ears were pierced by such a weird warble that he flinched and blinked, as the court seemed to be full of wings and gouts of flame, converging on the battered entrance to the Print Hall. Now human shrieks and screams reverberated amid sudden surprised shouts and protests. Tagetarl was on his feet, cudgel held high as he took the porch steps in two leaps, Rosheen right behind him, swinging her skillet.

Fortunately they were running down the left-hand side of the court toward the Hall because something large and gray settled to the cobbles, almost on top of them. Flattening his body against the wall, Tagetarl snatched Rosheen back out of the way, unable to imagine what other menace the intruders had imported. But the shouts from inside his Hall altered to angry, startled ones and shrieks of pain and curses.

"Get off my face!" "You're breaking my ribs!" "My face, my face!" interspersed with pounding on the outer gate and anxious calls. *"What's happening in there? Open up! Tagetarl! MasterPrinter!"*

"Master Tagetarl, it's Venabil! What's happening in there?"

"Watch out!"

"Shards! Do you see what I see?"

"Here! Back off! There now! Stand aside!"

There was a clearance of perhaps a meter and a half between the top of the outer gates and the arch, and that space was filled with two whirling, orange eyes.

"Tagetarl! Get this gate open!"

"In a minute! In a minute!" Pinch roared back. "Who has the hand lights? Torjus, Chenoa, dowse those torches! Macy, help me unfasten the bar!"

The court was suddenly awash with light. Someone in the Hall had had the sense to turn on the main switch. The large gray object Tagetarl had been trying to avoid turned rainbow-colored eyes on him and Tagetarl stared back at the white dragon, Ruth. And then at the man dismounting.

"So it's you Ruth wants me to rescue," was Lord Jaxom's slightly amused greeting.

"How did you *know*?" Not that Tagetarl wasn't remarkably relieved to see him.

"Only to come, here and *now*." Jaxom was unfastening his jacket and it could be seen that he was wearing casual clothing underneath, not full riding gear. "Ruth tells me Lioth and N'ton have also been summoned. Do I assume that you've had some intruders?" He pointed toward the broken doors and the wriggling mass hanging just above it. "Did you catch them all in the one net?"

Stunned by all that had happened so quickly, Tagetarl had not really noticed. So nets had been stuffed in those barrels? Hadn't Pinch mentioned that some of his helpers were seafolk? How ingenious. He then saw that the fairs of fire-lizards that had come swooping and flaming in were attacking those captive in the nets, pecking and scratching at arms, legs, and various other parts that were protruding from the mesh. The anguished and pained protests were almost louder than the furor of the crowd outside, demanding to be let in.

"There's one more," Rosheen said, breathless with relief and pride. "He tried to get into the hold and we knocked him out and pushed him down into the cellar."

"Clever of you," Jaxom said, raising his voice to be heard, "but whatever did you do, Tag, to annoy the Abominators?"

"Why are you sure that's who they are?" Rosheen asked.

"Who else would try to damage a Print Hall when most of Pern can't wait to own real books? And why else are N'ton and I here, too? As witnesses to a midnight attack on defenseless premises."

Just then, Pinch and Macy lifted the sky-broom bar and the outer gates were flung open to the considerable crowd waiting to enter, waving cudgels, knives, and more torches. They surged right up to the flattened leaves of the Hall's doors, halted and stared up at the swinging net.

"Jaxom? Are you all right?" someone cried above the angry shouting. A tall figure in riding leathers came striding through the crowd to join them. "Lioth was told to bring me to Wide Bay immediately. Tagetarl? Isn't this your Print Hall?" N'ton had rocked to a halt when he recognized those standing with Jaxom. Then his eyes went wide. He looked over his shoulder at the swinging net. "What's the haul?"

"That's what we must discover," Pinch said, stepping forward and nodding courteously to the Lord Holder and the Weyrleader. "I may have acted hastily but I did hear that the Printer Hall might be vulnerable. So, since it is such a valuable asset to Pern, north and south, I thought to prevent any untoward impairment of its facilities. Had a—beauty—of a message yesterday."

Tagetarl saw Jaxom and N'ton exchange glances but, Harper though he was, he could not read more than an odd regret on N'ton's face and a sadness in Jaxom's.

"There's no question harm was meant?" N'ton asked Pinch who shook his head.

"Three sent in over the roofs," and Pinch pointed, raising his voice to make himself heard over the tumult in the court, "to open the main gate, torches set to fire the paper stores, hauling the Printer Hall doors off their hinges."

"But the gates weren't opened," N'ton said.

"Not for lack of trying," Pinch said.

"One broke the glass and the door to the hold and Rosheen flattened him with her iron skillet," Tagetarl said. His arm still felt the repercussion.

"And there's the matter of the drugged wine, too," Pinch added.

"Drugged wine?" Jaxom repeated.

"So you netted those entering the Hall?" N'ton asked.

"Only after they'd battered down the doors," Pinch replied, eyes wide with injured innocence.

"Hey, the fire-lizards are having all the fun!" someone shouted from the crowd ranged about the entrance of the Print Hall.

Since it was obvious that the fire-lizards were also preventing the crowd getting near enough to have a go at the captives, Jaxom turned to Ruth, patting the white shoulder. "Do dismiss them, Ruth, with our thanks. They've performed admirably."

Ruth raised his head and emitted an unusual warble. Not only did it mute the noise of the crowd but also the fire-lizards departed in one final dramatic swoop, low enough to make the tallest onlookers duck. Gesturing to his friends to accompany him, Jaxom strode forward and the crowd parted to allow them to reach the battered doors on the cobbles, conversations dying down now that someone was taking charge.

"Lower the net!" Jaxom ordered and four of Pinch's assistants jumped to obey.

"Belay that!" cried a voice from the right-hand side of the crowd and a big man, capped as a fisherman and showing a Master's knot, stood apart. "If you leave 'em in the net, Lord Jaxom, we can just sling the whole lot of 'em aft of my ship and I'll tow 'em out to the deep water! Save a lot of trouble!"

The crowd roared its approval of such rough justice.

"Ah, but, Captain, I am here," Jaxom said and his expression was one of rueful regret, "and so is Weyrleader N'ton and the MasterPrinter. So we are obliged to follow established procedures."

"Which are?" the captain demanded, not pleased with the rejection.

"According to the Charter," and Jaxom swung slowly around to the audience, his eyes seeming to touch everyone in the front ranks, "by which we have been well governed for the past twenty-five hundred Turns, a Lord Holder, a Weyrleader, and a Master of any Craft may hold a trial."

"Hold it then!" roared the captain and the crowd roared back an affirmative.

"You can't do that!" one of the captives shouted, struggling in the net. "We've done nothing wrong."

A lump hammer dropped free of the mesh and then Tagetarl saw that it was not the only tool that had tumbled to the ground.

The captain threw back his head to roar with laughter. "Only because you didn't get the chance!"

The crowd howled with delight.

"Would you prefer the captain's justice?" Jaxom demanded.

"That isn't justice!" cried a woman's voice. "Stop grabbing me!" she added angrily to someone beside her in the net. *"You've no right to do this to us."*

Another heavy object dropped ringingly to the cobbles.

"Oh, clear all that hardware away, Pinch, and drop the net," Jaxom said, utterly disgusted with his attempt to make this an orderly procedure. "Let's see what sort of catch you've made. Black-faced iron fins? Did you get the whole school of 'em? D'you know the captain, Tag?" he asked in a quick aside.

"Captain Venabil," Tagetarl replied. "He's well known but no one would dare board his ship without permission."

The net came down hard enough to rattle everyone in it, provoking a new spate of cries, curses, and pained exclamations. The captives were then as unceremoniously dumped out of the thick mesh as a load of fish: some sprawled face-down, others on all fours, groggy after their time in the swaying net.

"All right there." It was Pinch who took charge. "Stand up!

Make a line!" Roughly, he pulled one man up and signaled for his assistants to get the rest to their feet. "Search 'em, too."

While that was being done, and knives, chisels, matches, and long spikes were added to the pile, he walked up and down the uneven line that was finally formed by the captives.

"Nothing else on them?" N'ton asked, remembering Fort Hold and the conspicuous absence of any personal identification.

"Clothes?" someone from the crowd suggested, laughing raucously.

"A bit worn, some of 'em," another man replied derisively.

"What a sorry bunch!" Captain Venabil said, fists thrust against his hips, shaking his head. "It's plain as the nose on my face this lot were up to no good sneaking into the Print Hall, faces blackened and all. Not to mention pulling the doors down and heaving torches about. Wide Bay's not a wild hold and we don't want such louts hanging about. What's this established procedure of yours, Lord Jaxom? I'd like to get back to my ship before dawn."

Jaxom accorded him a little bow.

"Shouldn't we send for Lord Kashman?" someone shouted from the crowd. "He's our Holder and he's supposed to deal with peace-breakers, thieves, burglars, and such."

"For general Hold matters," Pinch said quickly. "This is a Harper Hall matter. However, if any of you . . ." and he addressed the captives, "is from this Hold you may step forward and I'm sure Lord Kashman will keep you comfortably enough."

He was interrupted by a derisive snort and the comment from the crowd that the net was more comfortable than where offenders of the peace were held at Keroon Hold.

"As I was saying," Pinch continued with a faint grin, "if you are of this hold, you can be transferred to the Hold to await Lord Kashman's judgment."

None of the captives claimed that right.

"Name, hold, hall, and rank, if any," N'ton said, stepping with authority beside Pinch.

There was no response and N'ton shrugged.

"Then, since they have been caught in an illegal entry and in the willful destruction of an authorized Crafthall, Master Tagetarl, Master Mekelroy, how will you deal with them?"

Surprised by the anger and the sense of violation that suddenly fueled him, Tagetarl surged to Pinch's side, glaring at the captives. The false wineman he had already recognized by the ripped trousers—which hadn't fit properly even before he'd bounced about in a net—but he could not find Scarface or the woman sketched by Pinch after his first foray to the suspected Abominators' hill camp. Their absence from this line added worry to Tagetarl's very mixed emotions.

"Why did you wish to damage this Hall?" he demanded in a harsh voice, his fury palpable enough to make those captives nearest him recoil uncertainly. "WHY?" He jammed his fists against his side to rein in the urge to tear the truth out of those who would have destroyed what he had so painstakingly built. He took one more step.

"Lies!" Hands defensively raised, the man directly in front of him ducked back. "We have to destroy the lies!"

"What lies?" Tagetarl demanded, having expected no answer, certainly not this one.

"The lies Harpers are printing. Spreading all over Pern!" the man cried, gesturing wildly toward the Hall, to the wall where finished books were shelved.

"What's this about lies?" demanded Captain Venabil, turning to Tagetarl for an answer.

"I don't print lies!" Tagetarl cried, loudly.

"But you print books. You use the Abomination's vile methods. You distribute abominations!"

Captain Venabil, big fist raised, leaped toward the speaker who cowered away.

"Ha! Abomination, huh? These're Abominators!" He turned, eyes flaring with disgust, toward the crowd. "Nothing but a pack of cowardly Abominators, sneaking around in the night to destroy what they haven't the wit to appreciate."

"We must stop the lies. We must keep Pern pure!" cried a

woman farther down the line of captives. "We have to keep Pern free of abominations."

"Of all the daft ideas!" Captain Venabil's contempt was echoed vociferously by many of the onlookers. "Pern needs all the help it can get right now!"

"Where would we've been if Aivas hadn't warned us of the Fireball Flood?" a man in the crowd demanded loud enough to be heard, waving his fist at the captives. "Captain's got the right idea. Drown 'em!"

Shouts of "drown 'em" quickly became a chant, rising in ominous volume!

"Back in the net with them! Take the school back to the sea."

"That'd pollute our harbor!"

Ruth bugled loud enough to deafen those in the court. Outside, Lioth answered him and a muttering silence returned to those in the Hall court.

"You are Abominators?" Jaxom said in an oddly controlled voice. His eyes were on one of the taller captives who stared unseeingly ahead of him.

"We are!" the woman cried defiantly, just as the wineman shouted, "We admit nothing!"

"I think in this case," Captain Venabil said in a wry tone that carried to the edges of the crowd, "I'll believe the female."

"They're all together, ain't they?" asked the fist-waver. "All pulling the doors down, trying to fire the sheds."

"Yes, firing the sheds." A thin, stoop-shouldered man pushed through the crowd, waving wildly at the sheds and the back of the court. "You could've burned my hold, too! I'm Colmin, Journeyman weaver, and all my winter work's in the loft back there. I use only traditional patterns and you could have ruined me! Ruined me!"

"We don't like arsonists in Wide Bay neither," a woman shouted, cupping her hands to her mouth to be sure she was heard. "It's your say, Harpers! It's your Hall they attacked."

"Known Abominators require different handling," Pinch

cried and turned to face Jaxom and N'ton. "Or at least being isolated," he added in a low voice.

"Well, I'm glad to hear that," Captain Venabil said and then frowned. "What d'you mean, Harper Mekelroy?"

The onlookers hushed to listen for Pinch's answer.

"In offenses caused by those admitting to be Abominators, the Council recommends exile!"

It took another blast from Ruth and Lioth to still the clamor that was raised at that announcement.

"You can't exile us," the wineman cried, stepping out of line and trying to seize Pinch. He was instantly pinned by two of Pinch's assistants who, judging by the roughness with which they held him, had been just waiting for an opportunity.

"Why not?" Jaxom asked.

"All the islands were drowned."

"Oh," N'ton said in a quiet voice, "I think we can find a suitable one."

"We can't be exiled!" "We're saving Pern!" "That's unfair."

The captives broke from their sullen stance, dashing frantically about the court, looking for some way to escape or force their way past those blocking the gateway. The crowd was only too happy to recapture them. There were calls for rope to tie them, cloth to gag the screamers.

"So where're all these established procedures of yours, Lord Jaxom?" Captain Venabil demanded, heaving from his exertions.

"A Lord Holder, a Weyrleader, and a MasterCraftsman may enforce any Council decree," Jaxom said. "It is in the Charter, if anyone cares to check. We must do so before sufficient witnesses."

"WE WITNESS." "WITNESSED!" "WE WERE HERE!" "DROWNING'S EASIER. QUICKER!" "EXILE 'EM!" "AWAY WITH THEM!"

Raising his arms, Jaxom faced the crowd. "Those of you who do not care to be witnesses to the judgment of this incident may step back without prejudice."

Later Tagetarl was to remember that no one stepped away.

"Then the decree of the Council will be enforced. Weyrleader N'ton, you may send for assistance," the Lord Holder of Ruatha said formally.

"D'you just drop 'em off?" Captain Venabil asked, his expression severe as if stunned by the sentence of exile.

"They are not dropped," N'ton said, stressing the last word, his eyes hinting an inner conflict kept under stern control. "Sufficient food, supplies—" he paused briefly, "and water are provided to give them time to become established."

"But—but—"

N'ton stared Venabil quiet. "I," and he jerked a thumb at his chest, "am the only one who will know which island. And there are still many, many islands in both the Eastern and the Ring seas that can—isolate those who can be so destructive."

"Better than they deserve, Weyrleader. Better than they deserve!" Captain Venabil stepped back, giving all three men a respectful bow. Decisions involving the lives of others were never easy to make.

The crowd had quieted down from its previous high pitch though some low conversations were begun. Pinch sent two of his men to bring the unconscious man from the cellar, tying his hands behind his back before he was set with the other Abominators, placed in a rough line on the broken Hall doors.

Seeing Rosheen shivering, Tagetarl put an arm around her shoulders and drew her close to him.

"It is legal, you know," he whispered to her.

"I know. I've read the Charter. I just never thought we'd have to invoke it."

"It's perhaps as well to isolate them," Tagetarl murmured to her. Angry as he was, and he had been ready to batter the men, he was not a violent man. "They could escape from the mines and come back and try again. I think that I want to know they can't get to us—even if, at a later date, we decide to retrieve them."

She clung to him, shaking her head. He didn't tell her that two important members of the Abominator group Pinch had been watching out for were not in those captured tonight:

Scar-face and the awkward-looking holdless woman from Tillek. That meant that not all those who held Aivas an Abomination had been removed from hall and hold.

The dragons were seen in the sky, their eyes sparkling in serene whirls as they hovered above the court: a half wing of them. From somewhere, fire-lizards did sky-pirouettes around them, calling in an oddly melodious chorus.

"They'll land on the wharf," N'ton said and pointed in that direction.

It was only the next road over and there were plenty of strong men and women to carry the Abominators despite their writhing and struggling and the gagged pleas to be released. Ruth followed, perching on a bollard while the exiles were hauled up on the dragons, and tied alongside the sacks that were to be left with them.

Then N'ton vaulted to his dragon's back. "Riders, take your destination from Lioth!" he said in a voice loud enough to be heard by all watching. He lifted his arm, visible in the wharf lights, and gave the signal to leap skyward.

Tagetarl thought he had never seen a more impressive sight: twelve dragons leaping into the night, the fairs of fire-lizards escorting them and disappearing at the same moment.

In an unnaturally quiet way, those who had witnessed the night's incredible event left the wharf side or climbed aboard the ships anchored there for the night.

"It was what had to be done, Lord Jaxom, Master Tagetarl," said Captain Venabil in a low but firm voice. He shook their hands and then made his way down the wharf.

"Yes, it was what had to be done," Pinch said as they all turned to go back to the Hall.

Then Pinch dropped back to Jaxom who was walking more slowly, his head bent.

"Dorse was among them, wasn't he, Jaxom?" he asked so softly only Jaxom could hear. Jaxom flashed him the most quelling stare the Harper had received since he'd been an apprentice.

"No hold, no hall," Jaxom finally replied. "Even if he was my milk-brother, what else could I do?"

"I've been trailing him, Jaxom," Pinch murmured, "a long time."

"You have. I haven't."

"I know," and there was great compassion in the Harper's voice.

"Was he in this from the beginning?"

Pinch shrugged. "We don't even know when the Abominators were revived to plague us. Not all of those participating in these—events—are interested in keeping Pern pure or traditional. I've no doubt some of these people were motivated by blind adherence to what their fathers or mothers taught. I recognize some as hill folk who never took kindly to teachering: like the woodsy ones down in Southern Boll, or the mountain holds in upper Telgar and Lemos, or the desert nomads in Igen. Any and all of them simply fear change. They might even resent losing the Red Star as a permanent problem on which to blame 'things that go wrong.' Unfortunately, two of the people that I suspect have been churning up ill feelings against healers, and now the Print Hall's new technology, aren't among those in tonight's catch." He quickened his pace and fell in step with Tagetarl, leaving Jaxom to his own somber stride. "It would be wise, MasterPrinter, to issue a concise statement of what happened here tonight. The Runners can see that the truth is circulated."

A truth that would not name the milk-brother of Lord Jaxom of Ruatha Hold as one of the vandals who had been exiled that night.

A handful of men and women stood by the open outer gates of the Hall. Ruth could be seen quietly awaiting the return of his rider.

"If you need some help tonight, or tomorrow, Master Tagetarl," began one of the men stepping forward, "we'd be willing to do repairs."

Tagetarl thanked them, aware that the doors to the Print Hall would have to be replaced. Steel would have reassured

him but he didn't have enough marks and he doubted the
Smithcrafthall had the time.

"If one of you is a carpenter . . ."

"Five of us are, Master Tagetarl, the reason we bother you
right now."

"I am extremely grateful. Come when you can in the
morning."

He and the others had no sooner walked away than two
fire-lizards whisked out of the night, landing on the shoulders
of Rosheen and Pinch.

Jaxom walked straight toward his dragon and vaulted to his
back. Tagetarl lifted his arm in farewell but he didn't think the
Lord Holder saw him. In silence Pinch and Tagetarl closed
the gates. Then Pinch made his way to the loft where undoubtedly his assistants had taken themselves. Tagetarl and
Rosheen turned to the right and the steps up to their hold.

In the morning, while the five carpenters put up new
doorposts—made of sky-broom wood, they proudly informed Tagetarl—the Masterprinter took the report that he
and Rosheen had spent a sleepless night composing to the
Runner Station.

Pursing his lips, Stationmaster Arminet read the text.
"Well said, Master Tagetarl. Fairly said. It will go in every
pouch to come through here. I may even need more."

Tagetarl made a protest, wondering how much more the
night's work would cost him.

"Keep your marks in your pocket," Arminet added, pushing away the ones Tagetarl proffered.

"It's a Harper Hall announcement . . ."

"It's a community announcement," Arminet replied,
straightening himself to his full dignity though he was not as
tall as the well-built Tagetarl. He glared up. "I'm the one who
decides what should or should not be spread from my Station.
The people of Wide Bay were very much aware of the atrocity
committed by persons who would not claim hall or hold,
Master Tagetarl, and others must know about the matter so as
not to be left in doubt as to the exact details of the matter." He

tapped the bottom paragraph. "As I was one of those witnesses, this is exactly as I recall the incident. Thank you, Master Tagetarl. Let it not be said that the Runners did less than their best, too."

RUATHA HOLD—LATE EVENING—2.9.31

"You recognized one of them, didn't you, Jaxom?" Sharra asked softly, having watched his silence all day. She knew he had been called away that night. When he had returned, he had tried to disguise both fatigue and a preoccupied air. He had pushed food around his plate at both lunch and dinner. He had not been able to display any enthusiasm for the hour he usually spent so companionably with his sons.

She had waited, without appearing to hover close by, in case he might wish to talk about what was depressing him. She'd seen him terribly distracted like this only once before: when he had presided over the exile of those who had been responsible for abducting Master Robinton.

She waited until they had gone up to their own quarters and he was leaning against the deep window, looking out on nothing. Just as she was sure she'd have to pry, he gave a deep sigh.

"Ruth and I went to Wide Bay, to assist Tagetarl. There was an attempt to damage the Print Hall."

"More Abominators?" Who else could it have been, since the Print Hall had been so enthusiastically received by every Craft.

He nodded but did not elaborate.

In the silence that followed, Sharra watched her spouse, absentmindedly running his hand up and down the heavy brocade curtain that prevented the worst of the winter winds from penetrating into their sleeping room. She waited quietly. She knew when he was fretting over something.

"Dorse was one of them."

Sharra felt something within her lurch at that soft, chilling admission. Jaxom did not have many fond memories of his milk-brother but had kept giving him the benefit of the doubt, long after his foster mother had died. Dorse had left before one more outrageous act would have compelled Jaxom to send him away.

"I thought he had gone south. Worked for Toric." She gasped as soon as she finished speaking.

Jaxom nodded his head slowly. "He did not speak."

"But surely, love," and Sharra went to lay her hand on his shoulder, feeling the tension in his body, "he had only to—"

"They were asked to name hall or hold." Jaxom's grip tightened on the curtain so that the fabric was stretched from its rail, the upper hem tearing.

"Are you distressed because he *didn't* speak?"

"I'm not sure." Sharra could hear the anguish in Jaxom's voice. "I'm not sure! I—think," and now Jaxom buried his face in the folds of the curtain, "he was the leader. I think he was challenging me. Defying me and what I stand for. What did he expect me to do? See that they were only sent to the mines?"

Before he tore the curtain from the wall, she closed her hand around his fingers and gently detached them.

"I suggest that either way he is getting his own back on you, Jaxom," she said in a quiet nonjudgmental tone. "By any chance, did anyone else recognize him? Ruth said you did not go alone." He gave her a fierce look. "No, no, my love. I *never* asked him. He knows I worry that sometimes the pair of you might get into trouble and not tell me." She tried to speak lightly, to ease his distress. She didn't even get a rise out of him for what he usually termed unnecessary anxiety.

"Pinch has been on his trail, he said. It's possible N'ton recognized him, though he wouldn't have seen him in Turns." He was silent a moment then added, "I should somehow have had a word with him. To see if he would tell me more."

"More about what? Isn't it enough that he was caught destroying what he can very well recognize as a tremendously important asset for all Pern?"

Jaxom gave her a long closed look. That made her flinch

inwardly because they were usually so open with each other about everything in their lives.

"I thought he had been well placed in the south with Toric," he said finally.

"Oh!" Sharra had to sit down quickly as she absorbed the implications of that. Jaxom had been trying to shield *her*.

"It's preferable to think that he was on his own, perhaps just taking an opportunity to be paid for making the kind of trouble he enjoys. It wouldn't be unlike him," and Jaxom spun from the window and began pacing the floor, looking everywhere but at his spouse.

"My brother, Toric," Sharra said in a voice as taut as Jaxom's had been, "was greedy as a child and would allow no common sense to dissuade him from what he felt was his, or—" she paused a beat "—perceived was his by right. He has since, as you should know, forfeited the loyalty of all his brothers and sisters. Even his sons. I thought when he was brought up short several Turns ago by the Lord Holders and Weyrleaders that he might realize that there are limitations to what one man may hold."

Jaxom could not endure her anguish and took her in his arms, his cheek against her cheek.

"We do not know that this is another scheme of his, Sharra."

She clung to him, her fingers tight in his hair, pressing herself into the strength that always emanated from him. "Even if I, too, can see that Toric may be setting himself against the rest of Pern, just to prove he can?"

Comforted now turned comforter. "We shall know soon enough who has been giving orders for all this wasteful vandalism and unrest."

"We will? Did Pinch say anything?" Sharra leaned back, to look deep into his eyes. "We seem to recover from one disaster and another threatens."

"Sssh, sssh, love." He rocked her in his arms, slowly, lovingly.

Sssh, sssh, Sharra. We are here!

For just a fraction of a second, though she was accustomed

enough to having Ruth speak to her, she thought his reassurance was oddly amplified.

CORE HOLD—TWO DAYS BEFORE COUNCIL MEETING—2.26.31

From her seat in the window at Cove Hold, Lessa could watch those coming up the newly graveled path from the beach. It still amazed her that Robinton's Hold had survived the havoc that had spared few other places. After the Winter Storm, some of his possessions had had to be replaced with lovingly contrived duplicates and these had been removed in case the Kahrain Cape did not protect the Hold. So once again, the Hall looked much as it had before his death. She could still believe that he was only out on the porch, or fussing with his tunic in his room before coming to greet his guests. The essence of Robinton, the MasterHarper of Pern, subtly pervaded the place as if he still lived here with his friends, Lytol, old Master Wansor, and D'ram. What a quartet they had made!

Now she watched as dragons arrived in pairs, gliding down to waves that lapped quietly—again—up the beach. It was like a Gather dance, she thought, trying to think of something pleasant to quiet the nagging frustration that she had been experiencing ever since the Fireball Flood. From the north and High Reaches came the newest Weyrleaders, G'bear on Winlath and Neldama on Yasith—their mating had turned out felicitously, one of the few things that *had* gone right lately. Slightly west of them, in from Telgar flew J'fery and Palla on Willerth and Talmanth. A single dragon appeared from the west, with two passengers, Jaxom and Sharra on Ruth. She wanted a word with Jaxom and N'ton about the Printer Hall incident. A second Printer Hall must be established as soon as possible. Printed documents were too important: human memories couldn't cope with all the details and the tedious act of handwriting was a process rife with opportunities for mistakes.

The visibly larger Fort dragons, Lioth and Ludeth, with N'ton and Margatta, followed Ruth immediately. Igen's Gyarmath and Baylith with G'narish and Nadira entered facing north. Lessa could hear dragons bugling over the building announcing the arrival of K'van and Adrea on Heth and Beljeth. Then three from the east, T'gellan, Talina, and Mirrim. Well, Mirrim was to be expected and, while Lessa knew the girl could be domineering and arrogant, she had great sympathy toward a fosterling she had trained.

The newly made Master Erragon had particularly invited F'lessan and a Monacan green rider, named Tai, who was one of Erragon's apprentices. Her name was familiar to the Benden Weyrleaders for her part in thwarting the vandals at Landing and being indefatigable during the evacuation of Monaco.

As the Weyrleaders filed in, Master Wansor, their official host for the night, greeted them. He stood on the threshold, a serene personality in a room that held memories for all of them. He lifted a smiling face to each new arrival as if he saw them as clearly as ever. Erragon stood behind Wansor, wearing the diamond pendant that was the sign of his new rank, and well deserved for the way he had managed information and warnings about the Fireball. He was being introduced to those few Weyrleaders he had not previously met. Lytol and D'ram were fussing with papers at a table in one corner. Nine piles of paper: one for each Weyr and who got the last? She flicked her eyes back to the door, to scrutinize F'lessan as he reached the steps, one hand under the elbow of the tall, dark-haired woman accompanying him. What Lessa noticed most were her wide mouth and curiously slanted green eyes.

Zaranth's rider, Ramoth said, almost approvingly. Lessa cleared her face of the beginnings of a scowl. F'lessan was not a child any longer. He had come very close to total exhaustion after the Impact; moving dories among other things, Ramoth had reported with critical asperity. His feat of saving the Seaholder from sure death in the tsunami wave had been notable in a day that the harpers said had been full of incredible feats of courage. F'lessan's timing had always been exquisite and someday she must ask exactly how he'd achieved such an impossible rescue. He was at Benden only when Wingleader duties required him to be present, for he seemed to prefer living in Honshu now.

His choice, Ramoth added ambiguously.

F'lessan caught sight of his mother in the window seat, gave her that engagingly charming smile of his and turned to speak to Wansor. The very casualness of his greeting amused Lessa. She was more surprised when, as Tai held out her hand, the old Smith caught it in his, his smile redoubling, his eyebrows flaring up as if by widening his opaque eyes he might somehow see her more clearly: obviously this green rider was very welcome in Cove Hold. Erragon's greeting was that of pleased teacher to best student.

"Attractive but not pretty," F'lar murmured to his weyrmate after a very brief glance at F'lessan's companion. "No wonder he's so often at Honshu now."

He likes it there, Ramoth said in that same cryptic tone.

T'gellan, with Mirrim and Talina, came up the steps now and Lessa thought Monaco's Weyrleader was much too thin, his eyes haunted. He had been working all the hours of the day to rebuild his Weyr. For that matter, neither Mirrim nor Talina looked much better, but they didn't look as gaunt as the bronze rider: they didn't have the full responsibility that a Weyrleader shouldered.

Lessa realized that all were now assembled and F'lar led her to their places on one end of the long, oval-shaped table.

"We're all here, aren't we?" F'lar said with a weary smile. He waited until the others seated themselves.

Twenty-two riders, three men who should have been enjoying their last decades in leisure, two Masters, and a Lord Holder: twenty-eight men and women to solve what she felt in her bones was impossible. But then, killing Fax had been—once. And ending Thread. Why should she consider *this* crisis to be beyond their capabilities? She gave her shoulders a little shake and took her place beside her weyrmate. She heard his sigh. Then he, too, stood straighter, to address the assembled.

"I'm sure we've all heard that dragonriders should do something about anything that falls from the sky." He let the various angry and resentful reactions to that peculiar assumption fade. "Ridiculous as that notion is, I think we all realize that that's the first question the Council will put to us in two days' time. Somehow that Fireball has become our fault." He altered his voice, affecting a querulous tone. " 'Dragons can fly *between*. Can't they just push rocks out of the way? Can't they burn them out of the skies? Can't they *do* something?' "

"Didn't we do *enough*?" F'lessan said with a brittle edge to his voice that surprised Lessa. Then he shrugged and his expression altered to one of detached indifference as other bronze riders muttered about ingratitude and impossible demands.

"Dragonriders did more than enough," said Lytol, the former Lord Warder of Ruatha, his craggy face fierce.

"Every Weyr performed magnificently," D'ram added, prideful.

"In the time allotted," Jaxom said, his expression very bland, turning his head ever so slightly toward Lessa. That sly remark subtly defused the unspoken resentment. Some even chuckled.

"I never understood quite how you accomplished as much as you did," Wansor said in all innocence. But then his expression turned to respectful awe. "The miracles you managed! In the face of what could have been catastrophic. Why the Storm of 'Twenty-nine Present Pass was a shower in comparison!"

"Fortunately, we're not considered responsible for the weather," F'lar said satirically.

"Not yet," G'dened added in a sour voice. Though Ista had been spared the full impact of the tsunami waves, the island had suffered badly from the hurricane.

"You know, there are those who feel we failed them in that storm, too," G'narish said, shaking his head.

"This time we had sufficient warning," K'van remarked, "before the winds made it impossible to fly."

"Back to what you said, F'lar, it isn't as if dragons *could* flame rocks in space," N'ton said. "Dragons need oxygen to make fire."

"Meteorites are moving too fast to be caught by dragons," K'van added, "not to mention the fact that they're so hot, mere dragon fire would have no effect whatsoever and be a total waste of time and effort."

F'lar grinned broadly. "Other facts Lord Holders and Craftmasters tend to forget. Still, I'd like to take the initiative. We've been on the defensive since that sharding Fireball impacted."

"You mean, there *is* something we can do?" G'dened demanded, sitting up straighter and glaring around the table.

"Oh, indeed," Wansor said, smiling beneficently around the table. "My Craft hasn't been idle a single moment. We have solid recommendations to make to the Council."

"Recommendations?" G'dened snapped, scowling. "They want answers!" He thumped the table with one fist. He had been one of the youngest of the bronze riders to come forward to the Ninth Pass and Lessa could see that he was burned out by giving answers to Lord Holders and Craftmasters.

"They always want answers," G'narish agreed, shaking his head. He, too, had reason to be as tired as G'dened.

Lessa wondered if there was any way to suggest that those two older Weyrleaders should step down and let younger, more flexible bronze and gold riders take over. She was grateful enough that M'rand and R'mart had retired. The two new Weyrleaders tried to appear at their ease but it was certainly the first time G'bear and Neldama had attended this sort of tactical meeting.

"Well, they deserve answers, G'dened," F'lessan said at his most cynical. "Only this time, they also want us to *do* something." His grin was positively challenging.

"What *can* we do?" G'dened demanded, eyeing F'lessan as if the younger man were challenging him as Weyrleader.

As she was about to take exception to G'dened's manner, Lessa felt F'lar give her thigh a reassuring squeeze. Especially after F'lessan had laid claim on Honshu, it should have been extremely clear that he had absolutely no desire to accept Weyrleadership anywhere.

"It will, of course, require the cooperation of all the other Crafts and Lord Holders," Wansor went on, smiling with benign encouragement, "for the marks and craftskills required. We've already made the preliminary surveys and preparations and, with the assistance of our newest Master," and the old Star Master made a respectful bow to Erragon, "Master Idarolan, F'lessan, and Tai," and his smile included the two riders at the end of the table, "and three dedicated persons who are not included in this meeting, we have these ready."

"Preliminary surveys of what?" G'dened demanded.

"Preparations to do what?" G'narish asked, surprised.

"Which three dedicated persons?" Mirrim asked, turning to look at Tai in an almost accusing manner.

"Surveys to locate the most advantageous site for another of the telescopes from the Catherine Caves, to give us a twenty-four-hour coverage for that critically needed sky-watch program!" Master Wansor beamed expansively as if this provided the answer.

Turns ago now, Lessa recalled Wansor's triumph at finding a high resolution telescope, a Cassegrain—according to the metal plate on the mirror cell and the thick manuals that had come with it—in the Catherine Caves. Aivas had supervised its installation and lighting up during his first Turn in charge of the Red Star Project. F'lessan had found the one left at Honshu and had just recently, after a lot of hard work and delicate repair, got it functioning again. How a third one would possibly deter more comets, stony or metallic bits from pocking the surface of Pern she did not know. Whether or not the project would appease the nervous or parsimonious among the Council was, of course, in doubt. Was sky-watching what really kept F'lessan down in Honshu and so much in Tai's company?

Yes, was Ramoth's smug reply.

"If we hadn't had the *Yoko*'s telemetry reporting the Fireball as early as it did," Wansor went on, "or the unusual capabilities and devotion of the dragonriders, there would have been a complete catastrophe instead of a mere disaster."

"Mere?" T'gellan burst out, half rising from the table; his outrage reflected in the stunned expressions on the faces of both Talina and Mirrim.

"I am so sorry, dear boy," Wansor said, twiddling his fingers in distress, blinking his clouded eyes. Lessa knew that if Wansor had actually seen how Monaco's land had suffered, he'd have been more tactful. His next words tried to correct the damage. "I don't mean to imply that the incredible damage Monaco sustained was 'mere,' just that it wasn't as bad as it could have been had the Fireball landed without any warning. Everyone tells me how magnificently you have repaired almost all the damage."

"As much as we can until the land itself recovers," T'gellan murmured, reseating himself but still palpably upset.

"How will this sky watch help?" F'lar asked, trying to get back to the subject.

D'ram cleared his throat. "In the first instance, it will allay the Council's doubts to know that, since dragonriders are unaccountably responsible for anything in the sky, we are very much aware of our responsibilities, and the scopes are essential to identifying what's up there. In the second instance," and he paused, regarding those at the table with an oddly self-righteous smile on his lips, "if we make sky-watching our craft when this Pass is over, we will have a profession that is peculiarly suited to dragonriders."

There was a rather stunned silence as the various Weyrleaders assimilated that suggestion.

Beside D'ram, Lytol was also broadly smiling and Lessa thought that that must be the first real smile she'd seen on his face in Turns. The Oldtimer pursued the matter.

"By forming our own Craft, we will be able to significantly

reduce the tension among holders and crafters who fear we wish to dominate their traditional crafts."

"Well, well, sky-watching wouldn't take *all* of us," G'dened began, fuming with indignation.

F'lessan laughed out loud. "And a good many more, G'dened, if we're to make a proper job of it." His eyes sparkled. "In fact, Honshu already has images of the asteroid belt from its initial search patterns."

"Search patterns?" G'dened asked, scowling.

With a glance at Erragon, F'lessan went on, "We know which stars are constant in our skies. What we *search* for is something moving between those stars and us! Look!" He flipped several prints to the table. "See this one?"

"I see a streak on black and a blur," G'dened replied, dismissing the image.

"We've identified the streak as an asteroid. We're calling it Aliana." He ducked his head and gave the almost cheeky smile he had used as a small boy when he was hiding deeper feelings. "Tai thought we should give them names, instead of numbers, and I thought that perhaps we'd name it after one of the first dragonriders. We've got a lot of those."

"Which, asteroids or dragonriders?" Lessa asked, smiling to show that she liked the idea. She could see that both Wansor and Erragon obviously approved.

"Both."

"How'd you know it's an asteroid?" G'dened demanded impatiently, his scowl deepening.

"F'lessan cross-checked it with Cove Hold and *Yoko*," Erragon said.

"This blur, as you call it, is a star named Acrux. Acrux is fixed . . . at least in a forty-minute exposure . . . while the asteroid is moving fast enough to create the blur. By considering its position in the sky, we know that it is in the asteroid belt. By getting to know our night skies and taking images—" F'lessan tapped the print.—"we will find ones that might be moving dangerously close to Pern."

"One just did!" G'dened objected, feeling insulted, and pushed the print away.

F'lessan laughed. "We've had more than one near miss."

"Oh, not that Runner site again!" And the Istan Weyrleader swiped his hand in dismissal.

"If I may," Tai said in such a firm voice that everyone regarded her in surprise, "the Fireball was the first really hazardous impact noted in the *Yoko*'s records as far back as it kept them."

"Quite right, Tai. And, until the last ten minutes of its descent," Erragon said, "we weren't even certain that it would impact on Pern. And it is by no means the only one in a possibly hazardous orbit."

That was news to the inland Weyrleaders; G'dened's scowl deepened.

Lessa wondered if they oughtn't to have asked M'rand to come to this meeting. Usually he had balanced G'dened's pessimistic, biased attitudes.

"We have now had a chance to thoroughly examine the *Yoko*'s records," Lord Lytol said, his expression doleful, "and the Fireball was a visible light against the asteroid belt as far back as Turn's End."

"When we were occupied with other matters entirely," G'dened said wearily.

Lytol gave him a repressive glare and continued. "The *Yoko* has traced its inclination and now suggests that it was probably even then a possibly hazardous object, not merely one near Pern."

"What's the difference, Lytol?" Lessa asked.

"Oh, between 100,000 and 400,000 kilometers, Lady Lessa," Lytol said with a sad smile. "If Pern had been farther on its rotation around Rukbat, the cometary fragment would have passed us by."

"The point is, Lady Lessa," Wansor said, leaning toward her earnestly, "that if we had had a sky watch then, we would have known to track it more carefully."

"What *more* could we have done about it if we had known?" T'gellan asked wearily.

A depressed silence followed that heartfelt query.

"The situation for dragonriders was once much worse than

this," F'lar said in a quiet but firm voice, "when Benden had only a handful of riders to fight Thread, and you," he gestured to D'ram, G'dened, and G'narish, "came forward in time to support us. Now we have access to the Ancients' exhaustive records and, if I remember Aivas's lectures at the time, he told us that old Earth had its own share of problems in near space. Erragon, how did the Ancients handle that problem?"

Erragon gave a dry chuckle. "They watched through very powerful telescopes augmented by a dedicated group of men and women using lesser instruments. Aivas states that they had mapped the position of stars in their part of the galaxy—and objects in the Earth's system—with an accuracy measured by microarcseconds. Far beyond the abilities of the telescopes we have, of course. But we need only concern ourselves about Rukbat."

"Yes, yes," G'dened interrupted, leaning eagerly in his direction, "but what did they *do* to things that came too close to Earth?"

"They took—I quote—'action when required to divert a possibly hazardous object.' "

"With what? How?" demanded G'dened.

"That," Erragon said ironically, "they didn't say."

"But they must have done something!" There was a quaver of fear in G'dened's tone.

"They did have a sky watch," F'lessan said so firmly that he caught everyone's attention. "We can be accurate enough and, as Erragon says, we should learn what should be in our skies and track any newcomers."

"The astronomy files I've been studying clearly state that such destructive impacts are rare," Lytol added.

"Then why do we have to go through all this rigmarole of watching?" G'dened asked, more impatient than ever.

"In the first place, because it will prove to the Council that we *are* doing something," F'lar said. "In the second place, we would know if Pern would be in danger. Since the Weyrs were able to prevent much loss of life and property to reduce the damage done by the Fireball, we can certainly repeat that effort. May I earnestly recommend that we seriously consider

D'ram's second suggestion—that dragonriders would make excellent sky-watchers? Especially those riders who haven't yet found a suitable alternative."

Sky-watching, Lessa thought sternly, ought to be congenial to the less flexible bronze and brown riders. Blue and green riders were not so prone to stand on dignity and tradition.

"F'lar," and G'narish rose to his feet so suddenly that F'lar motioned for him to go ahead, "there've been rumors in Igen that the Fireball was the result of diverting the Red Star!"

"Shards, I hope you stifled such idiocy," F'lar said, disgusted.

"By Aivas, there is absolutely no possibility of that, G'narish," Lytol replied in vigorous protest. "I have made an exhaustive study of the physics and mathematics of that remarkable effort. Aivas was a superb astrophysicist. He was especially thorough in the matter of possible perturbations and every single equation of effect was faultlessly accurate. Waiting until the planet was far enough from Pern to assure that displacements would be negligible was one of the main reasons we had to delay the blasts, to achieve the maximum effect."

Abruptly Jaxom started to choke, a reflex that had him sputtering until Sharra thumped him on the back and the spasm subsided.

"Another reason being that we had to learn many new techniques to do so," D'ram said, his tone slightly acerbic.

"But if Aivas *knew* where everything else around us was," G'dened began in his rambling way, "then why don't we just use his records and not have to bother with this sky watch . . . rigmarole."

"Because," F'lessan began urgently before anyone else, "comets keep coming through, from the Oort cloud or beyond, because meteors and asteroids collide and fragments— possibly one like our Fireball—can spread in all directions, and we need to know where they are and where they're going! It doesn't matter that we haven't figured out how to *stop* them, but we certainly can learn how to spot them!"

Jaxom, N'ton, and D'ram cheered and clapped their hands,

Wansor positively beamed, Erragon looked immensely relieved, and even Lytol managed another smile.

"I think that should clarify the issue, G'dened," F'lar said, raising his hands for silence.

"It's certainly the plan we should present to the Council," D'ram said. "Put some heart into us, too, F'lessan! Do you happen to have any more prints like the one you showed G'dened? Perhaps a little clearer."

"We do," and he included Tai in his gesture, "so does Erragon from both Cove Hold and Stinar's link with the *Yoko*." Taking the prints in his hand, F'lessan glanced at each one before he began dealing them out to the Weyrleaders. "These are some that Tai has taken of what lies beyond our system." He shot a glance at Erragon. "She figured out how to do this 'unsharp masking' from her watches at Cove Hold. The technique reduces the intensity of the bright parts," he leaned over to tap the one in front of T'gellan, "and brings out sharp detail. That's a nebulosity—looks like a blob but there are stars imbedded in it. See? Those blurs are actually stars."

"Can stars be pink like that?" T'gellan asked, amazed and intrigued, holding the print up so that Mirrim and Talina could see it.

F'lessan chuckled. "Or blue, lavender, and white." He held up another for all to see. "We took this when we got the monitor up on the Honshu scope. This cartwheel is a galaxy far, far away. Actually, our sky is rather dark, apart from what Aivas called the Milky Way and the Magellanic Clouds."

"And these spirals?" asked Lessa, peering at the one in front of her. "There're so many." She was awed.

"Are these clusters all stars?" F'lar asked Tai, showing her the print he had picked up from the table.

"Global clusters," she replied.

"Good work," Erragon said, nodding approval. "You've made notes of time and position?"

"Of course, though these were random shots because I was actually experimenting with the filters Honshu has, trying to see more detail," Tai replied.

"And everyone can see these?" Mirrim regarded Tai with obvious respect. "You star-gaze for a reason?"

"That's part of it," Tai said, her dusky skin flushed with both pleasure and embarrassment.

"Just think what we could see and understand about the cosmos," F'lessan said, his eyes bright with such a visionary gleam that Lessa regarded the bronze rider with admiration, "if we had more observatories and people trained to watch."

G'dened grunted, unimpressed, flicking his fingers at the beautiful starscapes, and glared at F'lessan. "You said those were far, far away. Isn't it the nearby stuff you're supposed to be watching?"

"Oh, we do more of that." F'lessan splayed out another set of prints in front of the Oldtimer.

G'dened recoiled suspiciously. "Looks like a bug-eaten tuber." He picked up one, studied it briefly before discarding it contemptuously. "More holes than reef rock."

"Ah," and F'lessan waggled a finger at him. "Those asteroids are not far enough away. What looks bug-eaten is where other flying bits have made craters in the surface. Or where gases that were once in the asteroid blew out." Then F'lessan added, "The first one is ten kilometers long and the holey one is fifty. It's big enough to blow Pern apart."

G'dened swallowed, slowly turning his eyes to Erragon who nodded solemn affirmation.

"That's the whole point of tonight's meeting," Wansor said, "to establish a sky watch and train those who will keep their eyes on asteroids like that."

"There're only four scopes in the Catherine Caves," Lessa said, and wondered if they would be enough.

"Which," and F'lessan jumped to his feet, "makes me wonder if perhaps the Ancients hadn't planned to set up a sky watch of their own before Thread changed all their options."

"That has often occurred to me," Wansor said, nodding his round head thoughtfully. "And why there is no northern array. Though, of course, the Ancients had settled on the southern continent so they wouldn't have needed a northern array for many Turns."

"A northern array would have warned us of that storm," G'dened remarked sourly.

"Will four more scopes be sufficient?" K'van asked.

"It doesn't even take a large scope for night-watching, K'van," Erragon replied reassuringly. "Master Jancis has been making binoculars that many," and he turned to Jaxom, who nodded, "have been utilizing."

"All watch-riders use them and all of us have done our watches on Weyr Rims," N'ton added, glancing around for confirmation from the other Weyrleaders. "I think I can still name all the bright stars."

"Sadly, it's not the bright ones we have to watch, N'ton," Wansor said, "but they are important to recognize, to give the positions of the ones we must chart and register."

"It's also a very big sky, F'lessan," K'van remarked.

"Which is why it is such a very good idea for more dragon-riders to learn how to watch it," F'lessan said, giving K'van, the Southern Weyrleader, a challenge. "You've an admirable situation down there on the heights in your new Weyr."

"It's the sort of thing you young riders should do," G'dened said emphatically. Then he realized what he'd said. "You may be sure I'll encourage my riders."

"Before I Impressed Talmanth," Palla said, raising her hand, "I studied astronomy."

"Why, so you did," J'fery said, regarding his Weyrmate with surprise.

"An apprentice I was sorry to lose and would be delighted to encourage," Erragon said, nodding acceptance of her shy offer.

Aware that everyone was looking at her, she ducked her head and stared at her clasped hands. Lessa noticed that J'fery bent to say something in her ear and she gave him a quick smile, relaxing her hands.

"That sounds like it will take a lot of time," G'dened said, not sure he approved of such activity.

"Oh, it will," Erragon had to agree. "With your assistance, we will have a splendid register to present the Council. Already we have Master Idarolan quite willing to move anywhere he can be of assistance, in teaching or watching. He reminds me that most Fishmen use the stars to navigate and he isn't the only one who's retired."

"Which brings us back to making this sky watch efficient. What do you mean, Master Wansor, by twenty-four-hour coverage and another telescope?" F'lar asked.

"About time," F'lessan said forcefully.

"We have Cove Hold, we have Honshu," Erragon replied, "we need to site at least one of the Catherine Cave telescopes in the north as soon as possible." Erragon coughed. "For a proper twenty-four-hour coverage, we should consider setting up the first observatory on the Western Continent."

"There's nothing there," Lessa exclaimed.

"There are still stars above it," F'lessan reminded her, then hastily added, "We can worry about how to improve the place later."

"An observatory on the Western Continent must be established as soon as possible," Erragon said firmly, prepared to argue that point.

"To allow us to confirm sightings with as much accuracy as possible, we must have one there, despite its distance from any other major population center," Wansor said, bringing one hand down flat on the table. The noise startled everyone. Master Wansor was the mildest of men and his sudden insistence surprised G'dened and G'narish. "We must have one there or the sky watch can fail. Master Idarolan is of the firm opinion that a small settlement is feasible. He even suggests a sheltered harbor between the two halves of the western Continent and knows where clear water is available. Even some trees."

"Really?" Lessa asked.

"Really," Wansor said, nodding earnestly in her direction. "If we number dragonriders among the sky-watchers, establishing an observatory—even at such a distant point—will cause no great problem. They can be home daytimes, you see. It's only the night they need to watch."

His cheerful qualification caused several to grin; Palla and Mirrim turned chuckles into coughs.

"Then that's one observatory settled," he went on.

"But where will there be others?" K'van asked, still smiling as he leaned forward, a keen expression on his sun-tanned face.

Jaxom cleared his throat. "There's an excellent spot for an observatory at Ruatha Hold. Near the Ice Lake, accessible enough. I am quite willing to cede it—and the tithes of any holds in the immediate area—to establish a wholly independent Star Hall."

Wansor beamed in his direction while others exchanged glances at such generous sponsorship.

"With all due respect, Lord Jaxom," J'fery said deferentially, "since Palla has some training already and there is also a possible site not far from our Weyr . . ."

"Managing a Weyr takes all *my* time," Cosira said, pointedly looking away from Palla.

Lessa made a disparaging sound and dismissed that inference. "Palla's younger than either of us, Cosira. Since she's been Erragon's apprentice, I don't think any of us would object if she delegates part of her Weyr duties to the other queen riders."

"That's as may be," F'lar said, giving both Lessa and Cosira quelling stares.

"Yes, yes," Master Wansor said. "Thank you, Lord Jaxom, Weyrleader J'fery, Lady Palla. You will have to refresh and augment your original training. While I may not be able to see anymore, my memory is excellent. Master Samvel at the Landing school has a whole class of young people to whom I already teach basic astronomy. I suspect," and his opaque eyes appeared to twinkle, "that there may be many older people, aunties and uncles, retired from physically demanding work, like Master Idarolan, who would be delighted to have responsible work to do, even if it is at night. Frankly, I only need a few hours' sleep," he added with an ingenuous smile.

"It would be no problem for me and Tiroth," D'ram said, "to bring students *to* Master Wansor. It will take considerable time, especially with the workload that is currently carried by our best people, to build an observatory, so we must make strong representations to the Council to start as soon as possible. In the meantime, the production of binoculars from the Smithcrafthall has been increased—"

"By over half again as many," Wansor interrupted with one hand upraised in apology, "since the Fireball."

"Has been increased considerably," D'ram went on gently. "Master Jancis and Piemur assure us of a supply and Master Morilton has professed himself and his Hall willing to experiment with reflecting mirrors for small telescopes."

"And, when the dangerous objects are discovered, will dragons be required to push them out of the sky?" G'dened demanded sarcastically.

Lessa noticed that F'lessan exchanged a quick look with Tai. F'lessan also had a gleam in his eye that had always preceded some mad start of his as a boy.

"One never knows, G'dened," Jaxom said, "considering what strange things dragons have done in the past eleven Turns. I repeat, I'm quite willing to site and provide for an observatory in the Ruathan hills."

"I'll undertake to set another at Telgar. Master Fandarel will certainly approve of an efficient watch on the sky," and J'fery grinned, "and Lord Larad is more open to such projects than other Holders."

"It would be wise," Jaxom said, stressing the last word, "to include as many holders and crafters in this sky watch as possible."

"I thought it was to be a dragonrider responsibility," G'dened said.

Really, thought Lessa with a disgust she did not express, G'dened must step down. He was so hidebound.

"We will need everyone who's willing! Why, we'll need to train two or more Halls full of people," and Wansor held out both arms in an expansive gesture. "As Weyrleader K'van remarked, it's a big sky. And we must discover as many objects as possible. Most will prove harmless when their orbits are charted, like our Turnover Ghost cometary trails. Many may come close but proceed on their ways."

"That's all very well, Master Wansor," G'dened said, still unconvinced, "but that doesn't answer the important question: what *could* we do if another comet or meteor or whatever is close enough to impact Pern again?"

The silence in the hall was so complete that the incoming waves could be heard rippling up the beach, and the occasional splash of dolphins playing one of their evening games.

"We'll think of something," F'lar said into that silence.

"What's the matter with all of you . . ?" F'lessan cried, jumping to his feet.

Lessa could almost hear the words he had been about to utter: old dragonriders.

He recovered quickly, almost stumbling over the next words. "We've only started exploring the masses of information Aivas left us and somewhere in all that information there will be a way of dealing with them. When Thread first starting falling, our ancestors made do with what they had, and developed what they needed to survive—the dragons. They found ways to adapt that have sheltered and expanded a population that, had they been less resourceful and optimistic, would have perished without a trace in that first Pass. All due respects to you, Erragon, but Aivas had a habit of hiding information so we have to work to find it. Let us make the best of what we have—those telescopes and the brains we were born with."

Lessa regarded her son with considerable, if pessimistic, respect. And yet, what he said might well be true. Aivas had talked about weapons of mass destruction and she earnestly hoped that nowhere in those records were such particulars. But if there was hope . . .

"We had to learn a great many things to blow the Red Star off course. We still don't know the half of what there is in Aivas's records," F'lessan went on.

"There's more than half of that we don't *need* to know, F'lessan," G'dened said, scowling.

"Quite possibly more than half, G'dened, but, as dragonriders, we are committed to learn as much about our responsibilities of protecting this planet as possible."

Giving F'lessan an approving nod, F'lar rose. "The Weyrs will continue to serve. If we propose the sky watch to the Council in the most positive terms, and with complete accord," he glanced meaningfully at G'dened and the puzzled G'narish, "then, by the first Eggs that hatched here in Landing, we dragonriders will add a new dimension to our future!"

His fist came down on the table and, eyes brilliant, he stared around, daring anyone to challenge him.

Now *that*, Lessa thought with a surge of pride for her weyrmate, was plain speaking! The two new Weyrleaders, so determined to succeed in their new responsibilities, would have followed any strong lead. Between F'lessan and F'lar, they now had one and rose to their feet, cheering. T'gellan's dejection noticeably lightened and, if Cosira looked confused, at least G'narish seemed revitalized by F'lar's stirring words.

"I suppose it's best to show a united front," G'dened muttered, reluctantly acquiescing to the majority.

"Well now, that's most encouraging, most encouraging," Wansor said, nodding around. "So, let us summarize our plans. *Yoko,* Cove Hold, and Honshu will continue their search patterns of near-space; we'll request the Council to release three of the remaining telescopes; start work on the vitally required one on the Western Continent, another to be sited at Ice Lake—thank you very much, Lord Jaxom. The third at Telgar—if Lord Larad's goodwill and assistance can be obtained. Good of you, Lady Palla, Lord J'fery, to offer your services. Of course, we shall ask the invaluable cooperation of Master Fandarel. We shall also ask for volunteers— sky-watching will require many eyes as well as many of the dark hours—and instigate an accelerated training program. I'm sure the Harper Hall will encourage this. And I'll ask Master Tagetarl to print up one of his notices. The entire planet will know!" He swung his arms wide, his broad smile infectious.

"I think that does about summarize what the dragonriders will do," F'lar said. "Now, why don't we relax and have some wine? We brought some Benden with us for those who might like it."

There wasn't a person in the hall, save perhaps G'dened, who wasn't quite happy to take a glass. Mirrim bustled out to the kitchen with Talina, Adrea, and Sharra in tow. Tai started to join them but F'lessan held her back, to help him explain the prints to Palla, J'fery, and K'van. Erragon produced old Aivas projections, which showed how much currently unobserved sky would be the responsibility of the Western Continent installation.

Relieved that this meeting, which she had begun with little hope of any positive support, had ended on such a high note, Lessa felt incredible relief. The Weyrleaders of Pern would take their places at the Council with considerably more confidence and that, in itself, would impress the Lord Holders and Craftmasters. She especially looked forward to announcing the post-Thread occupation for which dragonriders were undeniably suited. She smiled to herself. Sharra brought her a glass of wine and a small dish of savories. She was roused from her private thoughts by G'dened's testy question to Master Wansor.

"You mentioned three other dedicated people? Who would they be?"

"Why, Master Stinar is one, the others are two of my old students from Telgar who are now masters in their own Halls, Tippel in Crom and Murolin in Southern Boll. They have even built their own scopes—reflecting telescopes, only one-hundred-millimeter—but adequate for the sky-watching. It is to Tippel's everlasting despair that he missed seeing the Fireball; it had been so cold he'd gone in early." Master Wansor made a comical face of regret. "However, I do have a suggestion for you, Weyrleader G'dened. Have a look at the sky tonight from the Cove Hold telescope."

Lessa sat straight up, grinning at G'dened's sudden confusion.

"Now, why didn't one of us think of that?" She stood up. "I should like a chance to see myself. Is it possible, Erragon?" She saw the brief hesitation on the Master's face. "Or would we be interrupting your search pattern?"

"All in a good cause, Lady Lessa." Erragon bowed with sincere courtesy.

"Who's there while you're here?" G'dened wanted to know.

"Lofton, a capable journeyman," he replied just as F'lessan came up to Lessa.

"Tai and I would be glad to demonstrate Honshu's scope," F'lessan said, grinning from ear to ear. "I've got K'van, Adrea, Palla, and J'fery coming."

G'dened and Cosira were the only ones who did not care to go on to view the stars, either at Cove Hold Observatory or Honshu. G'dened did agree that he would find out who among his riders would wish to train themselves for this sky-watch project.

"You did say, Erragon," said F'lar, joining Lessa, "that you have more prints we can show to relieve the fears of the Council?"

"And the majority of the holders and crafters," K'van murmured, adding so only F'lessan and Tai heard him, "not to mention the dragonriders."

It wasn't until Lessa and F'lar got back to their weyr that she remembered she hadn't had a chance to speak to Jaxom, who had slipped out with Sharra while others were finishing their wine. She missed a moment with F'lessan, as he, too, left more ostentatiously with the group going to Honshu, so that she didn't have any time to talk to this green rider of his. She had never seen him so protective of anyone. Tai did not look fragile.

"She'll do," F'lar murmured, once again touching her very thoughts as he slipped an arm about her shoulders and made her comfortable against him in bed.

PART 4

New Dimensions

HONSHU WEYRHOLD — 2.26–27.31

AFTER THE COVE HOLD MEETING that Tai had dreaded, she was as exhilarated as F'lessan. He had had to be unusually stern—for him—to get her to attend and only because Erragon had been equally insistent had she reluctantly complied. Then, during the meeting, both men had made so many references to her assistance that she had been embarrassed. When old G'dened had proved intransigent and supercilious, so—so *stupid* about the dangers, she had had to speak up. Erragon and even Lord Lytol, who often took the opposite side of any argument, had supported her comment. And encouraged her to speak. It had been a high and totally unexpected moment of acceptance for her. Neither Benden Weyrleader had taken exception to or even seemed surprised by F'lessan's remarks. She had been almost overcome with pride in him. When Mirrim would have marched her off to the kitchen, F'lessan had kept her by his side, to explain to the younger Weyrleaders how they established the scan, set the remote imager for timed exposures, and how to determine the significance of the images and why so many exposures of the night sky were required. Palla seemed almost as overwhelmed by the company she was in as Tai, and the two exchanged sympathetic glances. Palla was the only other young dragonrider who understood the immediate task.

Then F'lessan issued the invitation for those interested to

adjourn to Honshu. And eleven riders and dragons had flown to the weyrhold. That had been the heady part, especially with Mirrim present—showing off the observatory and bringing up images of the minor planets above the horizon. When F'lessan and Tai realized that Palla had remembered a good deal of her apprentice studies, they encouraged her to explain to J'fery, K'van, and T'gellan. Talina listened in the way she had of being of a group but not part of it. Mirrim pretended interest but Tai was aware of her restlessness, so when she offered to find out what there was to eat in the weyrhold, F'lessan told her by all means to find out and serve it up. He snagged Tai by the hand.

"She knows where everything is—" F'lessan murmured in her ear and paused significantly, "in the kitchen. Let her."

Revived by baskets of bread, cheese, fruit, cold river fish, meat, and klah that Mirrim served, the spontaneous first session of Astronomy for Weyrleaders—as F'lessan jokingly called it—went on till well after Rigel had set.

Having bid farewell to their guests, Tai began to clear the baskets, sweeping the remnants into one while F'lessan put the telescope to bed. She was gathering up the prints when he caught her starting to file them.

"Just make a neat pile. We need to get some rest tonight, my dear green," he said, curling his arms about her, pulling her into him and away from the chore. She leaned out of his arms to snag several more prints. "They'll come to no harm and filing will not only take you ages but you're tired enough to make mistakes." He kissed her neck. "You take the litter down with Zaranth. I'll close the roof and meet you downstairs."

"You walked up, I'll go down," she said firmly.

"No, I will. It's easier going down, and that way you'll have enough time to put the kitchen to rights after Mirrim's been messing in it and *then* we'll both take a quick swim in the river which I suddenly feel the urge to do."

F'lessan knew exactly how to manipulate her, Tai thought as she climbed the ladder to the roof and took the baskets that F'lessan handed up to her, grinning with his success. She heard the machinery that closed the roof begin to whir as she mounted Zaranth. Golanth's eyes blinked greenly at her.

I come with you, he said and dropped off the knob of stone he'd been perched on.

She left the two dragons on the terrace and made for the kitchen. All the lights were on and most of the cupboards left half ajar. There was rather more of a mess to clear up than she'd've thought. Had Mirrim done this on purpose? No, Talina had been with her; Talina might be indolent but she wasn't spiteful. Mirrim still didn't believe her about the pelts. Although Golanth had now managed, with just a little control from Zaranth, to alter the direction of trundlebugs only as much as was actually required, that had been as much experimentation as they had had time for. Images had had to be selected and prepared for the Weyrleaders' meeting and that had taken all their spare time. Well, almost all their spare time. Tai blushed as she cleared and wiped the worktops and decided that there weren't really that many dishes that needed more than a quick rinse. There was enough redfruit to make a pitcher of juice and she suspected that F'lessan would be thirsty. Any more klah and they'd never get to sleep. Maybe she wouldn't rest anyway, with so much of that meeting to review; vivid scenes in her mind. F'lessan would probably want to talk, and he always insisted that she have opinions and share them with him.

He looked tired when he finally got to the kitchen but his eyes lit up at the sight of the pitcher of juice. He had towels and two blankets over his shoulder, and clean clothes—for both of them—neatly folded over his left arm.

"How did you know I'd be dry as a bone, my dear green?" He poured juice into the two glasses.

She pointed to what he was carrying.

"Golanth has informed me that he now needs to wash the brine of Cove Hold off him and so does Zaranth, only she thinks we should all go to sleep. So I thought, if we went down to the river, they could get a good wash and we could watch the stars for what remains of the night. I really," and somehow he managed to stretch both arms out in a very dramatic gesture, "feel too elated to be cooped up! Drink!"

She did, laughing between swallows, because F'lessan in this mood was not easy to gainsay. And she did feel that she'd knocked down a few private walls tonight. So much had happened. So incredibly much. She'd been part of a special Weyrleader meeting, had spoken up and given information, shown examples of star images she herself had taken on the Honshu scope, and received commendatory glances from Erragon, Lytol, F'lar, and even Lessa. She felt for the first time that she was really a dragonrider, not *just* a green rider!

They finished the juice, mounted their dragons—F'lessan tossed over her clothes and a towel—and glided down from Honshu's heights to the river below the terraces. The pool was wide enough for several dragons to bathe in. It was deep on the Honshu side, where thick underbrush buried roots into cracked rocks, but the other side slanted up to a wide path packed down by centuries of herdbeasts watering there. Three wide terraces stepped up from the watering place before vegetation had found sufficient soil to nourish it. Many Monacan dragons had sunned here after the Flood. From the uppermost level, they could have seen the slate roofs of the cluster of holds. But daybreak was several hours away.

F'lessan had brought a pouch of sweetsand. Tai looked forward to a quick wash, even in cold river water. Cove Hold had been warm and she'd been in a nervous sweat there, worked up another in the crowded control room while showing off the fine clear sky view that the Honshu scope was capable of. They soaped each other, still with enough energy to make it playful. But fatigue settled on both of them soon enough, and the dragons splashed in gratefully to take their turn. Their antics sent sprays of water high up the bank. Laughing, F'lessan moved their things up on to the highest of the terraces and, throwing Tai her towel, began to dry himself. They dressed, since the dawn air could be chill, spread one blanket down, and pulled the other over them, using the towels as pillows against the rough ground cover.

Tai smiled, listening to the dragons' happy noises, and was at peace with herself in a fashion she had rarely experienced.

"I don't know if they sound more like fire-lizards or dolphins when they 'talk' like that," F'lessan said, cocking one arm under his head and reaching for her hand with the other.

"They're related, after all," she said, somewhat drowsily, quite content to lie there, next to him, letting his fingers twine in hers.

She heard him sigh.

"There are so many things to talk about," he murmured, "but I think they can wait until tomorrow, don't you?"

He turned his head toward her, though she couldn't see but a blur of his face and the whiteness of his teeth in one of his so charming smiles.

"It is tomorrow, you know."

"Well, a little further into the morning, then."

He lifted his head just enough to kiss her lightly.

Why was it that the tenderest of his kisses affected her more than the passionate ones—which she enjoyed, too? It was his tenderness toward her that undid her most.

She woke, sitting bolt upright, a second before everything happened, before Golanth roared, before Zaranth reacted to what she was staring at so intensely in the underbrush. That moment was graven on the back of her eyes as surely as the Fireball's explosion: she and F'lessan on the uppermost terrace, Zaranth just below them, her body taut for something Tai could not see and Golanth, head toward the river, sprawled lengthwise on the lowest level, his tail half propped against a thick bush.

Whether it was his tail which had enticed them or not would always be moot. Many felines were hunting that dawn. The sun had risen and sun-warm dragon hide exuded a scent all its own. Dragons generally sought heights for sunbathing. This morning, with all four deeply asleep, the dragons were accessible.

The felines had arrived stealthily. Perhaps thirst had initially drawn them to the river, only to find the sleeping dragons. Perhaps Golanth's tail had twitched in his sleep, attracting attention. Whatever Zaranth was staring at suddenly was flung backward at incredible speed and that was the signal for an orange-striped feline to clamp its teeth on Golanth's tail. At his roar the rest of the considerable hunting party attacked. Spotted, striped, and tawny hides, assaulting him from three directions, abruptly covered the bronze.

He reared to his full height, front legs clawing the air to remove the one that had sunk teeth in his left eye ridge. He tried to whip free of the one on his tail and kick off the third which had bitten into the fold of his flesh between rib cage and hip, to buck against the others racing in from the thick shrubs that bordered the river. Feline jaws clamped harder, determined to retain their hold.

Then others used Golanth's body as stairs to attack Zaranth, talons outstretched, heads angled to sink fangs in whatever flesh they could reach.

F'lessan moved so quickly that, in throwing the blanket from his legs, he entangled Tai in its folds. Springing forward and then vaulting over Zaranth's hindquarters, he launched himself at the nearest feline, brandishing the knife a rider always carried, though it was a blade that was shorter than the fangs of the nearest beast. Zaranth, too, reared, sending the one attacking her head spinning through the air.

These are NOT trundlebugs, Zaranth cried. *THROW them away!*

Golanth had torn the one off his face with one forepaw, but it turned in midair, legs at full stretch, and its right front paw raked down F'lessan's back. Its momentum took it to the ground where it instantly gathered and leaped toward the rider. F'lessan ducked, plunged his knife into the chest of the beast, and rolled away, the feline snarling with rage and trying to get rid of the knife lodged it in it. F'lessan grabbed a loose rock and, with it as a weapon, ran to help his dragon, despite the blood flowing from the claw marks on his back.

Trapped on one side by the terrace, Golanth had no way to unfurl his right wing. With his rider in peril, he would not go *between* where he could have shed the felines in the great black cold. Nor, in such close quarters, for fear of searing their beloved riders, could either dragon summon residual flame to deter their attackers. One feline was attempting to shred Golanth's left inner wing sail and others, sinking talons deeply into tough dragon hide, climbed all over him.

Not just over Golanth, Tai realized, frantic to get free of the blanket. Tawny bodies were flinging themselves at Zaranth as well but didn't seem able to do more than leave long bleeding furrows. The beast biting the soft part of Golanth's flank was flung into the river where it sank instantly. Zaranth howled, shaking her head as if ridding it of a burden, kicking out with a hind leg though Tai saw nothing but a darker green liquid oozing down the green leg. A tawny streak came at her from behind and disappeared. The one trying to run up Golanth's back was suddenly in midair, all limbs spread as if something had picked it up by the belly and punched it violently away. The one with jaws sunk into Golanth's left hind leg was similarly torn from him. Ripping at the blanket, Tai got to her feet, clutching it in one hand, wishing it had been any sort of a hard-edged weapon, wondering how she could get to F'lessan who now had two large felines circling him. Blood poured down his back.

The next thing she knew, she was beside F'lessan, the blanket billowing in the air behind her from the force of her arrival. Cracking the blanket like a beast whip, she hit the face of one of the felines who retreated, snarling, before she flung the blanket over the next one, catching the folds on its claws. F'lessan pushed her down and the second beast leaped on him. During the split second before the animal reached him, Tai could only think one thing: I've lost him! I've lost him!

Suddenly the air was full of dragons, wings spread, and flame spouting from their mouths. Tai was horrified lest the dragon fire sear them. Human flesh would shrivel—that powerful fire could char through dragon flesh.

WATCH ME! Zaranth's voice was like a thunder in the

innermost part of Tai's skull. *FLING THEM!* was answered by even more powerful external shrieks. Beset by fear and terror, by the horror of losing F'lessan and Golanth, she was utterly unable to absorb the strange things that were happening. Why was Zaranth telling the other dragons to watch her, to fling them? Zaranth never hurt the trundlebugs she moved! Now felines were spinning through the air without dragons touching them. Why had that one exploded into fragments?

Abruptly the creature struggling out of the blanket at Tai's feet was no longer there, just the blanket sinking emptily to the ground. The predator who had been positioning its hind legs to disembowel F'lessan was gone. Badly wounded, F'lessan turned toward Golanth, his body stretching out, yearning, but unable to rise and go to the bronze. Over the sound of dragon and feline roars and snarls, Tai could hear him calling Golanth's name!

Tai staggered to F'lessan, to help him to reach Golanth, staggered again as her eyes were blurred. Or was it because her legs buckled under her?

That was when she saw the predators launching themselves—all four at full stretch—from the terrace on which she and F'lessan had been sleeping. They must have crept around behind, concealed in the thick vegetation. Zaranth lifted her torso at precisely the right moment—as if she'd seen them from one facet of her red whirling eyes— and reacted. Three crashed into her body and were deflected away. The fourth was still in midair: it would land right on Golanth's shoulders, by the last neck ridge, where there was nothing to protect the dragon's spine. If jaws or talons connected, a single tear could end Golanth's life.

NO! NO! Later Tai would wonder why her throat was raw. She knew she pointed, unable to do more than that, aghast at what would happen if that predator made it to Golanth's back. The bronze dragon would die! F'lessan would die! She would die! "NO! NO! NO!" She'd lose them both! A blur of gold across bronze.

TIME IT! cried Golanth.

That shriek seemed to course along her bones, in her blood until her body trembled violently, and her head seemed ready to burst. Certainly her heart did. A huge blur of gold again rippled across bronze. She had one second to see its claws hooking briefly into Golanth's withers, tearing strips away. Then the feline burst into pieces, gore, entrails, shards of bone and pieces of hide splattering as far away as she stood, across F'lessan's inert, bloodied body. She saw Golanth staggering. Golanth dying? F'lessan would surely wish to die, too!

She dropped to her knees, bereft with the realization, staring at the green ichor staining Golanth's body. He was still swaying with the impact, his left eye oozing a green mixed with red beast blood. Yet he wasn't falling. Did a dragon fall down dead? Too shocked in that moment to go *between*? Somehow the predator had missed the vital spot. Golanth's head was hanging, canting to the left to favor the damaged eye. Could she cushion his fall? She couldn't even get her knees to work.

Then there were only dragons hovering! Bewildered she gazed up at the wrathful semicircle hovering, wing tip to tip, just above the uppermost terrace: huge golden Ramoth, Arwith, Mnementh, Monarth, Gadareth, Heth, Path, Ruth, and other dragons she did not recognize. She stared at Zaranth, stretched high on her hindquarters, wings spread glistening with smears of ichor—Tai felt the pain in her green's mind. As one, the dragons stretched their heads and bugled in fierce triumph at something she did not understand.

They live! A chorus assured her with such conviction that the devastated Tai collapsed, wondering and grieving at that response, crawling toward F'lessan before she lost consciousness.

She drifted in and out, aware of men and women, conversing in urgent whispers, of the coolness of numbweed easing the pain in her legs and other parts of her that had just started to be sore.

"No, leave *him* here until he's been seen by Oldive as well as Wyzall."

"Then the green won't leave. But we should move her rider."

"It's not far to a proper bed in Honshu after all."

"How many dragons will we need to shift him? He cannot be dumped on bare rock, you know!"

"Do we need all these people here?" Tai recognized the Benden Weyrwoman's caustic tones. "At least the dragons have the good sense to stay out of the way until they're needed."

When they lifted her, to bandage her clawed legs, pain roused her.

"No, no, Tai, don't thrash about. An artery must be repaired."

She thought it was Sharra who spoke.

"Golanth's dead! F'lessan?"

"No, no, they live."

"HOW?"

"They do live. Zaranth, tell her!"

They live, said her green in a whispery voice. *They live! You live! We live!*

She felt a prick in her arm and lost consciousness again.

When she woke, the chant—*they live! they live!*—was still in her head and she wanted so to believe it. And yes, there was Zaranth's mind, as close to hers as skin.

They live. The green sounded so very tired.

Rest, Zaranth. You can rest now, too.

Yes, Zaranth, another voice said. *You may rest now, too.*

A cool cloth gently bathed Tai's face and someone was holding her hand.

"Now, listen to me, Tai." The green rider was astonished to see it was Benden's Weyrwoman who sat beside her bed, holding her hand. "F'lessan has been badly wounded. Oldive, Crivellan, Keita, and two of his best surgeons have put him rather neatly back together. Golanth is actually . . ." Lessa's hands tightened briefly on Tai's fingers and she gave a sort of hiccup before she continued, "worse off. He'll need more repair work when he's stronger. He *will* live! Oldive and our best Healers have promised that much."

A memory of the bronze dragon, scored and oozing with thick green ichor, hunks torn out of tail and leg, his faceted eye blanked, weeping ichor, and that final leap to his most vulnerable spot flashed through Tai's mind.

"But he will never be the same," Tai said, her voice breaking.

Lessa tightened her hold. "Who could be the same after that mauling? But he'll fly again. With F'lessan."

Tai struggled up on one elbow to look directly into the gray eyes that were so like F'lessan's. "You wouldn't lie to me?" She was startled to see the fullness of tears in Lessa's eyes; the Weyrwoman irritably blinked them away. "No, green rider, I would not lie to you. Nor would that incredible dragon of yours. Nor will Ramoth or any other dragon on Pern. F'lessan and Golanth will require a great deal of care but Master Oldive is confident that they are physically strong enough to overcome their injuries."

There was something in Lessa's voice that fueled the fear in Tai. She tried to swing her legs to the side of the bed—she had to *see* F'lessan—but her legs wouldn't work and she re-lived that hideous moment when she couldn't get free of the blanket to help F'lessan.

She was pushed back, flat against the pillows. "You've wounds of your own that must heal before you go bouncing out of bed."

That was Sharra's voice.

What were they all doing here? Where was she?

You are in Honshu, and this time it was Ruth speaking to her. *Where else would you be?*

"And you said she was a biddable girl," Lessa said with characteristic testiness. She gripped Tai's face in both hands and forced her to meet her eyes. "F'lessan's in a fellis sleep. Zaranth, by the way, won't leave Golanth's side. It's as well. She wouldn't fit in this room or she might be tempted to leave her weyrmate."

"Where are they then?" Tai demanded. Honshu's main Hall would not be big enough for two dragons.

"The terrace," Lessa replied calmly. "There's no rain in this season, you know." She turned to one side for a glass. "Sharra will lift you so you can drink this."

"What is it?" Tai asked, suspicious. She didn't want to be put back to sleep. She wanted to check her brave Zaranth, to see F'lessan and Golanth no matter how badly wounded they were.

"Tell me, my dear green rider, how will you be able to care for F'lessan and Golanth if you jeopardize your own recovery?"

It was the phrase "my dear green rider" and the very kind tone in which Lessa spoke that so stunned Tai that she drank down the potion without further struggle.

"I think she did believe me," Tai heard Lessa murmuring as she felt the fellis juice easing the rawness of her throat, radiating through her body and mind.

"I knew she'd believe *you*," Sharra answered and that was all she heard before she fell into a deep sleep that was therapeutic.

Lessa had told Tai the truth about the other three injured in the felines' attack, but not the whole truth. F'lessan and Golanth were critically injured: the survival of one depended on the other. The experienced Weyrhealer Wyzall had been entirely honest about Golanth's ghastly wounds: the eye, with so many facets pierced by claws, might never function. He'd had fair results with a gel, which healed thread-char in dragon eyes, and he had used this heavily on Golanth's eye, more to provide surface relief than with any real hope of tissue repair or regeneration. He had repaired the wing joint as well as he could and, of course, the sail membrane would, in time, regenerate most, if not all, the torn tissue. There was the possibility that the joint, with judicious exercise and ma- nipulation, might regain partial flexion but "normal" flight was unlikely.

Oldive and Crivellan could be more sanguine about F'lessan. Physically he would recover from his wounds; the intestinal puncture had been repaired although the loss of flesh in the left calf, the tearing of the tendon and cartilage would almost certainly impair the full use of the leg. Right now, suffering from shock and loss of blood, they doubted he would survive the death of his dragon.

Neither would I, Lessa thought, grieving within the calm and confidence she projected publicly.

Both F'lessan and Golanth must be encouraged that the other, though wounded, would survive. Before F'lessan had lost consciousness, he—as Tai briefly had—may well have thought that Golanth was dying of his wounds and, had he taken that morbid thought with him into his fevered state, it was possible that he would slip away from them! They must also reassure Golanth, drifting in and out of consciousness from shock and weakness, that his rider was not mortally injured. Despite her own distress (numbweed deadened any pain), Zaranth kept assuring Golanth that F'lessan was alive, that his rider was only deeply asleep from pain and the exhaustion of their fight. Ramoth had given the bronze dragon the same reassurances and been a trifle testy when it seemed that Golanth put more reliance on what green Zaranth told him—when he was conscious enough to hear anything.

"So long as he understands that F'lessan lives," Wyzall told Lessa, "it doesn't matter who he believes so long as he *does*."

"Yes, yes, of course," she agreed, but it took a little rearrangement in her mind that *her* Ramoth should take second place to a green.

"Why not? They're weyrmates," F'lar told her, finding brief amusement in what Lessa had apparently not understood. "Each dragon speaks to the other's rider."

She gave him a long startled look. "But he's—" she began and stopped to reconsider. "Well, I suppose it's about time his *human* emotions were involved. I mean, he's very good with his sons, even if S'lan's the only one who ever lived in Benden. I just thought—"

F'lar put an arm around her shoulders. "Ramoth approves,"

he murmured in her ear. "Mnementh does. When you consider what that green did today . . ."

"What she did today—" Lessa broke off. "Well, we won't bother her about how she did what she did today. She did it and—and I'm more grateful than I can ever express."

"Me, too," and he rolled Lessa more firmly into his arms, holding her against him, comforting them both. It would be a long sleepless night.

Once Oldive and Crivellan had left the unconscious F'lessan with Keita to watch him, the two Masters had insisted that the Weyrleaders get some rest. Sharra showed them to a small room, just down the hall from F'lessan and Tai.

Propping pillows behind them, since both knew they wouldn't be able to sleep, they kept trying to figure out the sequence of the astonishing events of the attack and how to explain the extraordinary actions of Ramoth.

"I don't know as I can explain," Lessa told F'lar, "and she's my dragon. I linked with her mind the moment I realized she had gone in answer to Golanth's alarm. I saw what she saw, and that was too many of those wretched predators latched on to him and the green. The green was—somehow—picking them up and flinging them off. It was a—motion—that Ramoth imitated. So did the other dragons. Grabbing the felines and tossing them off the two dragons." She rubbed her forehead as if that would clear the confused images Ramoth had projected to her rider. "F'lessan was on the ground, being viciously attacked; he'd no more than his belt knife, you know. And—Tai—was jumping from the ledge with something flaring out behind her.

"Then," and Lessa paused, frowning, "I think Golanth shouted 'time it' and Ramoth saw the one feline Zaranth hadn't deflected with her body." Her frown deepened and she spoke slowly, measuring the words with the fleeting moment that had made all the difference. "If its jump had connected, the beast could easily have severed Golanth's spinal cord." A shudder ran down Lessa's body and F'lar pulled her head against him in a tight embrace as if he could press the horror of that moment out of her mind—and his. "It had to have been Golanth. Greens don't know the mechanics of timing it without guidance, and Golanth had done so much at Monaco and Sunrise Cliff," Lessa said softly. "The others had just come. Even Ramoth didn't grasp the danger immediately. So it had to have been Golanth who said 'time it.' He must have seen his peril through Zaranth's eyes. Or Tai's. And Ramoth perceived what action was imperative. To deflect the feline's spring. I lost touch with her—and you know that sense of blankness that is *between*?" she asked, looking up at him, her eyes swimming with tears. "I felt that. It's unmistakable. Ramoth timed it back to push the feline just far enough off balance so it missed its target. And didn't kill Golanth. Oh, F'lar, if it had, F'lessan wouldn't have been able to survive Golanth's death. Wouldn't have wanted to. We'd have lost them both!"

She crumpled then, having been calm, steadfast, and efficient for the past few hours. She burrowed into F'lar, struggling to hold him closer, closer, to drive away the appalling words she had just uttered.

"It's reaction," she sobbed. "I'm just reacting!" Tears streamed down her face; Lessa of Ruatha and Benden Weyr, she who had rarely cried, not even when Fax had slaughtered her family and everyone else in Ruatha Hold: now she wept!

She felt other tears drop onto her forehead, as she clung to her weyrmate and realized that he, too, cried even as he stroked her body and tried to soothe her, and let her weep. She couldn't stop, even if everyone or anyone else in Honshu heard her.

No one hears, Ramoth said, and her mental voice sounded very deep and echoing, *but us*.

It took time for both Weyrleaders to release pent-up emotions and regain composure. In the dark F'lar found the room's water basin and tap, discovered a towel, left behind when Monaco riders had been at Honshu, and they washed faces and hands. Still trembling, Lessa made an attempt to braid her hair and F'lar found a cup.

"Amazing!" he said, sitting beside her again, close enough

that their thighs touched, as if he could no more bear separa-
tion in the aftermath of their emotional storm than she could.

"The theory has always been that, if we knew the time, we
could forestall a—a fatal—accident," he said in a low, shaky
voice, reaching for her hand. "Like Moreta's death."

"Theory," she said with a derisive shrug. She sipped slowly
from the cup of water, willing her body to stop shaking.
F'lessan hadn't died because Golanth hadn't died. Golanth
hadn't died because Ramoth had prevented it.

It isn't theory, Ramoth said, her mental tone tart, *I timed it
to the exact moment. Golanth showed me just how he had
saved F'lessan and himself from being crushed by the tsunami wave. He was most resourceful to act on his own initiative. He learned something important that day and was too
tired when he got back to Landing to tell even me. Today,
Zaranth showed us how to push without touching. I admit that
I had never thought greens could do something so unusual. I
saw how she did it. Very clever of her. We two taught the
others. But it was I who timed it to save Golanth from that last
feline. Only I could have done that.*

Lessa managed a shaky little laugh. *Only you, my dearest.*

*I do admit that today I learned something from a green
dragon.* Ramoth sounded as chagrined as her rider had ever
heard her. *I have told the others what Zaranth showed me how
to do, how she* pushed *felines away,* she added calmly. *It is a
useful skill for all to know.*

Stunned by her dragon's attitude toward this new ability,
Lessa turned to F'lar, whose expression was probably as incredulous as hers. Lessa gave one last hiccup.

"In case you're wondering," he said, with a little smile on
his face, "Mnementh agrees. And Aivas was right."

She twitched her mouth and drew her brows together in a
scowl. "Right again and, while I'm glad he is, I'm annoyed,
too. He has complicated life."

"Maybe," F'lar said softly. "Maybe not. D'you remember
Aivas trying to understand the abilities of our dragons?"

Lessa scowled, perplexed. "He knew—we told him—that
they had always communicated with us mentally."

"Telepathy, he called it. And teleportation is the ability of dragons to go *between* from one place to another. Or, however briefly, one time to another." He finger-combed his hair back from his forehead. "Today they practiced the third of those special talents—telekinesis. Aivas could not understand why they could not do *that* if they telepath and teleport. Now they can. I wonder how he would have used this new ability to physically move other things without contact."

"They moved felines who would have killed Golanth, F'lessan, Tai, and Zaranth," Lessa said in a soft pensive voice.

They were both silent in consideration of these startling new concepts.

"As long as they think they can," she said, tightening her fingers on his.

"That's the requisite," he agreed, nodding, a smile twitching at one side of his mouth.

"Then that means there *is* something dragons can do about things in space."

He jerked straight up, hand gripping hers tightly. "Let's take this one slowly, shall we, my love?"

She swung her head back and forth. "Very slowly."

Someone tapped on the door and called her name.

She took a deep breath, felt F'lar do the same.

"Yes?"

"It's Manora. I just arrived to help. G'bol brought me on Mirreth."

"We'll be right there," Lessa called. When she turned her shining eyes to F'lar, they were no longer full of tears, but hope. He embraced her, cheek on her head, trying by the language of his body to tell her the words in his heart.

Calm and mutually supportive, they emerged from their brief respite to greet Manora.

Manora, headwoman of Benden's Lower Cavern, was seated beside the bed when Tai next woke, an honor that had Tai reeling until she felt Zaranth's mental touch, initially anxious and then relieved. *You are better! I am, too.*

"Ah, good," Manora said, examining Tai's face. "Your eyes are clearer and your fever is gone."

"F'lessan?" Tai tried to sit and wished she hadn't: she ached all over. This was much worse than the mauling she'd had from the men at Landing Healer Hall. She made no resistance when Manora pushed her back down.

"His fever has lessened, yes. His injuries were extensive. There was some internal damage, you see," and Manora's serious face made no light of that, "but Oldive and that clever-fingered Crivellan stopped the bleeding, repaired the damage the claws did, and he will heal."

Tai heard a note in her voice. "What else is wrong?"

She gave Tai's hand a reassuring clasp, her expression approving. "You're very quick, Green Rider Tai. Muscle was torn from F'lessan's left leg and not all the new skills that the Healer Hall has developed can replace that." She paused. "He'll have a few scars on his face but I do believe that once the wounds have healed they won't be so noticeable."

"F'lessan is not a vain man," Tai said, after a moment's consideration, "but he will hate a limp."

"You are quite right. How do your legs feel?"

Tai had to think because she felt awfully heavy below her knees.

"There should be little feeling," Manora added quickly. "I have only just finished dressing them with numbweed. You'll have scars."

Tai dismissed that with a snort. "How badly was Zaranth hurt and when may I see her?"

Manora gave her a slow look. "As I'm sure Zaranth has told you, she is better: not so stiff today. She was clawed and bitten, not as extensively as Golanth or in any way crippling to her. She is slathered with numbweed the moment she so much as twitches. She has been fed a plump and tender herd-beast, which Gadareth chose and brought for her. She is able to move and to fly if she should wish to."

Tai closed her eyes, all too keenly aware of how much worse the bronze's injuries must be. The predators had *savaged* him. She could *see* him struggling, Zaranth trying to defend them both. Oddly Tai felt no resentment that her dragon's primary concern had been for her weyrmate. Golanth had, after all, taken the brunt of the attack.

"G-G-Golanth?"

Manora's expression altered for a brief instant and then she smiled with gentle reassurance.

"He, too, is improving, but it will take much longer for him to heal. His injuries were—dreadful."

"They all went for him . . ." Tai's voice broke.

"The predators attacked both dragons. Zaranth has many claw marks on her; they are just not as deep as those on Golanth. Do you know—" and here Manora hesitated, "*how* she defended herself and Golanth?"

Vividly Tai remembered Zaranth staring intensely at something in the underbrush. She thought of deflected trundlebugs, such minor nuisances. She thought of the pelts that Zaranth had somehow retrieved. That night, she hadn't moved anything to prove to F'lessan that she could—until he threw the bowl at her. Nothing could have been more threatening than the felines! Neither dragon had hesitated in pushing them away. But Zaranth had had more practice with that technique while Golanth had had ever so many more to deal with. Until the other dragons came to help. She remembered now, too, something that Aivas had said in her hearing, when she was working in Admin. "The white one leads the way but why is it that they do not use telekinesis if they can telepath and teleport?"

As that incident had been prior to her unexpected Impression of Zaranth, she hadn't understood what he meant and certainly wouldn't have dared to raise a question then. She had puzzled over the remark from time to time. Aivas had been very interested in draconic abilities. He had also been somewhat disappointed, even after the incredible feat dragons and riders had performed to alter the orbit of the Red Star; no one had ever understood why, for the plan Aivas had devised had been impeccably carried out. Everyone had seen the explosion of the antimatter engines placed on the Red Star.

"It's something she learned on her own, to keep trundle-bugs from bothering her."

"Trundlebugs?" Manora asked in amazement.

"As far as I know, the species is limited to the southern continent," she said. "They're only a nuisance."

"And Zaranth would move them out of her way? So it is conceivable that she also moved the felines in the same fashion."

"There were so many." Tai could not stem the tears that flowed down her cheeks. Manora cradled her hand and stroked it soothingly, a tacit permission to cry as much as Tai needed to ease her distress. "She tried to help Golanth. There were more attacking him. Then more dragons arrived. They took care of the others. Except that last one. And Golanth told Ramoth to time it?" Brushing tears from her face with her hand, she looked up at Manora. "But what good could that have done? Only it seemed to. Golanth was not killed." With her eyes she begged some explanation of Manora.

Manora soothed her with a gentle stroke. "I believe that is the paradox of timing it. F'lar said something about causality. The beast had aimed, jumped, and even by timing back, Ramoth could only make the most infinitesimal alteration in the second she had, but she deflected a lethal blow. I gather that there was so much going on at that moment it is miraculous she managed what she did. And this started with a dislike of trundlebugs?"

Tai managed a little smile. "They've scratchy feet and if you swat at them, the female lets off the most incredible stink. So you have to move them carefully and before they know what's happened. So it takes a certain amount of skill." She paused, allowing the amusement of Golly's first attempt to flicker across her face. "F'lessan and Golanth saw her do it at Benini Hold. It wasn't anything much." Tai started to shrug one shoulder but it was painful. "Just Zaranth avoiding an inconvenience." Tai hesitated. "And then there was the problem with pelts."

"Oh, yes, the pelts. Mirrim mentioned those," and somehow Manora implied that, although Mirrim might have been talking a lot, Manora was not the sort of person who heeded gossip. Tai felt a surge of gratitude for Manora.

"I—think—" and Tai hesitated, trying to pick her words carefully; she didn't wish to lose Manora's good opinion of her. "I think—now—that's how Zaranth got the skins before the Flood reached our hold."

"Got them?" Manora repeated, miming her fingers picking something up and flicking it away.

"Without her being there."

"I think I understood that, Rider Tai. You were very busy helping to evacuate the children just then." Manora clasped her hands on her forearms and settled to consider what she understood. "I know what Weyrwoman Lessa said must have happened." She inclined her head respectfully. "An example of how pure blind instinct will react to the right stimulus. As Zaranth did yesterday."

"Yesterday?" Tai jerked upright, despite the discomfort, and was firmly subdued by Manora who, though everyone said she must be the oldest woman in Benden Weyr, displayed considerable strength.

"Yesterday."

"But today? We were supposed to go to the Council meeting." She struggled briefly. "To support Masters Wansor and Erragon."

The twinkle in Manora's eyes and her gentle and unusually broad smile surprised Tai by their unexpectedness.

"Yesterday, Rider Tai, you did more than you may yet understand to support the Masters. And the Weyrs. That is why I am here, with you, in the Weyrwoman's stead, overseeing your recovery." She leaned forward to pat Tai's shoulder gently. "Thanks to Zaranth and you, this will be an immensely interesting meeting, with broad repercussions and, I hope, changes. For the good of us all."

The Weyrleaders remained at Honshu overnight: Lessa looked in on F'lessan from time to time.

"I never have been much of a mothering person," Lessa admitted quietly to Manora when they shared a pot of klah.

"Why should you have been?" Manora asked mildly. "With you neck deep in Weyr business that only you could manage and every woman quite happy to take care of him? A much more sensible custom than what goes on in holds, Lady Lessa," Manora replied, "especially for as lively a lad as F'lessan."

F'lar spent time sitting between Golanth and Zaranth, Mnementh and Ramoth on guard on the terrace above. There seemed to be a plethora of dragons resting at Honshu.

Why aren't they at their own weyrs, Mnementh?

We are waiting until Golanth and Zaranth improve.

F'lar was flummoxed by the tinge of reverence in his bronze's tone.

All of you? And he indicated the many in attendance.

Yes. The affirmative seemed to echo throughout the valley below.

While it was true that the dragons were always solicitous about any injured by Thread or ill of the few ailments that could sicken one of them, this vigil was unusual.

Zaranth and Golanth have done the unusual. We wait with you, too.

So F'lar found himself content to sit, companionably silent with so many of the creatures who were keeping watch with him. Such a moment was rare.

When Lessa joined him later, murmuring that he should get some food into him, she took his place.

They sleep. They need it, Ramoth said so very, very softly, as if she did not wish even that intimate exchange to disturb the silence.

Tell me again, Ramoth, how it all happened. From the beginning.

I have been thinking of nothing else. I will speak softly. These here know what happened and yet—they don't know. I am not sure I do.

Lessa nodded her head. *Tell me. We will study it together.*

I am asleep. I am awakened by the most urgent cry for assistance. Mnementh wakes, too. It is Golanth who is in trouble. It is Zaranth who calls, fears for Golanth's life. She calls everyone. Everyone she knows. I get there first, Mnementh a breath behind. Then come Heth, Gadareth, Monarth, Path, Arwith, Ruth, and others. I see Zaranth tearing the felines from Golanth without touching them. Her mind has the fury of firestone as it comes from the mouth: never have I seen a dragon so angry. I see how *she does it. Golanth does it, too. Ruth learns quickly. All who came learned. We remove the furry killing things. We think only of removing the furry killing things. We do so. No other creature has ever attacked a dragon!*

She paused. *It is not the same thing as searing Thread from the sky. I feel good when a Fall is over and no Thread has reached the ground. This is very different. I see the leaping furries, coming from behind. Zaranth lifts as high as she can stand, to take their leaping—bravely done, the bravest thing a green has ever done—but one is aiming for Golanth's back where a rider could fend it off but there is no rider to help protect that place. The beast will not fail of its target.*

Ramoth grumbled briefly. *Golanth tells me to time it. Of course I know how. And I know what he means. It is what he did at Sunrise Cliff. There is so little time in that second. The beast is already leaping. It is too late to stop that. But I can change where it will land. Just enough to turn its strike. The claws do not reach the fatal place. They just nearly do.*

You saved Golanth's life that moment, Ramoth.

In truth it was Zaranth who saved his life.

Lessa had not ridden her golden queen for so many years to disregard something left unsaid.

And so, dear golden heart of my life, you will honor her.

She is a good green dragon. I had not thought to learn from a green dragon. I have. To Lessa's amusement, Ramoth seemed to be considering the source as even more important than the new ability. *But then,* she went on as if having finally settled that point, *this knowledge will require practice—without the spur of fear—to perfect the way to move things.*

Lessa digested that. *But you do remember how to do it?*

For one moment, Lessa feared that it might just be the circumstances of death and danger that had activated this new ability.

I would prefer more time to review what happened, Lessa of my heart, but I remember how. The moment is vivid in my mind. I will not lose it before I lose the light of my days.

Whatever Aivas would have called the emergence of the last of the linked telepathic abilities that dragons and fire-lizards possessed, Lessa did not know. She did wonder what use Aivas would have made of it, in those days when they were trying to alter the path of the Red Star. They'd altered it anyway. So did it matter?

And yet, subtly, it did. Every dragon lounging so casually on the cliffs around Honshu, down on the river terraces—soon every dragon on Pern—was aware of being more than they had been.

Practice? Ramoth said.

COUNCIL MEETING AT TELGAR HOLD—3.1.31

At last Lessa and F'lar slept, determined to be as rested as possible for what lay ahead of them at the Council Meeting. They went to the meeting by way of Benden, where they bundled up the notes they needed for the session and clothing appropriate to the occasion. No one stopped them at their weyrs, though people in the Bowl waved encouragingly and dragons bugled.

Though Benden Weyr had a more than adequate reason to postpone the Council Meeting, there were other extremely important matters—such as electing a new Lord Holder at Southern Boll, the Weyrleaders' presentation of their recommendations, made more cogent by yesterday's event (though the ramifications of *that* would not be open for discussion), the latest Abominator attack on the Print Hall—which made it impossible, as well as inadvisable, to reschedule. Nor, despite her immense concern over the patients at Honshu, would Lessa have absented herself.

F'lessan was in Master Crivellan's more than capable hands and those of Oldive's most experienced healers. The Masterhealer could return to Honshu if he was needed during F'lessan's recovery from the complex surgical repair to the worst of his wounds. Had she remained, Lessa would have felt superfluous, a role she did not play well.

The Weyrhealers attended Golanth and Zaranth. The green would heal as quickly as most dragons did, given the care she was receiving. The damage to Golanth's eye remained exceedingly critical. How the tattered wing sails would heal was another worry. The crack in the long bone of the left wing, splintered by fangs, might inhibit closing and be weak in stroke or falter during a prolonged glide. As long as the two dragons were lavished with numbweed, they would feel no pain. The fact that Persellan had attended Golanth's injuries five minutes after the attack had made a significant difference.

From the beloved Bowl of Benden Weyr, F'lar and Lessa went *between* and emerged above the hills of Telgar where a large crowd had gathered on the plain below the triangular jut of the Hold. As Ramoth, Mnementh at her right wing tip, glided in, Lessa could see the banners of many holds and halls displayed. A Council Meeting usually brought visitors, some waiting to hear about petitions, but she thought there were more than usual—especially in winter.

Then Ramoth's feet touched ground and people surged forward to crowd around Lessa and F'lar where they dismounted on the wide space before the V-shaped Telgar Hold.

"Well, I suppose I was naïve to think we could keep what happened within the Weyrs," F'lar remarked as the two dragons quickly took off again to find sun on Telgar Heights.

"Fire-lizards spread the word," Lessa said, her voice tight with irritation. *Does everyone on Pern know what happened at Honshu?* she asked her dragon.

That felines attacked dragons, yes, Ramoth said. *More is for you to say.*

Scattering replies to the questions about the injured—thank-you-for-your-concern or both-dragons-and-riders-will-be-fine, F'lar took Lessa's arm and, with some of Telgar's guards hastily opening a path for them, reached the ramp up to Telgar's forecourt. Lord Larad, his Lady Dulsay, and their tall, gawky son, Laradian, were standing there to welcome the official members of the Council. More guards, in fine new tunics bearing the Telgar shield of white, bright red, and medium blue, bowed them into the forecourt just as a triumphant bugling caused them to turn around and witness the arrival of the Ista Weyrleaders.

"By the Egg," F'lar said, "they seem to be glowing." He cast an amused look at his weyrmate. "What has happened to G'dened and Cosira?"

Lessa nearly missed a step. G'dened? Of course, he'd know about Honshu but she hadn't seen Baranth that bright in Turns. After over three decades of fighting Thread as well as the recent exertions during the Flood, it was hard to keep good color in the dragons. So long as some of the resurgence spilled into the Oldtimer and thawed him a bit! She couldn't be sure that G'dened would grasp the importance of this unexpected new facet of dragons, but maybe he would be encouraged. Certainly the vibrancy of his color—and even the restored gleam to the hides of Ramoth and Mnementh as she checked them and saw how bright they appeared—suggested that all the dragons of Pern had been renewed in vigor and purpose. Lessa took a deep breath. Now, if they could use this telekinesis effectively . . .

"The dragons and riders are all recovering?" Larad said, stepping down and holding out both hands to F'lar and Lessa. Taking his hands, she realized that he was genuinely concerned.

"Indeed, although truly," and Lessa projected her voice to be sure that everyone listening for news would hear, "if Master Oldive had not been provided with so much invaluable medical information from Aivas's records, we would have lost them both."

"Saved by Aivas?" Larad asked, likewise raising his voice

and implying gratitude. "What I don't understand is how did the felines get into Honshu?"

"The creatures were not in the weyrhold." F'lar gave the simplified version. "F'lessan and Tai had taken their dragons down to the river to bathe. That's where the felines attacked them. The area around Honshu hasn't been much bothered by the felines but the new holds nearby have been rounding up and domesticating more and more wild stock. Naturally the predators were attracted." F'lar shrugged as if dismissing the circumstances. "A concatenation of circumstances. Right place, wrong time. They'll heal."

"Oh, splendid! We are relieved to hear that," Lady Dulsay said and then her expression altered to concern. "And you have to attend a Council Meeting when you must yearn to be at Honshu with your son."

Lessa was momentarily surprised; few people referred to F'lessan as "your son." He was the one child she had been able to bear F'lar and she had once—briefly and keenly—regretted her inability to have more. But that was long ago. The Weyr was more important. Today it was vital for the Weyrwoman to be present at this meeting.

"As to that, F'lessan is very well attended and, being weyr-bred, he would not expect me to absent myself."

Lady Dulsay recoiled slightly. "My pardon, I do forget."

"This is one of those times," Lessa said as kindly as she could, for Lady Dulsay meant well, "when the customs of hold and weyr conflict."

Larad suddenly whipped binoculars to his eyes. Was everyone growing those things about their necks, Lessa wondered. "Here come N'ton with Margatta and the blue at his right wing is Boll's watch dragon, conveying Lady Janissian." He lowered the instrument and smiled self-deprecatingly. "I've only had them a sevenday," he apologized.

"At least you find them useful," Lessa said drolly.

"And hope to use them more," Larad said with a pleased grin.

Lessa swallowed. Could news of the Weyrleaders' meeting

at Cove Hold have leaked? No, Larad was merely showing off his new acquisition.

"There are more dragons, that much I can see with my own eyes," Lady Dulsay remarked, pointing to the skies. "Are any of them likely to be bringing contenders to Southern Boll's Holdership?" She turned to Lessa. "It was so sad when most of that Bloodline, and all four of Lord Sangel's sons, succumbed to the plague. Such promising young men, so my father said."

"Now, of course, with all the vaccines available to the Healer Hall, we won't have such tragic losses again," Lessa replied. She saw another pair of dragons enter from *between*. "I suspect this is G'bear and Neldama, Lady Dulsay. Have you had a chance to meet them?"

"Oh, yes. They arrived the very next day," and Lessa was surprised to see Lady Dulsay blush. "Most respectful to let us know how the Weyrleadership had been decided."

"Good of them to be prompt to introduce themselves," Lessa said, suppressing a desire to grin. Why was it that holders were invariably embarrassed by mating flights? It wasn't as if Dulsay and Larad hadn't been very much attached to each other when they had formally wed. "Are many of the Council here?"

Before anyone could answer, another triple-tone bugling— in Heth's unmistakably tenor voice—heralded the arrival of the Southern Weyrleaders. They, too, were gleaming, Lessa noted before she took the shallow stairs up to the main entrance.

"Would you like to change out of your flying gear now?" Dulsay asked.

"Since you've already met G'bear and Neldama, I think I'll take the opportunity, thank you, Dulsay," and, inside the imposing Hall, Lessa slipped to the left before she could be intercepted. It was a matter of moments to strip and put on the skirt and the more formal tunic she had brought, fold and leave her riding gear on the shelves provided. Menolly came up to her as soon as she emerged.

"They continue to improve?" Menolly asked anxiously,

Sebell close behind her. Sebell was rather spectacular in dark Harper blue, wearing the sapphire pendant of his rank. His eyes were tired and he was as eager to be reassured as Menolly.

"Yes, yes. It was sheer luck that both Oldive and Crivellan have been studying the Aivas files on perforated intestines—such accidents occur often enough to warrant study," Lessa said. "Once again we can be grateful to reacquire the skills that save lives."

Menolly pursed her lips. "Those wretched, narrow-minded, deceitful misfits. They really are abominable!"

"Are they making life miserable for harpers, too, Menolly?" Lessa saw the tension in Sebell's manner. Music might be Menolly's life but she no more liked Sebell distressed than she had Master Robinton.

Just then, trying to look completely at ease and not quite managing, G'bear came in with Neldama and smiled with great relief to be met by friendly faces and congratulations. Once again Lessa gave reassurances about the invalids' progress and then had it all to do again when K'van and Adrea walked in. G'dened and Cosira arrived, N'ton and Margatta, too, escorting Lady Janissian who halted, looking about her. Menolly went right up to the girl, putting an arm around her.

"You came!"

"I couldn't not come, could I?" Janissian replied, and then caught Lessa's eyes, relaxing when the Weyrwoman gave her an encouraging smile.

"No, you have to be here," N'ton said, grinning, "to get there," and he pointed to the closed door of the room where the Council would be held. "I'll get you some wine. Lessa, what would you prefer? You've had a rough few days."

"I'd prefer the klah. I suspect we must all keep our wits about us in this Council," she replied.

"Yes, I expect we will," N'ton agreed, his smile now for Janissian as he gestured for one of the servers to approach with the tray of drinks.

To Lessa's surprised gratification, fifteen minutes later the entire Council was in their spaces around the U-shaped table in Telgar's vaulted Hall. Toric was, as usual, the last to arrive. There were seventeen Lord Holders, sixteen Master-craftsmen and -women (since Joetta had replaced old Zurg as Masterweaver and Ballora was the new Beastmaster), and eight Weyrleaders and six Weyrwomen. Nadira and Talina rarely attended. The heavy sky-broom doors shut behind Toric with a resounding *thunk*.

Lips pursed, scowling, the Southern Lord Holder strode past Sebell, directly to K'van and planted his hands on the table, leaning aggressively toward the Weyrleader.

"Why wasn't I informed that dragons had been badly injured by felines?" he demanded.

"Because it doesn't affect Southern Weyr nor your interests," K'van said, blandly, not intimidated.

"Well?" and Toric swung round toward Lessa and F'lar.

Lessa gave him a bland look. Toric must have enjoyed hearing that F'lessan had been injured but it was in his usual bad taste to try to make it appear an omission on K'van's part.

"It's scarcely a Council matter," F'lar said. "Kind of you to be concerned."

"I'd like to know the details. It's seldom dragons are attacked, much less injured, by lesser beasts."

"As I'm sure the rest of the Council is already aware, Lord Toric, the injured are recovering. Now, do take your seat," Larad said with firm courtesy. "There is much official business to discuss."

Toric looked irritated but as no one would meet his eyes, he did take his chair. Immediately Sebell rose.

"We will deal first with the matter of Southern Boll's Holdership."

"Let us discuss the anarchic behavior," Lord Kashman said, speaking rapidly and angrily, rising from his chair so fast it crashed backward to the flagstones, "of Lord Jaxom, Weyrleader N'ton, and Masterprinter Tagetarl who arbitrarily exiled twelve people, alleged to be Abominators."

Larad looked up with surprise, and not a little annoyance, at Kashman's complete disregard for protocol. Newly appointed Lord Holders should not be so presumptuous.

"Yes," drawled Toric, smiling with considerable relish, "let's hear about this latest of the exiles so enthusiastically perpetrated by Lord Jaxom and Weyrleader N'ton."

"The Abominators did the perpetrating, Toric. Jaxom, N'ton, and Tagetarl followed precedent," Groghe said, slapping one hand down hard on the table. "I was present for two of those judgments. *I* was the one who passed sentence at Turnover. Furthermore, this Council decreed—you were actually present for that meeting," he pointed a thick, unwavering finger down the table at Toric, "don't deny it—when we all decided that exile was an appropriate deterrent for any more wasteful acts of vandalism."

"*This* issue will be discussed later," Sebell said, raising his trained voice that overwhelmed the beginning of a three-sided shouting match by Toric, Groghe, and Kashman. Old Lord Corman seemed to have passed his contentiousness on to this sixth son of his, who was not much past his thirtieth birthday.

"I came to discuss *that*," Toric cried.

"The first matter is, and will be, the confirmation of a new Holder for Southern Boll!" Sebell said in clarion tones.

"Why don't you just agree to the girl and let us get to the *real* issues?" Toric demanded.

"But she's a woman!" Kashman protested. "There hasn't been a Lady Holder, except in a temporary capacity for . . ."

"Not since Lady Sicca ran Ista," Groghe said. "My grandfather had great respect for *her*. For that matter, all of us here, bar you who are new come to the Council honors," and Groghe emphasized that, "know that Lady Marella's been running Boll for the past five Turns since Sangel began to deteriorate. Lady Janissian has been her steward and she certainly proved her worth to me during the Fireball Flood. Those cousins of hers removed themselves and their belongings to high ground and stayed there without lifting a finger. Neither of them should hold."

"For that matter," Lessa said, "Emily Boll held those lands in her own right. As I see it, that Holdership has come full circle and about time."

Lady Dulsay, Adrea, Master Ballora, and Palla were bold enough to second her.

"Shall we confirm Lady Janissian then?" Asgenar asked, looking around, a sly smile on his face, "And save time for the really important matters?" He glared at Toric.

"Like what the Weyrleaders are going to do to prevent more fireballs?" Toric demanded, glaring across the floor at Lessa and F'lar.

"Now, just a minute," Bargen said, annoyed, "that isn't as critical a problem—"

"I should hope it is," Toric interrupted at his most obnoxious.

Bargen gave him a furious glare and, raising his harsh baritone voice, continued, "as choosing a Bloodline successor, Lord," and he closed his lips for a moment, catching Lady Sharra's reaction, "or Lady."

"There are two males in the Bloodline, aren't there?" Lytol asked, supporting Bargen in order to keep to the agenda.

"Vormital, a great nephew of Sangel," Sebell said, eyeing Toric, "and Warlow, a first cousin. Sangel's sons died in the plague and there is no other male issue in the direct Bloodline."

"Never heard of Vormital or Warlow," Bargen said. "There has to be more."

"Not surviving," Sebell said. It was the Harper Hall's duty to check.

"There was, there was. I knew him when I was in High Reaches Weyr. Hillegel. Big man. Half brother to Sangel," Bargen insisted.

"He thought he'd go south," Toric said, grinning smugly. "I heard he went down one of the rivers and never a word since."

N'ton got to his feet. "When approached by the Weyr to help evacuate the vulnerable coast from the Flood, Vormital informed me that this was Sangel's problem, not his."

"Dismiss him from consideration," Groghe said, bringing his fist down on the table. "In my hearing, on five separate occasions, Sangel said the man was a fool and couldn't hold a cup without help."

"Does anyone know any good of this Vormital?" Sebell asked.

"If anyone does, it will be the first time," Groghe said in a voice meant to be heard.

"Who's the other one?" Bargen of High Reaches said. He had fought hard to return High Reaches to his Bloodline after Fax's presumptive holding and he saw nothing wrong with fighting to claim Bloodright—for males, of course.

"Warlow is the child of Sangel's youngest sister. He has a small farm and five sons, three of whom have served Lady Marella in minor capacities."

"If his sons served, and he hasn't pushed for himself, he'd be useless," was Bargen's immediate answer. "Are we left with the girl?"

"Lady Janissian has served as steward to her grandfather and grandmother—" Sebell began.

"More the grandmother's doing, I'm certain," Langrell of Igen remarked.

"It's more important that she was *doing*," Groghe said, scowling at Langrell. "And she is of the Blood."

"Oh, confirm her and let's get on with this meeting," Toric demanded impatiently.

"In that case, I will collect your votes," Sebell said.

"Isn't it a good thing," Lessa murmured to F'lar after they had both written their decisions, "that Janissian happens to be well qualified."

"Hold Blood's getting thin after twenty-five hundred Turns. And, with the end of Threadfall . . ." F'lar murmured.

"Holding began with Fort, with Paul Benden. There's nothing wrong with Fort's Bloodline. But that form of inheritance is not in the Charter, you know."

F'lar regarded her in mild surprise. "No, actually, it isn't. Holders and all those traditions came later." He looked at Toric who was impatiently tapping the table while Sebell was sorting through the slips.

Sebell held up two piles—one thin, one fat. Three slips remained on his lectern.

"Three abstentions, five nays, and thirty-seven yeas," Se-bell said. "Harper Hall votes yea."

Nothing more than murmured sounds of relief were expressed but Sebell strode quickly to the big doors, opened one leaf and gestured.

"Lady Janissian of Southern Boll, the Council would be pleased if you would take your seat as Boll's Lady Holder!"

There was cheering from outside as Janissian, a smiling Menolly giving her a little push, stepped in and the door was closed behind her. She stood there, her head no higher than Sebell's shoulder, and her dark hair fetchingly arranged around her pale, handsome face; the hem of her red gown matched the white shields and bright chevrons that were Boll's insignia. She wore the heirloom diamond and ruby chevron pendant that was supposed to have been handed down from Emily Boll and she gave the impression of great dignity. Sebell took her hand, and while everyone stood—even Toric, though he took his time getting to his feet—he walked her to the empty chair beside Lord Groghe. The old Lord Holder was red-faced with pleasure and kissed her on both cheeks as soon as she was seated.

Lessa approved of her calm in accepting such an accolade and her composed nod to the rest of the Council.

"Well, then, let's to real business," Toric said, remaining on his feet while the rest of the Council resumed their chairs.

"It's my autonomy that has been abrogated, Lord Toric," Kashman cried, standing up, his thin features reddened by agitation. "Those intruders should have been brought to *my* Hold for *my* judgment. I want to know why *my* authority was ignored."

Before the Masterprinter could get to his feet, Lord Lytol leaned toward Kashman, his gaunt face serene.

"Let me point out, Lord Kashman, a fact that you may not be acquainted with yet," he said, "but MasterCraftHalls enjoy autonomy within their halls and may set punishment or fines, depending on the nature of any offense committed within their confines."

"But—but the Printer Hall's new . . ." Kashman began.

"That does not," Sebell said, "interfere with its autonomy or internal discipline."

Tagetarl spoke up. "Let me remind Lord Kashman that the intruders refused—in front of witnesses—to name either hold or hall to which they could be taken to receive a hearing from another authority."

"It just *happens* . . ." and Kashman waved his arm in a sarcastic manner, "that Lord Jaxom who resides in Ruatha and N'ton whose Weyr is in Fort happened to be present in Wide Bay at such an unlikely hour?"

"The intruders picked the hour," Tagetarl said.

"The dragons responded to a summons for support," N'ton added.

"Who summoned them?" Kashman demanded, his nostrils flaring with irritation.

"Beauty, in my case," Jaxom said and turned to N'ton.

"In mine as well."

"Beauty?" Kashman echoed, confounded by that identification.

"Beauty is the queen fire-lizard that often conveys urgent messages from the Harper Hall," N'ton said.

"You *responded* to a message brought by a fire-lizard?" Kashman was incredulous. Toric snorted at his inexperience.

"When such a message comes from a main Crafthall," Sebell went on, "it is not wise to disregard its import, especially since other Crafthalls have become targets for vandalism. Twelve people do not simultaneously decide to sample Crafthall wares in the middle of the night, armed with torches, chisels, hammers, and spikes, Lord Kashman. They were discovered *inside* the main gates, which had not been opened to them, destroying the doors to the Print Hall itself. What conclusion would you have come to?"

"Yes, Kashman, what conclusion could you have come to?" Lord Groghe demanded.

"Something's got to be done about such impertinent men and women," Bargen said with considerable exasperation. "Wanton destruction—when it takes time and good materials to make anything these days—cannot be permitted. If we have already decided that exile would be a deterrent, then whoever sits in judgment—a proper court, with three judges and witnesses—has the right, indeed the duty of sentencing them to exile. Now, let's go on to the most important issue before this Council."

Beyond him, Kashman was gaping, infuriated that the older Lord Holders were so blithely setting aside *his* issue.

"What are you going to do about preventing fireballs dropping from the sky?" Bargen asked, surveying the Weyrleaders with a critical sweep.

"We have several recommendations . . ." F'lar said, rising to his feet.

"Don't want recommendations," Bargen retorted. "I want positive reassurance that such displays won't be repeated in the near future."

"Nothing in the *near* future has so far been discerned," F'lar said and found he had everyone's attention.

"What do you mean by that?" Groghe demanded.

"Such surveys of near Pern objects as Master Erragon has been able to complete with a dedicated band of sky-watchers suggest that nothing is close enough to descend on Pern's surface in the *near* future."

"And?" Bargen prompted, scowling. "In the further future?"

"We must place more telescopes in strategic positions to watch our skies, mobilize a body of dedicated people to support at least five major observatories—"

Toric leaped to his feet. "You want the Council to support *five*? Tithes are already in full use. Where would more marks come from for *five* observatories?"

Bargen was on his feet, so were Langrell and Toronas, shouting against such major projects. Deckter asked for details. Even Lord Groghe appeared concerned. F'lar stood still, ignoring the shouts, the arguments as Sebell struck the gavel for silence.

A burst of thunder—dragons shouting—penetrated the Great Hall and deafened everyone.

"As I was saying, if you wish to avoid more problems like

that Fireball, you have to be prepared," F'lar went on in a normal tone of voice. "We already have Cove Hold and Honshu," and he bowed to Lord Lytol and the Star Master, "which is generously maintained by Landing."

"A portion of our tithes," Lord Lytol said, "will be distributed to the other locations as well as to pay teachers."

"The SmithCraftHall cannot produce the telescopes required for observatories . . ." Master Fandarel began.

"There are four in the Catherine Caves," Master Erragon said, bowing respectfully to the Mastersmith for his interruption.

"Ah, well, in that case," and Fandarel raised a thick swollen hand in agreement.

"I have undertaken to supply a Star Hold," Jaxom said, rising briefly, "with appropriate tithes, and the cost of building one at Ice Lake as recommended by Master Erragon."

Toric's frown grew deeper when Lord Larad rose to his feet.

"Telgar does the same. Weyrwoman Palla completed most of her apprenticeship with Master Wansor."

"As a twenty-four-hour coverage of our skies is essential to its overall success," F'lar said, but Lessa could see how much he relished the shock he was about to give the entire Council, "an observatory must be constructed as soon as possible on a site, approved by Masters Wansor, Erragon, and Idarolan, on the Western Continent."

The Council was in an uproar. Even the usually placid Mastercraftsmen were excited, demanding details and plans while the Lord Holders were protesting such a drain on tithe-marks and labor. It took time for Sebell to reestablish order.

"But it was the *Yokohama* that saw the Fireball," Groghe exclaimed as the din abated.

"Why are so many needed?" Langrell asked plaintively.

"It's a big sky," K'van remarked.

"You have to *find* the near object before you can divert it," F'lar put in almost offhandedly.

"Divert it?" Groghe exclaimed, the smile that had been growing during F'lar's opening sentences turning into stunned

amazement. "But there are no more engines to divert anything since we blew the Red Star up, are there?"

"No engines, Lord Groghe, but dragons and their riders!"

Toric leaped to his feet, face suffused with blood, stabbing
his finger at the Benden Weyrleader, and shouted, "So you
think you can coerce the Holds to continue to support you
forever?"

"Not at all, Lord Toric," F'lar replied with calm pride.
"You cannot perceive how deeply every Weyr—" He paused
and the other dragonriders nodded or murmured emphatic
agreement with that statement. "—wishes to be as independent as any other person on this planet. Necessity has required our dependence on the holds we protect, but, by
the end of this Pass, we shall all have holdings or crafts
with which to support ourselves. We shall be journeymen
and -women, attracting apprentices to Star Holds and learning to be Masters of the Star Hall. We will study the stars and
watch the skies of Pern until we know exactly what might
threaten this planet again."

"And what will you do then?" Toric bawled the question.

F'lar regarded Toric with a smile on his face. "We will divert it."

"How? *How?*" Toric pounded the table. "You weren't able
to divert the Fireball."

"Now that," and F'lar paused significantly, without a trace
of apology, "won't happen again." His tone was so confident,
his manner so assured that the other dragonriders proudly
straightened, so obviously in agreement with his statement,
that the Southern Holder was perplexed.

"It is an ability that Aivas perceived in dragonkind," Jaxom
remarked as one chiding his audience to remember something they had not previously considered.

"Indeed, Lord Jaxom," F'lar said amiably. "The dragons
have always had the ability. We have been busy refining it."

"It takes time and practice," N'ton said.

"The older the dragon, the more adept, you know," K'van
put in.

"Combined with observatories and a sound knowledge of

the Rukbat system and our skies," F'lar continued, "we'll know exactly what's around us and what else the Oort Cloud spawns."

"As you all have reminded us," Lessa added, "dragonriders are the caretakers of Pern's skies. So let us continue to undertake that responsibility."

"Practicing and preparing for when the need for this potent ability presents itself," F'lar finished.

As draconic bellow had silenced argument, now everyone heard the carol that trilled the affirmative response of the dragons gathered on the cliffs of Telgar!

"Well, I for one," Groghe said, beaming at F'lar and the other Weyrleaders, "am deeply relieved to hear all this. Though I can't remember Aivas . . ."

"Naturally Aivas only discussed the subject with dragonriders," Jaxom said in a grave manner.

"Thank you, Weyrleaders," Sebell said. "You have relieved our fears considerably and I think I can speak for all the Craftmasters that there will be generous Hall support to match that already guaranteed new observatories by Lord Holders." He bowed to Jaxom and Larad.

"Tillek is the nearest port," Ranrel said to Erragon across the table, "we will donate shipping."

"Services in place of tithes?" Toric cried, infuriated.

"Oh, do sit down, Toric," Groghe said.

"There hasn't been a vote about approving more observatories," Toric complained.

"I can take a vote now," Sebell put in hopefully.

"The necessity for *three* new observatories hasn't been properly discussed," Toric shouted.

"I want to know more about the Western Continent," Master Ballora said in a loud voice. "We don't know what life-forms are there. What effect contact with new ones would have with our indigenous species."

"Not much is mentioned about it in Aivas records," Deckter remarked. "Will the project need much metal ore?"

"Of course it will, Deckter," Fandarel said, rubbing his big hands together in anticipation.

"Shall we deal with some of the minor petitions now?" Sebell asked, holding up a slim packet.

"No, no, not now," Groghe said. "Need to eat now and be refreshed for that sort of thing."

"What about the Western Continent?" Master Ballora objected. "I want to know more about *that*!"

"We'll talk," Erragon said while Sebell used the gavel to end the morning session.

So many questions were asked about where exactly the observatories would be placed, the form they would take, the personnel to work in them, the training required, that petitions were put aside for the next day. Toric called for a vote about *any* new observatories, much less three, none of which were evidently to be placed in Southern. He voted against the whole idea but the majority was in favor of it. Then he had to sit through talk about the Western Continent's urgently needed observatory and, while he fumed, everyone else seemed so enthusiastic about supplying engineering, construction, transport, labor, materials—without an increase in overall tithing, which he would have vigorously barred—the Star Masters and the sharding Weyrleaders got what they wanted. It never occurred to him that he had only himself to blame. He'd been prepared to argue about petitions and object to some—on principle—but none had been submitted for discussion. If he didn't stay, the Council might slip something new in, vote it into law and he wouldn't be able to gauge any new plans. He ought to make Besic accompany him. He'd be good for something then. Bargen had a son with him, so did Groghe. Such representatives were permitted to stand in for their Lord Holders at the petitions session: Fandarel had put Master Jancis in as his agent.

In the evening, Toric wandered outside, down into the Gather grounds. Dorse was supposed to find him so he had to be available. By morning, when Dorse didn't appear before the Council convened, Toric asked at the Telgar Runner Station for any messages for him. There were none but he encountered Kashman and had to walk back to the Hold in the man's company. Kashman was still furious with the trial at the Print Hall. He hadn't been *in* Keroon Hold that night but the matter could have waited until morning. He complained bitterly about the presence of N'ton, a Fort Weyrleader, far away from Fort's traditional authority, not to mention Jaxom. Who was not a subject to be mentioned in Toric's company under the best of circumstances! Corman had kept this son of his inadequately informed for Lord Holdership, Toric thought.

Late that evening, Toric wandered aimlessly among the Gather tents and then walked the perimeter, keeping to the shadows to give Dorse a chance to approach him discreetly. There was the other matter: this dragon ability that Aivas had mentioned? As far as Toric knew, dragons could speak to their riders, go *between*, and chew a rock that produced the flame that destroyed Thread. He must ask Master Esselin to trace any reference to what Aivas had said about the creatures. Everything Aivas said or had done was recorded. Esselin could find it and report.

He was halfway around the tents a second time when Toric wondered who had been among those exiled so precipitously. If no one had given hold, hall, or name, who *were* they? On the other hand, Jaxom had been one of the judges. He would have known Dorse. So might N'ton. And Masterprinter Tagetarl.

"Lord Toric!"

His name was spoken softly and in a deep voice. Dorse had mentioned that Fifth had a most unusual one. A most eloquent speaker, Dorse had said, effective in rousing people.

"Yes?" Toric stepped into the shadows. He had very much wanted to meet Fifth. Dorse had told him about the man's unusual obsession relating to the fact that the MasterHarper had been found dead in the Aivas chamber at the same approximate time that the Abomination had terminated itself. Was it possible that Master Robinton had indeed discovered some malign aspect of the Abomination and attempted to end its influence on Pern? Or had Aivas, suspecting that his evil designs to pollute and corrupt the planet had been divined by the human, killed the MasterHarper? It was well documented that Aivas had hidden defenses.

The conundrum had fascinated Toric from the moment Dorse had confided it in him. Now he could question the source.

HONSHU WEYRHOLD — 3.01.31

The moment Tai woke that morning, Sagassy appeared at her bedside.

"D'you need the necessary, Rider Tai?" she asked and whipped back the cover without waiting for an answer.

"Can't I walk by myself?" Tai asked. She was determined to put weakness and dependency behind her as soon as possible. Sagassy had been so practical that her help had not given Tai any embarrassment.

"I'll just put an arm about you in case."

Tai did need help getting to her feet but she tried to do as much as she could without Sagassy's help.

Her ankles and knees were still stiff; her calves felt more like blocks but they weren't painful; the left leg would even bear weight without great discomfort. So that brief excursion went well enough and, leaning against the heavy sink top, Tai managed to wash hands and face. She ate all the breakfast that Sagassy brought and then asked, as she did every time someone came into the room, when she could see Zaranth, F'lessan, and Golanth.

Having been asked that question frequently, Sagassy put her hands on her hips and gave her head a little shake.

"Well, I'm one as says it don't do *you* nor them any good not to. Leave it with me."

Tai wanted to burst out in frustration because everyone responded with—"leave it with me." So far it was left. She was surprised to see T'lion, bronze Gadareth's rider, enter the room, Sagassy behind him, grinning with smug satisfaction.

"Sagassy says I'm strong enough, and long enough," he said. "You look much better."

"How do you know?" And answered herself. "Oh, Gadareth was there that morning, wasn't he?"

"Indeed he was and has been extremely smug and glowing ever since. Now, put an arm around my neck."

"I can walk, I can walk!"

"I doubt it and I came to carry you because seeing all the invalids—not that Zaranth really *is* anymore—would definitely be too far for you to walk today." He had swooped her up in his arms before she could protest further and carried her out of the room. She'd had so many people moving her places that such intimacy no longer bothered her. "In reverse order of preference, perhaps, because I know you want to reassure yourself that Zaranth is fine, but F'lessan's just in here, so it's on your way to her."

There was a sudden alteration of the cheerfulness in his voice as he angled her into the largest of the sleeping quarters, not the one she and F'lessan had shared so often. She blinked back tears as she saw F'lessan's white face turning restlessly on the pillow, his lips twitching, his brows creasing, ricking the lines that now scored his cheeks. His body looked unusually bulky under the cover—bandages, she thought, snatching back the hand she had unconsciously extended toward him. He shouldn't be allowed to thrash so. Manora had said his wounds were deep. He could do himself more injury with this tossing.

T'lion placed her in the chair by the bed. She saw that F'lessan's dark hair had been cut back on the right side, clearly showing the stitches on his scalp. Holding her hand a scant few centimeters above his face, her fingers trembled as she followed the path of the other facial scars. They didn't look that deep but they were terrible to see on his handsome face.

As if conscious of someone watching him, he moved his head more restlessly from side to side and tried to lift first one hand, and then the other: the left hand slid limply to dangle beside the narrow bed. She picked it up, returning it to his side, and lightly touched his shoulder.

"Easy, F'lessan, lie still." She pushed behind his ear the strand of hair that had fallen across the stitched cheek. "Lie still. Golanth lives!"

"Golly?" The question was more breath than word, his brows creased slightly, halted when he felt the pull of skin. "Golly?"

His eyes opened, blinked, strained to focus on her face. He seemed puzzled by her presence. "Where've you been?" It was almost a complaint.

"They wouldn't let me come."

"She got clawed, too, F'lessan," T'lion said, leaning over the other side of the bed. "But I said I'd bring her and I have."

F'lessan's eyelids seemed too heavy to keep open but the corner of his mouth turned up.

"So you did. Don't go 'way, my very dear green. Don't go 'way."

His endearment caught at her heart and she had to wait a moment before she could speak.

"I'll see Golanth and then I'll be right back. You can rest now."

"Hmmm, yes. I can, can't I?" He turned his head to one side and, exhaling a deep breath, sank into a stillness that scared her until she saw his chest rise again.

"I'll convey you to bronze Golanth," T'lion said, picking her up and carrying her from the room.

"Why, just look at him, bronze rider," Sagassy remarked, pausing to look back at F'lessan. "He's much less restless already."

It was as well Tai had seen F'lessan before Golanth because the sight of the terribly wounded bronze made her weep.

"Now, now, he looks a lot worse than he is," the Monaco rider said, tightening his arms about her.

He is much better, Tai. He is much better, and Zaranth rose from where she was lying on the sunny terrace beyond Golanth's supine bulk.

"Oh, Zaranth! How can you say that?" Tai was sobbing.

Because it's true.

"Hey, now, Tai, don't go to pieces on me," T'lion said in a rallying tone. "He was badly injured, it's true. Flesh gouged out of him, bits gnawed off him, but they got the tail mended. That's what's in the splint affair. And he's not in any pain because we don't let him be."

That was when Tai noticed all the other people on the terrace and valiantly controlled her sobs.

"Ah, Green Rider Tai," and through the tear haze in her eyes, Tai recognized Persellan's familiar face. "I know the extent of Golanth's injuries seems appalling," he went on, "but we keep him comfortable." He gestured to the large gray pots in which numbweed was stored. "Having Zaranth here makes it certain that he is relieved before he can twitch a muscle in pain. She's been as close to him as a pulse."

Golanth's prostrate body made the terrace seem smaller than she knew it was. There was room for people to move around him. Near the main entrance, there were supplies, like numbweed pots and chests of dressings or other medications, chairs where carers could relax, a table for dining, like the ones that had been set out when half of Monaco had been staying here.

Golanth's body was cushioned from the rock of the terrace by many pads: an awning had been rigged above him—a sail, Tai thought, by the look of it. He seemed smaller somehow, diminished by the absence of his characteristic vitality: like rider, like dragon. She pushed that thought away.

There were marks all over the near side of him, where claws had torn and teeth had snagged. The patch over his left eye was most prominent and the casing around the end of his tail, which was positioned by his body. He lay with his head between his front legs but she could see his nostrils flaring slightly with every breath he took.

He is much better, Tai, Zaranth said with the heartiness of someone who has watched recovery. *Much better. Touch him. You will feel the strength in him.*

Zaranth had not moved from her position behind Golanth but now she cocked her head at her rider.

"I'll take you round," T'lion offered. "There's a place for you to sit and be private with Zaranth. Let me tell you, despite her own injuries, she has been conscientious in helping us tend Golanth."

T'lion deftly maneuvered her behind him and Tai nearly burst into tears again to see the slashes, hidden behind Golanth's body, that marred Zaranth's green hide. T'lion put her on the bench and stepped back, giving Tai's shoulder a firm reassuring grip before he left them. Zaranth took the small step that separated rider and dragon and put her nose down to Tai's knees.

I do not hurt, Tai. They tend me as well as Golanth but only I can hear to help him. He grieves for F'lessan's hurts. And that pain is the worst. Zaranth emphasized that with a little push of her nose.

It would be. And you've needed me!

In deep apology for her absence, Tai put her arms carefully around her dragon's nose, rested her face against Zaranth's cheek, aware of the dragon's warmth and the particular smell of her sun-warmed hide mixed with the astringency of numb-weed. Then, tenderly, lightly, she placed her right hand on the scored chest and felt the beat of the powerful heart, letting herself relax against her beloved. Reassured by the essential strong rhythm, she felt tension draining out of her body, soft-ening her muscles, and giving her back the sense of rightness that was the bond between dragon and rider. They remained in this silent communion until Tai was restored to serenity. And had renewed the strength in them both.

Caringly, she stroked Zaranth's nose, her cheekbones, was able to touch the deep gashes with gently inquiring fingers. She could see that they were shallow, worse than scratches but not as deep as the troughs that scored Golanth. Zaranth looked as if she were wearing stripes.

How did you do it, my heart? the rider asked the dragon. *How did you save us?*

I called. Ramoth and the others came quickly. I told Ramoth. The dragon's tone was squeaky with self-satisfaction. *She did what I told her to do. She saw how to do it and told the*

others. They did more than me. There were more of them.
Zaranth sighed gustily into her rider's lap. *And the felines threatened our lives: all four of us. But we were too much for them. I was very glad to see the other dragons arrive: especially Ramoth.*

I'm sure you were. So was I! Tai admitted, letting tears well up in her eyes, tears of exquisite relief now that she was physically close to her brave and clever Zaranth.

F'lessan has been anxious, Zaranth said with great concern. *He will not rest. Golanth sleeps a lot. I tell F'lessan not to worry but I don't think he believes me.*

He will believe me! Tai caressed Zaranth's sensitive eye ridges soothingly, just the way her green dragon preferred. Zaranth leaned her head more and more on Tai's knees until she became aware that this pressure was causing her rider pain. Zaranth opened her eyes and lifted her head.

I have called him.

Called who?

The bronze rider. The one who carried you. I thought about bringing you here myself, and Zaranth's eyelids lowered apologetically, *but it's one thing to do it because it's the only thing to DO but I couldn't risk dropping you and I'm not quite that good at it as I should be—to try lifting you carefully. So, first he will let you touch Golanth; this side isn't as bad. Golanth knows that you are here. You will touch Golanth and tell him that you have seen F'lessan. He will believe you!*

When T'lion duly returned, he supported Tai while she placed her hands on the bronze's side, carefully avoiding the grooves in Golanth's right shoulder that might, had they been a little higher, a little deeper, have ended the bronze dragon's life. And F'lessan's, too.

She blinked back more tears. This time death had not robbed her again of those she loved. She wasn't certain just how Golanth had escaped: the feline had been leaping in exactly the right arc/trajectory to land on Golanth's spine, teeth bared, talons extended. But somehow it had missed and she was profoundly grateful.

She spread her fingers on uninjured parts of Golanth's sun-warmed hide. She found a place where she could lean her forehead on his rib cage. She felt a rumble from Golanth and then a thought.

You have come.

F'lessan is weaker than you are, Golanth, so they will not bring him to you. But I have held his hand, I have spoken with him. Now I will tell him that I have touched you. And you will both start feeling better and healing as fast as possible. Do you hear me?

I hear you. The body beneath her hands heaved slightly and she felt him sigh. *I hear F'lessan. He wants to know if you are coming back.*

Now that I have seen you and Zaranth, I'll be right back.

"This may have been too much for you, Tai," T'lion said, picking her up. "I swear you feel lighter."

"That's as well for you then," she said.

"I'm stronger than I look, you know," he replied firmly as he carried her back into the weyrhold and down the hall.

"I must go back to F'lessan."

"Oh, I'm taking you there as fast as I can. And you must drink what Sagassy has concocted for you. Maybe even get F'lessan to sip some."

Which Tai did, after she had assured him of Golanth's condition. Most of the time he slept, his fingers twined in hers in a grip which alternately made her weep or feel intense pride that, of all the humans he knew, it was she whom he wanted by him.

INTERIM AT BENDEN AND ELSEWHERE

Despite F'lar's assurance to the Council, despite Ramoth's assurances to Lessa, not all the dragons were able to imitate Zaranth and the dragons who came to her assistance in Honshu that terrible morning. Although Ramoth had told Lessa that she had understood how Zaranth had managed telekinesis, anger, fear, and outrage had had a lot to do with the process. Cool thought, or gradually, more ardent wishes, were not as successful. And nowhere near as safe.

First, the path between the original position and the destination of an object being moved by a dragon's mind had to be clear of any impediment. The distance did not seem to be an obstacle, for inanimate objects. Even for smaller living creatures, like wherries or herdbeasts. But there could be nothing in the way. While stones didn't suffer from being moved telekinetically, they might be broken if they collided with anything; so might what they collided with. The speed was another problem. The transfer was instantaneous—which could, and did, affect what was kinetically moved.

"A case of all or nothing," F'lar said after the first few hours of imperfect results with Mnementh.

"Control," Lessa suggested cryptically, having had no better performance from her queen.

With the felines, there hadn't been a problem of safe transit or landing. Pieces had done very well. Ramoth disapproved of challenging more felines for practice or in groups large enough to provide the stimulus that Zaranth had had: sheer terror at seeing her weyrmate and the two riders attacked.

The dragons could send things straight up in the open air—and out of sight. To move an object telekinetically in a horizontal direction had taken a lot of control and required Mnementh and Ramoth working together, one slowing the other down. Ramoth and Mnementh practiced daily, *slowly* lifting small rocks vertically from the ground and putting them back down without crushing them into dust or pebbles. They could probably have thrown one all the way to the *Yokohama*, also not the desired destination, but one that was causing considerable speculation by Lessa and F'lar. *That* had been a significant forward step.

When queried by Ramoth, Zaranth recommended that dragons experience trundlebugs. If there were many riders who found that a bizarre way to awaken telekinetic ability, it proved to be the one that worked—on trundlebugs. Ramoth and Mnementh earnestly suggested that the experiment be carried out in pairs, female and male dragons, and preferably a good distance from any holdings and close to a stream, lake, or ocean.

Then, when Ramoth and Mnementh worked together, one controlling the other, kinesis became more practical, less hazardous to what was being moved without physical contact.

What purpose, other than repelling—and destroying—felines or disciplining trundlebugs was not immediately apparent to many, though the ability provoked deep thought and theorizing in many quarters. Meanwhile, the dragons and their riders continued to practice this counter-balancing of kinetic energy.

Master Esselin—who now complained bitterly about all the tasks set him—was supposed to see what records were available on early dragon training: going *between* and using firestone. Nothing legible remained from the old Record Aivas had transcribed and those who owned fire-lizards insisted that the dragons had learned from these smaller cousins.

No one had ever observed fire-lizards telekinetically moving something, unless the speed with which fire-lizards could gobble food from a plate could be considered a form of telekinesis.

Many other matters were being set in place, the most important of which was siting the Western Continent observatory. This so-called continent was two landmasses, a wide inlet almost completely separating them except for a straggle of boulders making a bridge at the northern end. Erragon had the plans Aivas had printed out for Cove Hold and, apart from a different telescope mount (he recommended the fork type), these would suffice: especially when those who had worked on Cove Hold volunteered their services to erect the new one. Lord Ranrel was as good as his promise and three ships were loaded with material and volunteers to sail, with Master Idarolan in nominal charge of the expedition, to the southern-most cape of the larger landmass. A pod of dolphins assigned by the dolphins' venerable leader, the Tillek herself, were to accompany the small fleet to a harbor she could recommend.

Green and blue dragons were to precede the ships, setting up a base camp.

The same general plans, with variations to the terrain, were to be implemented at Ice Lake and in Telgar. The most pressing need was training apprentices to serve the new facilities or to add to the Crafthalls that produced spyglasses that used to be called "far-seers," binoculars, and small telescopes.

Master Tagetarl's Print Hall was busy, first with printing the requirements of craftsmen and -women, lists of materials to be supplied—especially lists of people willing to be transported to such a distant location to help in building an observatory on the Western Continent.

That was a simpler task than the demand for printed instructions on how to build smaller non-metal telescopes: thick wher-hide would suffice so long as the interior was painted black and sealed against dust. Manuals must be written by the Star Hall, charts and diagrams of what objects were known to be in unthreatening orbits, instructions on how to sight, recognize, and make proper notations on possible discoveries. The GlassCraftHalls could supply mirrors for reflective scopes from 100mm to 400mm. Larger ones, of course, required time to shape and build.

When Thread, inevitably, fell near Honshu, the healers made sure the two injured dragons were so deeply sedated that they were unaware—except at some very primal level—that the ancient enemy was being met. Zaranth was recovering well but Golanth's injuries still concerned every Weyrhealer and Beastmaster.

HONSHU WEYRHOLD— TIME PASSING SLOWLY

"There's considerably more available about every other animal on this planet," Wyzall said after a long afternoon's study with Beastmaster Ballora; his best animal healer,

Persellan; and Tai, "than about the ones we're most dependent on." He pushed back from the table, rubbing his face to ease fatigue.

"That's because we have had bodies of every other animal to dissect for study," Ballora remarked. She was a big, athletic woman. She had started healer training with Master Oldive but found a real empathy and skill with animals so she had changed to the BeastCraftHall. Her manner was in general as reassuring to humans as it was to the animals she tended and bred. Now she sighed with deep regret. "But then the only anatomical studies ever available were those done on dead fire-lizard hatchlings that Ancient zoologists happened to find. And those most incomplete notes that Wind Blossom left that concerned unhatched watchwhers which, as we all know, were not *our* dragons."

"Records state that there were unhatched dragon eggs . . ." Tai began tentatively.

Wyzall dismissed that. "There was a prejudice against such study," he continued. "Not that I disagree, since any eggs that didn't hatch failed because of some defect." He gave a sigh. "Live dragons can at least tell their riders where they hurt, if it isn't visible. Unlike us humans who do not seem to be sufficiently in tune with our bodies because we—" He broke off, clearing his throat and riffling the pages he had been reading.

"Because we die when we wear out," Ballora said with detachment. "Did you ever discover which is the oldest living fire-lizard, Wyzall?" she asked with a grin.

Wyzall tut-tutted and shook his head. "It's an impossibility. They may tell dragons what they 'remember' seeing but I think it's analogous to the Tillek's knowledge of delphinic history. The fire-lizards weren't there to see it happen but they have passed the tale of it down so that it"—and he waved to the fairs that were either sleeping or lazily flying on the light breeze—"becomes a personal memory."

"Not all the fire-lizards remember seeing the spaceships in the ship meadow," Tai reminded him.

"Ah," and Wyzall wiggled a finger at her, "but which do? Back to the present," he said then, growing solemn, "I do think that gentle massage with the unguent will help circulation to Golanth's damaged wing joint. At least it no longer causes him great pain."

"How could it with five jars of numbweed soaked in!" Tai asked, since she had undertaken a lot of that massage.

"Well, no harm in trying this unguent," Ballora said, taking it from her pouch and placing it on the table with the air of exhibiting an item of rare value. "Helps with joint-ail on runnerbeasts but it's worse to produce than numbweed."

"Nothing can be worse," said Persellan, who was usually in charge of collecting, boiling, and rendering the weed at Monaco Weyr.

"It's a big joint," Tai said, dubiously.

"Rub it in well and we must be sure to wash our hands thoroughly. We don't want to absorb too much of it through the skin of our hands."

She removed the stopper to the pot and had been about to sniff but set it down quickly.

"The smell won't kill you," Ballora said. So willing hands massaged the substance into the dragon's wing joint.

There were other worries about Golanth that must soon be addressed. A dragon injured in a Fall usually went *between*— first to shake off Thread in the cold and second to emerge in his or her Weyr. Every Weyr, including Monaco, had an infirmary, which could accommodate a wounded, or sick, dragon. Honshu had only the broad terrace on which the queens had tenderly deposited the desperately wounded bronze after the attack. But Golanth could not be moved through *between* until his injuries were healed.

Another five days stuck in Honshu, with so many people around, was Tai's limit. She had to get away by herself, away from all the pressures there. She spent as much time with F'lessan as she could—when not dismissed by healers— because he really did seem less restless when she was nearby.

She could tell when he was speaking with Golanth, which was often, and also when his wounds were being dressed and he needed distraction from the pain, because his eyes went unfocused. Sometimes she worried that he was retreating too much into Golanth. Oddly enough, the healers could keep the dragon far more comfortable by use of numbweed than they could the rider.

There was, indeed, little she could do for F'lessan—which distressed her—and not all that much for Zaranth who, like most injured dragons, slept a lot. By the eighth day, she realized that the healing process was complete enough—no more grainy feel except to the deepest claw marks, though the new skin was very tender—and Zaranth could safely go *between*. Tai's leg wounds were red scars and peeling flesh. The sea would complete her healing, too.

We will go when they sleep, Zaranth informed her rider. *They will not then miss us.*

Sea will be good for you, too. Tai assuaged her conscience by saying, repeatedly.

Having made the decision, it was hard to get through the day. She worried about leaving F'lessan; Golanth wouldn't be aware. She felt as if she was deceitful and devious but she needed a respite. The sight of F'lessan crumpling in on himself when allowed to take a few steps from his bed had almost made her retch. He'd had to lean heavily on the crutch, for his left leg could still handle no weight and the abdominal wound kept him from straightening. Hair was beginning to grow over the head wound, but he was a far cry from the dashing, blithe, youthful Benden Wingleader.

So Tai and Zaranth made their plans and waited until the subdued, quiet, but constant activity of the carers and healers went into nighttime mode. At last Tai slipped out, wincing a bit as she jarred her leg on the stone floors: she had left her cane behind, for it had a metal tip and its click would be audible. Someone might hear her moving and investigate; very quick to investigate, they were.

She slipped onto Zaranth's back. The green padded carefully to the edge, slowly extending her wings above her head, and then, in a maneuver that they both knew was reckless, tipped over the edge. Wind caught under her wings and she glided silently a moment, just above the treetops, before going *between*.

They chose a little cove off the coast of Cathay, Zaranth expertly coming in over the placid waves to a white sand beach. They landed there long enough for Tai to strip off her clothing, leave her towel, and remount Zaranth. The green then walked slowly into the tranquil sea, chirping happily as the warm water caressed her, until she floated. Tai just fell off her dragon's neck into the sea, elated with the success of their escape and the caress of the warm water.

"We needed this, dear heart," she said, slapping Zaranth's wet wither.

The dragon let herself sink until only her eyes remained above the water, brilliant green and blue—and that unhappily reminded Tai of Golanth's eye. But suddenly dolphins arrived, squeeing and clicking in great sympathy for the red scars on Tai's legs and the black scabbed stripes on Zaranth's body, overjoyed at their unexpected arrival and scolding them, as much as dolphins scold, for staying away so long. And when were Golly and Fless coming to swim, too? Yes, they knew they had been hurt but seawater was good for all hurts, and swimming was good for sores, and they must come and tell them about the furry things. All these questions while sleek smooth dolphin bodies provided the dragon gentle massage and uncomplicated company for the rider. The moon rose as Tai, grasping two dorsal fins, was taken on a wild ride around the little cove, dolphins leaping high in escort and vying to take the place of any who lost her hand.

Indeed, it wasn't until Tai's hands slipped several times from fins that she realized she was tired. So much unexpected exercise.

"You rest," the dolphin named Afri urged, and cheed firmly about her, an order for the others to calm down. Tai was surrounded and supported by dolphin bodies, the light waves splashing over them, lulling her until she was all but asleep.

She came to awareness of how easy it would have been for

them to just succumb to such blandishments and find a weyr on the shore and forget the heartache and the dismal prospects at Honshu. But that was impossible, no matter how tempting. She had chosen.

"We've had our respite, Zaranth. We go back now. Dawn's not far away and you know that's when F'lessan is most restless."

Resolutely, she turned shoreward, letting Afri, or maybe it was Dani, tow her until her feet touched the bottom. She walked out, found her towel, dried herself, and dressed. Then she called Zaranth in and checked to be sure that none of the scabs had burst during all that diving and cavorting about in the water.

"Come back, come back. Good for you," Afri said, walking on her tail as she spoke. "Bring Golly. Much better for him."

It would be, too, Tai thought, except possibly for his eye. Buoyed by water, he could exercise his leg and his tail—the bone had healed but the muscles remained flaccid. He might also be able to spread his injured wing, ease open that stiff joint. If only they could *get* him up in the air and to the sea. Golanth had a much wider wingspan than Zaranth. Falling over the cliff at Honshu as she had done could have fatal consequences for the bigger dragon. Tai wondered if Ramoth and Mnementh had made any progress in refining the ability. After recommending trundlebugs, Zaranth had not heard anything from Ramoth except that she and Mnementh were practicing.

They returned to moonlit Honshu. Where shadows would mask their approach, Zaranth glided toward the edge of the lower terrace. All was peaceful below so their absence was unlikely to have been noticed. Because of the angle of their approach, facing the main entrance, Tai saw the halting figure making its way to the sleeping bulk of bronze dragon, pausing to hold the edge of a table. F'lessan?

What was the fool doing? He'd walked for the first time that morning. If he should fall, he could damage all the healing of the past two sevendays. What did he think he was doing? Fury for such recklessness dissolved as Tai realized what he *needed* to do: be *with* Golanth.

Come in slowly. If we startle him, he might fall, she told Zaranth. *D'you think you could support him if he falls?*

I could try. Zaranth's tone was doubtful. *He hurts.*

Of course he does, Tai said, almost glad that pain was slowing him down, making him cautious. Then, she could hear the faint click: he wasn't being entirely reckless, he was propping himself on a cane—hers, no doubt, since none had been offered him yet.

He was concentrating so hard on his goal, reaching his dragon, that he was unaware of being observed. He had ten more meters to move, painfully, slowly.

Golanth knows Tai comes. He does not move. Someone might hear that.

But I can hear the tap of the cane.

They may think it is you, Tai, checking on Golanth.

He managed another painful step in the moonlight, wobbling for a moment, uncertainly balanced.

If he falls. Oh, shards, Zaranth, just move him, as you did the trundlebugs. Move him to Golanth.

I—I. He's nearly there.

Not near enough. Just move him, Zaranth. Do it! You know how you moved trundlebugs!

Tai felt Zaranth gulp. If F'lessan made a sound, it was muffled against Golanth's neck as Zaranth complied.

Put me beside him.

And Tai—more abruptly than she had ever moved without Zaranth beneath her—was standing beside F'lessan who clung to the loose skin on Golanth's neck for balance. Tai put her hand under his left arm for support.

"How the shard did I get here?" F'lessan demanded in a low tense voice. "Where did you come from? There was no one else awake!"

"Zaranth!" Tai murmured by way of explanation.

F'lessan buried his head against his dragon's neck, gasping for breath.

"You could have opened stitches! You could have fallen

and hurt yourself more," she scolded him, speaking low, her lips to his ear.

"Why didn't you get Zaranth to bring me to Golly before?" He turned his head, his low fierce whisper conveying his fury, his pain, and his desperate need to be in physical contact with his dragon.

Tai grimaced. "Three reasons: one, because you've been badly wounded and needed to heal a bit. Two," and she allowed her irritation to color her voice, "because I just thought of it when I saw you trying to undo all the good done while you were forcefully kept in bed. Three, Zaranth doesn't really know how to control herself."

"Trundlebugs, my dear green, trundlebugs."

He took a deep breath and pushed upright, steadied himself on the cane before raising his arm. She saw the knife in his hand—one of the sharp ones that Crivellan used for surgical procedures.

"What are you doing?"

He gave her a shove. She stumbled and hissed as the imbalance sent a jab of pain through her half-healed leg. How had he managed to walk this far with his more serious wounds?

"I want to see his eye, Tai. I want to see it."

"Why?" No one had lied to him about Golanth's condition. Didn't F'lessan trust her to tell the truth?

"He wants me to." F'lessan's reply was grim and Tai's objections ceased. "They've got it patched over and sewn up and, despite all the numbweed and fellis juice, it upsets him. He wants his eye open."

F'lessan quickly severed the lower strips holding the patch to the eye. He gasped as he tried to pull the bandage free; the effort was too much.

"Give me the knife before you make a mess of what's left of his eye." Her concern for him—and Golanth—made her speak more brutally than she meant. The dragonrider in her knew that he had to know the worst, now, tonight, while he had steeled himself to accept.

Wordless, he passed her the knife, leaning against Golanth's nose and breathing raggedly.

Tai reached up to slice through the final straps and pulled the covering free. And stared at the dull circle where a bright dragon eye should shine.

Both lids are sewn shut, Zaranth said encouragingly from the shadows. *Nothing to be seen until the lids are unstitched.*

That won't hurt, Golanth said. *They always coat the outer lid lightly when they do the night dressing. It's the inner one that itches so.*

Belior's light now shone on that blank gray-white, slightly curved circle.

"Give me back the knife," F'lessan said.

He shifted, weight on his good leg, took a deep breath and carefully pulling the knot of the nearest stitch from the lid, severed it.

"There're a lot of them," Tai murmured.

Here. A second scalpel clattered to the stone at Tai's feet.

Ooops! Zaranth said. *Small things are actually harder to move than large ones.*

Thanks, Tai said, wondering if encouraging her dragon to spontaneous kinesis was wise. The ethics could wait until later. Zaranth had at least known what was needed and where to get it. Tai followed F'lessan's example and, since she was able to work quickly and stretch more easily, the stitches were soon removed from the vertically opening first lid.

She felt Golanth twitch. Gently she caressed his neck.

F'lessan should not stretch so high. Help him open the lid. I cannot. It has been closed a long time and is dry.

They did, careful to ease it over the stitches that closed the horizontal lid, gently pulling it to the rim of the eye. They removed the stitches from the second lid. Peeling it back was slow and disheartening. The first facets were revealed; the inner circles scarred black by the pointed claws that had irreparably damaged them. But, as Tai worked the upper lid, and F'lessan the lower, they could see that not all the facets were dark. The outer band, to the third facet in, showed a cloudy green; on the upper rank, four octagons were clearer. Along the dragon's nose, six more were brightening. Golanth had lost at least three-quarters of the sight in that eye. He might see directly in front of him in a narrow band and catch motion on the left and perhaps make out objects overhead.

Now, slowly, Golanth turned his head to his rider and Tai, and focused on them what remaining vision he had.

I see you, F'lessan. I see you, Tai. I see!

Dragons do not weep. F'lessan did, burrowing into his dragon's neck, clasping Tai's hand so tightly in his that some of her tears were for pain as well as joy.

Neither Wyzall nor Oldive, nor any of the beastmasters and healers they had consulted had thought that Golanth would have any use of the left eye. Nor did they know if the undamaged eye could compensate! While dragons often got their eyes full of stinging char and occasionally a direct score, the nictitating lids could close so quickly that rarely had more than a few facets been hurt.

I do not see much. But I see with two eyes.

Tai began to hiccup with sobs. F'lessan was gasping and hissing more than sobbing, sagging against his dragon, his injured leg sticking out to one side.

"I had to see, I had to know," he murmured.

Tai tried to support him, but he kept slipping, exhausted by his efforts, tears running down his face in a quiet despair that was far worse to hear than his initial sobs of relief.

Zaranth, put us in his room.

Where?

The bed!

Being moved telekinetically by Zaranth was not at all the same thing as going *between*. If anything, Tai thought, it was *between between*.

Notsofast! Tai heard Golanth say, like a tiny distant sound deep in her ear, not a phrase said aloud. And the breathless propulsion down the corridor eased somewhere in between the start and the finish, and by its finish, they were slowly falling onto a bed. The larger bed they had shared—a logical enough destination for Zaranth, who would have recognized from Tai's mind that this bed was preferable to the narrow one that F'lessan had left. Tai was able to ease F'lessan's descent to the mattress.

As she hastily checked for any blood seeping from his bandages, F'lessan lay there, supine, limp arms over his head, gasping for breath, his face pale even in the darkened room, his left leg jutting straight out over the end of the bed.

"A bit sudden, isn't it, Tai," he said, opening his eyes. "I'm thirsty." That was plaintive. The next was definitive. "And I do *not* want any fellis juice. I want water, lots of it. Cold."

Limping a little because she'd strained her bad leg, Tai paused at the door to listen for any activity in the hall, and then slipped as quickly as she could back to F'lessan's sickroom. She took the pitcher and the glass from the table and returned with them. Maybe she should have found some wine, or something sweet, for the shock. Now that she had had a few moments to get accustomed to the uncovered eye, it could have been worse: Golly had some sight. It must have been much worse for F'lessan, not able to check but very able to lie in that bed, numbed with the weed and fellis, thinking, thinking, and thinking. There would be considerable relief in knowing just how bad it was.

She got back with no one the wiser in the sleeping weyr-hold. She poured water for F'lessan, who dragged himself to a sitting position on one elbow. He drained the glass. She arranged pillows and pushed him back against them before she took a long swig from the pitcher to quench her own thirst.

"More, please." He held up the empty glass. When she refilled it, he sipped in mouthfuls this time. She drank again from the pitcher. The water was nearly gone. Should she get some fruit juice from the kitchen? Sagassy could be relied on to have a beaker cooling there. It wasn't just the sea that had made her mouth dry.

When she made a move to leave, he caught her hand. "Don't go, Tai. Don't leave me, my very dear green."

"Golanth's patch, I should replace it."

He grabbed at her hand, his fingers unexpectedly fierce. "No, he can use the lids if he needs to shield . . . what's left to see with. He hated that patch. I promised I'd get it off."

"If you'd only told us!"

Eyes closed with exhaustion, he gave a weak smile. "Would you, Tai? Would you have flouted Wyzall, Ballora, all of them?"

"Yes!"

His smile broadened, tinged with doubt, as he turned his head on the pillow toward her, his hand patting hers.

"Yes, I would have," she said firmly.

Then he scowled. "And what were you doing away from Honshu in the middle of the night, dear rider?"

She grinned. "We went swimming."

"Swimming in the middle of the night?" he cried, astonished.

"Belior's up and it did me a lot of good."

"Alone?" He tried to scold her.

"Not with nearly a full pod of dolphins about." Then, before he could continue, she added, "And all the good of that swim might be undone coping with your jaunt tonight."

He sighed, giving a weary shake to his head. "I think, my very dear green, my very dear Tai, we're all the better for tonight." Wearily he closed his eyes but his lips curved in a slight smile.

He is, Golanth is, I am, you are, Zaranth said.

F'lessan gave her hand a final pat before the fingers lay lax. She checked again for any seepage from the bandages. It would be like F'lessan to be unscathed by such a desperate antic. When she fumbled to draw the light cover over them, he was breathing evenly and the fretful lines on his face had relaxed. He almost looked like himself, except for the scar and the lack of hair around it.

He sleeps, said both dragons. *We sleep.*

She gave a happy sigh, ignored the ache in her leg and her bruised hand, put her head on the pillow beside F'lessan's, and turned her cheek against his bare shoulder.

Excited, concerned whispers and running feet awakened her. She was in that state of limp repose that allowed her to be aware of the distraction but unwilling to respond to the air of alarm.

Fortunately it was Sagassy who put her head in the door and stared at them. With a sense of mischief that astonished Tai as much as it did the hold woman, Tai put one finger to her lips to keep Sagassy from alerting the searchers. At that, Sagassy did give them a few more moments' peace, going back into the hall.

"The dragons are sleeping, aren't they? So the riders've come to no harm or be sure we'd've all heard the bugling. Now let's all be sensible . . ."

Then someone called urgently from the terrace. And Sagassy ran off.

Beside her, F'lessan moved, stretching a little. "I'll bet they found Golly's patch has been removed."

That was the startled news reverberating down the hall. F'lessan slowly slid his arm under Tai's shoulder and nestled her against him, his head on hers.

"It won't be long now," he murmured indolently and kissed her temple. Tai felt something inside her snap, as if all her guts and her ribs had been tangled in a great knot, which the kiss had untied. "I'm going to insist that we occupy this room from now on. It's big enough so you won't be bashing into me. You're a quiet sleeper anyway. I don't think you moved all night."

"They have to be somewhere," they heard Keita shouting.

"That is, if it's your choice, Tai?"

For a split second—wanting to throw her arms about him in an excess of relief—she didn't know where it was safe to embrace him. So she demurely rubbed her head against his left shoulder. "I choose. I choose you in any condition and any way I get to choose you."

By then, their refuge was officially discovered and they were the victims of some choice sarcastic official displeasure and tongue-lashing. Tai was ejected from the bed so that Keita could be sure that F'lessan had done no damage to himself.

The main puzzle—how had they gotten to this room—was the easiest to answer.

"Zaranth put us here," Tai said. "She can, you know."

"And brought F'lessan out to Golanth?" Keita demanded, still outraged by finding the patch removed.

Tai gave a negligent shrug and let them assume what they wanted to. Then the healer had F'lessan carried back to his sickroom where medicines and bandages were stored, to make sure that he hadn't done himself any harm. F'lessan's grin might have been a trifle off-center as Keita changed dressings to reassure herself that no stitches had broken, but he remained unrepentant.

"I'm soaked in numbweed," he said.

"You both should know by now," Keita said, reproachfully, her expression severe, "that the deadening effect of numbweed is deceptive. It is so very easy to damage tissue or tendon because you can't *feel* what strain you're inadvertently exerting. If the green dragon did indeed effect your unwise and unauthorized trip to the terrace, then that at least proves you're not totally bereft of common sense, bronze rider."

"And Golly's eye suffered no further damage?" F'lessan asked with a touch of arrogance and, to Tai, a wish to be reassured that it was, indeed, all right. "Persellan has seen it?"

"You're very lucky that the lids have healed as well as they have," Keita said, giving them full measure of her censure. "They were in shreds after the attack. Fortunately dragon membrane, unlike the more delicate eye facets, can regenerate."

"Yes," F'lessan said in a dry tone, "that's been explained. Golly knows he has limited vision but he does have some."

Keita had to admit that.

"He said the lids get very dry."

"Part of the injury includes an inability to generate sufficient moisture to lubricate the lids. I think we can help there, with a light gel, applied when needed. We coated the eye with it before we sewed the lids shut against sun damage."

"Then perhaps I can take over that duty now," F'lessan said, easing his body into a sitting position. Keita watched him, one hand lifting to suggest great care.

Then she said, "I'd very much like to see how green Zaranth does this telekinesis."

I can't do it slowly, Tai. Tai could almost hear her dragon gulp in anxiety.

I do the slow part, Golanth said. *You apply the lift.*

There is a chair out here, Zaranth added.

"Master Keita, would you have the gel handy?" Tai asked to distract her.

Keita turned to the chest where healer supplies were stored.

Stay very still, Tai heard her green say.

Out of the corner of her eye, Tai saw F'lessan disappear.

Notsofast! Golanth said. Her heart gave a thump of alarm, and she shot a glance down the hall in time to see F'lessan's body inserted in the chair, a look of surprise on his face. Trundlebugs had never appeared to notice.

We didn't even bump him, Zaranth said, highly pleased.

A matter of practice. You shove.

I don't. I move.

I slow.

We can try it the other way round, and to Tai her dragon's voice sounded wily.

You can practice on other *things*, F'lessan said firmly to Zaranth and Golanth but Tai could hear the amusement in his voice.

Hand reaching for a small jar, Keita swiveled, stared accusingly at Tai. She gave a deep sigh of exasperation. "I suppose it's similar to going *between*."

"Not really. It's sort of all at once, instead of by degrees. Is that the gel? I'll just take it out to him."

Tai left the room as fast as she could.

"Just so long as he comes out of it alive on the other end," Keita called after her.

When she reached the terrace, F'lessan was still in the chair, leaning down to look at Golanth's hind leg. One of the other healers was just staring at him. Zaranth, on the upper ledge, was blinking and looking, Tai thought, rather paler green than she should be.

Does it take a lot of effort?

No, Golanth helps. Last night I was afraid I might hurt him.

I slowed him down, Golanth said. *That's important, too. He isn't a feline.*

He also isn't a trundlebug. Heavier. Zaranth replied.

He seems to have survived, Tai said, walking quickly down the hall.

It may be just a matter of control. We must find out how the other dragons are doing, Golanth said.

Tai reached F'lessan in his chair.

"How was the ride?"

"It's *not* like going *between*," he said firmly, looking her in the eye. "But I got here and Golly's leg isn't near as bad as I thought it was. Couldn't really see it last night, you know."

"You had too much time to think. I told you it was healing."

"I had to see it."

"I know," she agreed affably but, when he started to get up, she pushed him back.

"I want to see all of Golly," he protested.

"Golly can turn around. You stay put. It'll do Golly good to move."

"But he's smeared with numbweed," F'lessan replied hotly. "You heard Keita lecture us."

"It won't hurt Golly to turn around in place. He has done it." Tai spoke firmly, sounding a bit like Keita.

I can do it. And Golanth ended that argument by rising to four feet, and whatever the turn might have lacked in grace, it did allow his seated rider to see all of him, glistening in ribbons and patches with recently and generously applied numbweed. Except for the deepest ones, the claw marks were now mostly black tracings; where the wing sails had been punctured, the membrane tissue was ringed with pale new growth. When F'lessan asked him to, Golanth obediently stopped so his rider could lean forward for a closer look at one deep groove or the imprint of claw tips. At the point where Golanth was facing Zaranth on her ledge, he raised his head and gave her an affectionate lick.

Tai tried to gauge F'lessan's assessment of his dragon's

condition but his usually mobile face was expressionless. His hands expressed his anguish, his fingers clenching and unclenching as if he wished he could erase the injuries, finally settling helplessly to the arms of the chair. Then Golanth halted, in front of his seated rider.

"Swimming would do F'lessan a lot of good," Tai murmured.

Zaranth made the most astonishing sound of surprise, her eyes whirling into yellow and she extended her head and neck in protest.

I'm only a green. I would need a lot of practice to move as much as Golanth.

F'lessan gave a burst of laughter. *When you bounced all those felines like so many wherries?*

I was angry. I was afraid. Zaranth's look was so apologetic that F'lessan laughed again, shaking his head at her. *I didn't bounce you last night.*

I helped, Golanth said with dignity, sweeping his weyrmate a kindly glance. *When I need to move, I will move myself. I can fall over the edge of the terrace just as you did last night.*

Not just yet, Golly, both riders said urgently.

Zaranth curved her head back. *You couldn't have seen me. And you can't go falling off the terrace. You've too much wingspread to drop off.*

When I need to move, I said, and his dignity increased. *I heard you last night. Nothing's wrong with my hearing. Swimming would be good for my rider. You must take him today. F'lessan, tell the healers you must swim.*

I'm not leaving you, F'lessan replied stoutly.

I am much better, you know. So are you, Golanth said, shoving his nose gently at F'lessan's knees, the good eye serenely steady. Then he cocked his head so he could see through the left eye.

"Keita gave me this to help lubricate his lids," Tai said, handing F'lessan the jar. It took her breath away to see the ruin of the left eye in full light and she knew it must be worse for his rider.

"Yes, that's a good idea," F'lessan said in an even voice and unscrewed the jar. With the tip of a delicately poised finger, he applied the gel. "Now close that lid and I'll do the other."

"Swimming would be very good for you," Tai repeated when he had finished that ministration. "Your wounds are closed. Going *between* won't affect them. I'm sure we can get you on Zaranth's back. The sea would do you good. Getting away from here would do you good."

F'lessan leaned back in the chair, regarding her steadily just as Keita approached.

"What's this about the sea?" the healer asked.

"It'd be excellent therapy, Keita, you know that. The dolphins will assist."

There was considerably more discussion about swimming. Basically Keita had no objection but she wanted a healer to accompany them, even offering to go herself, with perhaps T'lion and his Gadareth as support while F'lessan insisted that Tai and Zaranth would be more than adequate companions. Somewhat reluctantly Keita admitted that the presence of dolphins would suffice if Tai were certain they'd appear. F'lessan and Tai both reassured her.

"He doesn't need to get out of the water," Tai insisted, remaining firm but not pleading. "He can swim off and on Zaranth without requiring help or getting sand on him. We won't do much today, but the water is so—so buoyant."

"Let them have some time to themselves, Master Keita," Sagassy said firmly, giving Tai a wink. "The change would do them good and they'd be back in time for lunch and hungry for it. Golanth here won't be out of touch with them for a moment. Will you, bronze dragon?"

Not many non-riders were bold enough to ask a dragon's opinion but Sagassy had become quite comfortable with the bronze. He nodded and the remaining facets on his left eye began to exhibit whirls of enthusiasm.

That first excursion—short though it was—marked a decided turn in F'lessan's recuperation. And that night they shared a bed.

LANDING—3.21.31

On that last tack into Monaco Bay, Shankolin saw Landing once again ahead of him on its hill, the three volcanoes in the distance. He had had no warning from Lord Toric about the current size of the facility. Now he understood why the Lord Holder had advised him to come here and survey the area with the view of bringing total destruction to the Abomination, and all its adjuncts. Then the view was hidden as the ship tacked again, closing with the wharf where it would moor.

Even during their conversation at Telgar Hold, Shankolin was wary of coming to Landing but Toric had said that there would be no trouble at all to arrange entry into the Admin Building itself so that Shankolin could estimate just what method would serve their mutual purpose. Toric gave him a substantial number of marks and observed that he had best journey from one of the smaller seaholds on Nerat's Foot. Toric knew of a fisherman whose captain owed him a favor or two and would sail him directly to Monaco Bay. He remarked that gloves on Shankolin's hand would disguise the missing joint and a cap pulled down on the forehead would hide the scar.

"Someone saw you and the Harper Hall has passed a rough sketch of you around. You'd best cover what you can and change what you're wearing now."

Shankolin suppressed a smile at the Lord Holder's disgust but smell was as much a disguise as clothing. To most observers, Shankolin was a hill man whom few would approach for several reasons, one of them being the body odor.

Just before Shankolin reached Loscar port, he washed both himself and his stinking clothes in a stream. In the port, it was easy to buy good secondhand clothing, suitable for a sea voyage. He found the captain Toric had recommended and presented him with the first of the hastily scribbled notes Toric had provided. He gave his name as Glasstol from Crom and no one challenged it. He spent most of the journey either asleep or eating. One of the more sociable crewmen explained how much the Flood had improved the Loscar harbor, and was answered by an uncivil grunt. So no one tried again to enter conversations with a passenger who clearly wished to keep to himself.

On his arrival at Monaco Bay, Shankolin was struck by the repairs already made; even its shipbuilding facilities were back in place. He had heard that the area had been inundated by five major tsunami waves and significant smaller ones to extend the sea inland as far as a man could walk in a day. That the wharf was new—and the reek of its wood preservative dominated even the smell of fish—was inescapable. A weathered metal pylon with a bell at its apex had been erected. The captain pointed out the new floats on the seaward side where shipfish would come when the bell was rung. Sometimes, the shipfish would summon the Portmaster. Shankolin had been raised inland and doubted this unlikely story.

As he had once before, he found a carter who was taking supplies from the harbor to Landing and, for a half mark, allowed him to climb into one of the wagons. It was slow. He helped with the burden beasts pulling the heavy loads and the carter, not a curious man by nature, spoke more to them than to his passenger.

By the time Shankolin was left off by the carter at the edge of the widely expanded Landing, he was glad of the map Toric had given him so he could make contact with the Southern Holder's contact in Landing: a man called Esselin who could be found in the Archives. He also owed Lord Toric favors, which was why Esselin would oblige Shankolin by escorting him into the Admin Building and the Aivas chamber.

Shankolin found Master Esselin about to leave the main Archive Building, which had far too many windows. Perhaps that design shed light into the room and the shelving on which masses of books were visible, but all that glass would splinter so easily and destroy the contents. Shankolin began to assess how much explosives he would need. Perhaps Lord Toric knew of a man who could supply him.

Master Esselin was not happy to see the handwriting on the envelope Lord Toric addressed to him. He was even unhappier when he read the message; his sallow complexion turning paler and his fat face showing how irritated he was.

"Lord Toric felt that only you," and Shankolin knew how to flatter subtly, "would be able to grant my deep and abiding desire to see where the Aivas was housed."

That sentiment had the ring of truth and Shankolin infused his tone with reverent respect and awe.

"Just the briefest look would fulfill my life's ambition," Shankolin went on.

"Well, well, it is Lord Toric," Esselin said, as he tore the message into the smallest parts his thick fingers could manage.

At this hour, when most would be going to their homes for the evening, there were few on the neatly kept paths. However, Esselin made absolutely certain that no one else was nearby as he kicked a small hole in the nearest garden bed. The pieces of paper fluttered from his fingers into the hole and he stamped hard, looking all about him as he did so. One last look at his feet and he could see that not even a white corner was visible.

"Follow me," he said, straightening the lapels of his coat. "A brief look is all. I have work awaiting me in my quarters. As always." Esselin's tone was long-suffering as he waddled as quickly as he could pump his fat legs in the direction of the Admin Building.

Shankolin jumped as the lights illuminating the pathway blinked on in the twilight. He felt sullied by so much abomination around him. The sooner he could demolish all this, the better. There was, however, far more to Landing now than he had anticipated. It would make his ambition to destroy *all* the Abomination's work much harder but there should be a way. He might have to recruit more helpers. He wondered how deeply indebted the fat little man was to Southern's Lord Holder.

He was surprised when he saw that Esselin was leading him, not around the bulky building to the front door, but to a back entrance. Shankolin saw the guard seated inside, saw a look of dislike cross his features as he recognized the little Master, but he rose immediately to let them in.

"We'll just come through this way and go out the front door," Esselin said, waving Shankolin to follow him.

The guard stepped back to allow the portly man to pass. His expression was totally blank as if he was just as happy to avoid any conversation with Esselin and scarcely looked at Shankolin.

They continued down the corridor, and doors closed on either side. Probably he could peer in through the windows once he was again outside on the path. Perhaps. Then they reached the wider hallway that Shankolin remembered, part of the entrance he had used before. No one of those talking among themselves did more than glance at Esselin and quickly look away.

The rooms to the left would have to be inspected. Perhaps burning pitch from an outside window? No, an explosive would be needed to achieve the most destruction. Fire would never damage enough.

Then, there, at the end of the hall, was the softly lit Aivas Chamber. Shankolin felt no reverence at all, but an intense thrill of pleasure. He had never thought he could gain entrance to the facility so easily.

When he had planned Batim's raid on the main Healer Hall they'd thought it would be much harder to enter. Unfortunately for that expedition, it had been much harder to leave.

Should he prevail on Master Esselin to accompany him on his next visit here? The fat man's clothes would hide more than his excess weight. But first, he must get to the actual chamber. And take a quick look at what was in the room to the left. Light spilled out into the hallway and, by the sounds he could hear, a lot of machinery was being used and quite a few people were at work.

Suddenly a big man stepped from that room, frowned when he recognized Esselin, and gave Shankolin the briefest glance.

"Promised him just a look, Tunge," Esselin said, flapping his left hand to dismiss the man.

Tunge started to protest but by then Esselin stopped at the threshold to the chamber. He turned to beckon Shankolin to hurry along.

"There isn't much to see now, of course, since Aivas terminated . . ."

Shankolin ignored him. He was savoring this moment, heart pounding in anticipation as it had on that previous occasion. He stiffened with remembered fear of the awful noise that had deafened him. But Aivas had terminated itself. Impatient to view the site that he would soon see in rubble, Shankolin shouldered a startled Esselin aside and strode purposefully over the threshold.

That was as far as Shankolin got. From the opposite wall of the chamber two narrow shafts of light struck him on the chest at heart height. He was dead before he fell backward.

Master Esselin collapsed in hysterics, trying to scramble as far from the corpse as he could. Tunge yelled for help and then peered down at the dead man, scratching his head in perplexity. When he pushed back the cap and saw the scarred face, he bent down and picked up the left hand. The tip of the first finger was missing. Tunge dashed to the main hall, rummaging through the top drawer of the desk until he found the harper sketch that he remembered seeing. Master Stinar was now in the hall, to find out who was screaming hysterically and why.

Stinar immediately summoned a healer to attend to the Master Archivist. When Tunge showed him the harper sketch, Stinar then got in touch with D'ram and Lytol at Cove Hold and dismissed everyone in the Admin who was not essential, with the exception of the rear door guard who was mystified and kept repeating that he had never thought to question Master Esselin. The man was in and out of Admin all the time, wasn't he? When D'ram and Lytol arrived, Stinar escorted them to the body and requested Tunge to tell them exactly what he had seen.

"Like I've already told Master Stinar, I saw beams of light

come out of two spots high on the back wall." He pointed to the two places, not wishing to cross the threshold right now though he had done so many times to dust and keep the place tidy. "Far's I ever heard, nothing inside has been operational since Aivas and Master Robinton died in there."

Both Lytol and D'ram looked down at the dead man for a long time before they looked at each other.

"He got this far once before, you know," Lytol said in his slow sad voice. "When he and two others attacked Aivas. On that occasion, what Aivas called a sonic barrage deafened the intruders. Aivas said that he had been provided with self-defense units."

Surprised, Stinar turned from one to the other. "But that must have been twelve Turns ago."

"Thirteen, give or take a sevenday or two," Lytol replied. "Once a person entered that chamber, Aivas would know him or her again."

"You mean that Aivas's self-defense system is still operational?" Stinar asked in awe.

Lytol regarded him kindly. "I would hazard the opinion that some internal circuitry was never turned off. A system as sophisticated as Aivas's would have recognized this man as a previous intruder. Computers, as you should know, Master Stinar, have long as well as accurate memory files."

The Harper Hall was informed by fire-lizard message, and Pinch, who was the only person who had ever seen the Abominator leader, was conveyed to Landing to confirm the identification.

"No idea who he was, Master Mekelroy?" Lytol asked.

Pinch shook his head slowly. "Fifth" was only a convenient designation. He'd been called "Glass" at Crom Minehold 23, but that was no more the man's rightful name than Fifth. Pinch hoped it took a long while before Lord Toric realized that Fifth, too, was no longer available. Now, if he could just find Fourth and neutralize her, they might forget about Abominators.

Esselin did not recover from the shock he had received and

died a few days later of a hemorrhage in the brain. Or so the Healer at Landing said. The incident was forgotten as quickly as possible and Tunge soon resumed his duty of keeping the Aivas Chamber neat and tidy.

HONSHU WEYRHOLD—3.21.31

Once he started swimming daily, F'lessan improved in vigor, was able to concentrate, and asked for astronomy texts so he and Tai could study. He even sent someone up to the observatory office to examine the prints they had taken to show at the Dragonriders' meeting; that now seemed another lifetime ago. Perhaps it was—the notion passed F'lessan's mind briefly—but Tai saw a streak and they had to check that. Then a blur caught their attention and, although that print was marked as a time exposure and it took them all morning to update the orbit, it turned out to be an asteroid among the minor planets; nothing significant. The studying passed a morning and gave both of them practice in configuring orbits. Tai suggested that they could help Erragon by asking for more of the latest prints from Cove Hold. The Star Master might not have time to review prints with all he had to do supervising three new observatories—no name had been chosen yet for the Western Continent installation—and classes that Cove Hold had undertaken.

Golanth walked, limping at first but gradually with more confidence until he was pacing briskly up and down the length of the terrace. He kept trying to extend the damaged wing but it moved awkwardly, despite all the massage and smelly unguents. Sagassy's holdmate, arriving with fresh food, watched him for a long moment.

"Think we can do something about that. Not too far to the ground on the step side."

"Golanth couldn't manage the hold steps," F'lessan said. "He's too long."

"Ramp'd work. Double it, make it wide," Jubb said, rubbing

his chin thoughtfully. "Got the wood. Make it strong. How much does your dragon weigh?"

F'lessan and Tai exchanged glances, and F'lessan burst into laughter.

"What's so funny?"

"He weighs as much as he thinks he does," F'lessan managed to say and that set Tai laughing.

Jubb looked from him to Sagassy to Keita and the others and shrugged.

"No one ever weighed a dragon before? We weigh herd-beasts 'n' everything all the time." He threw his hands up in the air. "Well, thought it might help."

"It does, it does, it does." F'lessan caught Jubb by the arm, reassuring him and controlling his amusement. "I'm not laughing at the idea, Jubb. It's an excellent one. Golanth is tired of being stuck up here on the terrace." F'lessan's face lost all merriment. "He can't just take off."

"You are good to suggest it, Jubb," Tai said, coming to his rescue. "How long would it take?"

Jubb gave them a long speculative look. "About as long as you got folk handy enough to build it." Then he grinned.

It took three days, with dragons flying in timber, their riders, and folk who just "heard" that carpentry was needed, including the three dragons who flew in from Telgar Weyr with casks of nails, screws, new hammers, and saws, and brought whatever other equipment might be needed from the SmithCraftHall. Jubb; his workmates, Sparling and Riller; two Smithcrafters, and three of Lord Asgenar's best timber men designed a switchback ramp, with much discussion about the angle of incline, the size and bracing of the structure, the width and depth of the flooring, while men and women sawed and cut, and others hunted or flew in enough food to feed the volunteers. One thing F'lessan made clear: even for his dragon he would not mar the superb façade of Honshu Hold.

More important, F'lessan was immediately involved in the activity, taking time off only to swim, toning the muscles of his bad leg and his shoulder, regaining his tan. He also insisted on taking over as much of Golanth's treatment as possible and trusted no one else, not even Tai, with lubricating the eyelids. He seemed to ignore his own injuries: using a slower, more deliberate step to disguise his limp as he moved around with the cane. He was more his old self, though he didn't smile or laugh quite as easily. If she caught a darkness in his eye now and then, she knew it was all for his dragon, not himself. Several times, she saw F'lessan eyeing the drop from the ledge, measuring it, wondering if perhaps Golanth could indeed fall off its edge and manage a strong enough downward stroke with one wing to become airborne.

Once news of the project spread, Lessa and F'lar came to visit. While F'lar was looking over the plans with Jubb, the Smiths, and the Woodsmen, Lessa told them what was happening at Western—for lack of a better name that had stuck—and Master Erragon's resurrection of the telescopes from the Catherine Caves.

"Before he gets too involved with that," F'lessan said firmly, "we need him to rig a remote control console for the scope here on the main level. There's a room on the north face that would suit." He paused briefly, his eyes flickering. "There must be a way to trigger the dome mechanism, too. That spiral stair is ridiculous. Why did Kenjo hide everything away?"

"Who knows why the Ancients did what they did?" Lessa said, shrugging. "Have you asked Jancis and Piemur to help you? Didn't you persuade them to do the initial restoration of the observatory? Erragon's already grateful you're reducing his backlog of prints. I don't know how he fits everything in."

"He swears he needs only four hours of sleep a night," Tai remarked, incredulous.

"Neither of you can match him yet," Lessa said at her driest, "at your stage of convalescence, but as I understand it, there's more to sky-watching than lying on your back and looking at 'em. He says he needs references from Honshu."

Pausing, she looked out over the valley. "It is very pleasant here, you know, but we can't stay long today."

She and F'lar left shortly afterward, saying they'd be back when the ramp was finished.

They were. It was wide enough for Ramoth, the largest dragon on Pern, who demonstrated by walking down and up it without brushing folded wings against the cliff face. Bravely, Golanth set all four feet on it, F'lessan beside him.

"Now, put your weight down, Golly," F'lessan said, grinning broadly and cocking his head at the slight sound as the timbers gave a little under him. "Don't knock me off."

The spectators cheered dragon and rider as they proceeded down. Ramoth's eyes whirled as she watched from the upper terrace, Zaranth and Mnementh to one side on the cliff face, all three dragons alert. Gradually Golanth moved with assurance, able to lift his tail slightly, which was another improvement in his mobility. The first landing was more than wide enough for him to make the turn. When he and F'lessan reached ground level, he extended his head upward to bugle his pleasure and began to stamp round on the soft dirt. That was when the bronze dragon saw the door to the beasthold, the landing above and to one side of it.

I could weyr in this place, he told his rider. *It is wide and high enough for me to enter.*

F'lessan, who knew every plane and dimension of Honshu, now saw that the doorway was wider than it had been. Over the general hammering, sawing, and planing, he would not have heard the noise of masons making the enlargement. He knew—because he had mucked out the dirt that had accumulated over the centuries—that the interior of the beasthold was larger than Golanth's weyr at Benden. The ramp now gave him access to it and would certainly protect him from the winter rains.

"Rain," F'lessan thought and had to reach for one of the supports until the dizziness that had abruptly overcome him passed.

"What's wrong, F'lessan?" Tai asked, coming to see what

had attracted Golanth's interest. Her expression altered when she realized that he had had some kind of shock.

Rain! The silver fall of Thread was like rain! Golanth would never be able to fly Thread again. In fact, when Thread next fell over Honshu, Golanth would have to be shut into the beasthold, to keep him from *trying* to fly: the most powerful instinct of dragons was to fly when Thread was in the sky. Was that why the ramp had been completed so quickly? F'lessan tried to remember the sequence of Fall in this part of the south. He couldn't think. The realization that his days as Wingleader were over was too much to assimilate. He must have known it at some level. And denied it as he denied that Golanth was blind in one eye and too joint-stiff to work the left wing. As he had diverted such thoughts by plunging into Erragon's backlog of images. And Tai had encouraged him. Encouraged him to swim. To do *other things*! He wanted to think that she had been deceiving him but deceit was not a facet of Tai's personality.

Neither Lessa nor F'lar had said anything during their last visit. He should have noticed the avoidance, the talk about sky-watching and installing remote controls. Hadn't he mentioned it casually? Had they thought he was making the adjustment from Wingleader to sky-watcher? How could he have been so dense? This ramp allowed Golanth more freedom of movement—on the ground. But *into* the air! Golanth might not have lost his ability to go *between* but to go *between* from ground level presented hazards that no sensible rider would ask his dragon to face. What about an unsensible rider?

He could feel Tai beside him. He could hear the men and women who had made the ramp still cheering the accomplishment and encouraging Golanth to show how easily he could climb back up to the weyrhold. F'lessan took a deep breath and turned around: in Tai's eyes he could see she knew what he'd been thinking. Then, the second shock hit him.

A dragon must be in the air to "fly" his mate. He could not suppress his anguish at that realization. Hard enough to lose his right to lead, but to lose the ecstasy, too?

It took him a moment to realize that Tai was shaking him, her green eyes intense with denial.

"Nonsense," he heard Tai say in a whisper so furious it stung his ears. "There'll be a way. There's been a way for everything else! Come."

He grabbed her, pushing her against one of the thick stanchions at the base of the ramp.

"*Did* you know? Do *they*?" He meant his Weyrleaders. He gave her a shake when she didn't answer.

"I thought," and her words came out slowly, "that you realized someone would have to take over your wing—for a while."

"It's not just the wing . . ." He pushed her away from him. "I thought Honshu was my refuge. Now I realize it's Golly's prison!" He pointed to the beasthold and its widened doors. "He'll have to be put in there whenever there's Thread above. Not being able to fly drives a dragon crazy. We *always* assist an injured dragon to get far away until Thread has passed. But Golanth can't even do that!"

"You don't know that yet!" she said, whirling to stand in front of him. "We haven't even tried to get him to the sea."

"How in the name of the first Egg can we get him to the beach when he can't even get in the air?"

"Because," Lessa replied, walking in under the ramp, F'lar beside her, "we *know* how he can get into the air. Once he's in the air, he can go *between*. Did you think Ramoth and Mnementh—and other dragons—had forgotten what they learned that day at Honshu?"

F'lessan stared at her. She was almost reproachful. To his amazement, his father was more amused than critical. He couldn't quite grasp what they meant. His mind was tormented by the crushing revelations he had been too cowardly to admit to himself.

"The ramp is a good idea," F'lar said. "That—" and he waved toward the beasthold, "makes a fine weyr. Nothing else." His amber eyes held F'lessan's. "Certainly not a prison in time of Thread. By the time the Nine Fall is over Honshu, we'll have mastered lifting that bronze dragon of yours."

"But how?"

"It takes control, you know," Lessa said, walking up to her son and slipping her arm in his. "Which, I believe, your dragon was practicing the other morning."

"How did you know that?" F'lessan asked, startled out of his morbid thoughts.

"There's not much Ramoth doesn't know if she wants to find out," Lessa said, looking up at him and giving him an encouraging little smile. "Now, there is a celebration going on around us. I think we've inspected Golanth's weyr sufficiently to know it will suit and I think you'd better calm him down."

Golanth was bugling and his happy voice did not mirror the anguish of F'lessan's recent numbing thoughts. None had leaked to his dragon, for which he was intensely grateful. Now Golanth was happily prancing up the ramp. His mind was all about being free of the terrace. F'lessan concentrated on that positive thought, reinforced it by what F'lar had just said. Practice? Yes, practice. Zaranth and Golanth hadn't done so badly in the two movings they'd attempted so far. They could practice. He could feel the thud of Golanth's feet in the ground under his.

Lessa gave him a little shake. "Come, F'lessan, you've other things to do now," she said softly and then pulled his arm.

In the few steps back into the sunlight, he quenched that black moment of anger and mind-numbing despair, forced himself through them to grasp what hope allowed. He joined the applause as Golanth came charging back to the foot of the ramp, limping only slight on his left hind leg. His right wing was fully extended and, if the left was canted downward, it was straighter than it had been now the dragon didn't have to worry about banging into Honshu's wall.

Maybe swimming and dolphin massage would loosen that joint just enough—

"Don't consider anything else, rider," said his father in a low voice, striding past him.

F'lessan turned back and held out his hand. "Tai?" he asked hopefully.

She came out of the shadow of the ramp, too, and took his hand. They walked out to Golanth. "Remember, F'lessan, I have chosen you. I now reaffirm it." Her hand was tight on his as they began the walk up the ramp.

SOUTHERN HOLD — 3.23.31

Toric was overseeing the unloading of several prime breeding pairs of canines: big strapping animals, deep in the chest, thick-necked, well-set teeth, sturdy legs, dark to mid-brown short-haired—a necessary trait since parasites could cling to long fur to burrow into the host body. Shrewd calculating eyes, unafraid, despite a journey stuffed in a cramped forward compartment.

"They weren't seasick," the handler said approvingly, with a slight emphasis on the pronoun. "Name's Pinch, Lord Toric."

"Why the muzzles?" Toric asked, flicking his thick fingers in acknowledgment of the name.

"One of the females is near her heat. Couldn't have them biting, fighting."

"Aren't they trained?"

The handler, a medium-sized man with an angular face somewhat marred by tar stains and dirt, brown eyes, serious sort of expression, gave Toric a hard stare.

"If they wasn't when they came on board, they are now. *Sit!*"

All six dogs instantly obeyed, heads pointing at the handler. Though they didn't move, it was obvious by their rolling eyes and the movements of their nostrils that they were taking in such sights and smells as they could at the sit position.

"Stand!" On their feet in a shot. They took advantage and glanced about in every direction. One of them whined softly.

The man gave a sort of smug smirk. "Voice and hand." He demonstrated by firmly depressing his hand to the ground and the dogs sat down again. "Make sure you feed 'em by hand yourself and they'll be yours."

Toric had no time to feed dogs but his sons did.

"Here're their papers," the handler said. He fumbled in a clean but well-mended jacket, and passed Toric a sheaf. "Master Ballora guarantees fertility or you can return the dogs."

"Can you manage to get them to my hold?" Toric asked, eyeing the man. Any one of the dogs stood higher than the handler's knee: heavy collars as well as choke chains, paired up on three thick leather leads.

"Up to top, turn second left, up the wide stairs and Lord Toric's Hold is directly in front," the man said in quick phrases and then grinned, showing very white and even teeth.

"Get going then, and you're responsible if you lose one or any get damaged or do damage." Toric gestured him to be off.

"Come!" The dogs followed their handler down the gangplank, shoving a little with their shoulders to be closest behind him. At his order, they moved in front of him.

Toric watched as the dogs led the man up the stairs without pulling at him. Toric approved. He must remember to oversee his sons while they were getting accustomed to the beasts. Maybe, he'd keep one pair by him. Might be prudent. Ballora had offered him watchwhers. He couldn't stand the look of the creatures, and they were really only good watchers at night. They had to be blooded at birth to recognize the legitimate members of a Hold.

He pretended to read the dogs' papers as the rest of the passengers began filing off the ship, assessing the newest arrivals at Southern. More ragged ones who were unlikely to devote any time to that newest fad, sky-watching. If things fell out of the sky, they fell, and there was more water on Pern than land. What were really needed in the sky were more accurate weather satellites. That spaceship had only its southern array and the worst winds came down out of the north, which was what had happened two Turns ago and his coastline had been sharding ruined. Dolphin warning hadn't given anyone enough time.

He shifted his feet and glared as the last man off the boat led a small girl and encouraged three boys to move quickly now. Then the captain and the Runner Stationmaster emerged, the latter hefting the heavy message sack to his shoulder. The captain smiled and the Runner murmured something and made his way to the gangplank. He saw the Lord Holder and nodded courteously.

"You've nothing for me, Runner?"

"No, Lord Toric, or I would have had it to hand the moment I saw you come on board."

Toric swore under his breath, pursing his lips. The Runner Stationmaster angled past Toric, onto the pier, and up the stairs to the new Runner Station at Southern.

Sharding Fifth! He'd had no message since their meeting at Telgar. Fifth had indicated there were many men and women who obeyed his directions but not who or where they were; only the most discreet shared his theories about the Abomination and Master Robinton. Very prudent of Fifth but sharding infuriating for Toric. He consoled himself with the fact that there were plenty of men like that Ruathan renegade that he could recruit, but it meant starting out again. Dorse had been almost worth every mark Toric paid him.

Of course, he could approach Kashman! Now there was a man who had a legitimate grievance with the high and mighty Lord Dragonrider Jaxom. Toric might be able to work on that. Gain another freethinking man in the Council.

He also had had no word from Master Esselin about the meeting with Fifth that he had set up. Surely the old fool could do *that* much correctly. Unless, of course, Fifth had decided to take the marks and disappear. Toric rather thought not. The man's obsession would keep him fueled for the revenge he sought. Kashman might be a willing associate even if he'd been only a child when the beloved Robinton had been alive.

That was when he saw the thin woman, at one side of the wharf, watching him, standing in a very awkward position, one hand in front of her clasping the elbow of her other arm. He swaggered down the gangplank, knowing she waited to speak to him, Lord Toric. There was only one person she could be: Dorse had described her in unflattering terms, but had grudgingly admitted that she was meticulous with details, uncompromising in her devotion to Fifth, and determined to destroy all Abominations if she had to do it single-handedly.

And here she was, Toric thought, seeking him out. Did she intend to take Dorse's place? Or Fifth's? Whichever, he could control her as he had Dorse, as he hoped to manipulate Kashman. She'd be very useful in Toric's scheming. Dorse had once said that she had a knack of recruiting the disgruntled to their cause. At the very least, she could give him the names and whereabouts of those already "persuaded." She'd be convenient to use as an emissary to Keroon Hold.

He smiled at her as he approached. She met his glance squarely, her face a mask, her body motionless, facing him as an equal. Toric kept his smile, but thought that he had better make sure she didn't consider herself an equal in any respect to Toric, Lord Holder of Southern!

Neither saw that the dog handler paused at the top of the stairs and observed their meeting.

The dog handler remained in Southern Hold long enough to instruct Toric's twin sons in how to care for and use the commands to which the dogs had been trained. During that sevenday, he listened but heard nothing about any untoward incident at Landing or any word about Master Esselin's demise.

When Toric set off with Fourth to some destination along the coast, Pinch summoned Bista to him. She had been inconspicuous among all the fire-lizards that darted about Southern. He met with Sintary in Southern's Harper Hall and gave the Master a sketch of Fourth, asking him to keep an eye out for her. Then he sent Bista to Sebell, requesting a dragon to convey him back to the Harper Hall.

HONSHU WEYRHOLD—3.27.31

It took two days to recover from the party. Lessa had managed to talk F'lar into staying overnight as a snowstorm had blown in over Benden from the Eastern Sea and she wanted to stay warm. T'lion, who had helped build the ramp, talked one of the Monaco harpers into coming along for the celebration: Jubb had a gitar, Sparling a fiddle, Riller a drum. Keita sang a fine light soprano, Sagassy a rich contralto, and everyone, even Tai, laughed when F'lessan tried to sing the chorus with them. He didn't try to dance but F'lar partnered everyone, including Tai, though she excused herself from other invitations on the grounds of her sore leg and sat with F'lessan when he wasn't busy trying to keep his bronze dragon from walking up and down the ramp. But it was a fine evening.

The next morning both rider and dragon were so lame that Tai complained that they'd used up two whole pots of numbweed between them to ease their aches. Keita decided that she was redundant and asked T'lion for a ride to the Healer Hall. She'd send more numbweed.

The third morning saw the last of the party cleared up. Sagassy said they'd enough food left over for several days and she'd best get down to her hold. Tai offered to fly her back, with the favorite pots and pans that she'd brought up to Honshu to help out. Suddenly F'lessan had his weyrhold to himself. Taking a cup of klah out to the terrace, he sat, watching Golanth snoring, head on his forepaws.

His color's good, F'lessan thought and firmly turned his mind to wondering when Erragon would bring that new console so he could start working for his living. Which brought him right back to what he didn't want to think about! The facts that he would never lead a wing again and that Golanth might never fly Zaranth. *That* he didn't like—especially since Zaranth was a young dragon and would need a good male to keep her content. He, F'lessan, certainly didn't wish to share Tai with another rider—any other male. She enjoyed being with him now, relaxed, eager, and he wasn't going to have her response to him destroyed by some heavy-handed rider with no sensitivity for her marvelous, intricate personality. He felt himself getting quite roused by the very thought. And they had work to do, both of them, on the prints: they weren't half through that job. That was the channel he should concentrate on. The stars! The stars were important. Sky-watching was important work. He didn't need to fly to do that. He did need Tai to do that job properly. Truth be told, she knew a lot more about astronomy than he did, though he was catching up. They'd need more people in Honshu to help with that project. He couldn't keep up with Erragon's four hours of sleep a night. The daytime work, listing all the positions, seeing if there were other traces of the orbit from wherever Master Idarolan was working. Weren't there good men in Crom and Southern Boll already involved? He should meet with them. He should organize his life on a new basis—shouldn't he?

Abruptly another revelation occurred to him. Lytol, with his scarred and seamed face! *He* had been dragonless for Turns, ever since his brown Larth had died in a routine training flight at Benden: a training flight during which R'gul had allowed his dragon a chance to chew firestone and flame. Only Larth had caught flame in the face and so had Lytol. The dragon had managed to land his gravely wounded rider with the last breath in him. That should have been the end of the rider, as a person—a dragonless man.

Tradition said dragonless riders suicided rather than live without their dragon. But Lytol had defied that convention and had become far more than a dragonrider. He had been a Lord Holder for Jaxom's minority; he had then turned his hand to help Master Robinton and D'ram to manage Landing as a major Hold to the satisfaction of everyone involved. Now, Lytol and D'ram, in addition to bearing blind Wansor company, had accepted yet another role for which they were unusually qualified: as wise consultants for the complex society of the planet. Briefly F'lessan wondered, even as his soul cringed at the thought: would he have had the courage to build a new life—lives, in fact—as Lytol had done, if Golanth had succumbed to his injuries?

F'lessan gave a snort of disgust for his self-absorption. The time he had wasted. As Tai had said, there would be a way. Lytol had made several, and the example of the man's quiet heroism rebuked him.

Halfway through a snore, Golanth woke, alert, looking northward. When was the Nine Fall due? Close enough for Golanth to *know* it was near.

Five riders appeared in the sky, and a sixth came swooping up out of the jungle. It was Zaranth who reached Honshu first, hovering to let her rider dismount on the terrace before she turned on her wing tip, as if challenging the newcomers. F'lessan rose, wondering at her almost defensive attitude. Then the dragons were close enough for him to recognize them: Monarth, Gadareth, Path, Galuth, and Arwith, but they made no move to land.

They come to practice, Zaranth said. *Tai, I will get his jacket.*

"What do they mean 'practice'?" F'lessan wanted to know.

His jacket smacked into his chest and the reflex action of his hand kept it there.

"They mean to practice what they learned from Zaranth, Ramoth, and Mnementh," Tai said, as if reminding him of something he'd forgotten.

Lessa had said something about practice the other evening.

"Practice what? Who on?"

What happened next was as astonishing to Tai as F'lessan. As she watched—F'lessan went white and staggered in shock—Golanth rose vertically from the stone of the terrace, hissing in surprise. Instinctively, the bronze spread his wings, though he could not extend the left far or raise it to match the other. But he was being lifted into the air.

"WHAT ARE YOU DOING TO GOLANTH!" cried F'lessan, limping frantically to where Golanth dangled out of reach.

I'm all right, F'lessan. I'm all right.

"PRACTICE!" T'lion called.

"PRACTICE!" shouted T'gellan, Persellan behind him.

That was what C'reel and Mirrim were shouting, too.

"You have to practice, as well, F'lessan. All he needs is height," cried Mirrim gaily from Path's back. Her dragon was staring at Zaranth, indulging in some communication that neither rider heard.

"You knew about this?" he demanded of Tai, recalling her whispered reassurance under the ramp.

"Me?" she was affronted. "I'm certainly the last one they'd tell. Zaranth can't keep secrets from Golanth or you."

"PUT MY DRAGON DOWN!"

It doesn't hurt, Golanth replied, peering down at his rider, as he was supported in midair by the other dragons. *I'm high enough to go* between.

You can't go between *without your rider,* Monarth said and Golanth began to descend.

Stop! Golanth cried to reduce the pressure that was putting him back down on the terrace stones. *That's better. Be careful of me! I'm not a feline to be tossed about any old way.* Shaking his head, he righted himself and looked around for F'lessan. *Why can't I do it to myself?*

We don't know—yet! Arwith replied, blinking her lids with puzzled embarrassment. Queens were supposed to know everything.

"We're lucky we've got this far," T'lion shouted. "Get aboard!"

As Golanth crouched to allow him to mount, F'lessan hesitated.

"I'll try it from the left," he said and, trying to disguise his limp, hauled himself up to the neck ridge, though his left leg hung down stiffly straight.

Are you ready, F'lessan? Monarth said. *This time we'll lift Golanth high enough for safe passage* between.

Where?

Swimming. We're to get Golanth in the water, too, Tai said.

You're expected at Cove Hold today, Path told Golanth.

I can swim at Cove Hold, too, you know, he replied.

And Erragon has something for you to bring back. I don't

think he needs all *of us, you know,* Path added in an aside to the other dragons.

Ramoth says we are not to take chances with them, Arwith remarked. *Lift!*

F'lessan, once again in the air astride his dragon, felt Golanth's unmistakable elation. Within that joy was a core of deep fear that told F'lessan something else: as he had been hiding his fears from his dragon, Golanth had been concealing his from his rider—clowning up and down the ramp, exhausting them both so they could neither grieve nor think. Then he was aware of Zaranth on Golanth's left side. Poised to lend him her wing if needed? Well, he would certainly choose Zaranth and Tai as wing riders. Honshu Hold receded behind them until they were well clear of it. He could see as far as the clump of holder cots, the fields they had cleared for crops, the river—and the terraces.

It is good, and Golanth gave a sigh of relief, craning his head hard left to make up for his impaired vision.

Let's go to Cove Hold, Golanth. Bright in his mind were the blue waters, streaked with green over shallower bits: the observatory on the right. Unconsciously raising his arm in the Wingleader's command, he brought it down and told Golanth to go *between*.

BENDEN WEYR—3.27.31

They did it! Ramoth jubilantly told her rider. Then she added in a slightly critical tone, *Not as neat a landing as could be but, under the circumstances, it was well done. I don't think that five dragons were needed to lift Golanth. Just Mnementh and I could have done it.*

Most certainly, Lessa agreed but she herself was smiling with relief. *But the Monacan riders needed the practice and so many offered, that it might well require five to control each other.*

She had never seen the ebullient F'lessan so despairing as the moment he finally realized that Golanth would never again be able to fly Thread. And, by that disability, he could no longer be Wingleader.

She thought back to the day when she and F'lar had been overjoyed, the magical moment when F'lessan had Impressed Golanth at the first Hatching he'd been old enough to stand as candidate. The pair had been unusually well matched and had, almost without visible effort, succeeded in all the training and tests. At sixteen, he'd impudently encouraged Golanth to fly a female when the mating flight of a junior queen had been opened to all bronze dragons. The same Turn had seen the birth of his first child. Two Turns later he had been made Wingleader of a newly formed wing—Benden was at near capacity as a Weyr, so F'lar could take a chance on a new young rider assuming a full wing.

The Honshu attack had been a near thing, even though both F'lessan and Golanth had survived. Riders often had trouble accepting such severe, and limiting, injuries to themselves or their dragons. The ones who were not strong enough in character and resilience to deal with the reality would just go *between*. That had been the most important factor to the Benden Weyrleaders: that F'lessan, once he understood the severity of Golanth's crippling, would not suicide. Keita had dismissed that fear instantly. F'lessan did not have that sort of personality. Then there was Tai to comfort him. Frankly, Lessa had not foreseen F'lessan making such an attachment but the combination had lasted well past mating, and Zaranth was as supportive of the bronze as her rider was of the man. Ramoth had kept an ear open for Golanth and Zaranth every moment of the crucial period. So, Lessa thought privately, had F'lar and Mnementh.

Lessa could now be doubly grateful for F'lessan's keen interest in Honshu and she'd been much relieved to know that he and Tai had begun to pick up the sky-watching during the convalescence. F'lessan was too important—not just as their only living issue, but to Pern. How he had given heart at that Weyrleaders meeting! When she herself had despaired of finding a solution to what the dragonriders could do After, her one child had supplied a direction.

She gave herself a little shake, reliving that moment of cold terror when Ramoth had gone, without her rider, to aid Golanth and Zaranth.

"That moment is nearly a month ago," F'lar said, coming from behind to bend and embrace her. "I know you wanted to be there, but Zaranth is a Monaco dragon and having the support of her Weyr is as important as learning how to give Golanth just enough lift to get airborne. It's not as if we aren't getting plenty of practice in telekinesis lifting those telescope components for Erragon." He hugged her. "A fine control you and Ramoth have."

"And Mnementh's potential is seemingly unlimited," she said, returning a sincere compliment as she leaned against him, accepting the strength he always shared with her. "So many new things to learn in this new dimension of dragonkind."

F'lar gave a dry chuckle. "It's no wonder it's too much for some people to absorb."

"We've not had more trouble with Abominators, have we?" Alarmed, she turned in his arms to see that he wasn't hiding anything from her.

"Fortunately, we have enough to do."

"But you don't think we've heard the last with that death at Landing?"

F'lar sighed. "Pinch has evidently seen Fourth in Toric's keeping. Who can be sure? Such people are afraid of what they don't understand, won't understand. So they pretend to despise and reject it since they can't and won't understand. They retaliate by defiance and witless destruction. And claim they're acting on behalf of people and for reasons those people don't understand either. It may just be a sign of our changing times. And life on our planet is indeed changing."

"For the better?" she murmured.

He tipped her head up with one finger and lightly kissed her lips. "Definitely for the better!"

"You do believe that?" Lessa said, seeking reassurance.

"I wouldn't say it if I didn't believe it. After how many

Turns, don't you know I wouldn't give you false hope, dear heart?"

She put her hands on the arms that enfolded her. "We lived for nearly a whole Turn on nothing but hope."

"And I survived three days without any," F'lar said, kissing her as he reminded her of his own private despair when she had gone back in time to bring forward the five missing Weyrs.

COVE HOLD—SAME DAY, SAME APPROXIMATE TIME

As F'lessan counted the eight seconds in his head, he never thought he'd be so happy to be in the black coldness. Then they were above the blue waters. Golanth eased to the right, lowering the left wing's sail to compensate as they glided toward the lightly rippling surface.

This is good! I have missed this! Golanth said.

All right, my friend, how do you propose to land? F'lessan almost laughed as this problem had to be considered. And quickly.

I will settle as neatly on the water as I always do, Golanth said, but in his joy at being aloft, he'd briefly forgotten that the stiff joint would not respond as usual.

Later, Erragon and D'ram who had been watching from the deep porch of Cove Hold said that, considering the handicaps, it hadn't been a bad landing. Golanth, who had been gliding in without assistance from the other dragons, tried ineffectively to backwing. He couldn't balance and tilted, trailing his left wing tip in the water and that swung him round. Before the left wing could be wrenched by a rough immersion, he was skimming the water, supported by his guides. He had time to fold his wings before he splashed down, skidding forward another length. With no riding strap, F'lessan lost his grip, went over his right shoulder and into the water. He was able to turn his assisted dismount into a creditable dive.

Sorry! Monarth said. *Should have caught you, F'lessan. There's a trick to this we haven't figured out. Getting Golanth up is one thing. Getting him down is another. Water is at least soft.*

Water is not the least bit soft! was F'lessan's response.

Although his heavy riding jacket was sodden and hampered him, he surfaced and started swimming to Golanth, now bobbing on the sea, and looking anxiously about for him.

Is your wing all right?

I think so. Golanth demonstrated by cautiously stretching it out as fully as he could. Waves lapped across its surface, the stiff joint sinking into the warm sea. *That feels good!*

F'lessan had done no more than seven or eight strokes when his outstretched right hand was filled by a dorsal fin. He caught it gratefully and was conveyed toward Golanth at speed. Others surfaced beside him, squeeing with delight at his appearance, calling his name and Golly's and grinning at him as they arced above his head.

"Shore, Fless? Shore, Fless?" Alta asked him. Beyond her he could see Dik and Tom. Five more of the Cove Hold pod were tail-walking about Golanth. He could hear their excited clicking. "We take care of Golly. You leave clothes on shore, Fless."

As with everything this morning, F'lessan did not apparently have any options. He could at least submit with grace. The dolphin escort, squeeing and squealing, guided him inshore until he could get his feet under him and walk out.

A grinning D'ram was there to hand him a towel, offering to take his jacket and to make sure it dried properly. Zaranth landed Tai on the beach, Monarth hovering briefly as T'gellan leaned down to speak to the green rider. F'lessan saw her stiffen and then nod in acquiescence. Monarth veered off and gained height to go *between* with the other dragons. Zaranth splashed into the bright cove waters, swimming out to join Golanth and the dolphins who seethed in the water about him.

Tai hurried up the beach to join F'lessan, stripping off her jacket and helmet, but F'lessan knew that her conversation with T'gellan had been significant. She looked very thoughtful.

"Just the people I wanted to see," Erragon called out, waving for F'lessan and Tai to join him at the Hold. "I've got all the equipment you need for remote access to the scope."

Vigorously both F'lessan and Tai waved arms, acknowledging that good news.

Then Master Wansor, hearing the commotion, shuffled to the steps, Lytol beside him. As Tai reached F'lessan, he was wringing out his dripping shirt and trying to keep his balance on the slant of the beach.

"Clever of you to dive in," she said, giving him a proud, shy smile.

"Oh? You thought so?" he asked, teasing. Just then, his left leg gave under him. She gave him quick support until he recovered.

"I forgot the cane," he said through clenched teeth. The euphoria of his ride here on Golanth instantly dissipated. He glanced across the sands to the Hold, a long walk for a man with a lame leg. He did *not* want to fall on his face in front of Lytol or D'ram. Especially Lytol. How humiliating that would be. He was still incapacitated. His dragon was still injured. He would never again be what he had once been: the carefree self-indulgent bronze Wingleader from Benden Weyr!

"We did sort of leave abruptly," Tai said with an encouraging chuckle as she laid his bare left arm across her shoulders as if walking that way was customary. "Your skin'll be dry by the time we get to the porch."

"Give me that shirt, F'lessan," the old bronze rider said, taking it from the bronze rider's limp hand. "You'll want to be out of those wet pants, too. Come along to the house now. I'll just run ahead and get things ready."

F'lessan made himself match his stride with Tai's. He told himself that walking up the long beach to Cove Hold was really just another step on his way to recovery. After all, he and Golanth had nearly died a bare four sevendays before.

"What's all the fuss? Who just arrived?" Wansor was asking, his eyes wide in his sightless face. "I can't hear what those dolphins are screaming, they're so excited. Fless? Fless, they say? Surely it can't be F'lessan? Didn't you tell me, Lytol, that he and his dragon were badly wounded?"

"Yes, they were wounded, Wansor," Lytol said, coming to stand beside him. "They are here together to see you and discuss the Honshu scope."

They are here together. Lytol's sentence reverberated in F'lessan's mind and he felt tears spring to his eyes—not of pity, but for his new perception of Lytol's victory over the loss of his brown Larth. Lytol had re-created his life, not once, but three times.

Between one careful step and the next, the staggering concept that blossomed in detail in F'lessan's mind made him reel against Tai, who instantly supported him.

As she always had, as she always would! She and Zaranth!

You are all right? Golanth asked apprehensively, halting the water play in which he, Zaranth, and Tiroth indulged while dolphins leaped and played around them.

Quite right. Quite all right! F'lessan reassured his dragon.

Soon Zaranth would be practiced enough to be the only dragon whom Golanth would need for a lift to safe entry *between.* Tai and Zaranth were essential parts of the new future he had just stunningly envisioned for them—and for as many other dragons and riders who wished a part of such a bright, new adventure.

With such inner elation, F'lessan found it doubly hard to walk sedately when once he would have broken into a run. The ache in his left leg seemed irrelevant, even if he couldn't speed up their pace to reach Cove Hold.

"We're nearly there," Tai said, sensing the surge of excitement in her partner's body.

As he took hold of the stair post, F'lessan paused and grinned, almost reverently, up at Lytol. He saw surprise in

Lytol's expression, then D'ram moved past Lytol, gesturing for F'lessan to hurry up the stairs.

"Come, lad, you're not so completely recovered that you can run around in wet clothes and not catch a chill. This way." D'ram beckoned for F'lessan to follow him.

When they finally settled at the table on the porch where the three dragonriders could keep an eye on their water-sporting dragons, F'lessan was wearing clothes supplied by Erragon while his dried. They'd had fresh klah and fruit. Boxed and ready for transport were the remote units that would control the Honshu scope from the main level. A technician, highly recommended by Master Benelek, would install these and the circuitry necessary to operate the opening and closing of the observatory roof.

"What I want to know, F'lessan, Tai," Master Wansor asked, almost testy with impatience, "is what's happened to the feline problem?"

That was perhaps the last question the two dragonriders expected, and they stared at each other. Lytol and D'ram flinched at their blind friend's tactlessness.

"Yes, well, Master Wansor," Tai began, recovering more quickly than F'lessan. "None have been seen around Honshu lately. The holders protect their fields with dragon dung and firestone mash, so we've spread that mixture on our perimeter. Seems to do the job."

"I understand," Lytol added, shifting in his chair after Wansor's blunder, "that Master Ballora sent teams to investigate the habits and lairs of these creatures on Southern." He paused. "She's of the opinion that they were originally developed to hunt the large variety of tunnel snakes that preyed on herdbeasts in the early colonial days. The experiment went wrong, the creatures escaped, and, with no predators to inhibit their numbers, they proliferated unchallenged after the Ancients went north. It would be an impossible, as well as a very dangerous, task to eradicate them. Master Oldive suggests that it should be possible to decrease their numbers by using bait tainted with an infertility substance, but first the species must be examined. Master Ballora is not the only Council member who is adamant that we may not do away with any species that inhabits this planet."

"Except Thread," F'lessan murmured, his sense of mischief suddenly dominant.

Lytol gave him a long, almost amused look. "That organism is not indigenous."

"No more than the felines," D'ram put in, "since they were developed by the Ancients." He shuddered.

"I shouldn't like to think that there were any lurking near," Wansor added, his face furrowed.

"Not with Tiroth on duty," D'ram said stoutly, patting Wansor on the hand.

Erragon cleared his throat, taking charge of conversation. "Quite true. Quite true. Now I want to thank you, F'lessan and Tai, for the work you've already completed, analyzing the images I sent. What I'd like to know is—" and the Star Master hesitated.

"If we'd be willing to undertake regular reviews of the southern starscape," F'lessan finished. "I think from T'gellan's presence here today," he said, glancing at Tai, "that Tai must gradually return to her duties with Monaco Weyr. With their agility, speed, and control, greens are the most useful dragon in any Fall."

Lytol bowed his scarred face in acknowledgment of F'lessan's tacit allusion to the fact that he would never again fly a fighting wing.

"Perhaps you should consider spending the Nine Fall here at Cove Hold with us, bronze rider," Lytol said.

"I shall hope to be able to land more gracefully by then," F'lessan replied with a self-deprecating grin.

"Practice, I believe," Lytol murmured, his eyes alive with understanding and compassion, "always improves performance."

"I will, however," and F'lessan paused, "need to pursue another future for myself and my dragon."

"Well, you've already proved that you can be useful as a star-watcher," Master Wansor blurted out. "You don't need a dragon for that." His plump hand covered his mouth as he realized what he had said. "I mean, you still *have* Golanth, even if he . . ."

"Even if he is battered," F'lessan finished for him. "So, I entreat you, Master Wansor, Master Erragon, to allow me to study astronomy so that Honshu can become fully operational as the second Pern observatory."

"Oh, dear, there never has been a dragonrider astronomer," Wansor said, and then beamed in F'lessan's direction. "But then there wasn't even a StarSmith until very recently."

"Tai's already trained to near journeywoman status," F'lessan said, laying his hand on hers. "Isn't she, Erragon?"

"She is, indeed," Erragon agreed with hearty approval.

"We work well as a team," F'lessan hurried on, "and she'll need a profession, too, when Threadfall stops."

"True, very true," Erragon said enthusiastically, slapping his hands on his knees in emphasis. "Hope you'll be the first of many." Then, in an abrupt change of mood, he said, "Do tell us, F'lessan, how *did* you and Golanth get here today?"

"I was wondering when someone would ask," F'lessan replied.

"This new ability that the Weyrleaders mentioned in Council? Something . . ." Erragon clicked his fingers, impatient with his memory lapse. ". . . about the ability Aivas perceived in dragons that has some bearing on averting future dangers?"

"Given that dragonriders are apparently responsible for what falls out of the sky," F'lessan said with a touch of irony, "yes, it bears directly on that, and on my very keen interest in astronomy."

"What? What is it?" Erragon prompted.

"Actually you all witnessed a demonstration of that ability on my arrival."

Erragon, Wansor, and D'ram regarded him without comprehension, but a smile eased across Lytol's seamed face and he nodded.

"I thought so." When the grinning F'lessan gestured for him to continue, he did. "Consider, my friends, that Golanth sustained terrible injuries to eye and wing. I do not think

Golanth could have launched himself from even the topmost terrace of Honshu to gain sufficient height to go *between*. Also, he arrives in the company of five other dragons. He falters in landing and is righted—without any use of that damaged wing. The other dragons assisted him. Correct?"

F'lessan nodded. "While it doesn't require five dragons to lift Golanth, it does require a good deal of *control* to lift and land. From what the Monaco riders told us, it appears that female and male dragons work best as partners in such telekinesis."

"I still don't understand," Erragon murmured, shaking his head. "*How* did a wing-injured dragon fly?"

Beside him, D'ram was gaping open-mouthed at F'lessan and Lytol.

"Master Wansor, I know that you," and F'lessan nodded toward him, "remember that Aivas was fascinated by dragons, by a species that communicates mentally and moves freely between one place and another. He called these abilities telepathy and teleportation. He thought they should have a third: telekinesis. He very much wanted dragons to have that facet. They've evidently had it all along but—" F'lessan paused to grin at a speechless D'ram. "—until the feline attack on Golanth and Zaranth, had never *needed* to use it."

Turning to Erragon then, he went on. "What you saw today is a refinement of telekinesis. Controlled!" He paused to stress that. "Golanth can't—yet—use the damaged wing effectively. So the dragons lifted him vertically, high enough above Honshu to go safely *between*, which he can still do for himself." F'lessan leaned back in his chair, watching the reactions to his explanation: Lytol nodding, Wansor agape, Erragon frowning, and D'ram smiling in approval. "Today was the first attempt at a controlled lift of another dragon. It'll take more practice to perfect the skill. Especially landing. I'm sure, Lord Lytol, that we'll improve with practice."

Today was *my first try, after all,* Golanth remarked, somewhat irked.

Of course it was, Golly, Tai assured him, pinching F'lessan's bare arm.

"Just as he did with trundlebugs." F'lessan shot Tai a sly glance.

"Why can't Golanth 'lift' himself?" Erragon asked.

F'lessan shrugged. "Perhaps because he's too accustomed to doing it the usual way. It is, as Lord Lytol knows, very dangerous to go *between* at ground level. Golly may just have to change the way he thinks." He paused, a thoughtful expression on his face. "There's going to be a lot of that soon—a lot of traditional thinking altered to deal with our imminent future as aerial defenders of a planet no longer requiring protection against Thread."

"Hmm, yes." Lytol rubbed his chin thoughtfully, but his gaze gleamed with anticipation as he regarded the bronze rider. "So, today, to get Golanth aloft, the others supplied the initial lift and controlled the descent."

"To some degree," F'lessan said with a grin.

"Have you any idea, bronze rider, what use Aivas would have made of draconic telekinesis?" Lytol asked. Had the shrewd man already jumped to the same conclusion F'lessan had?

"Surely you don't mean he expected the *dragons* to alter the Red Star's orbit?" Erragon demanded, astounded.

F'lessan chuckled. "I don't know what he had in mind. Dragonriders did get the antimatter engines onto the planet. And the blast achieved an orbital shift. I have another, not completely dissimilar idea."

Erragon slapped both hands onto the table, his face mirroring complete skepticism. "And you are suggesting . . . that *dragons* will be able to deflect cometary fragments or asteroids?"

F'lessan gave the Star Master a long speculative look, amusement sparkling in his gray eyes. He caught a similar twinkle in Lytol's hooded gaze. If he had Lytol on his side, his preposterous notion might just have a chance.

"*Yoko*'s records showed the Fireball on an approach orbit months ago. If it had been moved *then*, by just a slight tap, if I can put it that way," and F'lessan could no longer suppress a broad grin, "the Fireball would not have impacted. Maybe it might not even have grazed the surface but trundled—"

He chuckled as he rotated his hand, index finger circling expressively. "—back out into space."

D'ram, Erragon, and Wansor gawked at him. Lytol's lips formed a smile of approval, and Tai stifled laughter at his description.

F'lessan went on. "I'm not saying that we can perfect this ability to have a significant effect on what's in our skies. But that doesn't mean we shouldn't try."

He looked around, satisfied by the thoughtful expressions. Lytol was nodding with comprehension. F'lessan leaned urgently forward across the table, the look in his eyes challenging them all.

"We already know that dragons can go into space without harm. They can manage a journey of fifteen minutes' duration before they incur oxygen debt. We lifted massive engines from three spaceships. We planted them on a dead world. The Red Star was much farther away from Pern than anything in the asteroid belt, or among the minor planets. What's to say we can't do *more* in our own space? We still have the helmets, suits, and the oxygen equipment. I think we should keep them in good condition. I think dragons should practice telekinesis and control their use of it.

"And another thing," he said, still noting that both D'ram and Erragon were having some difficulty in absorbing his remarks, "the Ancients may have had sleds. We have dragons. We don't have to waste time, or reinvent a fuel, to lift dragons from the surface of this planet. If a dragon knows where he's to go . . ." He waved his hand to let imagination finish the sentence.

"Just a minute, F'lessan," Erragon began, his eyes wide with confusion, "we can't afford to *risk* dragons . . ."

"They're risked every time they go into a Fall," Lytol said, having no difficulty with F'lessan's suggestion.

F'lessan nodded, his smile still in place. "We have the *Yoko* in its permanent orbit. It has the southern array of weather stations reporting to it. I often wondered why there wasn't a northern one."

"Perhaps because the southern continent was chosen, having the larger landmass and more temperate weather," Lytol suggested.

Erragon held up one hand. "Now don't tell me there are plans in Aivas records for weather satellites."

"There are," Lytol said.

"I was thinking of them more as links between the observatories," F'lessan put in, "which you know we'll need if we're to do a proper job of sky-watching."

With an exclamation of confused aggravation, Erragon rocked back on his chair, looking from Lytol to F'lessan to Tai, hoping for more explanation.

"Doesn't young Jaxom boast that his Ruth always knows where and when he is?" Wansor asked, twiddling his fingers as the tension in the room increased.

"Even in space?" Erragon's baritone voice rose to tenor levels in surprise.

"Well, not today, or even by the time the Western Telescope is lit," F'lessan said, "but we evidently have a way of putting objects up!" He pointed skyward. "Of course, it will take practice. Maybe," and he threw this out with a gleam of mischief in his eyes, "there is a prosaic use for this draconic ability—apart from defending themselves against felines."

"May we never have to do *that* again!" Tai said fervently. Outside, in the cove, three dragons echoed the sentiment.

"Meanwhile," F'lessan said briskly, gathering up the reports and prints that Erragon wanted them to study, "we have much to occupy us. Studying for our Mastery," and he gave Tai a sly glance, "and altering our ways. We must do as much as we can to make Pern fair up to our means, to make it the world our Ancestors hoped to create."

He felt his chest fill with determination to succeed in his new tasks. He could feel tears coming to his eyes as he held out his hand to Tai. She rose, inclining her body toward him, her eyes shining, too. He saw Lytol's face light up so that he seemed younger and more vital than ever. D'ram and Erragon got to their feet, while Master Wansor beamed benignly around the table.

The dragons continued to bugle and, in his head, F'lessan was certain that their call reverberated through every Weyr on the planet. He had the dragons' support.

"Whatever we have to do, we shall," he said in a choked voice. "There will always be dragons in the skies of Pern!"

THE PHYSICS OF PERN

by Anne McCaffrey

Did Anne McCaffrey plan the physics of Pern or did it develop along the way? Here's her response:

The Physics of Pern—ah, yes, well, they have been developed by Dr. Jack Cohen of Warwick University in *Dragonsdawn* and *All the Weyrs of Pern.* They are basically Newtonian physics and/or biology in which Jack holds both a Ph.D and a D.Sc. He is also a generalist, and was able to correct some of my basic errors, which were legion. I satisfied the science requirement at Radcliffe by taking cartography. Although I did not know at that point in my life that it would be a valuable asset in my life's work, being able to develop a map of new worlds has been extremely valuable. Even expert Karen Wynn Fonstad, whom I helped with details in the Atlas of Pern, remarked that most of my suppositions about Pernese terrain jibed well with what was geologically possible. It was a case of the subconscious running with an idea in the best of possible directions.

To Jack Cohen, I owe the biology of Pern, especially of the dragons and the fire-lizards who supplied the genetic material used to create—by a special and now-unknown process of the alien race—the Eridani, the dragons of Pern. (You can't just breed large examples of a species to other large examples and keep increasing the size in a few generations.) He also figured out how to decimate the malignant and possibly dangerous life-forms that inhabited the Oort Cloud with the zebedees (his name and creation, a creature that replicates itself despite its environment).

I had, you see, backed myself into a corner in *The White Dragon*, because there was no way the present day population of Pern could eradicate the mycorrhizoid Thread life form without the help of the original colonists. It was my notion to have a voice address artificial intelligence unit—AIVAS—as part of the settlers' equipment, and for the present day Pernese to discover this device and learn from it. I might have been ahead of the game in suggesting such a computer in 1970, but current computer techniques indicate that such a device is within the realm of possibility. What I desperately needed was a system by which the Pernese generation could access the technology left by their progenitors so that they could actively fight Thread and honor the Weyrleader's vow to end the Threat of the Red Star forever. Jack was ingenious in working out details that would forward this ambition. For instance, how the colony ships were powered. He figured out that, in order to move such a mass as a planet, there would need to be several attacks on it. He utilized the draconic ability to move between time and place, and also set up the zebedees to be sure that the mycorrhizoid spore did not again leave the Oort Cloud. According to the Hoyle-Wickramansingh theory (to which Jack does not personally subscribe but was willing to use as a mechanism in the story) about Oort clouds, many organisms might lurk within such astronomical features, as well as embryonic cometary masses, and it would be as well to disseminate a killer virus in the cloud to prevent any recurrence of Thread or similar nebular virii.

So, as far as the physics of Pern is discussed by me in the books, it is legitimate even if it hasn't happened elsewhere. Jack was adamant that I give a logical explanation of as much as I could, because then people would be more apt to trust the improbable. It's much easier to describe Pern as earth-like, and that is quite legitimate, too, especially now that we have discovered other star systems do have earth-type planets around their primaries. I try to have some basis for even the most drastic suggestions I make.

However, I went to the source, as it were, for correct astronomical dates for the latest Pern book, *The Skies of Pern*. I asked Dr. Steven M. Beard of Edinburgh Observatory, and Scott Manley of the Armagh Observatory for substantiating facts in deploying a fireball above and into Pern. I went up to Armagh, also meeting Dr. Bill Napier, author of *Nemesis*, and other members of the observatory staff to see Scott's Cosmic Impact Program from which he directed Pern's fireball. Coincidentally, earth itself had a Near Earth Object scare about the time I finished writing the manuscript, and many concerned scientists were watching the rather busy skies near our planet to identify and forewarn of other close encounters with NEO's and PHA (Possibly Hazardous Asteroids). Such movies as *Deep Impact* and *Armageddon* gave me visual evidences of such a disaster, but the dragons of Pern are unusually designed to help mitigate the worst effects of such a catastrophe. The thrust of *The Skies of Pern*, the need for the inhabitants to become more aware of their spatial environment, and the critical need to set up additional observatories to help prevent a recurrence of such a cosmic impact, is as modern and timely as the one currently in operation on earth, even if it requires the dragons of Pern to implement.

So, Did I plan the physics of Pern or did it develop along the way? The answer is, I didn't plan. It developed along the usual lines for any earth-type planet, and I dragged in whatever experts I needed to substantiate any unusual actions or positing. People want Pern to be believable: I've tried to make it logical as well. I also hope that the general attitude of the Pern People within the books has reflected their growing awareness of science and technology. I tried to infer this by their less restricted vocabulary and general acceptance of their historical origins.

Dragondex

THE WEYRS IN ORDER OF FOUNDING

Fort Weyr

Benden Weyr

High Reaches Weyr

Igen Wyer

Ista Weyr

Telgar Weyr

Southern Weyr

THE MAJOR HOLDS AS BOUND TO THE WEYRS

Fort Weyr
  Fort Hold (oldest hold), Lord Holder Groghe
  Ruatha Hold (next oldest), Lord Holder Jaxom, Lord
    Warder Lytol
  Southern Boll Hold, Lord Holder Sangel

Benden Weyr
  Benden Hold, Lords Holder Raid and Toronas
  Bitra Hold, Lords Holder Sifer and Sigomal
  Lemas Hold, Lord Holder Asgenar

High Reaches Weyr
  High Reaches Hold, Lord Holder Bargen
  Nabol Hold, Lords Holder Fax, Meron, Deckter
  Tillek Hold, Lord Holder Oterel

Igen Weyr
  Keroon Hold, Lord Holder Corman
  Parts of Upper Igen
  Southern Telgar Hold

Ista Weyr
  Ista Hold, Lord Holder Warbret
  Igen Hold, Lord Holder Laudey
  Nerat Hold, Lords Holder Vincet and Begamon

Telgar Weyr
  Telgar Hold, Lord Holder Larad
  Crom Hold, Lord Holder Nessel

Southern Weyr
  Southern Hold, Holder Toric

CRAFTMASTERS AND MASTERCRAFTSMEN

Crafter	Rank/Craft	Location
Andemon	Masterfarmer	Nerat Hold
Arnor	Craftmaster, scrivenor	Harpercraft Hall, Fort Hold
Baldor	Weyrharper	Ista Weyr
Belesdan	Mastertanner	Igen Hold
Bendarek	Craftmaster, woodsmith	Lemos Hold
Benelek	Journeyman machinesmith	Smith Hall
Briaret	Masterherder	Keroon Hold
Brudegan	Journeyman harper	Harpercraft Hall, Fort Hold
Chad	Harper	Telgar Weyr
Domick	Craftmaster, composer	Harpercraft Hall, Fort Hold
Elgin	Harper	Half-Circle Sea Hold
Facenden	Craftmaster, smith	
Fandarel	Mastersmith	Smithcraft Hall, Telgar Hold
Idarolan	Masterfisher	Tillek Hold
Jerint	Craftmaster, instruments	Harpercraft Hall, Fort Hold
Ligand	Journeyman tanner	Fort Hold
Menolly	Journeyman harper	Harpercraft Hall, Fort Hold
Morshall	Craftmaster, theory	Harpercraft Hall, Fort Hold
Nicat	Masterminer	Crom Hold
Oharan	Weyrharper	Benden Weyr
Oldive	Masterhealer	Harpercraft Hall, Fort Hold
Palim	Journeyman baker	Smithhall
Petiron	Harper	Half-Circle Sea Hold
Piemur	Apprentice/journeyman	Harpercraft Hall, Fort Hold
Robinton	Masterharper	Fort Hold
Sebell	Journeyman/Masterharper	Harpercraft Hall, Fort Hold
Sharra	Journeyman healer	Southern Hold
Shonegar	Craftmaster, voice	Harpercraft Hall, Fort Hold
Sograny	Masterherder	Keroon Hold
Tagetarl	Journeyman harper	Harpercraft Hall, Fort Hold
Talmor	Journeyman harper	Harpercraft Hall, Fort Hold
Terry	Craftmaster, smith	Smithcraft Hall, Telgar Hold
Timareen	Craftmaster, weaver	Telgar Hold
Wansor	Craftmaster, glassmith	Smithcraft Hall, Telgar Hold
Yanis	Craftmaster	Half-Circle Sea Hold
Zurg	Masterweaver	Southern Boll Hold

SOME TERMS
OF INTEREST

Agenothree: a common chemical on Pern, HNO3.

Between: an area of nothingness and sensory deprivation between here and there.

Black rock: analagous to coal.

Day Sisters: a trio of stars visible from Pern.

Dawn Sisters: an alternate name for Day Sisters.

Deadglow: a numskull, stupid. Derived from glow.

Fellis: a flowering tree.

Fellis juice: a juice made from the fruit of the fellis tree; a soporific.

Fire-stone: a phosphine-bearing mineral which dragons chew to produce flame.

Glow: a light-source which can be carried in a handbasket.

High Reaches: mountains on the northern continent of Pern (see map).

Hold: a place where the common people live; originally they were cut into the mountains and hillsides.

Impression: the joining of minds of a dragon and his rider-to-be at the moment of the dragon's Hatching.

Interval: the period of time between Passes, generally 200 Turns.

Klah: a hot stimulating drink made of tree bark and tasting faintly of cinnamon.

Looks to: is Impressed by.

Long Interval: a period of time, generally twice the length of an interval, in which no Thread falls and Dragonmen decrease in number. The last Long Interval is thought to herald the end of Threads.

Month: four sevendays.

Numbweed: a medicinal cream which, when smeared on wounds, kills all feeling; used as an anesthetic.

Oldtimer: a member of one of the five Weyrs which Lessa brought forward four hundred Turns in time. Used as a derogative way to refer to one who has moved to Southern Weyr.

Pass: a period of time during which the Red Star is closed enough to drop Thread on Pern.

Pern: third of the star Rukbat's five planets. It has two natural satellites.

Red Star (sic): Pern's stepsister planet. It has an erratic orbit.

Rukbat: a yellow star in the Sagittarian Sector, Rukbat has five planets and two asteroid belts.

Sevenday: the equivalent of a week on Pern.

Thread: (mycorrhizoid) spores from the Red Star, which descend on Pern and burrow into it, devouring all organic material they encounter.

Turn: a Pernese year.

Watch-wher: a nocturnal reptile distantly related to dragonkind.

Weyr: a home of dragons and their riders.

weyr: a dragon's den.

Weyrsinger: the Harper for the dragonriders, usually himself a dragonrider.

Wherries: a type of fowl roughly resembling the domestic Turkey of Earth, but about the size of an Ostrich.

Withies: water plants resembling the reeds of Earth.

Visit Del Rey Books online and learn more about your favorite authors

There are many ways to visit Del Rey online:

The Del Rey Internet Newsletter (DRIN)
A free monthly publication e-mailed to subscribers.
It features descriptions of new and upcoming books,
essays and interviews with authors and editors,
announcements and news, special promotional offers,
signing/convention calendar for our authors and
editors, and much more.

To subscribe to the DRIN: send a blank e-mail to
join-ibd-dist@list.randomhouse.com
or you can sign up on Del Rey's Web site.

The DRIN is also available for your PDA devices—
go to www.randomhouse.com/partners/avantgo for
more information, or visit http://www.avantgo.com
and search for the Books@Random channel.

Del Rey Digital (www.delreydigital.com)
This is the portal to all the information and
resources available from Del Rey online including:

•Del Rey Books' Web site, including sample chapters
of every new book, a complete online catalog, special
features on selected authors and books, news and
announcements, readers' reviews and more

•Del Rey Digital Writers' Workshop, a members-only,
FREE writers' workshop

Questions? E-mail us...
at delrey@randomhouse.com